ALL WE WERE
PROMISED

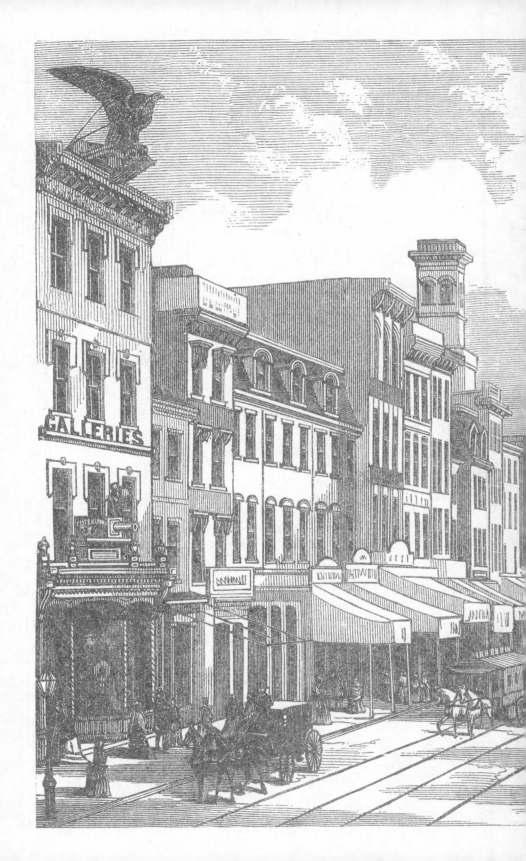

ALL WE WERE PROMISED

A Novel

ASHTON LATTIMORE

BALLANTINE BOOKS

NEW YORK

Copyright © 2024 by Ashton Lattimore

All rights reserved.

Published in the United States by Ballantine Books,
an imprint of Random House, a division of
Penguin Random House LLC, New York.

BALLANTINE is a registered trademark and the colophon
is a trademark of Penguin Random House LLC.

Hardback ISBN 978-0-593-60015-3
Ebook ISBN 978-0-593-60016-0

Printed in the United States of America on acid-free paper

randomhousebooks.com

2 4 6 8 9 7 5 3 1

FIRST EDITION

Book design by Barbara M. Bachman

For my grandmothers

ALL WE WERE
PROMISED

———

Chapter 1

CHARLOTTE

———

Philadelphia, 1837

THE CITY OF PHILADELPHIA WASN'T WHAT IT CLAIMED TO BE. But after four years of living here with her father, Charlotte knew there was a lot of that going around. It was unseasonably warm that November morning in Washington Square Park, enough to leave Charlotte and her friend Nell sweating under their dresses even as amber and gold leaves crunched beneath their feet. In Philadelphia, a stray hot day was as good as summer, when folks would gather at parks and carousels and crowd onto the cobblestone streets in messy, loud-talking clumps that circled and melted into one another. But warm weather also meant rioting season: when all the city's resentments between Black and white, freedman and immigrant, working folks and the struggling poor boiled over. Though the near-holy parchment at Independence Hall claimed all men were equal, the words told only half the story—in the heat, the city's people rarely shied from acting out the rest. And in the cooler months after all the ruckus, the city would hush and turn itself inward, with everyone huddled into stately brick town houses and tumbledown back-alley tenements alike, as if embarrassed by all the thrashing and carrying on.

Charlotte had seen the same cycle play out for four years going, and that morning she knew that all the conditions were ripe for a mob scene. Still, as she and Nell sat together fanning themselves a few rows back from the open-air wooden stage waiting for Mr. Robert Purvis's speech to start, she was lulled into a fool's sense of safety.

After all, it had been Nell's idea to attend. With her hair pulled back into a neat bun, two perfectly curled tendrils framing her deep brown face, and an immaculate lace shawl draped over her lavender wool and silk dress with pleated sleeves, Nell looked every inch the daughter of the city's monied Black elite—not the sort of woman you'd expect to lead you into a street tussle. Beside her, Charlotte self-consciously smoothed down her drab gray housemaid uniform. The color did nothing for her tawny brown complexion, but even such a sorry palette didn't dim the natural prettiness of her face: deep mauve lips shaped in a Cupid's bow beneath the wide-set mahogany eyes she'd inherited from her father. Those were among the many things he'd given her that she'd never asked for.

These days, Charlotte was in the habit of going more or less wherever Nell suggested, if only to get out of the little row house on Fourth Street that her father—no, boss—meant to serve as both her charge and her cage.

"I'm so pleased you decided to come," Nell said, "but are you certain your employer won't mind you stepping away from your duties this morning?"

"He'd have to notice before he paid it any mind," Charlotte said. Lately her father was far too wrapped up in his work to have any idea what she got up to while he was at the workshop, which was just how Charlotte liked it.

"Well then, I suppose neither of us exactly has permission to be here," said Nell, leaning over conspiratorially. "I let my mother think I was off to meet with my sewing circle."

Charlotte laughed. "I won't tell if you won't."

Though she and Nell ought not have been there in the first place—in their parents' eyes, anyhow—at the start there hardly seemed anything to worry about. The gathering was only meant to be a simple public talk, but the topic was a touchy one. Pennsylvania might be a free state, but that didn't always amount to much—the state legislature was floating a plan to strip free Black men of the vote, and to hear Nell tell it, Mr. Purvis was one of the scheme's fiercest critics. That's why the sight of him was such a shock. When the clock struck eleven, a tall, slim man with olive-colored skin and deep brown, wavy hair strode across the stage dressed in a finely tailored deep blue morning jacket with the chain of a gold watch glinting from his breast pocket. Charlotte gasped so sharply at the sight of him that Nell leaned over to ask if she was unwell. She gave a shaky nod in reply, but couldn't stop staring.

If Mr. Purvis had taken a notion to pass for white, he'd have fooled most anyone who saw him. But from the very first lines of his speech, it was clear the man's interests didn't run across the color line in that direction. Charlotte listened intently as he held forth for nearly an hour in a voice both elegant and booming, laying into the state legislators who held out their left hand to collect taxes from free Black Pennsylvanians even as the right hand busily drafted more laws that insulted their dignity—"the dignity of colored people like me," he declared. Before long, his speech waded into the thick of things: slavery, and what the government owed to the freedmen and fugitive slaves who poured into the city by the hundreds.

The audience in the park was rapt. Trouble was, they weren't the only ones listening. Mr. Purvis's words carried onto the sidewalks surrounding the little corner of Washington Square Park, and before long, Charlotte realized that nearly three dozen passersby—all white, mostly men—had slowly filled in around the audience. A handful loomed behind the stage as well, with their hardened, unmoving stares fixed on the man at the podium.

Even as they pressed in closer, Nell was too much in her element to notice, constantly leaning over to Charlotte and whispering helpful facts to put the speech in context. Charlotte knew more about the subject of slavery than her genteel friend realized, but far be it from her to deprive Nell of a teaching opportunity. Nell knew her only as a housemaid, and that made their keeping company strange enough without bringing up the small matter of Charlotte's also being a runaway slave.

As Purvis drilled in on making the city safe for abolitionists and the fugitives forced into the shadows by fear, Charlotte's mouth went dry. She suddenly felt sure that everyone could tell—that she was marked. Was the earthy musk of the plantation cabin's hard dirt floors still hanging on her skin, even after these years away? Could people spy a house slave's stooped back and shuffling steps in her walk? And in the shape of her utterly plain garments, Charlotte could almost trace the pattern of a slave's linen rags—how easily must everyone else see it? Her cheeks burned.

But she hardly had time to stew in her shame, because when Mr. Purvis reached the section of his speech calling for the legislature to punish rogue slave catchers, his words were a spark on a pile of dried leaves. The white men's agitated murmurs picked up, until finally someone snarled, "Shut your mouth, you high-yellow sonuvabitch!"

Mr. Purvis put up his hands and called for calm, but not a second later, a sharp gray rock hit him square in the shoulder and another only narrowly missed his head. He stumbled back as a gang of white men rushed in toward the stage and the crowd alike. The mob started to grab Black men from the outer rows of the audience and beat them mercilessly, raining down blows with fists and folding chairs. Charlotte and Nell, frozen in their seats, looked at each other. They were women, but no less Black, and mobs weren't in the habit of making distinctions—they had to get away. Now. They scrambled up and ran.

In the rush, Charlotte tripped and smacked her face on the leg of an overturned chair. The sharp pain pierced deep into her cheekbone, throbbing even as she and Nell dashed for the street. But before they could get out of the park, they were met with a wall of twisted, screaming faces. Raging men grasped at them, blasting hot, sour breath into Charlotte's nose. One man's filthy hand tore the sleeve half off her dress, adding the pop of ripping threads to the overwhelming racket of the brawling around them. Incredibly, Nell started shouting back into the men's faces, apparently convinced they'd give way after a loud but polite request. "Move aside, please! Excuse me!" When they finally pushed through an opening in the crowd, Nell and Charlotte took off running down the block. Behind them, the brittle sound of breaking wood cut through the shouting as the rioters tore apart the stage, smashed the folding chairs, and tossed them into a pile for kindling. Of course—fire. Always fire.

Charlotte and Nell ran for several blocks, until Charlotte's chest was ready to explode. When they finally reached Chestnut Street, it was quiet enough for them to stop and catch their breath, but Charlotte scanned the area warily. Dangerous as the city streets could be, the rioters weren't her only worry. Her father's woodworking shop was blocks away, but even a city as grand as Philadelphia seemed dangerously small when the person you were trying to avoid might be around any corner.

She kept her head down, but her damp, ruined dress and increasingly swollen face made her feel like a spectacle. Beside her, Nell brushed dirt off her own dress and Charlotte wondered if all this was old hat to her—born into a free family, Nell had lived in the city her whole life, after all. She did seem a little shaken, but more than that, Charlotte realized, Nell was furious.

"Mr. Purvis didn't speak an untrue word, whatever those ruffians have to say about it," she huffed. "The way this country enslaves and abuses colored people is shameful! As a free state, we ought to be doing everything we can to spread abolition, but those men want us to be no better than the South!"

Charlotte shifted her weight from one foot to the other and offered only a halfhearted "mm-hmm" as they stepped off the sidewalk to make way for a man carrying an armful of fabric into a nearby tailor's shop.

"I'm so sorry about all this," Nell said. "I should've known, I just thought since the speech was only meant to be about voting . . ."

"We're fine now, don't worry," Charlotte said, sounding more at ease than she felt. What time was it? She really did need to get off the streets before anyone at home realized she was gone.

"But look at you!" Nell reached out to touch Charlotte's exposed shoulder through the rip in her dress. "Here, take this," she said, wrapping her lace shawl around Charlotte. "I'm so, so very sorry. I hope this won't put you off our plans. Everyone in the Wheatley Literary Association is so looking forward to meeting you next week."

Charlotte smiled. "I don't rattle too easy, and neither do you, by the look of it."

No matter what had happened, there was no way she'd go back on accepting Nell's invitation to her exclusive book club. For Charlotte, the Wheatley Association promised a path toward a life that was her own, instead of one in the margins of her father's. She'd been preparing for weeks, combing through the few books she had at home to find the perfect reading, and stitching herself a passable new outfit to wear. Well, near new, anyhow.

"I'll be there," she reassured Nell. "But I really ought to get home, this dress wants mending. Will you be all right?"

Nell shrugged almost casually. "I'll keep to the back streets on my way home. Promise me you'll look after yourself—make sure to put a cold compress on your face," she said. "And I'll see you at the meeting next week! I can promise it'll be a much quieter time, at the very least." She winked and waved goodbye, and Charlotte started eastward for Society Hill.

Hustling past the rows of redbrick townhomes with painted shutters in subdued tones of beige, powder blue, and forest green, with bored white ladies gazing out the windows, she walked as fast as she could without breaking into a run. The sight of a Black housemaid sprinting down the street of such a well-appointed Philadelphia neighborhood—even one where she worked—would attract attention, and she had no time for that kind of trouble.

When she finally made the turn onto Fourth Street, where the blocks of wide four-story brick town houses gave way to simpler row homes, she breathed a sigh of relief: no one was watching. She quickly unlocked the green door of her house, pushed it open, and in one fluid motion slid off each shoe and shook off the dust over the shrub beside the front steps. She'd done the same thing dozens of times since the summer, a few months ago, when she'd first met Nell and started slipping out of the house while her father and the household cook, Darcel, were away. She was careful to leave no evidence that she ever set foot outside the house, but after the commotion in the park she'd barely made it back on time. Every Tuesday, Darcel returned from the market at 12:30 on the dot, and it was 12:27 by Charlotte's pocket watch.

She crept up to the attic in her stocking feet. Her tight quarters there were drafty and dim. The only bright spot was her sewing corner, a straight-backed wooden chair and a wide table set against the wall to take advantage of what little light peeked in from the tiny circular window. The table was laid out with needles of varying sizes, two thimbles, scissors, a pincushion, and thread, mostly in shades of gray, brown, and off-white for mending her own uniforms and her father's shirts. After stitching her sleeve back onto her dress, Charlotte spent the rest of the day attending to her chores in a fog of boredom and irritation, with her face throbbing.

In the years since she and her father had run off from White Oaks plantation, he'd transformed her from Massah and Missus Murphy's slave to his own housemaid, and from his daughter, Carrie, to his domestic servant, "Charlotte." Meanwhile, he'd reinvented himself too: a runaway slave no more, in Philadelphia he was an up-and-coming white tradesman whose success financed their new lives. Charlotte supposed she ought to have been grateful, but for what? Trudging someone else's laundry out back to the boiling pot in the cool of an early morning, sewing up the busted threads of another pair of britches, and dusting the same ornately carved end table for what must've been the hundredth time, most days her "freedom" felt the worst kind of familiar, a miserable echo of the old days on the plantation: slow and small, with her eye always fixed on what someone else needed.

But the loneliness, that was new. At least at White Oaks she'd had little Evie. For as long as Charlotte could remember, the two had worked together to look after their mistress, Missus Kate: washing and mending her clothes, dressing her, keeping her room tidy. In those days, when Charlotte smoothed down a bedspread, there was always another pair of little brown hands smoothing right along with her, a giggling face cracking little girls' jokes amid the drudgery. Now, as she worked her way through the city row house, there was no one, and not a sound.

In the parlor, she narrowed in on the spindly-legged, sharp-cornered end table beside the rust-red damask sofa. Though it was one of the furnishings her father was most proud of having created in his increasingly prominent workshop, the grooves on the surface and the intricately carved floral patterns atop the legs made it a daily thorn in her side. No matter how doggedly she'd wipe the table down, by the next morning the sun would light up the thin film of dust that had settled itself into the crevices like new fallen flurries. That afternoon, she made up her mind she'd never dust it again.

After all, she was on the verge of much more important doings outside these four walls. If some tidying slipped, her father would just have to live with it. If he noticed, that is. In truth, the parlor didn't see much use, making it a perfectly safe space for Charlotte's small personal stand—another one of the minor mutinies fueled by a mix of weariness and resentment that had piled up over the last few months, entirely out of his sight and, so far, mercifully overlooked. Still, when she strode out of the room to attend to the rest of her duties, she glanced back at the dusty table and smirked. As she moved through the rest of the house, the silent hours bled into one another as the sun sank lower in the sky.

That evening, extra footfalls and laughter on the front steps announced that her father had come home from his woodworking shop with a friend in tow. Charlotte smoothed her starched apron over her dress and met them at the door, keeping her head down in hopes he wouldn't notice the tender red spot on her cheek. Her father walked in first, exaggeratedly ducking his nearly six-foot frame underneath the door lintel. He didn't need to, but must've liked calling attention to what Charlotte guessed was his second-favorite feature.

"Good evening, Charlotte," he said, handing her his hat.

"Evening, Mr. Vaughn." She had long since stopped calling him "Papa." When they'd fled the Maryland plantation, they spent two wearying days trudging and scrambling through the forests between White Oaks and the nearby towns, constantly alert for the sound of baying hounds or twigs snapping under a slave catcher's footsteps, until they finally came to a road that would lead them north. But they'd made it only a few miles before a man stopped them. He'd sized them up, and Charlotte prayed he wouldn't notice their mud-caked clothes in the waning dusk sunlight. Whatever else he saw, though, his attention must've settled on James's cream-hued face and wavy brown hair, a stark contrast with Charlotte's brown skin.

"You headed up toward Delaware, sir?" he'd asked. James froze and nodded warily. Before he had a chance to panic, the man went on. "Storm's coming down from that way. There are a few taverns about a mile up. You'll want to settle in somewhere for the night with your slave."

Upon the last word, James had exhaled and the deeply etched lines of worry melted off his face. Just like that, they weren't two runaway slaves anymore, or even a Black father and daughter. No, he was a white man and she was his enslaved maid. In that moment, a sickening heat rose up underneath Charlotte's skin. For one wild second, she'd imagined peeling it off in a single layer, stepping outside it, and running away.

They'd walked on in silence. Of course, Charlotte understood the ruse was the best way to keep from being caught until they reached the free North. But in the years since, what had begun as a convenient cover had hardened into a way of life. And so it was that evening.

"My business associate, Mr. Ethan Wilcox, will be joining me for dinner," James said, gesturing toward the sandy-blond-haired white man who'd come in behind him. Charlotte looked the man over and raised an eyebrow as she took in the gaudier details that adorned his finely tailored light gray suit: a peach silk cravat, silver buttons with what looked like flecks of sapphire in the middle, and a polished gold pocket watch chain dangling on one side of his chest. He seemed out of place beside James, who was in an unadorned suit jacket and plain waistcoat of the same deep blue shade Mr. Purvis had worn. Even as

Charlotte eyed Mr. Wilcox, he didn't bother to acknowledge her, and James offered no introduction. She took a step back and stood beside the coatrack.

"Please go and tell Darcel we'll have one more for supper this evening."

"Yes sir." Charlotte nodded and started toward the kitchen as James led Mr. Wilcox into the parlor.

The rhythm of their conversation and laughter picked up and echoed through the house. Past the back stairway, Charlotte poked her head into the kitchen, where the scents of browned butter and garlic flooded her nostrils. "Darcel—" she began. He held up a spoon and cut her off without even turning around.

"I know, I know, I heard 'em come in. There's plenty, and just about ready, too. Now go on with you," he huffed. That was about as much as Darcel ever said to her. After all, he was probably near her father's age or even older. He was short and stocky, and with a round, balding head and deep bronze skin. When he spoke, his words were gruff, but the cadence of his speech had a lilting musicality that was like no accent Charlotte had ever heard.

In the dining room, Charlotte laid down another place setting. The dining table was another one of James's showpieces, perfectly carved by his own hand: a long, flawlessly polished oval made from cherrywood, with turned legs. While he'd once filled their cabin at White Oaks with cast-off pieces too irregular to sell on Massah Murphy's behalf, since they'd settled in Philadelphia, he'd gradually started keeping some of his best work for himself. The table was slightly too large for the room's modest size and could seat a dozen— James's grand ambitions of entertaining made manifest.

At dinner, James and Mr. Wilcox tucked into plates piled with roast chicken in a savory butter sauce, garlic wild rice, and boiled carrots sprinkled with cinnamon. Snippets of their conversation carried into the pantry, where Charlotte waited quietly, leaning against the wooden counter. They were putting their heads together on a scheme to expand James's workshop, and for Mr. Wilcox to introduce him around to some new potential buyers. Though the details of her father's business didn't interest her, Charlotte kept listening until Mr. Wilcox left and her father retreated to his office.

Off to the side in the pantry, Darcel had left her a plate that included a few extra scoops of wild rice, Charlotte's favorite. With her father gone, she settled into her seat at the dining room table. She always sat just to the left of the head chair, where she imagined she'd place herself if she and James ever took a meal together. Idly, she wondered whether Mr. Purvis was somewhere across town, eating with his own family and telling them the horrors he'd narrowly escaped that morning.

Charlotte ate alone and in silence, slowly and carefully, practicing for some far-off evening when she hoped to have dinners of her own to attend and company to share them with, somewhere outside the stifling confines of this house. Until then, as she did every night, Charlotte would clear her dishes away and smooth the tablecloth down, running her hand over it to gather any wayward crumbs. Before leaving the dining room, she blew out the last of the few remaining candles, leaving no trace.

Chapter 2

NELL

Gently at first, Nell pulled on the door of the Arch Street Meeting Hall. It didn't give way. As the women of the Philadelphia Female Antislavery Society gathered close behind her, waiting, Nell swallowed hard. Maybe she'd been turning the knob in the wrong direction—she twisted it again and this time tried pulling the door open with a little more force. It gave only half an inch before sticking resolutely in place, forcing Nell to take a step back that caused a ripple of backward stumbling among the other ladies. Nell squinted up at the Independence Hall clock tower just two blocks away: 10:00 A.M. exactly.

"I'm certain we've got the right time," she said, staring at the door as if she could will it to open. "It appears we're locked out." Her frustration mounting, she exhaled sharply. Behind her, the others murmured: The delay was using up valuable meeting time, and perhaps they ought to just go somewhere else, and was Nell sure she'd remembered to pay the room rental fee?

As the group of more than two dozen women moved out of the middle of the sidewalk to avoid making a scene, Nell glanced at the window. Inside, a curtain swished, and the shadow of a short man scurried just out of sight.

Nell knocked on the door. "Mr. Smith, is that you? Perhaps you've forgotten our meeting time today. Would you please let us in?"

She waited, determined not to turn around and meet the others' eyes.

"Ahem, Miss Gardner?" The voice came a moment later from the side of the building, where Mr. Smith, the building manager, had slipped out of a less conspicuous door and now stood beckoning. He was a small-framed white man wearing a pair of bifocals.

Nell came around and he drew closer, his eyes darting side to side. He spoke so quietly she could scarcely hear him.

"I'm afraid we'll have to cancel today's rental."

Oh, for heaven's sake. This again? But as ever, Nell was polite. "We would have appreciated more notice, sir, but we're perfectly able to take our business elsewhere. If you'll kindly return the fee, we'll be on our way."

The man reached into his shirt pocket and pulled out a handful of crumpled bills that looked nothing like the neatly folded currency Nell had given him three weeks ago when she'd made the arrangements.

"I'm sure you understand," he said as he shoved the money into her hands. "Haven't you heard what happened?" Before she had a chance to respond, he hurried back inside and the lock clicked behind him.

News of the riot at Mr. Purvis's speech had clearly made its way around town, the latest in a years-long line of riots sparked by white Philadelphians who couldn't abide the city's growing free Black population and lashed out violently for any reason or no reason at all. In Washington Square Park, the debris from the skirmish had already been swept out of sight. All that remained was a rectangular patch of grass, flattened and burnt brown, where the mob had broken up the stage and set it on fire. As if that weren't bad enough, earlier in the month there'd been that dreadful business with poor Mr. Elijah Lovejoy. The story was in every antislavery newspaper in the country, and some of the other newspapers too: in the nominally free state of Illinois, the abolitionist newspaperman Lovejoy had been shot to death by a mob that was trying to destroy his printing press. The antislavery message wasn't popular in other parts of the country either, apparently.

This was hardly the first time the women's Antislavery Society had been turned away from a rental space. More and more, building managers were afraid to host meetings for groups like theirs, and lately that had meant being left out on the street too many times to count. Still, with this latest incident, Nell couldn't help being annoyed. As the self-proclaimed cradle of liberty, Philadelphia was already a city of broken promises, with accommodationists straining to silence antislavery speech and Southerners shuttling their very much not-at-liberty slaves in and out of the city's borders. Where abolitionists were concerned, it was fast becoming a city of broken contracts as well.

Nell pulled her coat tighter against the chilly November morning and rearranged her face before rejoining the ladies on the sidewalk. She must always appear calm, unruffled. "It's another set of doors closed to us, sadly," she said. There were murmurs of frustration. As people walked by, a few cut their eyes or stared angrily at the mixed-race group, Black and white women gathered side by side.

"That's all right," said Sarah Mapps Douglass, sensing the change in the air around them. "We can meet at my schoolhouse. Follow me quickly, let's not linger in the streets." The Antislavery Society helped to fund the school's operations, and in turn Sarah offered up the building whenever the society found itself in need of a place to meet. Nell fell in step beside her as they walked. Apart from being a teacher, Sarah was a daughter of one of the city's most prominent Black families and a dedicated abolitionist as well. At thirty, she was nearly a decade older than Nell, who had always looked up to her, especially the way she never let anything distract her from the work—not riots, not political infighting within the movement, and not marriage either. Hers was the kind of focus Nell could respect. Over the years, as their age difference mattered less, they had become friends.

"I'm impatient to wash our hands of all this to and fro," Nell said, looping her arm through Sarah's. As they crossed Sixth Street, Nell looked longingly up a few blocks at the building frame for what would be Pennsylvania Hall. In the distance, dust rose around the builders working to close the frame before the winter snows arrived and the ground hardened with the cold.

Sarah nodded. "The hall opening will be a dream come true, and not a moment too soon! As long as I've been at this, I'm impatient for it myself." Fed up with being shut out from venues across the city, Philadelphia's abolitionist groups had banded together to raise money for a grand meeting hall of their very own. There was no denying this was a city that fell far short of its ideals. For Nell, the construction of Pennsylvania Hall was a reminder that it didn't have to.

Once they arrived at the small brick schoolhouse, the women squeezed into the administrative office to talk until one of the classrooms opened up. A few members of Nell's all-Black book club, the Wheatley Literary Association, were there, making up the handful of Black faces mixed in among the white women who'd also taken up the abolitionist cause. That day, they were gathered to discuss plans for the fundraising fair, to be held in December. After scheduling sewing circles to make goods to sell and planning baking assignments, finally they came around to the question of a venue. Nell piped up without hesitation.

"I've got just the place," she said. "We ought to try the Fire Men's Hall near the market, and then we can also set up a table in the market itself to drive more traffic to the hall. We'll catch people coming and going," she said. Sarah smiled at her proudly.

"That's a wonderful idea, Miss Gardner," she said, addressing Nell formally given the official setting. Nell was increasingly well known for her powers of persuasion in both fundraising and petitioning, so this sort of event was where she tended to shine.

"Will you be handling the rental arrangements on your own?" asked her sometime friend Lillian Forrester. "After what happened today, we wouldn't want any mishaps with such an important event." She rarely missed an opportunity to twist the knife. Nell smiled warmly at her in response.

"Perhaps you can help me set up and keep everything in order, Miss Forrester," she replied. "You're quite right this is far too important to rest only on my shoulders. And I'll work on bringing in some other ladies to help as well," she continued, thinking of Charlotte. "It'll be an opportunity for people to see what we're all about, and consider getting involved." The women's Antislavery Society was overdue for attracting members outside the narrow crowd of monied white women and the handful of upper-class Black women who'd enrolled since its founding, and Nell had made it her personal mission to expand its reach.

Sarah nodded, and with her stamp of approval, everyone else voiced their support. Lillian's lips stretched into something that might've been a smile, on a different face.

Once the meeting wound down, Nell started for home. The section of Lombard Street where her family lived was quiet, refined, and comfortable, much like Nell herself. Freestanding brick houses occupied half a block's width and sometimes more; the sidewalks were shaded by cherry trees and magnolias peeking out from courtyards. Carriages rolled along the wide streets, with horses' droppings mingling with the scent of flower box blossoms to give the air a thick, sweet odor. Nell's grandparents had made their fortune in book printing and binding with the press they owned in a small shop on Broad Street. Her father had kept up the family business over the years and added to their wealth through real estate, including purchasing the stately house where the Gardners now lived.

Nell had stepped inside and was delicately brushing the dust off her dress when her mother came into the foyer. "Nell, is that you? Were you out walking the streets again?"

Nell smiled indulgently. "I had important matters to attend to, Mama. All good things."

Her mother cocked her head to the side. "I suppose being turned away from yet another meetinghouse is a good thing to your mind?"

Honestly, the city was far too small.

Her mother continued. "Lunch is in just half an hour; go and straighten yourself out."

As Nell changed clothes, the prospect of a family meal brought to mind an idea she'd been quietly mulling for weeks: Beyond just inviting Charlotte to the holiday fair and the literary association, why not ask her over for dinner too? The logistics might take some work, of course. It wasn't entirely clear whether Charlotte's employer actually allowed her once-a-week outings, merely tolerated them, or even knew about them at all—Charlotte was cagey on that score and Nell was too well mannered to press the question. Nell also had to contend with restrictions of her own—her parents held narrow, old-fashioned ideas about how and with whom she should spend her time, and lately she found herself straining against them. But, ever the optimist, Nell wondered if her family might become more open-minded if she started introducing them to her changing social circle.

New to these egalitarian ideas, Nell had only recently started spending time with working women like Charlotte. As she came of age in Philadelphia, Nell had watched with curiosity as the city's population of working-class Black residents swelled, alongside the families like her own who'd been free in Philadelphia going back generations, even before the Revolution.

While some of the more closed-off Black members of the Antislavery Society and her own parents tried to hold themselves apart from the city's Black underclass—once slaves and indentured servants, now free domestics, laundresses, dockworkers, factory hands, and the like—it hadn't escaped Nell's notice that the violence and indignities from white Philadelphians seemed to fall on all their heads just the same.

When she was eighteen, Nell had been all dressed up for one of the first social dances she would attend following her debut, but as the Gardner family coach pulled up to the assembly hall on South Street, they weren't met with lively music and smiling faces. Instead, a pack of white hecklers had come to gawk at the Blacks they felt had gotten above themselves, and to put them back in their place. They yanked men and women out of their carriages, tore at girls' dresses, and threw young men into the gutter, their faces showing sick satisfaction at muddying the men's fancy evening clothes. As they attacked the Black crowd, the mob certainly didn't bother asking whether any of them were born free or newly emancipated, rich or poor. Nell had scrambled back into her carriage unscathed, but she would never forget that night.

For Mr. and Mrs. Gardner, the more tense the city grew, the more they retreated into their elite circles. But for Nell, the constant racial tension prompted questions, and she dove into reading about the realities of Black life in Philadelphia. Her research turned up an old newspaper article that was particularly explicit, vividly describing the struggles of other free Black people in the city—most of them poor, some of them fugitives from the South. And, to a person, undereducated or not educated at all. Brimming with righteous empathy, Nell showed up at her next sewing circle meeting, broadsheet in hand. "We've got to help these people!" she pronounced, smoothing the article out on the table.

In front of her, a half dozen perfectly plucked eyebrows raised in unison. "But we *are* helping them," one of her friends said, "by offering an example of what they can aspire to." Another nodded in vigorous agreement. "Yes, and my family often donates clothes and money to shelters and such," she added. Nell supposed they were right, but their methods seemed so impersonal, so distant. And after what had happened at the dance, she no longer saw the sense in the more fortunate Black people so jealously guarding their class boundaries.

Since then, in fits and starts, she'd begun keeping company with laundresses and domestics she met through church or her charitable work, learning all she could about their shared struggles as Black women, but also certain that she had much to teach these women as well.

When Nell had met Charlotte, a housemaid with no local family to speak of, she'd seemed a bit rough around the edges, but also bright, and curious.

"What do women like you do all day?" Charlotte had once asked her over coffee. "I figure anything would have to be more interesting than dusting and mopping for hours. I've been at it my whole life and can't see keeping to it much longer." At that, Nell had smiled warmly. After years of complex social customs, shrouded motives, and thinly veiled digs from women of her own social class, she appreciated Charlotte's straightforwardness.

"Rather than tell you what I do most days, I'd be so pleased to show you," she'd said to Charlotte at the time. Nell took the young woman under her gentle wing, and they'd been in the swing of their regular meetings for months since, with Nell sharing how she filled her time with the women's Antislavery Society, teaching night classes, and doing charitable work, along with social engagements. Charlotte seemed to absorb it all eagerly, while considering where she might fit in.

Though Nell's and Charlotte's backgrounds couldn't have been more different, Nell found it refreshing to spend time with someone else who was still figuring out what she wanted to be, and who—like herself—seemed to know only that it wouldn't be what was expected of her. Just as most of the other women in Nell's sphere seemed happily headed toward marriage and child rearing or already embarked on that course, many of the working-class women she'd known before Charlotte had seemed either resigned to their day-to-day toil or too exhausted to think of much else. But Charlotte was something else entirely: a young woman at the outset of her own path, with the energy to carve out something new. Nell found her company invigorating, and was eager to bring Charlotte more fully into her circle.

Over lunch, as Nell, her parents, and her brother, George, sipped iced tea around the table, Nell let the conversation unfold before gingerly pressing her case.

"Did you see, Nell? Mrs. Marion brought over an apple pie," her mother said, pointing to the glass pastry case sitting on the sideboard. Their neighbors across the street, the Marions, brought treats over often, extra bounty from the family's booming catering business. "She mentioned Alex has been keeping himself busy working with his father. He really is a fine young man."

"Mm-hmm," Nell said, keeping her gaze on her plate. Any reply more engaging than that might invite one of her mother's monologues on how Nell ought to take her marriage prospects more seriously and spend more time with the Marions' older son. Never mind that Alex was basically a brother to her, or that she'd already told her parents—much to their dismay—that she aspired never to marry, just like Sarah. She changed the subject.

"Mrs. Marion was kind enough to join my sewing circle last week; we're making quilts for the new orphanage," Nell offered.

"How lovely and kind, that's just the sort of thing you ought to be doing," her mother replied. Helen Gardner was a subtle woman, so the "instead of befriending laundresses and housemaids" part was left unspoken. Having inherited her mother's powers, though, Nell picked up the subtext all the same. She took it as a challenge.

"You know, I've started inviting some new women into my sewing circle and into our literary association, to help us keep up those kinds of good works. You might be interested to meet some of them, perhaps I could invite one or two over for dinner. My friend Charlotte—"

"Is that the young woman I've seen you walking through the neighborhood with lately? With the rather drab dresses?" her father interrupted. Mr. Gardner was decidedly more direct. Nell's mother wrinkled her nose delicately.

"I do so enjoy our little dinners as a family, my dear," her mother said. "Why not just keep things amongst ourselves for the next little while?"

There was something overly precious about the way Nell's parents regarded their home. Generous as they could be outside its doors, Mr. and Mrs. Gardner were downright miserly with their hospitality, at least for anyone outside the innermost circles of Philadelphia's Black upper class. Even nestled as it was into the wealthiest part of Cedar Ward, the Gardners' stately brick colonial was still firmly inside the boundaries of the center of Black life in the city, which meant all kinds of folks could be found within just a few blocks' radius of their double front doors. From refined Black families with names older than the young nation to runaways whose backs were still bent and scarred from the cruelties of some faraway plantation, there were endless sorts of lives buzzing through the busy streets of the neighborhood. But only a very particular sort was ever invited to cross the threshold of 78 Lombard Street. All that was going to change, though, if Nell had anything to say about it.

"Surely there's room for us to open ourselves up a little—" she began.

"You can always invite Alex over," her father interrupted. "Always happy to see him and the Marions! They're just our sort of folks, and those pies . . ." He glanced longingly toward the sideboard.

Nell laughed, and decided to let the matter drop for the moment. Her parents may have been out of step with her burgeoning politics, but she could play a longer game. And in the meantime, there were plenty of other ways to spend more time with her new friend while working to broaden her horizons.

Chapter 3

CHARLOTTE

IN THE DAYS FOLLOWING THE RIOT, CHARLOTTE THREW HERSELF into a frenzy to get ready for the Wheatley Association meeting. She spent her free hours in her attic room, elbows deep in fabric and thread, pins hanging from the side of her mouth as she squinted down at the yellow church dress she was tearing apart and restitching for the occasion. After all, this wouldn't just be her debut as the newest member of Nell's book club—she was stepping fully into another life, one she hoped would be far less lonely and tedious than existing in the shadow of her father's growing ambition. Nell and the Wheatley Association offered Charlotte a new community, and she had no intention of showing up in such fine company as a dutiful housemaid wearing a dull gray dress. With a few alterations to the shape and some small details added, Charlotte's church outfit wouldn't exactly be high fashion—she could work a needle and thread, not a miracle—but it would do.

The evening before the meeting, she sewed by candlelight, straining her eyes in the near darkness. While she worked, her mind wandered back to White Oaks, where Auntie Irene had taught her how to make dresses for Missus Kate. Auntie Irene had always worked quietly, wordlessly—probably too worn out from the tobacco fields to talk—but she was a teacher through and through. She'd lay her warm, steady hand over Charlotte's, guiding her small fingers along a straight-lined stitch or through the tricky work of attaching a button. She never had a cross word if Charlotte dropped a piece or accidentally skipped a stitch—she'd just tap her finger twice, and point. Under the gentle pressure of her heavy callused hand, Charlotte had wondered—was this the feel of a mother?

Her own mother had died when she was just three, and Charlotte barely remembered her. In the years after, Charlotte settled beside Auntie Irene gratefully—though they shared no blood, Irene was one of the few women left on the slave row to look after her. And while they worked side by side, Charlotte would steal fond glances at sweet baby Evie, Irene's daughter and almost as good as a sister, as she dozed on the pallet nearby. When Evie grew older, Charlotte sewed little frocks for her from scraps of fabric, dressing her up like her very own doll. Now, in quiet moments, Charlotte still ached for Evie and Auntie Irene. But that old life—that old family—was lost to her. All she could do was go on.

With the moonlight streaming into her small attic window, at last she attached a set of deep blue buttons to the wrists of her remade yellow dress, which she'd embroidered at the shoulders with three intertwined roses in the same shade of blue. As she stepped back to admire her handiwork, she was surprised to hear her father's soft knock on the attic door. Since things had begun to pick up with James's business and his partnership with Mr. Wilcox, he'd been around less and less. His lack of attention was a lucky thing, since it had given the deep purple bruise on Charlotte's cheek time enough to fade.

"Carrie? Got time for a lesson?" When they were alone, he called her by her old name. Over the years, it had started to ring false. But "Charlotte" didn't feel like the truth either—not yet. She closed up the dress in her armoire before inviting him in.

James stepped into her room, holding a package wrapped in brown paper under his arm. He settled himself in the old worn chair beside the writing desk, where Charlotte kept the books they'd been studying: *The Legend of Sleepy Hollow,* the collected works of Shakespeare, and James's favorite, *The Odyssey.* After they'd arrived in Philadelphia, he had borrowed books from local charitable organizations and the Library Company, to which his apparent whiteness granted him access. Under Massah Murphy and Missus Kate's roof at White Oaks, slaves had been strongly discouraged from reading, though under Maryland law it wasn't forbidden. Recognizing that James was a craftsman, though, Murphy had seen the value in teaching him at least enough literacy to enhance his skills and keep him in steady and profitable work.

When he and Charlotte found their way to freedom, James leapt at the chance to pass along what reading and writing ability he had, and he pushed her to study the classics. Maybe with that knowledge she could rise above the sorry state of the many other Black people in the city: illiterate, poor, and overworked—that's what he always said. If only he knew the kinds of fancy people Charlotte had started keeping company with on her secret jaunts out of the house, he might even be a little proud. Angry, but proud. After all, in Nell, Charlotte saw her father's ambition and his wish, all she could've been had she not been born where and what she was.

As he sat down, James slid the package across the desk. "I've brought you something." The paper crinkled as Charlotte un-wrapped it, and inside were two lengths of fabric—one gray wool, and one plain muslin in a lovely muted peach color. She ran her hands over them, one rough and the other softer, with more give. In an instant, her mind was running with what she might shape them into, though it was clear enough what he had in mind for the gray.

"I thought you might like to make a few new pieces for yourself, maybe a new uniform and a dress for church," James said with a small, nervous smile. "You do such fine work with your stitching."

"Thank you," she said. And then, without thinking, she went on. "I've just been trying to keep up with all Auntie Irene taught me."

The smile dropped from his face. "Yes, well—I'm sure you'll make something very nice, and well suited to your needs." He cleared his throat and straightened up in his seat. "We should begin," he said stiffly, reaching across the desk to hand her *The Odyssey*.

Of course. Any mention of White Oaks and the walls went right back up. How was it so easy for him to shut out their old life? He'd taken everyone away from her and offered her no one in return—not even himself. Wearily, Charlotte shook her head and started to read aloud.

As she worked her way through the text, she considered her situation. It was plain enough that James wanted her focused on the present, not their past. And if he was branching out into the world, inviting new people like Mr. Wilcox into their home, maybe he was finally ready to loosen his grip on her. Otherwise what were all these lessons for? Besides, all the sneaking around was starting to wear on her, and permission after the fact was better than nothing at all. A book club sounded safe enough; no risk of anyone discovering James, and no risk it would ignite into a mob scene—she hoped so, anyway.

After she finished reading the last assigned chapter and answering James's questions to show her understanding, Charlotte ventured her suggestion. "You know, since I've come along so well with my reading, I wonder if I might join one of the local libraries for colored people, or even a reading club," she said.

"Reading club? Where'd you hear about a thing like that?"

"Someone mentioned it in passing at church, and I've been thinking it over," she said. Asking permission didn't mean she had to tell him the whole truth. It wasn't like he'd know what folks did or didn't talk about in the Black section of the church they went to some Sundays. He always sat down front with the white parishioners, tossing back apologetic glances while Charlotte climbed three stories up to a cramped balcony to sit with the other Black congregants—all second-class children of God.

"I've told you not to spend too much time talking to people at church, Carrie," said James. "You're there to listen, not make friends—you know how important it is that we keep to ourselves."

"It was just a quick invitation, nothing more," she said, trying to tamp down her frustration. "It'll be good for me. You're always saying how important reading and education are."

"You're reading plenty here, and I don't want you around the sorts of folks who'd be in a club like that. Gathering all those freemen and heaven knows who else together, it attracts the wrong kind

of attention—Southerners, slave catchers, and worse," he continued. "No, I won't have you around it."

Before Charlotte could protest, he repeated himself. "No. And
that's final. You have everything you need here in this house."

There was no point in arguing. He was blind to his own hypoc-
risy, utterly convinced it was perfectly fine for him to go out and do
as he pleased in the world, all while Charlotte was stuck at home to
prop up his cover story. She returned to her book and continued
reading aloud. James didn't say any more, but she felt his eyes on her.
At the end of the night's lesson, he reached into his pocket, gave
Charlotte a dollar—her wages for the week—and left.

THE NEXT MORNING, CHARLOTTE bided her time doing chores until
James left for his woodworking shop and Darcel set out for his
weekly trip to the market. When she was certain they'd both gone,
she bounded up the stairs to change. She laid aside her uniform and
redressed herself carefully, pulling on her transformed yellow dress,
reverently running her fingers over the embroidery. In the mirror,
she admired how the color complemented her skin. She smoothed
her hair's fluffy coils into a bun, the way Nell always wore hers. Before leaving the attic, she grabbed a small journal and a pencil to take
notes and write down ideas at the meeting. She intended to be taken
seriously.

Outside, the air was crisp. Charlotte walked through the city
streets, past the row houses and parks that gave way to shops and
taverns on the main roads. Even as far as she was from the river's
edge, a breeze curled into Charlotte's woolen shawl. Closer to the
library, she melted into the crowd as more and more free Black people walked the streets alongside her. At the city's center, they'd made
many of these neighborhoods their own. Along the sidewalk, café
doors swung open and little bells announced customers' comings and
goings. The pepper-pot soup women and fruit peddlers shouted
their wares as curious customers looked over the goods, and took in
the meaty, peppery scent steaming up from the soup pots. In the

street, the clip-clop of horses announced the passage of the wealthy, peeking out the sides of their carriages to watch their fellow freedmen at a remove. Here, noise and freedom were all bound up with each other, and Charlotte welcomed the break from the house's lonely quiet. It was almost enough to distract her from the fluttering in her stomach, where her excitement mingled with her nervousness.

Charlotte got to the library a few minutes before the meeting was set to start. Built up from the book collections of well-to-do Black families in the city, the library's interior was small and close, but inviting. The shelves were lined top to bottom with beautifully bound books, and the scent of ink, leather binding, and parchment mingled in the air with the wafting of cinnamon and sugar from a plate of cookies on the front table.

Heads turned at her arrival, and a few women offered polite smiles that barely concealed their question: *Who are you?* There were a dozen Black women, all elegant and at ease with one another. Most were outfitted in day dresses of taffeta and organdy silk striped in jewel tones of ruby and sapphire, all with fashionable leg-of-mutton sleeves that ballooned out above the elbow. The style was all the rage now—Charlotte had seen it in the windows of dress shops on Chestnut Street but hadn't had enough fabric to do that to her own dress. With the women's eyes on her, suddenly the rougher muslin of Charlotte's narrow sleeves chafed against her wrists. She reached down into her lap, feeling for a string to make sure she hadn't left her apron on. Finding none, she veered to the side of the room, hoping to take the most out-of-the-way seat she could find.

She was just sitting down when she looked up and saw the room's lone familiar face approaching.

"You came! I'm so glad." Nell learned forward and gave Charlotte two kisses, one on each cheek. Was this how they were supposed to say hello? Without asking, Nell nudged Charlotte toward a seat closer to the center of things. As they moved, Nell laid a hand on the shoulder of Charlotte's dress, running a finger over the embroidered blue rose. "What lovely work! You made this yourself?" Char-

lotte nodded, and Nell smiled warmly. "You've got such an eye.
Have you been all right since . . . ?" Nell trailed off, letting the guilty
look on her face call the memory of the riot to Charlotte's mind. "I
truly cannot apologize enough for putting you in that situation."

Charlotte waved her friend's worry away. "We got away safe,
Nell—it's all right." Though Nell had no way of knowing it, that
hadn't been Charlotte's first time dangerously close to a crowd of
white men with their blood up, not by any stretch. Back at White
Oaks, when Massah Murphy's friends came visiting, Charlotte and
Evie would huddle together in the dark and stale air of the closet
beside the parlor, pushing aside muddy boots and the heavy wool
overcoats that hung down onto their heads, praying Kate didn't call.
They'd listen as the men got rowdier with every cup of rum they
sloshed down their throats, whipped up by news of some faraway
slave rebellion or just their unruly variety of holiday cheer. Even as
young girls, Charlotte and Evie had known it was safest to keep out
of the men's sight—there was no telling what they'd do if the notion
struck them. After the visitors finally went home or dozed off on the
parlor couches, the two girls would creep out of the closet, shaking
off their frazzled nerves by pulling faces and mocking the men's
slurred down-South drawls as they ran back to the cabins in the slave
row. But this was hardly the time for Charlotte to lose herself in
plantation memories. "Will we be starting soon?" she asked.

"Of course, you're just in time," said Nell.

"You always say, 'punctuality is the surest sign of good breeding,'" Charlotte said.

"Good *manners,* Charlotte, manners. I'd just as soon we not talk
about breeding ourselves like livestock. That's what they do to those
poor wretches on the plantations, you know. I've read all about it."

Charlotte nodded, trying not to wince at Nell's apparent exper-
tise about what went on down South.

"I'm going to be leading today, so I'll sit up front, but let me introduce you to Lillian." Nell glanced at the woman walking over to
sit in the chair beside Charlotte's. "Miss Lillian Forrester, I'd like you
to meet my friend Miss Charlotte Walker," she said. Charlotte tried

not to be thrown off—the last name she'd invented for herself always sounded distractingly odd in her ears.

Lillian smiled primly and extended a gloved hand.

"Of course, Nell's told me so much about you," she said. "I'm pleased to make your acquaintance."

"Um, pleased to be met," Charlotte said, and immediately regretted it. Lillian only blinked at her, then went back to leafing through her book.

Finally, Nell opened the meeting. Everyone had brought something to share with the group, which they would read aloud, going around the room in turn. The woman to Nell's left started things off with a column she'd written for *The Pennsylvania Freeman* on the importance of setting up mutual aid societies to help poorer folks in the neighborhood: washerwomen, laborers, and domestics. Charlotte blushed, though no one was looking at her. The next woman stood and smoothly recited several lines of verse by Phillis Wheatley, the club's namesake, who Nell had explained was a poet who'd once been enslaved. Reading her work here seemed a little on the nose, but Charlotte appreciated the turn toward literature rather than politics. As the woman moved through the verses, others nodded in unison, and when she reached the final lines, a few voices murmured them along with her. "*Remember, Christians, Negros, black as Cain, May be refin'd, and join th' angelic train.*"

Charlotte shifted in her seat as the group moved on to the next reader, and the next, drawing ever closer. There was more poetry, a short essay on self-improvement and temperance, and a passage from David Walker's *Appeal to Colored Citizens*. With just one person left before her turn, Charlotte reached into her shoulder bag and felt for the sheets of paper she'd brought. The paper dampened as she clutched at it, the sweat from her palms making the ink bleed. Nell nodded in her direction, giving an encouraging smile.

Charlotte stood up. With every eye on her, she cleared her throat. "My name's Charlotte Walker, thank you all for welcoming me." Each woman smiled, a few said "Of course," and "Welcome!" Then, just as quickly, the group lapsed into expectant silence. Charlotte cleared her throat again. "This, uh, it's a selection from the collected works of William Shakespeare." More silence. She began to read. Her cadence was slow and halting. Between her shaky hands and the ink stains, she could hardly make out the words. As she read, from the corner of her eye she caught a few puzzled faces staring back amid the masks of politeness. Others glanced sidelong at each other, though Charlotte couldn't figure out just why. On the last line, she tripped over the final word and sat down in a hurry. Nell piped up right away.

"Thank you, Miss Walker, that was a very diversifying addition to our reading list, to be sure."

What on earth did that mean? Charlotte smiled as if she understood, then exhaled gratefully as all the eyes swung to the next woman in the circle. Though she tried to listen, a ringing in her ears drowned out all but her own thoughts. Had she chosen the wrong sort of thing to read? Had they noticed her stumbling and figured out she wasn't really one of them? With their well-practiced politeness, the women in the literary association were as hard to read as Charlotte's "diversifying" excerpt. Even as they all seemed to move on, Charlotte felt exposed.

When the meeting ended, Nell stayed behind to tidy up and Charlotte lingered to help her.

"Everything all right?" Nell asked, scooping up the last remaining cookies. She was boxing them to give to people on the streets.

"Oh, I'm just fine, that wasn't what I expected it to be, is all. But not bad," Charlotte replied. "Not bad." She left her questions unasked.

When they stepped out onto the sidewalk, Nell took Charlotte by the arm.

"We ought to go book shopping together one of these days and look for something for you to read next time around," she said. "I'd be glad to help you find something fitting, and we could even practice together ahead of time. I teach literacy, you know, at Sarah's schoolhouse in the evenings."

Charlotte nodded, trying not to parse Nell's words too closely. "I'd like that," she said.

"Good. Now, say you'll come with me to the market please. I feel just awful about what happened to your dress at Mr. Purvis's speech, and I'd like to make it up to you."

Charlotte froze. She'd never been to the market, and this was hardly the moment to explain she had to stay away from there to keep from being spotted by the household cook. But as she searched her mind for an excuse, Nell started walking. There was nothing to do but fall in step beside her.

The market was a crush of people, both Black and white, all bustling around aisles of stalls and carts beneath tall open-air sheds that stretched on for blocks. To one side, deep-red cuts of meat hung from hooks over a butcher's counter, and across the way, the shelves of a fruit stall overflowed with sweet-smelling and possibly overripe apples. Even as she gaped at the teeming aisles, every few minutes Charlotte looked over her shoulder. In such a huge crowd, anyone could be watching her.

When they finally reached the cloth merchant's stall, the richly textured and patterned bolts of deep purple, amber, and bright yellow muslin, wool, and silk were a welcome distraction. There wasn't a single stitch of cotton to be seen—no doubt the clothier shared Nell's politics, and didn't deal in any slave-made goods. While Nell browsed and fingered the fabrics, Charlotte hung back, embarrassed to be made such a fuss over.

"Here we are!" Nell exclaimed after a few moments, lifting a stunning bolt of pale blue silk. Charlotte stared, taking in the gorgeous cloth. It was the same color as the irises that had grown in the little garden Charlotte and Evie had tended together at the end of the cabin row. It was Evie's favorite color as a little girl, because it reminded her of the sky, she said—big, blue, open, and stretching far, far away from the tobacco fields. "How do you like it?" Nell asked.

As Charlotte gawked, she caught sight of the eleven-dollar price tag. Six square feet of that fabric cost more than all of Charlotte's possessions combined. "Nell, it's too much. You don't need to do this; I've already mended my dress—it's all fine."

"Nonsense. This is the least I can do," she said. "Please accept it as my apology."

Charlotte sensed it'd be rude to keep arguing, so she shrugged and nodded. Nell paid for the cloth and had it boxed up. On their way out of the market, Charlotte walked with the box under her arm and quietly battled with herself, trying to drink in the sights and smells but also somehow keep her head down so no one could see her face. There'd been no sign of Darcel yet, so she was nearly home free. Maddeningly, before they could step out from under the sheds, Nell stopped to chat with the baker while she paid for two spice cakes, fragrant with nutmeg and cloves. Charlotte stood by, making another anxious scan of the crowd.

As she looked, Charlotte caught sight of a girl on the market's middle path, walking with a group of other uniformed Black servants. The girl couldn't have been more than sixteen, and had deep brown skin the color of acorns. Her face held a familiar pair of deepset, wary eyes and a button nose. Charlotte held her breath. The girl looked for all the world like Evie. But what would she be doing here? Charlotte took a step closer, squinting.

"Charlotte?" Nell called. In the split second Charlotte looked away, the girl disappeared.

When they finally left the market, Charlotte walked back home in a daze, trying to shake off the mirage she'd just seen. Evie had been just a twelve-year-old girl when Charlotte and James left White Oaks, so Charlotte couldn't say for certain what she'd look like now. But there was no reason to think she'd be here. She was far too young to have run away on her own, and the people with that girl didn't look like Evie's mother and brother—Charlotte would've known Auntie Irene and Daniel anywhere. Evie had just been on her mind, that was all.

At home, she arrived to find she'd gotten there ahead of Darcel and exhaled gratefully when she shut the front door behind her. With her adventure into society done for the day, Charlotte had to begin her chores. She tucked away the box of cloth at the bottom of her armoire and slipped off her yellow dress. As she peeled off the layers of her outside clothes, she felt a part of herself draining away, and with it all the newfound freedom life in Philadelphia was supposed to offer. She pulled on her drab gray uniform. As she trudged downstairs, the collar's rough fabric pressed tight around her neck.

Chapter 4

EVIE

EVIE'S HEART WAS POUNDING. IT SPED UP EVERY TIME SHE thought back to that moment at the market earlier that day. The woman there next to the bakers' stall—it was Carrie. It had to be. So this was where she and Uncle Jack had run off to.

Since the night they'd disappeared from White Oaks, Evie had rolled through one emotion and into another, from fearful disbelief to brokenhearted abandonment, and finally—once the plantation mistress had sold off her family, ruining Evie's life for good and all—to a quiet, slow-burning rage. That was where she existed now. There, and, for the last couple of weeks, here in this strange city. The place was new, but life was just the same as it had been in Maryland: attending to Missus Kate, looking after her every want and need, bending to her moods, and trying to keep focused on just one day at a time.

After keeping Evie close since they'd arrived in town, that morning Kate had finally decided she could spare her for a few hours and let her go to the market with the other house servants. The price she extracted was that Evie had to bring her back a little treat, something she'd pick out special for Kate. "You know me best, my dear," she'd said. "We've been together so very long."

On her way to the market, Evie had wondered at the scenes she passed. The houses were packed together cheek by jowl with hardly any space between them at all. Even Kate's rich cousins lived in a huge town house that nevertheless sat wall to wall with the neighbors. Still, inside, it was plain as day that Kate's family had much more money than Massah Murphy ever did. While White Oaks was all rough-hewn wood, chipped plates in the dining room, and threadbare rugs that looked even older than the wizened Massah Murphy, the Jackson family town house boasted fine china in shades of eggshell and blue, heavy tapestries over brightly wallpapered walls, and plush velvet sofas set atop exotic-looking rugs in deep shades of crimson and gold.

And white folks weren't the only ones doing well in this city. On another street, Evie had wondered at the sight of rich-looking Black people striding the sidewalks dressed in the same finery as the whites. Still, she could see the city wasn't all wealth and good times. In fact, on some blocks people were dressed in little better than rags, and Black women walked the streets with backs stooped from heavy loads of laundry. They reminded Evie of her mother, and how she'd strain under the weight of bagged tobacco leaves at the end of a long day.

Far as she could see, freedom in Philadelphia was as good as a coin flip—easy enough to catch the wrong side of it, but promising at least a fair shot at winding up better off. Even a quick glimpse of Carrie had shown Evie that much: at the market, she'd looked at ease in her neat, brightly colored clothes, and with the fancy company she'd been keeping—some woman in a fussy silk dress and shiny satin shoes—it was clear enough how *her* coin had landed. Mighty far from White Oaks, that was for sure. But how had Carrie done it?

When Evie got back to the house from the market, she stepped into the dark, stuffy pantry off the kitchen to drop off a loaf of cinnamon bread for Kate, the same kind the cook back at White Oaks used to make. From there, she headed up the back steps to the second-floor bedrooms to retire to her small room inside Kate's suite until the woman rang for her. While the house's other slaves stayed in separate quarters out back in the courtyard when they came to the city for their massah's visits, Kate insisted on keeping Evie close, even if it meant housing her in what could only have been built as a closet. The room was hardly wide enough to lay down across it lengthwise, and had no window to let in any of the sunshine or moonlight in the evenings. At least it was warm.

Inside was a narrow, soft bed with a pillow and a plain down-stuffed blanket. A little wooden table with a drawer stood beside the bed, and that's where Evie kept her meager possessions: the straw doll her mother had made for her, and a small wooden box her brother, Daniel, had carved with the image of a rose. It was all she'd had left of them to cling to for four long, lonely years. On the table-top sat her jug of water and the candle she blew out before lying down to sleep each night, praying to wake up and find Kate had been carried off by wolves or struck by a passing carriage. Anything that would free her from the loathsome company of the woman who'd sold off Evie's family like so many sacks of tobacco. But every morning, there she still was, and Evie had to swallow her hatred like a hard, dry lump and go on serving her.

Alone in her room, Evie left her door open a crack to let in the light and sat on the bed. She lifted her feet to rub away the ache of the long walk back from the market and all her other errands. Kate would be along soon looking for help to get ready for the evening's dinner party, and she'd be all a-twitter to look her best since her new beau, Henry Brooks, would be there.

Evie had seen the man only once, and he wasn't much to look at, but it was clear as day he was both younger and richer than Kate's first husband, old Massah Murphy. Neither quality was a very high bar to jump, but Kate was thrilled and wasn't shy about saying so to Evie. That or anything else. Evie closed her eyes for a moment and leaned against the wall. The next thing she knew, that familiar ring of the summoning bell clanged in her ears, and then came the voice. That voice.

"Evie? Evie, are you here? I need you." The sound was a breathy singsong, always half-whisper and half-whine.

Evie clenched her teeth at the sound, making the pain in her jaw flare up. Still, she jumped from the bed, rubbed her eyes, and pinched her cheeks. Always had to look alert, ready. She took a deep breath before opening the door fully.

"Here, Miss," she said, hurrying to Kate's side. Kate sat in the chair at her vanity and rolled her neck and shoulders like she was tired, though heaven only knew from what. Maybe doing needle-point all day and gossiping with her cousins was more wearying than it looked.

As was her daily habit, Evie walked over and stood behind Kate, picked up the hairbrush from the vanity table, and began a series of long, slow strokes, carefully pulling sections of her mistress's hair apart to work out the tangles. Carrie had taught her that.

"We'll need to put some of those curls into it tonight, Evie. I need to look positively radiant—my first time out with Henry I can't afford to put a foot wrong." Kate sighed.

She couldn't afford much of anything, let her family tell it—her cousins gossiped endlessly about the penniless, widowed relation they'd so kindly welcomed for a lengthy visit, and the whispers made their way down to the slaves' quarters. As Kate spoke, Evie nodded.

"Yes, Miss." Nights like this, the ridiculousness of calling Kate "Miss" pushed itself to the front of Evie's mind. She'd seen the woman live as man and wife with Massah Murphy nearly as far back as she could remember, but when he died it was like those years went up in a puff of smoke and blew away with the wind. Now, just in time to find a rich new beau, Kate was no longer the near-middle-aged widow of a white trash Irish planter who'd never made good. No, she was a somewhat less fresh-faced maiden again, ready to make her perfect match far from Anne Arundel County, Maryland, where anyone might be too fussed about the facts. At least until her rich cousins got tired of letting her stay in their town house and buying her fine clothes—but Kate hoped to be mistress of a plantation again well before she'd wear out her welcome here. With her own parents dead, she couldn't expect to bounce around from one family member to another forever. The way Evie had heard it, neither her siblings nor her cousins meant to support the aging widow for very long.

"Get all the tangles out, now, then we'll let it rest a few hours before doing it up. I've got to look fresh for tonight, not like I've been sitting around all day just waiting for it to be time to go," Kate said. "But we know I have!" She giggled like they were old friends.

Evie giggled back and squeezed Kate's shoulder. By now she was well practiced in playing the part of a confidante. Carrie had taught her that too.

Back at White Oaks, when Evie was still just a girl and Carrie was the lead housemaid, Kate had started treating Carrie like some unholy mix of slave and peer. Evie had done a lot of watching then: the way Carrie lifted each section of Kate's stringy brown hair and guided the boar-bristle brush through; how she beamed at Kate in the mirror while Kate preened and tried on newly sewn dresses—first made by Mama's hand and later by Carrie herself. All along as Carrie tidied up the stitching or nipped them in at the waist, she'd laugh and chat with Kate like they were girlfriends, the two nudging each other with their elbows. Kate would talk at Carrie into the late hours as Evie nodded off, both slave girls late for their dinners with rumbling bellies while Kate prattled on about which plantation belle had snubbed her, which tobacco buyers were late with their payments, or how she'd mercifully made it another month without getting caught up carrying old Massah Murphy's baby. Old man could hardly do it anyhow, she'd whisper to Carrie. At the time, Evie'd had no idea what "it" even was.

Once, the evening of Uncle Jack's birthday, Carrie had tried to cut Kate's prattle short to go and bake her father a cake. But Kate was beyond even her usual form that night, weeping and wailing because she'd had a letter from her parents refusing to let her attend her little sister's debut ball. They didn't approve of Murphy, she'd wailed, clutching at Carrie's brown linen rag of a dress and dripping tears on her shoulder.

Evie had watched from the side of the room as she dusted a chest of drawers, and Carrie subtly tried to pull away from Kate.

"It's all right, Missus, you just need a little rest and you'll feel all right again in the morning. I'll bring by a bite for you to eat and you can lie down," Carrie had said. "I'll go and give you some time to yourself."

At that, Kate reared back like she'd been struck. "You're just trying to put me off! I'm so good to you, and you can't even be a friend and help me through my troubles?"

"No, Missus; I wasn't——" Carrie began.

"Where could you possibly have to be that's so important, any-how?" Kate's wounded-looking eyes were wide and filled with tears.

"Nowhere, Missus. I'm so sorry. I'm listening," Carrie had said, defeated. Her shoulders slumped and her eyes went blank, dark, though Kate was far too wrapped up in her family drama to notice. But Evie had seen, and remembered.

After Carrie vanished, Kate grew to depend on Evie the same way. And though her cloying mistress set her teeth on edge, Evie had understood there was nothing to do but go along.

"Which gown do you think I ought to wear tonight? The green taffeta and silk or the velveteen sapphire?" Kate asked, breaking through Evie's reverie.

"Hmm, why don't we take a look at both and see what strikes us?" Evie said. "We," "us," and on and on it went. The sham of their equality sickened her. She put down the hairbrush and stepped into Kate's enormous dressing room, hung from end to end with the rich-est fabrics and nicest frocks her distant family's money could buy. Evie figured they saw it as an investment: the better she looked, the sooner they could see her married off and out of their pockets, some-one else's problem at last. Evie envied them their hope. She draped the two contender gowns over her arms and carried them out to meet with Kate's judgment.

"The blue is more luxurious, isn't it? But maybe a little bit too warm?" Every statement was framed as a question.

"I like the green," Evie agreed. "It brings out your eyes." Kate called her eyes hazel, but Evie thought the hue was closer to dishwa-ter with nearly all the bubbles gone out of it—some reflection and glints of color but mostly a dull and grimy gray.

Kate beamed. "The green, then," she said. "And for jewelry? Hmm." She pursed her lips and furrowed her brow, like she was working through a difficult problem. Evie couldn't understand why—it wasn't like she had a wealth of jewels to choose from. There was the single strand of barely convincing false pearls from Massah Murphy, a bronze rose-shaped brooch handed down from some way-back ancestor, a pair of alexandrite earrings borrowed from her cousin Maggie, and a silver pendant necklace. Evie had grown to loathe polishing the last of those, stretching out drops of polish from the one bottle Kate had held on to since Murphy died. It had come with them from White Oaks, to the Jackson family home in Virginia, where Kate slunk back to reconcile with her people once she finally ran out of money, and now here to the family's city town house up North. "Let's go with the pendant, no? No need for reminders of ghosts tonight."

Over the next two hours, Evie painstakingly transformed Kate from her lounging robe, undone hair, and plain face to something rather more appealing. Evie brushed, curled, and pinned her hair, pulled her into the green gown limb by limb, and plumped her up in just the right places, sucking her in at others. She stood by and made supportive murmurs while Kate rouged her face, pinching and painting and primping until she was well pleased with the reflection looking back. Finally, Evie clasped the necklace around her mistress's neck and clipped on the earrings.

"We've outdone ourselves tonight, Evie," Kate said expectantly.

"We sure have. Mr. Brooks is liable to lose his breath at the sight of you, Miss."

"Isn't he just?" She grinned at Evie and patted her hand. "And let's hope he does more than that! I'd better get myself downstairs, he'll be here soon to drive us over."

Kate hoisted herself up from the vanity chair and started for the door. Evie could feel her own shoulders relaxing, anticipating the moment she could finally lie down and exhale for the day, alone at last.

Kate stopped just before the door and turned around. "Wait up for me tonight, Evie. I know you'll want to hear all about it!"

She breezed out. With the door shut, Evie breathed a sigh of relief—at last, silence. She tidied up Kate's vanity and stepped into her small room, where she dropped onto the bed like a sack of potatoes. Her mind drifted back to the market, and her anger bubbled up again. Carrie had four mind-numbing, miserable years of Evie's life to answer for, including the last few hours, but there she was running around the city, free and surrounded by new friends like Evie had never existed at all. What did she have to say for herself? Was she even sorry? Evie lay back, stewing.

SHE'D DRIFTED OFF FOR what felt like only half a second, only to wake and find a huge deep green stone waving in her face. Hours must have passed, and Kate was back and standing in Evie's room holding up her hand nearly close enough to gouge Evie's eye out, impatiently awaiting her murmurs of admiration. Evie sat up. The moonlight flooded in through Kate's window and Evie's wide-open door, casting a sheen on the emerald and the yellow gold band in which it was set.

"That's a mighty fine ring, Miss," Evie offered.

"Oh, isn't it just divine? Henry said it reminds him of my eyes, and that's why he chose it," Kate said. She went over to her bed, expecting Evie to follow, and swooned backward. "Get my shoes, will you?"

Evie bent down to pull them off.

"Tonight was the night, Miss?"

So invited, Kate launched into the tale of the proposal: how Henry took her out on a carriage ride to Franklin Square in the middle of the city and walked her through the gardens in the moonlight and the cold evening air. When they reached a gazebo, he got down on one knee and asked if Kate would do him the honor of being his bride. She feigned surprise and put on her best flustered Southern belle, of course, she explained winkingly. At least with Evie, she didn't try to disguise the fact that she'd been angling for this moment practically since she'd set eyes on the man and heard talk of all his money.

"And then, do you know, he said just the sweetest thing. He took me in his arms and said, 'I promise I'll keep you warm all your life. After the wedding I'll bring you down to my home in South Carolina, where the sun shines bright and hot all year. It's no less than a flower like you deserves.'" She sighed. "What a dream, to leave this cold, filthy city and get back down South, where we belong. I can hardly wait, Evie, and I know you must miss it too."

Evie stood frozen in horror, slowly trying to take in what Kate was saying. How could she possibly think Evie missed the South? There were *some* things Evie longed for from her old life: her mother, her brother, the stillness of the woods around the plantation. But the fact of being down South itself? As much promise as it held for Kate, for Evie it meant only misery, and loss. And the threat of going even deeper into the South only sharpened her fears.

Evie hadn't been much of anywhere in her life, though she'd heard things. But what was far worse was what people *didn't* say. Mama had grown up far down South, on a giant plantation in Georgia, and had carried the scars from it with her to White Oaks: raised welts that crisscrossed her back where the whip had laid into her skin, the constant ache in her right foot where she said a toe had been broken and never healed up right, and the nightmares. Sometimes Evie and Daniel would wake up to find Mama on the hard dirt floor on her knees, repeating the same set of names over and over while silent tears poured down her face in the moonlight—Maddie, Nat, Willie, Jessamine; Maddie, Nat, Willie, Jessamine, like a prayer, or a spell. They might've been Mama's brothers and sisters, or babies she'd left behind—there was no way of knowing since Mama never once uttered their names in the daytime, and Evie and Daniel didn't dare ask. Mama only said she'd sooner die than go back down South. Her words echoed in Evie's ears now, and she was scared. Anything south of Virginia was dark and undiscovered country to Evie, and she wanted to keep it that way. But how?

As Evie helped Kate out of her clothes, Kate went on about her June wedding plans. They'd hold the ceremony at the Jacksons' family home in Virginia. It would be the talk of the social season: Miss Kate Jackson, washed clean of the Murphy name, finally married up with a proper Southern gentleman and received back into polite company.

The next morning at breakfast in the slaves' room off the kitchen,

Evie sat still and quiet, staring into her porridge. One of the family's drivers, Peter, and the others milled around her like she was just another chair. They barely sat down for a rushed bite before hustling back to the day's work. All had gotten up with the sun to tend to the Jacksons and they didn't have much time for whatever was troubling Evie. It was just as well. She wasn't really one to gripe.

Only Ada, Cousin Maggie's maid, paused long enough to spare a word for her. Ada was probably twice Evie's age and seemed to have taken a motherly shine to the girl. For her part, Evie welcomed the kindness but was wary of getting too close. She was all politeness, pleases and thank-yous and no, ma'ams, but anything more familiar than that would've felt like a betrayal. The only mother she needed was her own, and she was long gone. Ada slid Evie a cup of warm milk across the table.

"Something troubling you?"

"Just a lot of excitement coming, is all." Evie stirred her porridge, and didn't look up. She pulled the cup of milk closer to her, grateful for its warmth with the early winter wind blowing through gaps in the rough plaster wall.

"Weddings do bring excitement, that's for sure. Excitement and change," Ada said. Evie looked up. "Miss Maggie was chattering all about the news, but maybe a change of scene would do you good. It's plain enough this isn't where you want to be." With that, Ada picked up her plate and left.

Evie sighed, feeling uncomfortably exposed, like everyone could see through her. She had kept Ada and the others at arm's length since she arrived, but there was no point trying to make a home of the place—Kate had said from the beginning that they wouldn't be in the city long, even if Evie had silently hoped otherwise. Of course, it was never her hopes that mattered. Stay or go, Philadelphia or Maryland, city or country, Virginia or South Carolina, it was all in whatever notion Kate took—and so it would be again. Unless Evie could get ahold of Carrie. If she'd found freedom here in Philadelphia, maybe Evie could too.

———

A COUPLE OF WEEKS later, Evie saw a crowd of well-dressed Black women, all with clipboards in their hands, milling around near the Second Street entrance to the market, across from a firehouse. At the center of the group was the same woman who'd been with Carrie before. For the past few weeks, Evie had been going to the market alongside the house servants to do the weekly shopping, hoping to run into Carrie herself, but she hadn't had any luck. But this woman would do. When she spied the familiar face, Evie slipped away from the other servants and went over to the group.

"What's all this?" she asked the young woman politely.

"A petition drive! We're writing to Congress to speak out against the ills of slavery. Would you like to read and sign?" The woman's voice was friendly, and her speech crisp and refined.

"Ah, can't do either." Evie looked over the woman's shoulder at the rest of the group. No sign of Carrie.

"That's all right, everyone has their ways to contribute. We'll be back on Tuesday holding our fair, selling cakes, handkerchiefs, and other trifles to support construction of the new abolition hall. Why don't you come back around then? Buy a sweet and call it politics," she said with a smile.

That, Evie could do. And if anywhere, this was where she was likely to find Carrie. She'd always had a sweet tooth—both of them did. Once, when Evie was about seven, she'd stolen a caramel off Kate's dressing table after trying and failing to resist the temptation all day. But when Kate complained to old Massah Murphy about its going missing, Carrie piped up and took the blame. Kate had pouted, and didn't say a word when Murphy rapped Carrie on the hand with his cane so hard he broke the skin and cracked one of her knuckles. Carrie couldn't close her hand around the duster for weeks after that, but Evie had taken up the slack. Evie wondered if Carrie still had the scar—if she still remembered any of it at all.

Chapter 5

CHARLOTTE

ON A TUESDAY IN DECEMBER, CHARLOTTE AND NELL MET AT THEIR usual spot in Washington Square Park. Charlotte was nervous but game—Nell had invited her to join the women's Antislavery Society for one of their most important annual events, and Charlotte had pinned high hopes on the occasion.

"You'll be great," Nell said as they shivered their way through the streets, bundled up in their scarves and heaviest coats. *I'd better be,* Charlotte thought. After her embarrassing showing at the first Wheatley Literary Association meeting, for weeks she'd been trying to dig herself out of the hole with the other women in Nell's social circle, and so far she wasn't having much luck. Even without knowing what Charlotte really was, they knew she wasn't one of them, and that was enough.

No one said anything directly, of course—they were too polite. But it was obvious in their little remarks, the glances at Charlotte's neat if somewhat plain clothing, and always the questions about why exactly she was confined to meeting only on Tuesdays. Eventually, she'd at least picked up that the point of the Wheatley Association was to share the writings of other Black people rather than to pore over the works of long-dead white men like James's beloved Shakespeare. Still, at meetings, Charlotte was wary and quiet when talk turned political—she felt very much the outsider. Nell tried to help her along, slipping her copies of books and the latest issues of *The*

Pennsylvania Freeman, where the stories slaves had written about their lives made Charlotte shift in her seat for all their familiarity. Last time they'd met, Nell had slid yet one more sheet of paper into Charlotte's bag, a flyer: "Pennsylvania Female Antislavery Society, Holiday Fair—December 19–22, Arch Street Fire House." When Nell invited her to join them for a shift at the fair, Charlotte finally saw her chance. There, Charlotte could sit alongside the women and really make conversation, the best kind, which comes from working toward a common goal. While there was clearly no social cachet in *being* part of the city's downtrodden Black lower classes, helping such people was something else entirely, and that's what the fair was all about.

As they walked toward the firehouse that morning, Nell went over all the details one more time: together, they'd sell trinkets, cakes, and other trifles to raise money to underwrite operations for the statewide Pennsylvania Antislavery Society and support the running of a school for free Black girls. They'd donate any remaining funds to groups that provided food and shelter for the poor and for fugitive slaves. With some of the proceeds, the women's Antislavery Society also planned to deck out their future meeting room at Pennsylvania Hall with fine furnishings and artwork. Their fundraising goal was fifteen hundred dollars, a sum so huge it hardly sounded real. But if Charlotte turned out to be helpful in raising the money, maybe the women would finally warm up to her.

She followed Nell through the city, listening eagerly. But when they reached Market Street, Nell started to turn in toward the market sheds. Charlotte stopped short. "Where are you going? I thought the fair was at the firehouse."

"Oh, that's where the main part is, but I had this idea to set up a table right inside the market to catch more shoppers, and everyone loved it. So that's where we'll be!"

Charlotte suddenly felt a roll of dread in her stomach. Even being in the neighborhood was bad enough, but the market itself—this wasn't where she wanted to be. She'd avoided the place since that day—that girl. She'd decided it was best to stay away, even as she reassured herself over and over that she couldn't have seen who she thought. No, Evie was still at White Oaks, right where Charlotte had left her.

The night James took Charlotte and ran, she'd sobbed for having left Evie and the others behind in that life, where all of them had nothing and were nothing, with no future to look forward to but being sold, or bred, or worked to death. All her father had for her then were gentle pats on the head and a hoarse whisper—"Hush, hush, now, we've got to go on." And so she had. For four years, Charlotte had tried not to think of them, and now she was finally beginning to look toward her own future. But knowing they were still back there—Auntie Irene, Evie, and Daniel—was always a dull ache in the pit of her stomach, one that sharpened with every reminder of them: the prick of a sewing needle on her finger, a bouquet of spring wildflowers on a table, or the smile of a handsome brown-skinned boy on the street. It wasn't Evie she'd seen at the market that day—it was a guilt-conjured ghost. She was certain of it. Still, Charlotte wasn't in a hurry to go back for another haunting. She stopped walking.

"Are you all right?" Nell asked, staring at her. "I'm sure someone will have brought an extra scarf if you're worried about sitting outside. And we'll be close together, so we'll stay warm." She smiled.

Charlotte forced her lips into a tight smile, nodded, and continued onward. What else was there to do? At the market, Charlotte and Nell found Lillian ready and waiting to set up. Together, the women arranged chairs behind a long table near the northern entrance to the sheds. The tabletop held all the wares for sale—cakes, confections, and embroidered handkerchiefs and quilts—each neatly arranged between signs attesting to the group's antislavery cause. Many of the handsewn items were embroidered or printed with an icon from the Philadelphia Female Antislavery Society's seal: the striking image of a kneeling, half-dressed Black woman with her wrists chained, hands clasped, and eyes fixed upward at some unseen superior. Above her head were the words AM I NOT A WOMAN, AND A SISTER? Though the motto gestured at equality, Charlotte stared at the woman frozen in her pleading pose and saw what she feared: for women like Nell, a slave was no peer but a beggar to be lifted from the dirt as an act of charity. Uncomfortable, she smoothed her dress and tried to push away the thought.

It was chilly though the December sun shone bright, with the roof of the market shading the tables from its warmth. Shoppers trickled past, some uninterested, others walking up to look over the merchandise and chat a little, and still others meeting the women with hard, angry stares. However righteous their cause, the abolitionists were by no means popular. For her own part, though, Charlotte was establishing herself as a favorite as the morning wore on. She expertly cajoled customers into spending more, and even directed some into the firehouse across the street, where tables had been set up so they could shop in relative warmth.

"You're like our very own lucky charm," said Lillian. "We're so glad to have you here!" Nell must've overheard, and she looked over at Charlotte with a small, satisfied smile at the sound of Lillian's icy façade cracking. Inside, Charlotte beamed, but she worked to keep her face neutral—that seemed more refined.

With the sweets in front of her selling out so quickly, it wasn't long before she needed to restock. Charlotte got up from the table and went behind the chairs, bending down to grab as many boxes of confections and miniature cakes as she could keep in her arms. She nearly dropped them when she felt a tap on her shoulder.

"Excuse me—Carrie?" a girl's voice spoke quietly.

At the sound of her old name, Charlotte whipped around.

Evie had grown in the years since Charlotte had last seen her, from a girl into a budding young woman. Even though she'd already glimpsed her a few weeks back—without admitting as much to herself—Charlotte was overwhelmed at the sight of her. Her young friend had been frozen in her memory just as she'd left her at White Oaks. But standing in front of her now, Evie had grown—her big dark, deep-set eyes had lost the innocence they once held, and her rounded cheeks had resolved into something flatter and more defined. She was dressed like Charlotte used to be, a neat if not stylish housemaid out in town. But most wonderfully, she was alive, and safe.

Not wanting to make a scene, Charlotte resisted the urge to pull Evie into a hug. Instead, she grabbed both of Evie's hands and squeezed them intensely, and pulled her aside several feet from the table. Lillian, Nell, and the others glanced over but soon had to return their attention to the customers in front of them.

"It *is* you," Evie and Charlotte both said at the same time, then broke into laughter. Charlotte was overcome with relief. Evie was here, and she was all right. But Charlotte's joy quickly curdled as she realized what it meant that she was seeing her old companion in the midst of her new life. She looked over her shoulder, hoping none of the other women were paying them any mind, and wondering what Evie must think of all she'd come upon.

"What are you doing here? Did you run away too?" Charlotte asked.

"No, Kate brought me here. We moved into a house near the river last month."

"We?" Charlotte's breath caught in her throat. "You mean Daniel and Auntie Irene? Are they . . ." She started looking around the market for them before even finishing her question. At the thought of seeing Daniel, she smoothed down her hair without thinking.

"No, they're not with me." Evie's voice was oddly flat. Charlotte deflated. They must be back at White Oaks. It was just as well. But there was still the problem of who *was* with Evie.

"Does Kate know me and my father are here? Is that why she's in the city? To take us?" Charlotte felt the panic rising. Her heart was racing and she was beginning to sweat. She didn't know exactly what would happen to James and her if Kate caught them after all these years, but she could guess the consequences of disappearing for such a long time would be severe. Kate herself always playacted kindness, but she never stood in the way of any of the plantation men doling out punishments. With Massah Murphy dead, who knew what man she had by her side now to enforce her will.

"She doesn't know a thing," said Evie. "She came here and took up with some man from South Carolina who does business in the city, and she's set to marry him soon. She dragged me along since I'm her ladies' maid now, and I come to the market with the other slaves sometimes when they do their shopping. That's all."

If Kate wasn't here to claw Charlotte and James back, and was on her way down to South Carolina, maybe she wouldn't pose a threat if Evie handled things quietly. Maybe James didn't even need to hear about this. No one did. Charlotte glanced at the table again—Lillian, Nell, and the others were happily bargaining.

"You'll keep this a secret, won't you, Evie? She cannot know that we're here!" She looked around, still nervous someone might be watching them.

"I won't tell, don't worry," Evie said. "But I don't want to go down to South Carolina either."

Charlotte drew her hands back from Evie. It wasn't clear there was anything to be done about that.

"But won't your family be with you at least?" she asked Evie.

"I've got no family anymore, not since you left us behind," Evie said.

"Well of course you do, don't be silly—your ma, and Daniel—"

"No," said Evie. "When Kate couldn't pay off the debts on the place after old Murphy passed, and with no money coming in from Uncle Jack's workshop, she sold Ma and Daniel." Evie had no idea where they'd been sold off to, and she never saw them again, she explained, her face showing her anguish.

Auntie Irene, gone. And Daniel. *Daniel.* Of everything her father had taken away from her when they ran, all the hopes he'd dashed and plans he'd interrupted, this was the one Charlotte could least forgive. What had just begun between her and Daniel four years ago had been sweet, and new, and carried with it the promise of family— a real family, where she and Evie would truly be sisters. And now even that family had been torn apart by her going, and Daniel was lost to her all over again. Charlotte felt sick as she listened to Evie's story, and her eyes burned, but she pushed her tongue to the roof of her mouth to stop the tears before they could fall. Charlotte didn't deserve to cry for them. She'd left.

Evie went on.

"With you gone, I was the only one left there to be Kate's personal maid, though I suppose she felt I was never as good at it as you were," Evie continued. "I was mostly indoors, at least I had that much. But her brothers came round to visit her often after Massah Murphy died, and the way they started looking at me—I don't even like to think of it. But they never lifted a finger to help us, and with no money coming in, there were plenty of nights we all went hungry," she said. She paused for a moment and pressed her lips together, willing herself to stay in command of her emotions. Charlotte grabbed her hand and squeezed it, wishing she could take some of the pain onto herself. She'd known Evie would miss her after she left, but how could she have known the girl's whole life would unravel?

"Things have been a little better since we came up here," Evie said. "After Kate went home to Virginia, her brothers convinced their Philadelphia cousins to take her in, give her some distance from Murphy's stench and let her start over. At least we aren't starving anymore. But I've still got no one to talk to. Kate's cousins mostly split time between here and Virginia and bring their slaves along, but I keep to myself," she said. Charlotte could relate to that. With only the taciturn Darcel and her distant father at home, she didn't have much in the way of company either. At least not company she could be completely honest with about where she'd come from, or where she hoped she was headed. Since leaving White Oaks she hadn't told her story to another soul. There was no one she felt she could trust, and maybe no one who would even care. But against what Evie had suffered, her complaints suddenly felt like they didn't amount to much.

"I'm so sorry for what you've been through," said Charlotte. "You have to know, I didn't want to leave you—any of you. My father just woke me one night and said we were leaving right then, and that's all there was to it. He didn't even tell me why. It wasn't until we reached our first stop that I realized no one else was coming with us. Best I can tell, he wanted to make himself a new life somewhere and saw a chance to do it when old Massah Murphy died."

"You mean a new life for the both of you together? He's here too, isn't he?" asked Evie.

"He is," Charlotte said carefully. She shifted her weight from foot to foot—Lillian, Nell, and the others had started glancing over at her and Evie curiously, and the attention made her nervous. She needed to get back to her seat, but she knew she owed Evie answers. She continued explaining. "But as far as anyone around here knows, he's a white man and I'm just his maid, not his daughter. I still spend all day keeping house, I just get paid for it now."

Evie's eyes went wide at that. "Uncle Jack always did have that look about him," she said. She took a deep breath. "Look, I don't want to be any trouble to you, but I don't know who else I can go to. I've got to get away from Kate. I know there's free Black folks here in the city, and folks who help slaves get away from their masters. Isn't that what these ladies do?" She gestured at Nell and Lillian. "If you'll just introduce me—"

Charlotte's throat tightened.

"I'm not so sure," she said, cutting Evie off. She bit her lip while she took a beat to think, and placed herself more squarely between Evie and the others. "The political abolitionists are one thing, but I can't tell if they're the same people as the folks actually helping fugitives escape. I don't even know who I'd take you to."

"You must know someone," said Evie. "Otherwise, how did *you* get here?"

"That's just it," said Charlotte. "After we left White Oaks, we spent a few nights working our way through the woods, but after that, with my father passing, we set ourselves up here on our own, and didn't need any help since we could blend right in," said Charlotte. "He had a little money saved up from his carpentry work on White Oaks, what Massah let him keep when he hired him out."

Evie's shoulders slumped. Charlotte looked at her with pity, and more than a little guilt. Charlotte wanted to help her, but how could she get involved without turning her own life upside down when it was just getting started? Charlotte knew that plenty of people, white and Black, helped fugitive slaves around the city, but there had to be some kind of planning that went into it.

"My friends might be the right people to help, or know who is," said Charlotte. "But I need time to think, and find out whether they can be trusted." Trusted not to throw Charlotte over if they found out what she was. There had to be a way to get Evie sorted without undoing her own plans.

"I don't know how much time I have," said Evie. "The wedding is in June, but if Kate wants to go back to Virginia before then to plan—"

"I understand," Charlotte interjected. "We should talk again soon. You come here every week?"

Evie shook her head. "Just every so often," she said.

"That's just as well, it'll give me more time to figure things out," said Charlotte. "I'll come back and check for you each Tuesday, and give you updates if I have any. But I'd better get back to the table now. And won't your people be looking for you?"

Evie nodded and walked off, leaving Charlotte standing amid the extra merchandise. She grabbed a handful of confections and settled herself back at the table, trying not to appear rattled.

Lillian looked at her suspiciously. "Everything all right?" she said. "That took an awfully long time."

"Everything is fine, there was just a girl asking about the recipe for the confections, she'd tasted one earlier and liked them so much. I told her to come around to a meeting one of these days and we could talk it over," Charlotte replied. "Any way to get folks involved, right?"

"That's what Nell always says, isn't it?" Lillian's tone of voice didn't make clear whether she thought that was good or bad.

At any rate, Charlotte was well and truly involved now.

She hadn't promised Evie much—just another meeting—but even that promise wasn't one she was sure she wanted to keep. One thing was for certain, though—her father couldn't know about any of this. He'd only try to run again, shaken at the faintest whiff of Kate, and then Evie and Charlotte would both be lost, each in her own way. No, this was one escape Charlotte would have to manage without his help. But that didn't mean she had to do it alone.

Chapter 6

NELL

It WAS A WEEK AFTER THE HOLIDAY FAIR, AND CHARLOTTE AND Nell had spent the morning browsing the shops. Charlotte had been unusually quiet and fidgety, so it was plain something was distracting her. Nell wondered whether the Christmas holiday had dampened Charlotte's mood—though the day had passed, the festive atmosphere was lingering with a light dusting of snow on the ground, and wreaths still decorating every shop door—and after Nell mentioned her own family's celebration, Charlotte mumbled sadly that she'd just spent the day on her own in prayer and reflection. It sounded lonely, and Nell felt for her. Charlotte hadn't said much since. But just as they got up to leave the café on Spruce Street where they'd been sipping hot coffee to warm up, it seemed Charlotte was finally ready to talk.

"Can I ask a favor of you? It's important. And private," Charlotte said.

Nell nodded and the two walked, shivering in the late December cold.

"I've got a project I think you'll be interested in, and I wondered if you'd want to help," she said. Charlotte's voice was tentative, but her nerves only made the prospect that much more interesting. What intrigue was this?

Nell leaned closer and took Charlotte's arm. "Tell me all about it."

"Well, I've met a young woman, a slave from Maryland brought here by her mistress. Before she's forced to go back down South, she wants to run. To get free." Charlotte's eyes were on the ground, and she picked at the edges of her sleeves as she spoke. Whether her hesitance was owing to the dangerous subject matter or something more, Nell couldn't quite decide. Her voice had a faraway tone, and she was vague on the details of how she'd encountered the girl, who was named Evie. She'd only say that she'd met her at the market on the day of the fair and felt moved to help—maybe that's who she had been talking to when she stepped away from the table for so long. Privately, Nell was warmed by the idea that she'd been such an influence for Charlotte to do some good. Still, it felt like there was something she was leaving out.

"I need help to figure out how I can get her to safety, and with all your abolition work I thought you'd be the right person to ask," Charlotte said, turning to Nell with hopeful eyes.

If only that were true. There were plenty of Black families in the city deeply involved in the dangerous business of emancipating slaves one by one, but the Gardners weren't one of them. Nell's parents tolerated her involvement in the women's Antislavery Society, sure—it was a respectable charitable and social outlet for well-born girls like her. But that was as far as it went. The risks of taking things beyond committee meetings and bake sales were too great to even consider. For her parents, anyway. But here—here was an opportunity for Nell to live out all she'd been reading in the newspapers and books. And how unexpected! For all her plans to bring Charlotte into her world, it appeared the tables had turned. Or maybe they were both being pulled into this Evie's. Either way, the work wasn't to be taken on casually.

"It's not exactly abolition work you're talking about, Charlotte," Nell said slowly. "We wouldn't be changing the law by helping this girl; we'd be breaking it. We could be arrested and fined hundreds of dollars." Or worse. Mobs around the country were willing to kill people for even discussing the notion of freeing slaves, let alone actually doing it. And right here in the city, plenty of folks had been attacked on suspicion of helping runaways. For everyone's safety—and reputation—there could be no mistakes.

Charlotte's shoulders slumped.

"But," Nell continued, "that doesn't mean it isn't the right thing to do." Nell could hardly say no. She'd be proud to have a hand in helping this young woman, and it was high time she started doing more about abolition than just talking and fundraising. She'd longed for a way to make a real difference, and here was one—it didn't get any more real than this.

"Thank you. I wouldn't ask it lightly," Charlotte said, squeezing Nell's arm. "What do we do? I'll see her again in a few weeks and I don't know what to tell her."

What *would* they do? Confronted with the rare question she didn't know the answer to, Nell figured she'd do what she always did: read. While lately the Wheatley Association had been more focused on political tracts and poetry, she'd heard that in recent years there had been accounts of court cases involving fugitive slaves and a few first-person accounts of slavery written by some who had escaped, published in full-length books. The trouble would be getting her hands on them. There was a decent enough book collection at home, but Mr. Gardner was careful not to personally print too much controversial material, and he certainly kept none of it in the house. That left the library, but while they let women's groups rent rooms there, actual circulation was confined to male patrons. Fortunately, later that week Nell ran into just the man to infiltrate on her behalf.

Outfitted in a wool dress and her heavy winter coat, Nell had just stepped out of the house when Mrs. Marion waved from across the street, where she was seeing her son Alex off for the day.

"Good morning, Nell!" Mrs. Marion called out brightly, tapping the snow off the winter holly bushes decorating her front steps. With a pointed lack of subtlety, she gave Alex a sharp elbow in the side that Nell couldn't miss, even from a distance.

He laughed. "I cherish your gentle cues, Ma. Out for a Sunday stroll, Nell?" It was Thursday.

Nell shook her head. "It must be some kind of life you've got,

Alex, never needing to know what day it is," she said. "And good morning, Mrs. Marion! I hope you had a lovely holiday."

Alex fell in step beside her. "I'll walk with you a ways, I'm in no rush this morning."

"No, you never are," she said. Her tone was good-natured and easy. She and Alex had been neighbors for years and had been ribbing each other just as long, having grown up like brother and sister.

"And where are you off to in such a hurry?" Even with Alex's long-legged stride, Nell noticed it took some effort for him to keep up with her determined pace. He was nearly a foot taller than she was, with golden brown skin and bushy red-brown hair that glinted in the sun.

"I'm delivering some quilts to the shelter." Her sewing circle had finally finished their gifts for the new Shelter for Colored Orphans, stitched together from scraps of dresses Nell had outgrown. A lace fringe here, a free-labor cotton pattern there, a ribbon of silk, the blankets were a patchwork of dainty teas and formal dinners, a girl-hood ensconced in the city's Black elite. It seemed fitting, now, to take what remained of all that and give it away to children who possessed nothing, and no one.

Alex stopped walking and gave her a once-over. "Where are they?"

"I've only got two in my bag, they're quite heavy so I'll need to make a few trips to drop off all seven." There was no way Nell's thin arms could carry them all at once, nor would she have tried. But here was a better idea. "You've got time this morning, Alex," she said after a pause. It wasn't a question, but her phrasing ensured Alex heard the request all the same. He smiled.

"They're in the wooden trunk in the parlor," she said. "You're a gem."

He took off jogging back down the block. "When I catch back up," he called, "you'll have to tell me all about your friend."

Alex was yards away in an instant, so he didn't catch Nell's defensive flinch. He could only mean Charlotte, of course. Of all the women she'd recently walked through the neighborhood with, chatting, discussing books, and laughing, Charlotte was the only one Alex could conceivably need to be told about. The rest were well-known members of their social circle who lived in the neighborhood. They'd all grown up together, taking teas and dinners in one finely appointed parlor or dining room, then another, and another.

But not Charlotte. Of course Alex would've sensed she wasn't one of them, though it remained to be seen whether his interest was good-natured curiosity or snobbery, like Nell had come to expect from her family. She was feeling especially tender on the subject given the unexpected turn their friendship had taken as they conspired about how to help Evie.

She walked on and Alex soon caught up, a thin film of sweat forming on his forehead as he trotted up beside her, his arms laden with loose quilts. At the sight of him, Nell laughed her quick, sharp laugh despite herself. All her careful folding, undone by Alex's special brand of "help."

"What?" he asked, knowing the answer.

She ignored the question. "What was it you'd wanted to ask about my friend? She's new to the city and I've begun inviting her to the Wheatley Association," Nell said. "Or, I think she's new. She doesn't get out too much—domestic work, you know."

"I don't, actually. But I've seen you with her what seems like every Tuesday morning going back months now. Why not introduce her around properly?"

"Who's to say I haven't? We're working on an important project together," said Nell.

Alex raised his eyebrows. "And how's that going over with your parents?"

"About as well as your hobbies are going over with yours, I'd imagine," Nell said, laughing. For all he liked to play the scamp, Alex was a conscientious son. Nell had watched him for years dutifully helping his father build up the family's catering business. But he had other interests too. Earlier in the year, he'd started helping to run *The Pennsylvania Freeman,* the paper the Wheatley Association often read and sometimes wrote for. Though he mostly kept his involvement quiet to avoid disrupting his father's business, it was still a source of some family tension. But it could also be useful.

"Alex, what do you all at the paper hear these days about runaways in the city?" she asked as they wound through the streets.

"Only that they're all around us, despite the best efforts of the legislature and the slave catchers," he said. Then, leaning in conspiratorially, "I hear some fugitives can even be found hidden away behind trapdoors in the homes of some of our better-known fellow Philadelphians, but you won't read that in the *Freeman*."

Trying to keep things light, Nell pulled an exaggeratedly shocked face at Alex's information. But there—that was an idea.

"Could I ask you a favor?" she said quietly. "I'm trying to learn more about the laws governing slavery, and about the goings-on down South—I've gathered a lot through the women's Antislavery Society, but I'd feel more confident if I could make a bit of a study of things."

"Down South? There's plenty of the same going on right here, you know, and worse—"

"I know, Alex, I was at Mr. Purvis's speech, remember? But that's the thing—I'd like to understand what people are running from, and perhaps also, exactly how they're getting and staying free. Could you pull a few books from the library for me to fill in the gaps?"

"Of course," Alex said. "What did you have in mind?" She rattled off a list of the slave narratives she'd heard about but had not yet been able to lay hands on, and asked for any texts Alex could find that would help her better understand the legal landscape surrounding slavery.

As she did, Alex's eyes widened. "What exactly are you getting into here, Nell?" His voice was low, the danger obvious to both of them.

Nell gave a light shrug and said nothing, as they were finally coming up to the shelter.

The director met them at the door of the cavernous redbrick building and gratefully accepted the quilts.

"How kind, Nell, thank you," she said. "Thank you both."

"You're quite welcome! My sewing circle and I are glad to be able to help," she said, carefully making sure to share the credit with the other women. Silently, she drank in the feeling of accomplishment the donation gave her. "I won't take up any more of your time. Do let me know if there's anything else we can do to contribute—the work you'll do here is so very important."

With that, she and Alex said their farewells and left.

"This is where I get off," Alex said after a few blocks, stopping short to pull out his pocket watch and confirm the time. "Pleased as I am to be your delivery boy for the day, I do have a few places of my own to go."

It was just as well. Alone now with nothing left to carry, Nell was free to reflect, and she suddenly wondered whether the solution to Evie's problem wasn't right in her own house. If other respected families were helping runaways, maybe Nell's parents just needed some persuading. With Evie's plight pressing in on her mind, this was as good a time as any to try, and the family's monthly evening with the Marions would be the perfect opportunity. She considered for a moment, then called after her neighbor.

"Oh, and, Alex—when we all get together this weekend, do me a favor and follow my lead, will you?"

He turned back to her, winked, and then he was off.

THE GARDNER-MARION GAME NIGHT that weekend came at the perfect time. Nell always looked forward to these evenings. As tedious as many of her social engagements could be, the game nights were the rare occasions she got to catch up with Alex and his younger brother, Theodore, and enjoy some of the experimental recipes Mr. Marion dreamt up for his catering business: aromatic broths, crispy chicken croquettes, lemon pudding. There was always something delectable to try, and tonight's menu was sure to be special since the evening doubled as a New Year's Eve celebration.

Across the street, the Marions' house was nearly a mirror image of the Gardners' and just as grand, only with deep crimson shutters rather than green. At the door, the Marions' maid took their coats and beckoned them into the parlor, where Mr. and Mrs. Marion and the boys were waiting, with the elders already seated at opposite ends of the card table.

"Come in, we're all ready for you," Mrs. Marion said, waving the Gardners over to join them for a game of whist. Nell's mother nudged her toward the piano, where Alex was seated and plinking along the keys.

"Why don't you go over and accompany him, dear? We love to hear you sing."

Nell didn't protest, she'd wanted to talk with him anyway. On the narrow piano bench, she sidled up close to him. "Go on and play," she said. She hummed along for a few songs, until their parents became absorbed in their game and stopped paying attention.

"Were you able to find everything?" she asked, just under the volume of Alex's expert rendition of Mozart's "Rondo alla Turca." He nodded, smiled, and kept playing.

"Quite an interesting list of titles you asked for, but I got them all. I set them aside for you in a bag in the foyer, so you can take them home whenever you'd like. I'm guessing not tonight," he said, smiling. Even as he spoke, he never lost track of the melody, and Nell found herself swaying along as she always did. "I'd ask again what you're up to, but—"

Nell shrugged. "Just learning more about the world outside these fine walls, is all," she said lightly, looking down at the keys as Alex played. She noticed an ink stain running along his thumb and forefinger. "I could ask you the same, you know. Been writing love letters?" She playfully nudged his shoulder with her own, knocking him off the rhythm.

At her touch, he smirked and stopped playing for a moment, causing their parents to look up from their cards.

"Has our talented pianist gotten weary?" Mr. Marion said genially. "Why don't you two come and take our place, we've just lost this game."

"Just follow my lead," she said under her breath as they walked over.

As they settled into their seats, Mrs. Gardner dealt the cards and Nell assembled her hand.

"So, Alex, what's new with you?" Mrs. Gardner asked him.

Before he could answer, Nell piped up, leaning in as if pushed forward on a tide of gossip. "Well, Alex was just telling me about all he's been hearing at the newspaper," she said. "It seems there's been an uptick in runaways coming to the city, and more and more families like ours taking them in, quietly. Hiding them away somewhere in the house."

Alex glanced at Nell, and seeing her unblinking stare, he nodded in agreement. "It's true, there's lots of this kind of underground organizing going on in many northern cities," he said. "Even formal structures being put in place for it."

Behind him, Mr. Marion, who'd been looming over the card game with his wife, coughed. "You heard this at the newspaper, did you?"

"If it's going on so quietly, why is it in the papers?" Nell's brother, George, interjected from across the room. Nell ignored him—she couldn't let this be derailed, though her father didn't seem to be taking the bait from her and Alex. She'd have to engage more directly.

"Pa, Mr. Marion, have either of you heard anything about this? I understand it's happening more and more among the good families in our neighborhood." That was wishful thinking. Nell couldn't say for certain how much covert, direct action against slavery was actually taking place on their particular block, but upper-class Black families in the city *had* grown more politically active over the years, leading and inserting themselves into local debates over slavery, the vote, and even women's proper role in public life. Nell's parents were traditionalists on that last score.

"Taking in fugitives, is that so?" Pa shifted a card from one side of his hand to the other, considering. "I suppose that's something one might do, yes."

"I wonder what it's like," her mother chimed in. "It seems terribly risky—not just for getting caught, but having a complete stranger in your house."

"Me too, I wonder what it's like," Nell echoed, ignoring the second half of her mother's comment. "What a kind thing to do. Brave, really."

"I suppose all of us came from someone who was a stranger in this city at one point," Mrs. Marion said.

"Well said, Mother," Alex piped up. "It's necessary, brave work."

"What's brave about hiding someone?" George interrupted again. "It seems to me the brave thing would be to do it openly, declare oneself along with the abolitionists, that sort of thing. Or go and pick up the slaves from down South and run them up to freedom— *that* would be brave."

Nell chalked up her brother's belligerence to his age—she wouldn't expect much different from a seventeen-year-old. At twenty-one though, Nell had more discretion, and didn't shy away from teasing her brother for his lack of it.

"Yes, George," she said. "I'm sure you'd be the first to take up arms against the slave owners and smother their children in their beds as well. We've got the gist of how you conceive of bravery, thank you." Her words were cutting but her tone was light.

"Nell . . ." her mother chided.

Nell put up her hands in surrender. Her brother just rolled his eyes.

"I'm simply saying, going about things quietly seems to be more effective," Nell continued. "All the cloak and dagger may be less satisfying than brute force, but it's working—people are getting away freely, and in the long run isn't that what we all want?"

"Of course it is, well said," her father replied. "And there are plenty of different ways to work toward that. George has the methods he endorses, some people will hide runaways, and then there are things that families like ours can do."

"But hiding runaways *is* one of the things families like ours can do," Alex interjected. Nell looked up at him and gave a quick, small smile.

"I suppose, but why go through all that fuss and intrigue when we can be so much more helpful just by sharing our resources? We've only got one house to hide people in, but our money can help clothe, feed, and shelter dozens. Or we can work the political angles to free thousands. It seems to me that's the part of this we belong in, and never mind about the rest of it."

"You make a good point, Pa," Nell said, covering her disappointment.

"He couldn't have gotten this far in life without occasionally doing so," said Mr. Marion, laughing. "Now, let's all try some lobster salad—I've been working on a new recipe."

That seemed to settle things. Everyone smiled and went back to their cards, playing through to the end of the hand until the food was brought out. Before long, Nell's mother spoke and changed the subject to an upcoming ball.

Amid the quiet, Nell weighed her options. She wasn't surprised by her father's stance, but it had been worth a try, and at the least her family was none the wiser about why she'd raised the subject in the first place. Still, the conversation left her without an obvious way to help Charlotte's friend. If there was one thing Nell couldn't abide, it was feeling useless. One way or another, she'd get out in front of this problem. She just needed to figure out how.

At least in Alex, she had an ally, even if he didn't quite know what for. As he shuffled the cards for the next hand, she looked up at him across the table and mouthed, "Thank you."

Chapter 7

CHARLOTTE

WEEKS HAD COME AND GONE SINCE EVIE HAD ASKED FOR HELP, and a whole new year had been rung in, but the dawn of 1838 brought Charlotte and Nell no closer to a plan. So far, Nell's reading hadn't turned up any answers, and it sounded like her family had no plans to get involved. Charlotte had suggested turning to someone in the Wheatley Association, thinking that maybe one of the women's families, rather than the Gardners, could offer Evie a safe haven. Trouble was, it was impossible to know who could be trusted enough to ask—given all the secrecy it took to keep fugitives safe, hardly anyone ever seemed to talk about it. At loose ends, the two of them had taken to walking the city streets, talking and racking their brains. Charlotte found that the bracing cold air cleared her head enough to think, and Nell mostly seemed to enjoy showing her around the city.

One morning in January, Nell led Charlotte past the Pennsylvania Hall building site. With the structure's frame closed, the carpenters were perched on wooden scaffolds putting the finishing touches on the exterior, and on the street, one couldn't pass by too close for fear of getting covered with dust and flying debris. Charlotte's clothes weren't valuable so she didn't fret too much, but she could tell Nell was a little precious about this sort of thing. Dressed in all her finery, she picked her way along the sidewalk, carefully positioning herself a step ahead of Charlotte and dead center in the path, the farthest possible point between the dusty road on one side and the carpentry on the other. Charlotte smiled. For all Nell's pride in her investment in this planned monument to abolition, she still liked to keep some space between herself and its gritty reality.

"It'll be magnificent, just wait until the opening this spring," Nell said. "People will come from all over to push the abolitionist cause forward, all in a space of our own—one not so easily mobbed and torn apart like a little stage in the park."

As she spoke, Nell looked at her meaningfully, and Charlotte chuckled, then stopped. "Nell, what exactly does the Antislavery Society do when you're not hosting fairs?" she asked. "I mean, what's this building for, exactly?"

Nell seemed to perk up at the sign of Charlotte's interest. "The hall will be a meeting space, mostly. The women's Antislavery Society and the men's abolitionist groups as well will hold gatherings here, work on our efforts like petitioning Congress for abolition, and invite the public to learn more by hosting speakers who can talk about the issue. In fact, there's even talk of inviting Miss Angelina Grimke to speak at the conference this spring!"

Charlotte cocked her head to the side, and Nell grinned. They were past the point of Charlotte having to ask "Who?" every time Nell brought up the name of some new luminary.

"She's a renowned abolitionist, a young woman like us," Nell said. "She comes from a family who holds slaves down South, in Charleston."

"So not *too* much like us, then," Charlotte said slyly.

Nell laughed but went on. "She and her sister have turned their backs on slavery and now they speak out against it. She wrote an essay in recent years that caused quite a stir, *An Appeal to the Christian Women of the South*. I'm rereading it myself ahead of the next Antislavery Society meeting." She reached into her bag and held the slim pamphlet up.

Instantly, Charlotte became more aware of their surroundings. "Put that away!" She grabbed it and stuffed it into her own bag just to get it out of sight. People didn't casually wave abolitionist literature around on the street—not unless they were looking for trouble.

And with the unstable balance of Charlotte's double lives, she most assuredly was not. Especially with the incident at the speech, she'd had more than enough chaos to last her a good while. Getting Evie taken care of quickly and quietly would be the best way to put her life back on safer ground. And maybe the Antislavery Society could be the answer to their problem.

"At this next meeting, do you think you could find someone to help us with Evie?" she asked. "I mean, that's what all the work is about, right? Freeing people?"

Nell paused for a minute to think. "I'm honestly not sure," she said. "Most of our work so far has been on paper—antislavery petitions to Congress and fundraising, things like that. I don't know."

"Have we got any other options?"

Nell shrugged. "There's no harm in trying, I suppose. I could at least plant a seed on the subject." She hesitated. "If the opportunity presents itself."

"I'm not sure we've got time to wait for an opportunity for a seed to grow. Couldn't we just raise the subject ourselves?" Charlotte asked, stepping closer to Nell. "Let me come with you." She'd already met many of the Antislavery Society members at the fair and through the Wheatley Association, how much different could it be to attend a meeting? And this was too important to sit on the sidelines while Nell figured it out alone—Evie was practically family. But Charlotte could see that Nell didn't seem quite sold on the idea.

"Are you sure? It's not so freewheeling as our literary association get-togethers. There's parliamentary procedure to be followed, and things can get quite political. There's less room for emotion."

"You're saying you don't want me there?" Charlotte took a step back, wondering what Nell thought of her. Maybe Charlotte was good enough to come to the threshold of her world, but not to step all the way inside.

"It's not that I don't want you to join, I do," said Nell. "But these things take time, and with the situation being so urgent— The Philadelphia Female Antislavery Society is many things, but it's not a place for urgency, that's all I'm saying."

"I'll follow your lead at the meeting, Nell, I promise. I just can't sit this out—it's too important. Just like you're always saying at our Wheatley meetings—everyone has to get involved in the cause of freedom, and that's what I'm trying to do."

Charlotte's appeal to Nell's own words must've convinced her, because she relented. "All right. It's in two weeks," she said. "But we always meet on Wednesdays—are you sure you'll be able to make it?"

Charlotte felt her heart skip a beat, but she tried to look assured. For Evie's sake, she'd have to find a way to get there. Her only option would be to slip out while Darcel was at home, and just hope he'd be too absorbed with his cooking to notice. It was a risk, but she couldn't let Evie down.

"Don't worry," she said, resolved. "I'll work something out."

ODDLY ENOUGH, WHEN CHARLOTTE wasn't mixed up in scheming about Evie, life went on more or less as normal: she sullenly did her chores at home, and spent what free time she could with Nell, trying to see the shape of what a life in Philadelphia might look like after things were settled with Evie.

Later in January, in the days before the meeting, the two found time for a shopping trip—Nell had a midwinter ball coming up and wanted the benefit of Charlotte's eye when she picked out a dress. In the parlor of a dress shop on Chestnut Street, in Nell's neighborhood, Charlotte sank into the luxuriously deep sofa and admired the shelves of fabrics lining the walls while Nell tried on one dress after another. Charlotte waved away one champagne-hued silk gown whose waist sat too high up on the bodice, wondering aloud if it had been resewn from an older pattern, back when empire waists were still in fashion. Next, she handily rejected a powder-blue satin gown—the waistline was at least in the right place, and the stiff-hemmed pleated skirt cut a lovely silhouette on Nell's lithe, slight figure, but the color did nothing for her complexion. Finally, after an hour, they found a winner.

Nell stepped forward in an emerald-green silk gown with a fitted bodice and lace-trimmed bishop sleeves. The wide pleated skirt was covered with a woven rose pattern in gold, and it gave a satisfying swish when she turned around. "That's the one!" Charlotte said. She smirked as she eyed the dress's low neckline. "But you'll have to go without a shawl if you want the full effect. Or is high society afraid of shoulders and all the rest?" she asked playfully, discreetly gesturing toward Nell's bosom.

Nell laughed. "I hardly think anyone's interested in my shoulders or 'the rest'; it's just going to be the same old people as usual," she said.

"Not even that one boy? The one you said your parents are trying to push on you?" said Charlotte, giving Nell a sly side-eye as she stepped out of the dressing room.

"Alex?" Nell said, all innocence and light. "Don't be silly, we grew up together. He's almost like a brother to me," she said.

"Uh-huh. Does *he* know that?"

"Ha! I can't deny he's a flirt, he always has been. But honestly, I'm immune—who has time for all that silliness when there's so much work to be done?"

"Mm-hmm," Charlotte said, nudging Nell in the side.

Once Nell was dressed again, they went to the shop's front desk. The shop owner, an elegant older Black woman, nodded to Charlotte and slid her two issues of the *Lady's Book* fashion magazine. "You've got a good eye, you know. Maybe you can use these," she said. Charlotte flipped through them while she stood waiting for Nell to arrange delivery of her dress. Inside were full-color panels showing all the latest fashions, along with dress patterns detailing how to create some of the looks. Charlotte thanked the woman as Nell beckoned her toward the door.

"Well, at least now I know what's got you so preoccupied all the time," Nell said as they walked.

"Magazines?"

"Romance! You were teasing me with all that talk about Alex, but I bet you're the one with a beau. Tell me about him!"

Charlotte tried to laugh it off, but her mouth went dry. There was no one, of course—there hadn't been for years, not since her father ripped her away from Daniel. She could halfway understand Nell's denial about Alex, and the idea that someone who'd grown up right alongside her could suddenly be something more. But it hadn't been so sudden, really, had it?

With Daniel, it was like the ripening of a peach: on the tree all along, but one day suddenly heavy with juice, and sweetness, and readiness. That first kiss under the willow tree had made him something more than Evie's big brother, unattainable and seemingly all-knowing. Charlotte had always nursed a little girl's crush on him, but that moment transformed Daniel from a boy who'd belonged to his family, and his massah, to a young man who belonged to Charlotte. And her into a young woman who might belong to him. But who did he belong to now? Charlotte pushed the thought away and shook her head.

"Nope, no beau for me," she said. "You're right—too much to do." She tried to keep her tone light, but something in her voice rang hollow even to her own ears. Nell smiled warmly but let the subject drop. Mercifully, they'd reached Charlotte's turn to head home, and she stepped away from her friend, promising to get together again and plan for their approach at the Antislavery Society meeting. But Charlotte couldn't muster up any excitement. Weighed down by her thoughts of Daniel, she felt numb as she walked on, with the late morning sun throwing shadows into her path.

———

Chapter 8

EVIE

———

WAITING MADE EVERYTHING WORSE. EVERY FORCED CONVERsation, every painful and tedious chore—combing Kate's hair, lugging pitchers of hot water up and down three flights of stairs for her bath, pressing her dresses and sweating from the heat of the heavy iron. Every single day hanging in the balance, under one woman's thumb, watching and waiting to see if another woman would keep her promise or break it. At least a month had passed since Evie had spoken to Carrie at the market, though she'd seen her a few more times, but never for more than a moment, and sometimes only from far away. Carrie would shake her head and mouth "hold on," from a distance. Evie could only hope that meant she was working on some sort of plan, but there was no way to be sure.

In the meantime, Evie had little choice but to continue her life as usual. Since that visit to the market, she wasn't sure if Kate could tell something had changed in her, but despite Evie's best efforts to be patient, she'd grown short-tempered with her mistress. One evening before bed, Kate was sitting in her vanity chair waiting for Evie to plait her hair and droning endlessly about her latest big problem: whether she should invite Mr. Brooks's parents to visit for supper when they came to town, and whether the cook should serve roast lamb or a game hen instead.

"I want to make the best possible impression as their future daughter-in-law, do you know what I mean?" She paused and heaved a great, dramatic sigh. "Well of course you don't, but honestly, it's so complicated managing all these affairs, Evie, and I—"

"Might be less complicated if you weren't hiding so much," Evie snapped.

Kate pouted and cast down her eyes. When she lifted them back up, they were filled with tears, and she held Evie's gaze in the mirror.

Evie tried to soften her face, and Kate launched in again.

"Oh, I know, it's just so much to bear, all of it," she whined.

Of course. How could anyone that self-absorbed take any notice of what might explain Evie's tone? Kate was too busy feeling wounded to realize the change in the air. It had been the same after Carrie disappeared from White Oaks. Evie had waited anxiously for Carrie and her father to come back, but Kate hardly noticed the shift in her mood. It was only Evie's own family who saw the full measure of her worry.

For weeks after Carrie and Uncle Jack left, she'd sit close beside her mother at dinnertime and ask in a pleading whine, "They come back yet from the trip?" Her mother just silently shook her head and kept at her work, stirring a pot or setting the table so that now just the three of them could carry on through their sadness. Until one night, Evie sat at the table across from her family and put on the most serious voice her twelve-year-old self could muster.

"Mama, I'm worried something might've happened to Carrie and Uncle Jack on their trip," she said. She sat up straighter in her chair, and then made the pronouncement: "We have to go and find them. Help bring them home."

Daniel rolled his eyes and leaned forward. "For God's sake, Evie, they—"

"Excuse me!" Mama interjected. "No one takes the Lord's name in vain at my table." Daniel shook his head furiously. He'd been sullen and brooding since they'd gone—he must've missed them as much as Evie did. He went on.

"Sorry, Mama, but she needs to understand—"

"Hush. It ain't your place to tell me what she needs to under-

stand. Eat your dinner." The look their mother gave Daniel brooked
no argument, and he stood up and stormed out. Mama's face softened when she turned to Evie and placed a hand on top of her daughter's.

"Baby, they don't need no help from us. They ran away up North.
I don't think they got caught, we'd have heard about that by now, so
they must've got all the way free."

"And just leave us here? They wouldn't do that, Mama!" Evie
shook her head in disbelief and turned back to her meal. Even as she
refused to accept that Carrie and Uncle Jack would've left them behind, her mother's words planted a seed that the coming weeks
would water. It was three months before Evie's fear of the truth finally blossomed into the open, when she trudged back up the big
house stairs one night after emptying Kate's chamber pot, a task that
had once fallen to Carrie's older, steadier hands. Evie couldn't say
whether it was the smell, or the ache in her legs from what must've
been her tenth trip up the stairs that day, but in that moment when
she realized Carrie wasn't coming back, the betrayal stung so sharply
that she broke down in tears. And the question—"Why?"—had
continued to haunt her until they met again in the market. It tugged
at the edges of her mind even now, both an unasked question and an
accusation.

Now here she was again, waiting on Carrie—or Charlotte, as she
now called herself. And it wasn't clear if she could trust this new
woman any more than she could the old one. Carrie had left her behind to deal with Kate once—who could say she wouldn't do it
again?

As Evie stood behind Kate and lifted one section of hair over another to braid it, her fingers tensed with anxiety. Was waiting always
this hard, or had city life just made her impatient? Since they'd come
to Philadelphia, the whole tempo of life seemed to have speeded up.
At White Oaks there were slow days made even quieter by the selling
off of Evie's family, and she had passed the hours puttering around
the house after Kate, tending to the needs of a woman with nowhere

to go and nothing to do. Now, in a crowded house with ever more comings and goings, cousins and callers, and parties to attend, the sense of hurry crept into Evie's bones.

Of course, there was only one thing Kate had any sense of urgency about, and she kept up her patter about it as Evie braided her hair.

"I know it's been such a long road here, but we've only got a couple more months to go, Evie, then we're home free," Kate said, without a trace of irony. "Oh, a June wedding. Isn't it just divine to imagine? The flowers, the sunshine, and I have it on good authority my aunt is having her head kitchen girl serve her famous sweet iced tea, folks will be so delighted . . ." On and on she went, and Evie tried to tune her out.

"And then the honeymoon! We'll want to visit someplace cool before heading down to South Carolina. We're thinking of Newport—won't that be something, Evie?"

Evie's breath caught in her throat. Summer. South Carolina. Just a few months in the balance before she'd be shipped off way down South—farther south than she'd ever been, to the place folks told horror stories about. If she was going to make her move, it would need to be soon.

THE TEMPTATION TO JUST take matters into her own hands rather than wait for Charlotte was becoming overwhelming to Evie, not least because it was so hard to keep acting normal with the other slaves in the house: Peter, Ada, and the cook, Fannie, along with those who'd come and go with other visiting relatives.

They were kind to her. In the evenings, they'd invite her to sit with them in the little room off the kitchen, and sometimes Evie would oblige. She didn't say much, but she listened. Most of them had been with the Jackson family a good while, traveling back and forth between the city and Virginia. While some of the family spent time in Philadelphia just to pass the summer in more congenial weather or for social calls, some of them—like Massah Frank—had business interests that kept them and their slaves in town for months at a stretch. Then there was Miss Maggie, Kate's much older cousin, who seemed to live here almost year-round because the climate suited her health better.

As for the slaves, they got along all right. Peter said they mostly stayed in the house, apart from errands. In fact, the family forbade them from speaking to other Black people at all—they weren't even allowed to go to church.

" 'Too many of these free Blacks running around putting ideas in perfectly good slaves' heads' is what Massah Jackson always says," said Peter, explaining Frank's opinion one Sunday afternoon. Evie had noticed a few Black houses of worship in passing, built of sturdy bleached brick and wood, looking grander and far more permanent than the lean-to church shack she'd grown up with down South. Parishioners went in and out at will, all dressed in their best, even on weekdays—the buildings seemed to be prime meeting places for the city's free Black folks, so it was no surprise Frank insisted on keeping the slaves away. Fannie had made the mistake of asking the family's permission to go to a Sunday service a few months back, and the next morning she limped downstairs from the slave quarters aching and stiff-legged from where Frank had beat her with his cane—only on the lower half of her body, he'd told her, so she'd still be able to make the family's food. None of the others said a word about seeking worship ever again.

One afternoon, Ada came around looking for Evie in Kate's bedroom. "You got a minute to help me?" she asked, poking her head in the doorway while Evie was pressing Kate's gown for yet another dinner party.

She followed Ada downstairs. "We've got to clean out Fannie's room and make space for the new cook who's coming in. Didn't get a name yet."

The two crossed into the slave quarters at the back of the courtyard behind the house. The building had three floors with a single narrow room on each level, and Ada had shared the second-floor room with Fannie. When they got up there, Evie could hardly understand what Ada needed help with. The place was so sparsely furnished there was barely anything to move, just a bed with a thin mattress and a washrag on a hook beside it.

"Looks like Fannie took everything with her," Evie said.

"Oh no, she never brought much to begin with. No point, folks don't tend to stay here too long."

That was strange. Fannie never caused any trouble—and she hardly spoke at all after wicked Frank did his work on her. She seemed like a perfectly fine cook. On more than one evening, Evie had happily tucked into her fish stew, sopping it up with pieces of the soft brown bread Fannie had baked almost every night.

"What's the trouble, is the family picky about cooks up here?" Evie asked.

"Oh, it's not that. There's just a lot of coming and going. City life, I reckon," said Ada. "But when a new cook comes up, the family likes me to scrub down their quarters—got to have it extra clean since the person will be making the food."

Evie shrugged. Ada had carried up a bucket of soapy water, and they set about washing the stone floor and the rough-hewn plaster walls until they looked passable, though far from the standard of luxury the Jacksons had in the main house.

"You ever been sent away?" Evie asked Ada quietly as they finished up.

"Not for a long while. But sometimes I wish Miss Maggie would send me back," Ada said sadly. "She only visits Virginia maybe once, twice a year now—and going with her is the only time I get to see my son. But Miss Maggie don't care—she hardly lets me out of her sight."

"I know how that is," Evie said, putting a hand on Ada's shoulder. A habit of tearing families apart without a second thought seemed to run in the Jackson family.

They carried the washing bucket and rags back downstairs and across the courtyard. Just as they sat to rest for a moment in the room off the kitchen, a little bell rang in the corner. It was Miss Maggie summoning Ada.

"And here we go," said Ada, sounding resigned. "Thanks for up-stairs."

Evie tried to distract herself and shake off the sadness that had settled on her after hearing Ada's story. At least there'd be a new cook to meet. That was something halfway interesting to look forward to while she waited for Charlotte to plan.

In the meantime, Evie cherished her time outside the house, catching little glimpses of the city as the weeks went on, always under the watchful eyes of Peter and Ada. The family had started letting the slaves use a wagon to get their errands done more quickly, and as they rolled along, Evie would sit in back and pass the time imagining what sort of house she'd like to live in once she finally got away from Kate. On trips into the center of town they drove through all sorts of neighborhoods. One week she'd taken a shine to the fine brick town houses they passed on Third Street. Living in one of those as an owner, not a slave or a servant, must feel like being a prin-cess in a palace—or maybe just how Kate felt all the time. Other days, she noted the tenements closely packed down side streets and wedged into alleyways. Though they were tumbledown and rough-looking, the near absence of white faces in the streets surrounding them made the whole place feel a different kind of comfortable.

But it was the modest row houses of Chestnut Street that eventu-ally captured Evie's heart. They were small enough to feel cozy, real homes like the cabin where she'd lived with Mama and Daniel, but worldly and just a little grand, enough to give freedom a different feel than the life of a slave. When she looked into her future, she saw herself in one of them, reunited with Mama and her brother, though she hadn't quite worked out how she'd make that happen. In some quiet part of herself, she worried that leaving Kate meant giving up any hope of finding them.

In the weeks after they were sold, she'd rifled through Kate's pa-pers looking for any mark that could maybe tell her something about where they were. Though Evie didn't know her letters, Uncle Jack had taught them all how to read their own names at least, and she could recognize numbers. But she'd never found a thing—not a scrap that might've told her how far south they'd been sold, or who to, or for how much. And there was no reason to hope Kate would ever tell her where they were, or that she wouldn't do the very same to Evie someday. Married or not, there was nothing to keep Kate from deciding she needed money more than she needed her "best girl." Evie couldn't wait around for that. If there was any way out of this life, she had to take it. And if the fancy people Charlotte was mixed up with could figure out how to free her, there had to be a way they could find her family too—maybe look up the bill of sale, or get them a message somehow.

More and more, she couldn't stop herself thinking about what it might mean to be free from the tight grip of Kate's ownership squeezing the joy from her life, her movements, her every moment. Maybe she could finally breathe. But the prospect of a life without a constant companion would be intolerable to Kate. However sweetly she seemed to treat her housemaids, Evie well knew how she couldn't abide anyone getting away from her. Evie remembered how she'd dissolved into a puddle of tears at Charlotte's escape, first forlorn and then enraged, and how in reaction she'd clung to Evie that much tighter. What girl would she be sentencing to Kate's company if she ran away now?

Even as she waited, Evie's hope swelled dangerously alongside her impatience, and the life she imagined felt more within her reach every time she rode through the streets. Anything seemed to be possible in this city, for both good and ill.

There was a part of Evie that felt silly, spinning out fantasies about some freedom that might never come. More than that, she caught Peter looking at her warily, almost as if he could see into her head and was catching on to the outline of her plans, or judging her foolish dreams. But for the moment, dreams were all she had.

Chapter 9

———

NELL

———

I f NELL WAS GOING TO CONVINCE THE WOMEN'S ANTISLAVERY
Society to get involved with helping Evie, she realized she'd need at
least some idea of what the society could actually do. Ahead of the
next meeting, she returned to the books and old newspapers Alex
had brought her, hoping for inspiration. She found some hope in the
story of a former slave named Ben, who'd gotten his freedom more
than thirty years ago with the help of the statewide Pennsylvania
Abolition Society. Ben's master—a signer of the Constitution and a
senator from South Carolina—spent years living in Philadelphia,
mostly while the city was the U.S. capital, and kept Ben at his side
the entire time. But the senator lingered in the city for two years
even after retiring from Congress, and that was his mistake: once he
was out of office, the legal loophole that let Southern congressmen
indefinitely keep their slaves in Pennsylvania no longer applied, and
the Pennsylvania Abolition Society swept in to help Ben sue for his
freedom, and win.

Reading about the case sparked Nell's hopes: perhaps the wom-
en's Antislavery Society could help Evie go to court and do the
same—her mistress was no senator, after all. But as Nell read on, her
excitement evaporated: it wasn't only elected officials that Pennsylvania made exceptions for when it came to slaves' freedom. In fact,
she learned as she parsed through the dense legal texts, the state had
abolished slavery only gradually and incompletely, leaving so many

loopholes and contradictions in the law that even decades after so-
called abolition, many Black people in Pennsylvania were still trapped
with their masters as either slaves or indentured servants. And all the
while, the supposedly free state still welcomed Southern travelers to
bring their slaves within its borders for months at a time. Though
Pennsylvania had at least tried to outlaw kidnapping runaway slaves,
even that bit of good work had been undermined since the federal
government still let slave owners chase runaways into free and slave
states alike. As Nell waded through the morass of state-level half-
measures and national compromises, she found herself more disillu-
sioned than ever at Pennsylvania's halfhearted commitment to
abolition. It seemed that if the Antislavery Society was going to help
secure Evie's freedom, they wouldn't find refuge in the law—they'd
have to help her run.

But running was no safe proposition. The slave memoirs Alex
had brought her were wrenching glimpses into all that could go
wrong. One story described how a man and his wife were mutilated
after a failed escape attempt: an overseer used a hammer to shatter
their foot bones just enough to keep them from ever running again,
but not enough to stop them from working. Horrified by the cru-
elty, Nell wept for the unknown strangers as if she were standing
beside them and not tucked away in her room, surrounded by paper.
With the threat of such harsh penalties for getting caught running,
Nell wondered what had made Evie brave enough—or desperate
enough—to want to try it.

Of course, these accounts gave some hint of what it was like to be
enslaved: never-ending, backbreaking labor, no control over your
own movements or time, and the constant threat of white men forcing themselves onto slaves in the shadows—whether the self-
anointed masters or the low-class sorts they set up as overseers. All
this in the sweltering heat of the Southern sun, and cut off from
family, friends, and loved ones who'd been sold to faraway plantations.

The books were useful up to a point, but there was no one in
Nell's life she could turn to for firsthand insight. Given her social

standing, it was unsurprising that she didn't know any formerly enslaved women. The closest possible connection she had was to a
woman named Hetty, who was a founding member of the city's Female Antislavery Society. Nell had seen her around at meetings and
had heard that she'd fled slavery in New Jersey a decade ago. But
she'd been free so long that the fact of her enslavement felt quite
abstract—at least to Nell, who'd never even spoken to her. Apart
from that singular woman, runaway slaves were rare sightings in
Nell's circles, even though it was their plight that drove her group's
activism. Rather, former slaves and other poor women were orna-
ments pulled out for special occasions, to drive home the point of it
all at just the right moment, then set out of sight again. The handful
of Black members of the women's Antislavery Society came from
the city's most elite Black families, and white members outnumbered
them ten to one. All the privileged women's good intentions weren't
enough to disrupt the group's insularity, and their work often felt
frustratingly aloof from the city's Black community.

With Charlotte at her side, Nell was prepared to march into the
meeting and make the case for much closer—and more dangerous—
involvement. Politely, of course. But refocusing the attention of the
women's Antislavery Society onto helping fugitive slaves would be a
challenge, with the grand opening of Pennsylvania Hall just four
months away. Planning for the mid-May event was in full swing, and
dozens of abolitionist groups from around the country would celebrate the hall's completion by gathering there for antislavery conventions to coincide with the opening.

When the day arrived and she and Charlotte walked into the
meeting, Nell was struck by how strange it must seem to someone
new, the sight of white and Black women sitting side by side, talking, swapping papers, planning, and interacting with one another on
some approximation of equal footing, even if not in equal numbers.

Nell always felt at ease in the schoolhouse—any place with that
many books was like home to her. But Charlotte moved closer to
Nell the farther into the room they got. Nell had prepared Charlotte
as best she could, explaining the basics of parliamentary procedure

and the etiquette of the space. A mixed-race but majority white group like this demanded different niceties than an all-Black one like the Wheatley Association, and Nell reminded Charlotte more than once to follow her lead. Her attire was appropriate, at least— Charlotte wore a neatly tailored peach-colored day dress with a matching capelet, and blended right in. Some of the women had already taken their seats when Nell and Charlotte entered; they were in rows of chairs facing the blackboard and the teacher's desk, where Sarah kept a collection of minerals to give students direct experience in her science courses.

When Nell saw Sarah across the room, she hurried to greet her. Here was someone Charlotte ought to know. It had been Sarah who drew Nell into the society last year, talking it up during one of the spring balls and sparking Nell's interest. Now she was standing near the blackboard deep in conversation with Lucy Stewart, one of the group's white members, a chestnut-haired woman with ivory skin.

"Mrs. Stewart, Miss Douglass, please allow me to introduce my friend Miss Charlotte Walker. You might remember her from the holiday fair. She's passionate about these matters and is here to listen and learn." Each offered Charlotte a handshake and a quiet "How do you do?" before turning back to Nell.

"Mrs. Stewart and I were just talking about our speaking program for the hall's opening. Hundreds of women from groups like ours in Boston, New York, and other cities will be in town for the opening and the Antislavery Convention of American Women, and our society has been offered the chance to put forward a guest speaker," said Sarah, growing more animated as she spoke. "We're hopeful that Angelina Grimke will agree to join us."

"It's terribly exciting," Lucy said. "Have you read her work?"

Before Nell could reply, Lucy produced a slim volume from her bag. Holding it out to Nell and Charlotte, she started speaking with great intensity.

"I so admire her activism, and her brutal honesty about slavery," she said, opening the book. She read a passage where Grimke described in lurid detail the horrors of slavery she saw growing up in

Charleston. Men and women sent to the workhouse for merciless whippings, children overworked and starved, slaves denied basic necessities like light, heat, and bedding, family members sold off, and worse. With each sentence, Lucy's voice rose gradually, never out of control but clearly emotionally stirred by the words. Sarah and Nell just listened, but Charlotte kept shifting her weight from foot to foot and looked almost haunted by what she heard. Noticing her reaction, Nell could understand that—it was very upsetting.

Charlotte stared at Lucy for a moment, and then spoke. "You mean Miss Grimke saw all of that and never once did she lift a finger to intervene?"

Lucy's mouth dropped open. Sarah looked sidelong at Nell. What on earth was Charlotte doing? "What I think Miss Walker means to say is—" began Nell, rushing to smooth things over.

But Charlotte plowed on. "What Miss Grimke wrote is true enough, that's what happens to families down there. All of that and worse, much worse. I suppose her leaving the South and speaking out afterward is better than doing nothing, but I'm not ready to throw a parade for this woman just because she felt bad after benefiting from slavery for years. Not when there are women right here in Philadelphia who lived those horrors and can describe them firsthand. Folks owe it to the people down there to listen to what colored folks up here have to say about it. Why not ask one of them to speak?"

Nell, Sarah, and Lucy stared at her, mystified, even shocked, trying to puzzle out exactly where Charlotte's sudden passion had come from. She spoke as if something in her had come uncorked.

Lucy was the first of them to find words. "Perhaps, but people can be so conservative, especially those who are coming from out of town. They already get so uncomfortable about women speaking in public at all. Adding a colored woman on top of it . . . I just don't know." She paused, and then spoke again more definitively. "I'd hate to see us hurt our cause out of some misguided desire to assert our views too aggressively, do you know what I mean?"

Nell felt caught in between. Charlotte wasn't wrong, but she still

had a great deal to learn about how things worked in these circles—
a mostly white audience wasn't likely to listen to a colored woman
speaker, no matter the subject. And pressing them on the issue wasn't
likely to win her any allies, especially not if it meant snubbing Angelina Grimke, one of the most prominent white women in the movement, a personal friend to half the abolitionists in the city, and a
former member of the women's Antislavery Society as well. In any
case, whatever had come over Charlotte was distracting from their
goal for the day. Nell tried to steer them back onto safer ground.

"Oh, Miss Douglass, before I forget, will you be at Lillian Forrester's family ball next month? It's been so dreary out, getting an
early start to the season might be nice."

Sarah laughed, looking grateful to have the tension broken. "I
think not—I've just about aged out of all that, I think, and officially
entered my spinster season of life!"

"Lucky you," said Nell, laughing. She couldn't wait for the day
her family would stop pestering her about finding a husband.

Charlotte stood by quietly.

"Why don't we take our seats, Charlotte? Things will be getting
started soon." Nell took her arm, ushering her over to a table far
from Sarah and Lucy.

"What was all that a moment ago?" Nell asked as they sat down.

"Evie has shared a lot with me," Charlotte said. "I suppose I was
just overcome."

Nell patted her on the shoulder. "Just stick with me," she said.
"Let me do the talking."

Charlotte nodded distractedly, then sat staring toward the blackboard with a faraway look in her eyes.

The president gaveled the meeting to order, and the women spent
the next hour talking through their plans for the convention. When
it came time for new business, Nell was feeling even more uncertain
about their prospects for helping Evie. Beside her, Charlotte leaned
over anxiously and whispered.

"This is the time to bring it up, right?"

Nell nodded, raised her hand, and then spoke carefully.

"I wondered if we might set aside the convention for a moment and discuss a more pressing matter—the issue of fugitive slaves in the city," she began. "As conditions deteriorate down South, we've been seeing more and more of them come through here in desperate need of help to flee farther North. As leaders in the antislavery movement, I propose we have a responsibility to do something for them."

In the silence that followed, eyes shifted from face to face. Lucy broke in tactfully. "I agree, we're responsible. That's why I'm pleased we do so much for them already," she said. "We've advocated for suspected fugitives to receive jury trials before being stolen away to the South, and donated clothing and food to the shelters where many runaways end up. And that's to say nothing of our future plans—surely you haven't forgotten about our standing committees to explore how we might offer job placement and educational assistance!"

Standing committees didn't exactly translate to help, but Nell tried to remain evenhanded. "All that is well and good," she said, "but I do sometimes wonder if there's more we could do." She looked to Sarah for support. Sarah shot her back an uncertain glance, unsure what Nell was driving at. Suddenly, Charlotte piped up.

"What I think Nell means is, beyond trying to change the laws and giving money, what are we doing to actually, *directly* help slaves get free?"

Heads turned. Breaking the stony silence, Lucy spoke. "Begging your pardon, what was your name again?"

Nell swallowed hard.

"Miss Charlotte Walker, ma'am, and I'm just saying Nell—I mean, Miss Gardner—has got a point. If we can take people out of slavery directly, why not do it?" Every head turned back to Lucy.

Nell put a hand on Charlotte's arm, signaling her to stop. This was exactly why she'd been hesitant to bring her. These women needed to be slow-walked into these kinds of things, not browbeaten and shoved.

"My goodness," Lucy said. "Isn't that our entire purpose? Moral suasion is the key to ending slavery, and that's where our attention is best kept—on changing hearts and minds. Political action, public speaking, and fundraising are the surest tools for that work. Unless there's something else you're driving at, Miss Gardner? I think we've heard plenty from your friend." Nell felt her cheeks flush.

With no one else speaking up alongside her—besides the increasingly unruly Charlotte—Nell sensed she'd waded out too far into deep waters. "I'll have to give it some more thought," she said quietly. "I welcome anyone who'd like to join me in crafting a proposal to start a committee."

Charlotte huffed and crossed her arms. But Lillian, Sarah, the Forten sisters, and a few others murmured their interest in working with Nell on it. Finally, the president interceded.

"Very well then, we'll be glad to take it under consideration and form an exploratory committee once your proposal is ready for review," she said. Nell sat back and folded her arms. Committees and taking matters "under consideration" were classic tactics for an officer wanting to scuttle a plan outside the semipublic eye of the meeting. "In the meantime, though, if you're finished, Miss Gardner, we have other business to address."

Nell nodded and smiled, and the meeting moved on. With the need for a proposal, a committee, and all the intricacies of parliamentary procedure, the Antislavery Society was as good as a dead end for Evie. That was the trouble, of course. For a pack of radicals, so many of them were terribly uncomfortable with the notion of doing anything overt. Still, Charlotte ought not have pushed so hard—Nell was just as frustrated as Charlotte was with the focus on talk rather than action, but there was an art to these things, and it seemed they hadn't won anyone over.

At the end of the meeting, though, a woman came and tapped Nell on the shoulder. "I don't disagree with you one bit, but you won't find what you need here—not yet."

Charlotte and Nell nodded. "I don't believe we've been properly introduced yet," Nell said.

"Miss Hetty Reckless," the woman said, extending a hand. She was somewhat familiar to Nell: tall, stout, and a little rougher hewn than the rest of the group. Her two front teeth were missing, sup-

posedly having been knocked out by a former master. A rare former
slave who'd found a way into the city's most elite circles, she continued speaking as Nell and Charlotte stood and listened. "I'll be in
touch about your committee. Meantime, try the menfolk—the Vigilant Association is ahead of the women's Antislavery Society on
these matters. They'll get you and whoever's in trouble straightened
right out." She winked at them and walked off.

Chapter 10

CHARLOTTE

BETTER THAN ANYONE, CHARLOTTE KNEW SILENCE COULD BE just as sharp a rebuke as an unkind word. After the meeting, Nell never exactly *said* Charlotte had embarrassed her—she was far too polite for that. But she was awfully quiet for the rest of that morning, and it was easy to understand why. As much as Charlotte knew about Evie's day-to-day life, in Nell's world she was still out of her depth, and had let everyone at the meeting know it. She'd stepped way over the line by speaking out the way she did, and had almost nothing to show for it—nothing except Hetty. Charlotte would've given anything to sit and talk with her, to hear the story of how she'd clawed her way into such high society after being a slave. How had she gotten folks to take her seriously, to treat her like a real person and an equal, instead of just pitying her for what she'd come from?

For now, it was enough that Hetty had told her and Nell where to turn next. Of course, looking to the menfolk was easier said than done. Of the two men in Charlotte's life, neither was very likely to put her in touch with the Vigilant Association! Darcel hardly spoke to her at all, and in any case his whole world was in the kitchen—though that had turned out to be a lucky thing, since at least he'd seemed not to notice the day she went out for the meeting. As for James, if he'd ever had any zeal for helping slaves escape, it began and ended with himself and Charlotte. The man he was today was about a hundred miles away from being an abolitionist. Not to mention, he seemed busier than ever.

The last few evenings he'd shown up for dinner late or not at all, and he hadn't come up to the attic to give Charlotte a reading lesson in weeks. Instead, when he wasn't at the workshop, he was holed up in his office at the house. With James being so scarce lately, he hardly crossed Charlotte's mind except when she cleaned his room. One Saturday as she replaced the bed linens and swept the floor, her eye was drawn to his vanity table. Laden with containers of face powder and a pomade he used to smooth down any telltale kinks in his hair, the crowded surface revealed how over the years his grooming routines had grown more elaborate even than Kate's. While Charlotte was staring, James came in unexpectedly.

"There you are," he said. "Come with me please, I've got somewhere to take you. It'll be very edifying, I think."

Warily, she followed along a few paces behind him as he led her downstairs and out onto the street. It felt strange to be in public with him, and his mood seemed different today—a mix of anxious and hopeful at the same time. She could only guess it had something to do with his business. Mr. Wilcox had been back for dinner twice in the past few weeks, and while serving, Charlotte had overheard the two of them planning some grand affair they hoped to host in the spring. As James led her onward through the city, her suspicions were confirmed.

"I'm going to be very busy for the next few months," he began. "As you likely know, Mr. Wilcox has joined as a partner in my workshop, so we'll finally be able to expand now," he said, unable to keep the tinge of excitement out of his voice.

"I'm sure you must be very proud," said Charlotte. But what did any of this have to do with her? She paused and let the silence fill up the space between them.

James continued. "What I mean is, I'll be at the workshop and away from home more in the coming months as we get things up and running. But once the expansion is finished, life will begin to look very different for us, Carrie. Things will change. It's exactly what I need after what happened."

"What happened" was the euphemism he always used for the grave mistakes he'd made soon after they came to Philadelphia. After hiring a Black apprentice at his workshop, he'd been accosted on the street by a small but determined mob incensed that a Black boy had "taken" such a plum job. That day, James returned home badly scraped up, and Charlotte had spent the evening scrubbing blood out of the collar of his shirt. He managed to skate by afterward by firing the boy and moving his workshop to a different location, and he hardly ever spoke of it again. Instead, he'd set his sights on the road to establishing his good name. And that meant keeping a long, long distance from anything that might look like sympathy with the city's Black residents. Free city or no, business had come first ever after.

Charlotte peered at him as she stood there, trying to figure out exactly what he was promising. The unusual situation in their house had gone on so long she couldn't imagine what a different life there would look like. Would they live openly as father and daughter instead of pressing on with this charade? For an instant, she let herself hope: she could move into one of the bedrooms downstairs, and wouldn't have to eat dinner alone. Maybe they could find a church that would welcome them both on equal terms. Maybe she could even tell him about Evie, and together they could find the rest of her family. Maybe. But she didn't dare ask.

On Second Street, he paused in front of a construction site, where the wood framing for a building was going up on an empty lot. Men were at work cutting and measuring, standing up more boards and filling in between the beams. Beside it was a small storefront with a hand-carved and glossed wooden sign, VAUGHN'S WORKSHOP—FINE CUSTOM FURNISHINGS AND GOODS. They weren't too far from the waterfront—Charlotte could smell the river.

"I just thought you'd want to see what makes all this possible for us. And what will make even greater things possible, with the expansion," he said. Charlotte peered in through the windows. Tables, chairs, and rows of elegantly carved bookcases stared back—her father's other creations, and the only ones he truly seemed proud of. He'd come a long way from his ramshackle workshop on the side of the White Oaks barn. When she was a very little girl, he'd sometimes bring her to visit the shop, and she'd sit at his side and watch him for hours as he made magic with his hands: once, she remembered, he started with two small hunks of oak and, cut by exacting cut, transformed them into two smooth dolls, a sheep and a pony. In his determined face, she'd seen the thrill of creating something beautiful from what had been scrap. As she grew older, she recognized the feeling herself when she sewed. That day in his old workshop, he'd given Charlotte the pony and sent her scampering off to deliver the sheep to Evie. But today on Second Street, he didn't invite her into his shop, and he had no gifts for her—only words.

"I know at the house it can all feel very removed, but we truly do have a foothold here in this city now. As long as we protect it, we'll never want for anything," he said. "We can look forward to a new and larger home, and many more nice things. The world will be open to us, there will be nothing we cannot afford, perhaps even a carriage."

There was pride in his voice, the same tone that always crept up when he talked about his trade. As they stood across the street watching the builders work on the expansion, a few would-be customers drifted in and out of the shop—wealthy, finely dressed white folks. But James was looking at Charlotte, not them, and his eyes were full of expectation. This wasn't the first time he'd come to her with news of a business expansion, and promises of wealth and fancier possessions, with a look on his face like that of a cat bounding up to its master with a mouse in its teeth.

It was clear these were the things that mattered to him, and so he couldn't see how little they mattered to Charlotte. She cocked her head to one side and said only "Mm." But one thing he'd said brought her up short, something about a new house. "What's wrong with the house we have? Seems perfectly good to me," she said.

"For now, maybe," James answered. "But there's no reason we can't work and hope for better. For more."

"You mean bigger?" Then, under her breath, she muttered, "That's just more for me to clean."

"Maybe not," said James. "With a growing business and a bigger place, we could bring on more staff, folks to do more of the day-to-day cleaning and cooking and all that—"

"We have Darcel to cook for us," Charlotte said.

"Sure, for now, but supposing he doesn't want to come along, there's always better out there. We've got to stay in motion, Carrie." He paused. "And there's room for you to advance too. With more staff, you could be more of a supervisor and wouldn't have to do as much yourself."

So that was it. That was his grand vision for her: more people to help her clean an even bigger house. It never occurred to him that there was an entire world outside that might have something to offer her, or even that she might have something to offer it. That with a real education, the right connections, she could make something of herself the same as he had. Maybe teach, like Nell, or open a seamstress shop. Anything—anywhere—but this.

The door of the workshop swung open and more patrons came out. One tipped his hat to James as he departed, and another came over with his wife.

"We were just checking in on the wedding chest you're carving for our daughter. Your apprentice showed it to us—it's beautiful!" The man shook James's hand. Both he and his wife ignored Charlotte entirely.

"Nothing but the best," said James. He turned to Charlotte, as if to say "See?"

As the couple walked away, Charlotte huffed. "Can we head back now? This has been very interesting, but I've got chores."

"Things will be even better, you'll see." But the excitement had drained away from his face, and his expression went cold. "Anyway, I didn't want you wondering after me or worrying Darcel about preparing dinner for me most nights, since I won't be around," he said. "But I'll need you to start getting the house into shape for the dinner party Mr. Wilcox and I are planning. It may be a few months away but you know how quickly time can move." Could it really? It didn't feel that way to her.

Standing beside him on the street, Charlotte wondered when and how her father had gotten so very far away. The more he gained a toehold in his new circles, the less he seemed to see her. But she had a new community of her own too—one that could help her find real freedom for herself and Evie both. She didn't need James or his blinkered promises.

They walked back to the house in silence. Along the way, Charlotte stayed three steps behind her father, a servant's respectful distance, shivering in the biting February air.

JAMES DID HAVE AT least one thing right—there was freedom and possibility in what folks could do with their hands. Not long after they spoke, Charlotte finally sat down in her attic room and started looking through the *Lady's Book* magazines the dressmaker had given her. She pored over the pictures and patterns, marveling at the kind of sculptured elegance that could be created with just fabric, a needle and thread, and some time—dresses much more complex than she'd ever made herself.

With no formal training in seamstressing, Charlotte had always worked by sight. At White Oaks, there'd been no choice. Kate couldn't afford expensive magazines, patterns, or bespoke pieces by dressmakers in town. No, what she had were slave women—so few of them on the plantation that even field hands like Auntie Irene had to take on the work of keeping their mistress clothed, at least until Charlotte's hands grew large and steady enough.

For dress patterns, all they had to go on were memories of what some plantation belle had worn months ago when she'd come to White Oaks for a pity call. Kate had a greedy eye for the fashions of other, wealthier women and could call out the broad strokes: if a dress had lace, if the fabric was finely spun cotton, if it was a light shade of purple, that sort of thing. But with Auntie Irene's guidance, it was Charlotte whose young eyes learned to observe the women closely and pick out the details to answer her questions: Had there been three buttons down the back of the dress, or four? Sure, there was lace around the collar, but did the fringe hit at the shoulder or stop at the bottom of the neck? And just how billowy were those sleeves? Working from magazine patterns instead of memory would feel downright luxurious.

And these new patterns would give her something to do. After how poorly things had gone at the Antislavery Society meeting, Charlotte wondered if maybe it wasn't such a bad idea to avoid the group for a while, until she and Nell could find a new plan. But that didn't mean she had to leave her hands idle. She glanced over at the armoire, wedged into a low-ceilinged corner of the room.

Inside, underneath her hanging dresses in shades of gray, rich-soil brown, and yellow, the open box holding the iris-blue bolt of cloth from Nell lay waiting. With the peach dress she'd made from the cloth James had given her, Charlotte's growing fabric collection was starting to remind her of her and Evie's beloved garden.

The day James had taken Charlotte and run, she and Evie had just finished their planting for the season. Every spring for as long as Charlotte could remember, they'd tended their little plot of earth down at the end of the cabin row. At first, when they'd both been small, it wasn't much more than two little girls playing in the dirt, feeling the cool of the earth as they plunged their hands in and turned it over. Grit crunched under their fingernails while Auntie Irene called instructions to them from the cabin window, where she sat sewing.

Evie and Charlotte had saved the flower seeds they'd found and carefully planted and covered them up. Charlotte showed Evie how to work the spade as they got older, her bigger hand over Evie's little one. And every May, the flowers would burst into bloom—shocks of sunny yellow marigolds, pale blue irises, fire-pink wildflowers, and orange milkweed tempting the butterflies, which made a bright contrast to the green sea of grass and broad tobacco leaves that blan-keted the rest of the White Oaks fields. On Sundays, they'd put flowers in their hair—always irises for Evie, and marigolds for Charlotte, bright spots above their coarse sand-hued linen rags.

Maybe there was at least one thing Charlotte could do for Evie while everything was being worked out. Something to remind Evie she still cared, even with all the distance between them.

Charlotte lit a candle, opened the magazine to a page with a pattern for a silk dress with a ruffled hem and matching cape, and settled into her sewing corner.

———

Chapter 11

NELL

———

ON A FRIDAY NIGHT IN MID-FEBRUARY, NELL WAS PACING BACK and forth in her bedroom, ruminating. Just where was she going to find a man who'd help free Evie without it getting back to her parents? Philadelphia was so small sometimes, there was no way of knowing whose discretion she could rely on. As she brooded, a knock came at the door.

"Your ma and pa told me to say the carriage will be leaving in ten minutes, Miss Nell, so you'd best get on downstairs. You need help with your dress?" Beth-Anne asked from the hallway.

"I'm all right, thank you. I'll be right down." Nell was already dressed, outfitted in the emerald-green gown Charlotte had helped pick out for the ball. Lillian Forrester's family was hosting the occasion in honor of her father's forty-fifth birthday, and all the city's most prominent Black families would be there. The Gardners and the Marions were set to drive over together, a scheme no doubt orchestrated by Nell's and Alex's mothers. They were determined women. All the same, Nell knew where she'd inherited her own single-minded disposition from, and she was grateful for it. That, and she never much minded spending time with Alex, especially not now.

Downstairs, her mother, father, and brother weren't waiting for her at all; they had already climbed into the carriage. Instead, Alex stood alone in the front entryway visibly tapping his foot as Nell swept down the stairs. His eyes went wide at the sight of her.

"You must be chilly," he said, brushing a hand over her shoulder and breaking into a broad grin.

Nell rolled her eyes. "Very funny." With Beth-Anne's help, she put on her coat.

For all Nell's elegance, there was no denying Alex cut a dashing figure himself in his black evening coat and dress boots, with his wavy red-brown hair slicked back from his face. He offered his arm, and in return, she gave him a slight peck on the cheek. She was still distracted.

"What's the matter?" he asked, leaning in close as they walked to the carriage.

"Let's talk at the ball," she said. He helped her into the carriage, where she sat beside her mother with her father and brother across from them. Alex rode just behind them with his own family.

They arrived to find scores of people streaming into the building, a two-story brick hall the Forresters had rented and outfitted for the celebration. The energy inside was electric, with the intricately carved high ceiling letting air circulate while the dancing crowd drove up the temperature. Along the sides of the room, waiters passed trays offering punch and light fare—almonds, figs, and lemon tarts, plus savory olives and buttery miniature puff pastries—to keep up everyone's strength. There was plenty to eat and drink, but the evening's main business was to dance.

The atmosphere was a welcome change from the more buttoned-up social calls and meetings Nell usually attended. But still, she wasn't quite ready to join the fray of the dance. It was distracting to have the loose ends of Evie's escape dangling, and Nell was also still smarting over the way her ideas had been dismissed at the women's Antislavery Society meeting. A few of the other members were there at the ball, and seeing them brought her frustration back to the forefront of her mind. If she could at least air her worries with Alex, Nell hoped, maybe she could clear her head enough to enjoy the party.

Nell stood on the side of the room, watching others dance as she waited for a chance to talk to him. He'd had no trouble getting into the swing of things, and Nell watched with her arms crossed as he moved from one pretty dance partner to another. She considered stepping into the withdrawing room to collect her thoughts and figure out the best way to explain her dilemma, but before she could, Alex came over. They couldn't have been there more than twenty minutes, but his hair was already tousled and a light sheen of sweat was forming on his brow. He offered his arm.

"I'll make you a deal," he said, leading her out onto the floor. "For one waltz, you can tell me all your troubles, and I'll do my best to help. But for the next two songs afterward, we'll just dance and forget everything else. All right?"

"That sounds like a fair bargain," Nell said, slipping her arm through his. This was an old trick. Growing up, whenever Nell was unhappy, Alex would use music to cheer her up—playing her a song on the piano in the Gardners' parlor, or sweeping her around in a mock waltz while his mother played the harp at the Marions' house. As they'd grown older, their interactions had become more formal, but they kept that same heart.

The band struck up a gentle waltz. As the music picked up, Alex looped his strong arm around Nell's back and the two began to step and spin, step and spin. They fell easily into each other's rhythm.

"What's going on?" he asked. "Is this something to do with all those books you asked me for during the holidays?" Their faces were close, and no one could hear them over the music. It was as safe a moment as any.

"Part of it is the Antislavery Society," Nell began. "But that's not all of it. I've got someone in desperate need of assistance, and you'd think an abolition society would be just the people to ask, but no. I'd always put so much faith in the society, I believed—I *knew*—we were truly making a difference. But what does it matter if we can't help even one young girl get free?"

Alex nodded. "I can imagine how frustrating it is. What did the society say exactly?"

"Essentially that direct action isn't our place as an organization—that we're working to change the law, not break it. But, Alex, it can't all be hosting speeches, running fairs, and writing petitions!" She huffed and blew hair off her forehead.

"No, but everyone has their entry points, I suppose, and writing does have its place," he answered. "In fact, at the *Freeman,* the editor, Mr. Lundy, has been trying to persuade me to write a column. I haven't decided yet, but he thinks adding more voices may convince the legislature to change course on the voting issue at least."

That was all well and good, but a newspaper article wasn't going to free Evie, or anyone else. Still, it did sound like Alex was doing well at the *Freeman.* He'd only started working there to learn the printing trade and branch out from his family's catering business; Nell had assumed the paper's abolitionist politics were just incidental to his work. But if he was making the kinds of inroads that led to the offer of a column, perhaps he was just the person Nell was looking for.

She leaned in closer as they swept around the ballroom. "Alex, do you ever come in contact with members of the Vigilant Association in your work at the paper?"

He raised an eyebrow. "I'm connected with them, you could say. But I can't see a group like that interfering in the affairs of the women's Antislavery Society."

"They're not the ones who need interfering with. Not yet, at least." Step, step, turn. Too out of breath from the dance to mince words, Nell spoke plainly. "If I tell you something, can you promise to keep it to yourself? And help me if you can?"

He pulled her closer. "Who could resist all this intrigue?"

Nell couldn't help but grin. "Be serious!"

He put on an exaggerated frown. So invited, she laid out the entire story for him. "My friend Charlotte has made the acquaintance of a young woman in the city, a slave girl. She wants to run away from her mistress before she has to return to the South, and we're going to help her."

Alex pulled away, his eyes wide. "Help her what?"

"Escape!" Nell whispered beneath the music.

As the song came to a close, Alex took a step back and swept a grand bow to Nell before straightening up and staring into her face with wonder. "I knew you'd been reading about all this, and had joined the Antislavery Society, but I don't think I understood how serious you were until this very moment. This is crazy, Nell! And dangerous."

"I know it is. But the poor girl has been waiting nearly two months for us to devise some sort of plan to free her, and I've tried to go through the proper channels up until now, and gotten nowhere."

"Going through the 'proper channels' to break the law?" Alex said, stifling a laugh. "You're nothing if not consistent."

She lightly smacked him on the shoulder. "Alex, come on. Will you help me?"

"Well, I can't very well let you do something this wild without me, can I?" he said, eyes twinkling.

Overcome with gratitude, Nell kissed him on the cheek in her excitement, twice. With Alex's connections, her plans with Charlotte could get back on track. The notes of the next song floated down from the stage.

"So, what's our next step?" she asked.

"A turn, I think." Alex pulled her back into his arms, twirled her around, then dipped her. She laughed loudly with her head back. There would be no more talking. Nell swirled into the next dance with gusto—a deal was a deal, after all. Over Alex's shoulder, she caught a glimpse of her parents watching with approval. Though that usually would have bothered her, she was having too good a time to care.

As the evening wound down, Nell and Alex slipped away from the dance floor and found a corner to sip punch and put their heads together, with her filling him in on Evie's situation, and him thinking through the who, where, and when of how the Vigilant Association might set about freeing her. Deep in conversation, neither of them heard approaching footsteps over the music, and so they startled when someone finally addressed them.

"All right, you two—out with it!" Nell and Alex raised their eyebrows and looked up to find Mrs. Marion and Mrs. Gardner standing over them, smiling with satisfaction.

"Ma?" Alex said tentatively.

"Oh stop," Mrs. Marion said. "You've kept us in suspense long enough, but we're your mothers! We deserve to hear such important news from you."

Nell and Alex looked at each other. How could they possibly know what they were planning?

"We're just—" Alex began again. Nell was quiet, working out the angles in her head, watching her mother watching them as the rest of the revelers danced in the background, the fiddler driving them on with a lively quadrille.

"All the time you two have been spending together—with Alex bringing gifts, and the way you're always so deep in conversation. There's no need to play coy," said Mrs. Gardner. "We're just glad you two have finally come to your senses."

Ah, so that's what they thought was going on: the romance they'd pinned their hopes on, made real at long last. Nell very nearly denied it but she caught herself as the thought popped into her head—what if they just played along? Better to keep their mothers off the scent of what they were *really* up to, and she'd at least get a break from constant nagging about her marriage prospects. Why not?

"You've found us out, Mother!" she said, grinning. She looped her arm through Alex's and patted him on the hand. "We're engaged!" She smiled and held tight to his arm, squeezing it to signal him to keep quiet. Side by side, the two mothers beamed.

"I knew it! At last!" Mrs. Gardner exclaimed. Nell and Alex stood, and their mothers hugged them both tightly—overjoyed, and best of all, vindicated.

"What wonderful, joyous news!" said Mrs. Marion, clapping her hands. "Your fathers will be thrilled. Come, Helen, let's go find them and give the two lovebirds a moment." With that, they practically floated away, already tittering about what would be the wedding of the season.

Left behind, Nell and Alex looked at each other and burst out laughing. For a moment, it all seemed too sudden and too silly to be real. But as they waited for the women to return, the gravity of what Nell had just done slowly settled down on them.

"Nell, what are you thinking?" Alex asked.

"Well, I couldn't very well tell them what we're actually doing!" she said. "We'll sort it all out later—my parents know I've never wanted to marry, so if I change my mind in a few weeks or months it won't be too much of a surprise. In the meantime, at least they won't have questions when they see us together."

Alex shook his head and smiled. "Whatever you say, my dear fiancée."

In a flash, their parents had returned, with Mr. Marion carrying a chilled bottle of champagne tucked discreetly under his arm.

"Where'd you get that, Pa?" Alex asked, surprised. Society was largely temperate these days, and even at parties the punches were dry.

"Never you mind, I have my ways," Mr. Marion said, leaning forward to give Nell a kiss on each cheek. "After all, this news calls for a special celebration."

Mr. Gardner reached out to shake Alex's hand. "Welcome to the family, son." With stemware appropriated from the punch table, Mr. Marion poured six glasses of bubbly.

"To our dear Nell and Alex, best wishes, and the Gardners and Marions—one family at last. Cheers!"

"Cheers!" they all repeated. Clinking their glasses, Nell and Alex looked at each other, shrugged, and took a sip. The champagne was sweet and clear, and the fizz went straight to Nell's head.

Chapter 12

CHARLOTTE

WHEN CHARLOTTE ARRIVED TO MEET NELL AT THE PARK benches and her friend said she had exciting news, Charlotte figured that meant Nell had found them a connection to the Vigilant Association. That would've been plenty, but it turned out Charlotte was only half right. After keeping up the suspense while the two of them walked to the newspaper office on Arch Street, Nell finally came out with it when they stepped inside.

"Charlotte, please allow me to introduce my fiancé, Alexander Marion!" He was hunched over a printing press, his hands smudged with ink as he worked the plates for the next day's edition. He looked up and smiled at them and nodded at Charlotte like he'd seen her before. He was equal parts elegant and impertinent, a combination Charlotte recognized as the telltale sign of a young man born into wealth.

"Fiancé?" Charlotte sputtered. "Since when are you—"

Before Charlotte could even get the words out, Nell and Alex looked at each other and grinned. "What? What's going on?" Charlotte asked.

"It's just a ruse," Nell said, laughing. "We've been friends for ages, and at the ball our parents were asking too many questions about why we suddenly had our heads together, so I just grabbed for the first explanation that jumped to mind."

"Lovely work choosing the dress, by the way," Alex said, winking at Charlotte. "My fiancée here looked stunning, shoulders and all."

"Why, thank you, my dear," Nell said in an exaggerated voice, looping her arm through Alex's. Then, she turned more serious. "Honestly, I'll be sad to disappoint our parents when we have to call this off later, but with all the work and meeting we'll be doing, it seemed easiest to just give them an explanation they'd happily accept without too many questions."

"Uh-huh," said Charlotte, taking in Alex's handsome face and bright, kind eyes. He was well connected, and apparently beloved by the rest of Nell's family, and what was more, if Nell had roped him into their plans with Evie, he must also share her politics. There was probably a good reason an engagement was the first cover story that popped into Nell's mind, but Charlotte wasn't one to stick her nose where it didn't belong.

"But seriously, Charlotte—Alex believes he can help us, he's connected with the Vigilant Association."

Then he was exactly what they needed! "Connected how?" Charlotte asked, a chill of excitement running through her.

"It's not for me to say," Alex replied vaguely. "The association's most sensitive work is kept secret, of course—along with the identities of the full membership. But they'll be looped in, don't worry."

After Hetty had mentioned the organization at the meeting, Nell had filled Charlotte in on the details she knew. Led by men like Robert Purvis and other prominent members of the Black elite, for the last year or so the association had been openly providing aid to runaway slaves, setting them up with housing, money, legal advice, even jobs—anything to get them on their feet—and also arranging patrols to keep the wider Black community safe from slave catchers. At the same time, behind the scenes, the association had started helping folks run away, providing safe houses and hideouts, and connections to fellow abolitionists in cities farther north who'd do the same. The association was all-male, so Nell and Charlotte didn't have a way in themselves. In truth, being so new to the city and its abolitionist

ALL WE WERE PROMISED

circles, Charlotte was beginning to feel she didn't bring much to this effort beyond a gnawing sense of obligation. Fortunately, Nell was savvy and well connected enough for the both of them—especially with her new companion.

Once Alex finished his work at the printing press, he ushered Nell and Charlotte into a private office toward the back of the building and sat in the grand chair behind the desk. The nameplate on the desk read BENJAMIN LUNDY. Charlotte raised an eyebrow.

"Mr. Lundy has been absent lately due to ill health, so I've taken over the office while we await the new editor," he said by way of explanation. "In any case, I'm sure he won't mind us using the room for such important work. Charlotte, Nell has given me the broad strokes, but can you tell me a bit more about your friend?"

"Of course. Like I told Nell, she's originally from Maryland but her mistress brought her up here recently, and they've been staying at a town house somewhere in the city. She isn't sure how long she's got before being taken south again. We've got to move fast," said Charlotte.

He stared at the table for a moment, then looked up at Nell, his face serious. "This is risky, you both know that?" His words spoke of danger, but there was a hint of admiration in his voice and in his eyes. Charlotte suspected it wasn't directed at her.

"We know," they said at the same time.

He leaned back and thought, going silent for a minute or two. "I'll start carefully putting out feelers to determine who can help us line up an escape route," he said slowly. "They do this all the time, so it shouldn't be too difficult. And once your friend is free, we can help get her set up to live independently. She's owed more than just freedom, after all."

"Very well then," said Nell. "How quickly do you think we can move her? And to where?"

"It could take days, or even a few weeks. It's all about who we can convince to take her in, and how soon she can safely get away. Where's she living?"

"She didn't say exactly, she doesn't know the city that well. It sounded like a big brick house on the edge of town. She said she could see the river," Charlotte said.

"Which one?" asked Alex.

"I don't think Charlotte has that information," Nell interjected. "Evie wouldn't have known the river's name, and one river looks pretty much like the next one."

That's not quite true, Charlotte thought to herself. When she and James had first gone on the run, they had to know the difference between the creek southeast of White Oaks and the one to the north to get their bearings. Charlotte remembered her father paying close attention to what kinds of flowers were blossoming on the banks, how the grass looked, and what color the mud was to ensure they could tell the creeks apart. They knew if they saw dark brown mud and a rash of purple petunias near the water, they could be assured they were headed in the right direction, while lighter, drier dirt and patches of red honeysuckle meant they'd lost their way. Of course, this was the city—there might be no flowers growing beside these rivers. But they'd have other distinguishing features.

"She didn't tell me the name of the river," Charlotte murmured, puzzling it out, "but she told me about something she saw from the banks—docks, and large ships coming and going."

"That sounds like the Delaware River," said Alex. "The other river, the Schuylkill, only has smaller boats, canoes and the like. She must be on the far eastern edge of the city."

"That would make sense, given the location of the market where I ran into her," Charlotte said.

"How clever," Nell said. "Have you studied much geography in your travels, Charlotte?"

Charlotte tensed up at the question. "No, can't say I have. I just notice my surroundings, I guess—and Evie does too."

Charlotte shifted in her seat, regretting her words. It would have been wiser to keep her skills learned from life on the run closer to her chest. After her unexpected outpouring at the Antislavery Society meeting, she'd been calling far too much attention to herself.

"So, we've got a location—or at least the beginning of one," Alex said. "That's a place to start. Why don't you give me some time to set things in motion, and we can catch up in a week or so? If you see Evie again soon, make sure to get her exact address."

"I will," Charlotte said, gathering up her papers.

"Thanks, Alex, you're the best," said Nell. She kissed him lightly on the cheek before breezing out the door ahead of Charlotte. "We'll talk soon," she tossed over her shoulder.

Out on the sidewalk, the two fell in step together as they walked down the street.

"Just good friends, huh?" said Charlotte.

Nell laughed, but on her cheeks, Charlotte could've sworn she saw the beginnings of a blush.

Chapter 13

———

EVIE

———

SINCE SHE'D FOUND CHARLOTTE AT THE MARKET THAT FIRST day in December, time had moved strangely for Evie. Somehow, it seemed like these had been the slowest days of her whole life even as she felt the date of Kate's wedding rushing closer, a runaway wagon set to flatten her unless Charlotte pulled her out of the way. It was obvious that Charlotte hadn't made any headway at all on plans to get her away from Kate, since for two months she'd had little to say when they passed each other in the market, if she showed up at all. But it was nearly March—surely by now, she and her friends should've come up with *something*. When Tuesday rolled around, Evie woke up before first light, roused from sleep by the sheer anticipation: today she was going to demand some answers. Charlotte usually arrived at the market around ten o'clock, so Evie had to find a way to break away from the other house servants and wait her out.

Eyes straining in the dark of her room, Evie took extra care as she decided what to wear. With the fancy company Charlotte kept now, her clothes seemed to be getting more elaborate each time Evie saw her; they sure were nothing like the rag dresses she'd sewn for Evie back at White Oaks, though as a child Evie had twirled around the cabin in them like they were a queen's robes—they were special, just for her. Now Evie had a few simple homespun frocks, most of them fraying at the edges and sporting more than a few patches. But as she'd begun growing into her body, Kate would sometimes make a gift of castoffs from her own wardrobe. Maybe wearing something more adult would make Charlotte listen to her.

Evie grabbed one of Kate's hand-me-downs from the separate pile under the little table across from her bed. As the sun rose and the light from Kate's windows peeked through the crack under the door, she caught a glimpse of what she was picking up—a yellow-brown calico frock unadorned with any patterns or embroidery, but nice enough. Having sat under the table for so long, the dress had a coin-size pat of wax on one of the sleeves where a candle had dripped before Evie blew it out. Not the tidiest sight, but it flaked smoothly off, and Evie hoped no one would notice the oily spot left behind. As she dressed, Evie planned what she would say to Charlotte.

On the ride to the market, she, Ada, and Louise, the new cook who'd been sent up from Kate's family in Virginia, piled into the back of the wagon while old Peter drove. They didn't talk too much, content to just watch the city go by. Evie took in the buildings. She was still getting used to how tall some of them were, much higher than anything she'd ever seen in the Maryland backwater she'd grown up in.

The ride over the cobblestone streets was bumpy but not too long, and as they traveled Evie made a mental map of their route. If she was going to run away sometime soon, she'd need at least some idea where she was starting from and which way she was going.

As they came up on the turn to Market Street, Evie's impatience had her heart beating fast. But then, without a word, Peter jerked the horse's reins and made a sharp right turn, taking the wagon up toward Race Street instead. Evie and Ada were nearly tipped over, and in her surprise at being jostled Evie couldn't help crying out.

"What do you think you're doing!"

With the wagon steadied, Peter turned his head slowly to look at her, raised an eyebrow, and then turned around again without a word. The others just stared at her. Her cheeks grew hot and her throat dry. Feeling suddenly exposed, she took a deep breath to regain her composure.

"I'm sorry, Peter—you just startled me is all. I thought we were going to the market."

"We are," interjected Louise. "But Miss Maggie asked us to drop by the fishmonger first and pick up some of her favorite trout."

"Haven't they got trout at Market Street?" Evie asked.

"Maybe, but she's real particular about this kind of thing, and I'm too new to get on her bad side," Louise said. "Besides, we need a lot of it, sounds like she's planning some big affair on account of your Miss Kate's engagement."

They pulled up to a storefront with a painted sign and a blue wooden fish hanging over the doorway. Louise hopped out of the wagon and walked inside, moving at a pace that suggested no kind of rush at all.

Evie tried to sit still, but as she grew agitated, she couldn't keep herself from chatting to try to fill up the time. "How long does it take to pick out a fish anyhow?" she asked Ada after what felt like an eternity. "Seems to me they'd all look the same, one's just as dead as another." Ada raised an eyebrow and shrugged. Evie looked at the door. No sign of Louise. She scanned the street for some sign of how much they were delaying her—there was a clock tower atop a nearby bank. It was already 10:30.

She looked down the block, trying to guess how far they were from the market. Could she jump out and make a run for it? No, that'd cause too much fuss.

"Peter, can't we go on ahead to the market and circle back to meet Louise? We don't have all day," Evie said.

"What's the hurry?" He cocked his head to the side and looked back at her.

What indeed. She stammered as she tried to come up with a good-enough-sounding reason. "It's just—we've been sitting here so long already, and there's shopping to get done, and . . ."

"It'll get done. Just set tight, she won't be but another minute."

Evie exhaled in a huff and sat back, crossing her arms. Ada nudged her with her elbow and raised her hands, wordlessly asking just what was going on. Evie said nothing and sat miserably—she was going to miss Charlotte. To make things worse, there was a cold drizzle outside, and a fine mist had settled onto Evie's cap, chilling her head and neck in the icy air. As she sat and shivered, she went back and forth between watching the door of the fish market for Louise—who, unbelievably, still hadn't come out—and racking her brain for the right thing to say to get Peter to move. Then it came to her.

"Peter, Miss Kate said we've got to get to the market early. She only likes the fresh spice cakes the bakery has in the morning, not the ones that've been sitting in the air all day," Evie said. "We've just got to get on. If we bring her back stale cakes . . ." Evie trailed off, letting the others fill in the rest with their imaginations. They didn't know Kate like she did, but they knew enough to be wary of her. She was growing a reputation around the house as someone whose moods came and went like summer storms, too changeable to be trusted. Some of that talk was true, but when Kate was upset she usually just whined and complained to Evie, rather than doing all the yelling and carrying on and calling for whippings that others must've expected since she was Southern. No, she always let others take care of that for her.

But playing on the other slaves' fear of Kate worked. Peter perked right up and slapped the reins of the horse to get the wagon going again. "We'll come back around for Louise, or she can find us at the market. She'll understand," he said, half to himself.

It was nice and dry under the market sheds. Near the fruit stall where Evie and Charlotte had agreed to meet, the air was sweet, crowding out the yeasty scent of fresh bread that had filled and delighted Evie's nostrils as she passed the baker. The shelves of the fruit stall were laden with late-season pomegranates and apples held over from the fall, bright shocks of color against the brown of the baskets that held them. But as she looked around, she couldn't see Charlotte anywhere nearby. Evie turned in every direction, trying not to panic—had she missed her chance? Peter and Ada wouldn't take long to finish their shopping, so there was no time to waste. Just then, she looked over at the fabric stall and saw Charlotte hurrying off with a package under her arm. Of course, more new clothes. So much for their meeting.

Evie marched over and grabbed her by the arm and yanked until she turned around.

"Let go of me! What are you— Oh," Charlotte said as she recognized who it was.

"Oh?" Evie snapped. Didn't she feel even an ounce of shame? "You were leaving! Again!" In her anger, all Evie's carefully planned words flew clean out of her head. Onlookers stared.

Charlotte crossed her arms. "If you'd just let me explain, I was waiting for you at the meeting spot just a minute ago," she said. "But you were late! I can't hang around all day—I might be caught myself."

A harsh, humorless laugh escaped Evie's throat. "Well at least I know who *you're* worried about."

"That's not fair, Evie." Charlotte looked at the ground. "I'm doing everything I can to help you."

"And to avoid me too," Evie said. They'd hardly spoken since that first meeting, and her body flushed with an angry heat as she remembered how it seemed like Charlotte had stayed away from the market after catching a glimpse of her the first time. It was like she was a bother, an interruption to whatever Charlotte had going on here.

"Look, let's not do this, all right?" said Charlotte. "I had good news to bring you today. Nell and I know someone who's connected to the people helping slaves escape, and he's working with us. So next time we get together, I should be able to tell you the full plan. You've just got to hold on a little longer."

"How long? I can't just keep waiting! Once this wedding is done with, Kate will drag me down to South Carolina, and what then?"

Passersby moved around them, and as Evie spoke Charlotte pulled her to the side of the path so they'd be out of the way. She didn't even bother hiding how Evie was embarrassing her.

"You said the wedding was set for early June, so we've still got a few months, right?"

"*Months?* You've strung me along for two months already!"

"I'm not saying it'll be that long. I can't be sure—planning an escape is tricky, and complicated. But there's still plenty of time—there's no need for you to panic."

"Easy for you to say, you're already away from Kate!" Evie shot back. "And if it's so complicated, shouldn't you hurry up so we don't run out of time? You can't just leave me with her until the last minute!"

"I don't intend to!" said Charlotte. "I'm *trying,* Evie. You've just got to hold on, please."

"And while I'm waiting, you just get to keep playing around with your new friends?" Evie asked. "I bet they don't even know who I am."

She saw Charlotte blush. As if Evie didn't know. Charlotte probably spent her time going to parties and teas, all the lovely places she could wear her lovely new things, while Evie was stuck at Kate's beck and call. What good was Charlotte's easy new life if she couldn't—or maybe *wouldn't*—help anyone else?

Charlotte shook her head. "I don't want to fight." She checked her pocket watch. "I've got to get back. And so should you. Let's try to meet again in two weeks, over in the pastries section, where the bake sale was. I'll look for you."

"Fine," Evie said. It was just as well. Peter and Ada would be looking for her any moment now. "I guess there's nothing else I can do anyhow. Nothing but keep waiting."

"We'll sort this out, Evie." Charlotte squeezed her hands and walked off.

Evie couldn't decide whether she believed her or not.

Chapter 14

CHARLOTTE

CHARLOTTE COULDN'T SHAKE HER LAST CONVERSATION WITH Evie. She wasn't proud of how she'd kept her at arm's length, but how could Evie understand? She might've had nothing to lose the day they'd found each other again, but Charlotte had, and still did. It was true, she wasn't exactly suffering while she was getting Evie's situation sorted out—she was shopping with Nell and taking tea and cookies with the Wheatley Association, and Evie was just "that poor girl" they were trying to help. What had she said? *They don't even know who I am.* But that wasn't what made Charlotte feel so queasy about it all. No, the trouble was they didn't know who *Charlotte* was.

Busy as she was trying to be someone else, she grew more and more anxious to have everything sorted out—both Evie's situation and her own. She was relieved when the next week, Nell and Alex wanted to meet and catch up on where things stood with their plans. That early March morning, the last of winter's chilly wind was in the air and it was pouring rain. Charlotte fought to keep her umbrella right-side-out as she hurried toward the offices of *The Pennsylvania Freeman.* When she got inside, shutting the door behind her against the deluge, Nell and Alex were already there, chatting and laughing as Alex scribbled at a desk in the corner of the front room.

"Deep into wedding plans?" Charlotte called out from the door-way. "Don't tell me, you've settled on a dress?"

Nell smirked. "Without your expert eye? Never."

"We're leaving all that to our mothers," Alex said, sidling up beside his bride to be. "It's their dream come true after all."

"You two don't seem all that put out by it, by the look of things," Charlotte said.

"Oh stop. Heaven knows how we'll break it to them when all this is done," Nell said, chucking Alex in the shoulder. He absorbed her playful blow, but his look at Nell lingered just a moment too long.

"That day isn't too far off, as it happens," he said, leaning forward. "Everything's all set."

All set? How could it possibly be that easy? Alex went on. "The family Evie and her mistress are staying with, the Jacksons—they've held property in the city for a long while now, splitting time between here and down South, from what I'm told. With spring coming, they've recently started sprucing up the exterior and fixing up the courtyard of the town house. One of the Vigilant Association's allies is a white man who runs a gardening and landscaping concern; he goes out that way sometimes to do some work for them."

"That's all well and good, but how does gardening help Evie?" Charlotte asked.

"Hold on now, listen. He brings a covered wagon with all his supplies every time he goes over there, so all Evie's got to do is get herself into that wagon without being seen next time he's there, and he can take her out with no one being any the wiser."

"But how will she know who he is?"

"He'll have a blue ribbon tied to one of the wagon wheel spokes. That'll tell her it's safe to get aboard."

"What do you think, Charlotte?" Nell asked. Charlotte had been listening carefully as Alex laid out the scheme, but she wasn't quite sold.

"You're sure this man can be trusted?" she asked.

"The association's worked with him before," Alex said. He was a Quaker and a longtime abolitionist, and he knew people outside the city with safe houses where runaways could hide until they fled farther north. "He's the real thing. She'll be in good hands."

Nell smiled proudly. "I knew we'd been right to bring this to you." Alex had come through for them, just as Nell had said he would. But Charlotte couldn't fight the urge to keep pressing on the details.

"But what happens next? She's out of the house and then what? She can't hide in a covered wagon forever," said Charlotte.

"The Vigilant Association has an arrangement with a family who lives north of here, in Bucks County. He'll bring her to their house, and from then on, she'll make her way from one spot to the next until she gets to Boston, where the last family is. She'll be free there, but if she wants to go even farther north to Canada, that's up to her," Alex said. "We'll get her as far as we can."

It didn't sound like a bad plan. Maybe it was even a good one. Working with people who'd done this before, and the gardener a known ally—it all sounded like the best they could hope for. But something was still tugging at Charlotte.

"So, she'll be gone, then," Charlotte said. Her voice was small and quiet. Alex leaned forward and laid a hand on hers, but the look on his face was confused. He glanced over at Nell, inviting her to help figure out what was going on.

Nell spoke gently. "She'll be gone, yes—safe, and free. Isn't that what we all want?"

Charlotte looked up. "We?"

"You, me, all of us. Evie too. That's what we're doing this for, isn't it? So that she can get away?" Charlotte supposed Nell was right, but something about sending Evie north all alone felt wrong—like she was still abandoning her somehow.

She swallowed and tried to reconfigure her expression into something less sad.

"Of course, yes," said Charlotte. She spoke mechanically, like something had switched on in her mind. "Alex, when is this man due to visit the Jacksons' house next?"

"A week from Friday."

"I'll tell Evie. She'll be ready," Charlotte said. With that, she stood up and smoothed her dress. "I've got to get back to work. Thank you. Thank you both."

She was out on the sidewalk before either of them could say another word. Trudging through the streets, Charlotte struggled to push her feelings down. Everything was happening so fast—Nell engaged, and Evie set to leave town. It was like everyone's life was suddenly moving on to the next phase. And where did that leave her? Having just gotten Evie back, she couldn't square her feelings about the fact that in just over a week they'd be separated again. But there was nothing easy about Evie being here, Charlotte reminded herself; she was finally setting a new life in motion, and Evie was nothing if not sand in the gears. Things had been tense between them, though somehow even that felt familiar—the way they watched out for each other, irritated each other, trusted and mistrusted each other the same as they ever had. They'd been near as good as sisters once, grown up together. If Evie were well and truly gone, Charlotte wondered if she'd ever be known the same way again.

But a promise was a promise. She'd dangled the hope of freedom and had to see it through, even if Evie leaving Kate behind meant she'd leave Charlotte and this city behind too. It was no less than Charlotte had done herself. And in helping Evie now, maybe she could begin to make up for it. With everything settled, she'd tell Evie the plan next time they met, and maybe find it within her to say everything else she needed to say, too.

At least she wouldn't show up empty-handed. With just a week to go, Charlotte could finally finish the dress she'd been sewing for Evie, working from the patterns in the *Lady's Book* magazine she kept splayed out on her writing desk. After leaving the newspaper office, she spent the rest of the morning wandering the streets in the rain, bouncing from dress shop to dress shop, and soon grew impatient. She'd been working on the dress for weeks and structured it precisely according to the pattern: she had folded pleats into the bodice before closing it with an invisible whip stitch that concealed the thread, added button-up cuffs at the ends of the sleeves, and sewed corded panels inside the skirt to hold its shape. Still, there were a few final details missing, and the precise shade of yellow buttons and thread she wanted were proving nearly impossible to find. None of the shops had it. She carried a swatch of the fabric that showed bright blue against the dismal gray of her maid uniform.

Charlotte glanced at her pocket watch. It wouldn't be long before she'd have to head home unless she wanted to be caught out. At the corner of Seventh and Chestnut, she lingered in the doorway of a dress shop with an inviting raspberry and floral-print day dress made of Indian chintz standing in the window. The shop owner, a white woman probably in her forties, glanced up at Charlotte and then looked away, disinterested. That was as warm a welcome as she could hope for, so she went in. The woman eyed her closely as Charlotte bypassed the ready-made dresses on offer up front and headed toward the back to look through the satin-covered buttons and other closures for sale. Her hand had barely made contact with a bolt of dyed-amber wool before the shop owner materialized behind her and cleared her throat. "Something you need help with?"

Charlotte's shoulders tensed, and she replied without turning around. "Just browsing, ma'am. Looking for a final touch on a new dress."

The woman put a hand onto the fabric and pulled it away.

"A dress for your mistress?" Of course. One look at Charlotte's uniform and what else could be assumed except that any little luxuries would pass straight through her hands and into some white woman's. Four years ago, the shop owner's words might've cowed Charlotte into a more submissive posture, but she was long past all that now and didn't feel like playing servant.

"It's for a friend, actually, ma'am. She's got a special occasion coming up and wants to look her best." She tried to mimic Nell's high-born diction, and lifted her chin.

The woman's eyes narrowed. "I see. Well," she said, laying a hand on Charlotte's shoulder and nudging her toward the door, "I don't know that we'll have anything appropriate for what you might want. Why don't you try one of the shops down on South Street, they might be better suited to your taste and budget."

Better suited to her color, she meant. Half-shoved back onto the street, Charlotte huffed and glanced at her watch. She'd hoped to speed up her errands by sticking to a shop close to her neighborhood, but prejudice in this city never lacked for ways to waste one's time.

Out on the sidewalk, she hurried west along Chestnut Street, glancing into dozens of shop windows and seeing one white face after another, until finally she came to the one past Fifteenth Street where Nell had taken her. There, a friendly and familiar brown face welcomed her in.

"Hello again," the owner said.

Charlotte smiled warmly and stepped into the shop. She felt herself blend comfortably into the scene as the dressmaker worked with a young woman near her own complexion, fitting her for a ball gown.

"Nip it in another half inch at the waist," Charlotte muttered under her breath as she browsed the thread for the perfect shade. The dressmaker glanced over and smiled—"I was getting there," she said.

Charlotte went back to rifling through the smaller items until finally she found them—a set of rounded, cloth-covered yellow buttons, and matching thread. She'd add the buttons to the sleeves of Evie's dress and embroider the cape with the thread. At the front of the shop, the dressmaker spoke kindly to Charlotte as she boxed up her purchases.

"I meant it when I said you've got an eye, you know. If you ever get tired of domestic work, you know where to find me," she said. She handed Charlotte a card: MAE BRATTON, DRESSMAKER. Now there was something to think about. When all was said and done, maybe she could start taking in piecework or apprenticing. Anything but going back to sitting around the house again.

She walked back home feeling both hopeful and lonely. When she opened the door, the house was quiet, and she slipped off her shoes to tiptoe down the side hall toward the stairs with her bag slung over her shoulder.

"Charlotte!" Her father's stern voice boomed from the parlor, breaking the silence. She flinched and stopped short. Turning back to answer him, she took a deep breath. She would act calm.

"Mr. Vaughn," she said with unnatural lightness. She stepped into the parlor. "Something I can do for you?" He was sitting in a chair at the corner of the room, shrouded in shadow. He'd been lying in wait.

"Come into my office," he said.

Charlotte tensed. "I'm fine here."

"Where have you been, Carrie?" He kept his voice low.

"I just went out for a walk, to get some air for a few minutes," she said carefully.

"A few minutes?"

"Yes. What's the problem?"

"You've been gone at least an hour, if not longer. *Where were you?*"

She crossed her arms and looked at him coolly. "I've already said. I'm going upstairs now to get changed and do some tidying up, if you'll excuse me, *Mr. Vaughn.*" She drew out the speaking of his name, her words laced with false deference.

"You're not going anywhere!" he roared. "Sit down."

Charlotte slowly took a seat on the couch. She never broke eye contact as she sat, and waited in silence. He'd found out she'd left the house, sure, but how much else could he really know? If she kept quiet enough, maybe there was a way out of this conversation without too much trouble.

Or at least she'd hoped as much, until James rose from the couch and yanked the bag off her shoulder. He dumped the contents onto the end table, and out tumbled her notebook, several Philadelphia Female Antislavery Society pamphlets, Nell's copy of Angelina Grimke's essay, and the latest issue of *The Pennsylvania Freeman.* They slid into the layer of dust lining the tabletop. The small drawstring bag holding the buttons for Evie's dress fell onto the floor, and three of the buttons rolled out next to Charlotte's feet.

"What is all this?" James picked up Grimke's essay and leafed through it, his face growing redder by the second. Charlotte's palms started to sweat. As he read, she grasped for a lie, but in her nervousness, the best she could muster was a half-truth, edited to its least dangerous form.

"They were given to me by a young woman I met," she said. That

was true. "We're in a literary association together—a reading club."
Also true. "You've been so eager for me to read more, I thought
you'd be pleased." Not quite. She decided to stop there before digging herself any deeper.

"Would this be the precise club I told you *not* to join? Exactly
what sort of 'reading club' is it that has you walking around with
abolitionist propaganda? Do you have any idea how reckless this sort
of thing is?" The questions came rushing out, as if with each one
James realized how little he knew about the way his own daughter
spent her time. Charlotte didn't get the chance to answer before he
went on, barely stopping to catch his breath. "I don't know how
many times I've said that it's too dangerous for you to be out of the
house on your own, let alone talking to strangers and joining abolitionist clubs! This is exactly the kind of thing that attracts slave
catchers and mobs. Why not just paint a target on our front door?"

"You go out and talk with strangers all the time," Charlotte said
sullenly. "You even bring them here." She never understood why he
always acted like *she* was the one who'd put them at risk of being
exposed as fugitives even as he gave himself permission to build a
whole double life outside the house and bring people like Mr. Wilcox home with him. Even if Charlotte's activities were risky, she'd
just taken her cues from James. But he didn't see it that way.

"That is obviously quite different. And whatever connections
I've needed to make for business, I'm mature enough to keep our
secrets and avoid unnecessary friendships. You're hardly more than a
child, Carrie!" She winced at the sound of her old name. James raged
on. "Who is in this club and what have you told them about yourself
and where you come from? About me?"

She shook her head, disappointed but not surprised by his lack of
imagination.

"Not everything is about you," she said.

"That is not an answer."

"I've got nothing to answer for. You've got no call to question me
like a criminal just for meeting with a few friends to read and talk a
little. I'm not a prisoner, am I? Or a slave?"

James's eyes narrowed.

"No," he said. "But you're putting us at a terrible risk by getting involved with these antislavery types, especially now that I'm working so hard to set us up for better. We may be free here, but this kind of talk can get people killed," he said, waving one of the tracts from Charlotte's bag. "Between the riots and everything else, it's far too dangerous. We're not so far north that there aren't plenty in the city who'd be happy to see us all in chains."

"*Us?*" Charlotte let out a peal of humorless laughter. The way he slid in and out of Blackness whenever it suited him was galling. When he needed some white man to invest in his business, Black people were all "them" and "those colored people." But now that he needed to guilt Charlotte into protecting his interests by staying at home, all of a sudden he was one of "us" Black folks again. But she wasn't going to let him off the hook.

"Most of 'us' *are* in chains—down South and even some in this city. Not everyone has your . . . *advantages*. How can you of all people begrudge them help? What's more antislavery than running from it like we did?" Charlotte paused. She knelt and picked up the buttons and slipped them back into the drawstring bag. "We can't just leave people behind. It wasn't right—it isn't right. We owe it to them to try and make things better."

"Destroying my livelihood and getting us sent back to Maryland isn't going to make things better for anyone. Our own freedom will have to be enough. And look how well we've done. Why would you want to jeopardize that?" James said. Charlotte didn't answer.

He took a deep breath. "The risk of what you're doing is too great, even if you're too young and foolish to see that. I won't allow it to continue." With that, he picked up her notebook, newspapers, and books, and dumped them into his trash can.

Charlotte crossed her arms tightly. "You're a very selfish man," she said quietly.

At that, he looked wounded. "I'm not just doing this for myself. I'd be no kind of father at all if I didn't keep you safe, whether you approve of my methods or not. I can't let you endanger yourself and me in the bargain after all we've struggled to build these last few years. If keeping the house tidy isn't enough for you to do, we'll just have to find other ways to occupy your time."

With that, he went to the parlor door and shouted toward the back of the house.

"Darcel, will you come in here please?"

"What are you doing?" Charlotte whispered, leaning forward. James didn't respond.

Darcel was out of breath when he showed up outside the parlor, with his shoulders tensed up almost to his ears.

"Everything all right, sir?" he asked, his voice on edge.

"We're fine, there's no cause for alarm," said James. Darcel's shoulders dropped as he exhaled.

"But I've been thinking, given your rare gifts in the kitchen, there's a lot Charlotte here could stand to learn from you," James continued. "From now on, she'll shadow you during the day to get the ins and outs of cooking under her belt. Wherever you go, she'll go, every day. She's not to leave your sight."

Charlotte inhaled sharply and stood up. Darcel looked from James to Charlotte and back again as he tried to work out just what he was being enlisted to do. After a moment's pause, he shrugged, and nodded. "All right, sir."

"Good," said James. "And the timing is ideal. I've got a dinner party coming up that I'm cohosting with Mr. Wilcox to increase our business, so I'll need both of you to help prepare. This will be just the thing."

Perfect, now her life was being ruined all so James could have a party. Charlotte stormed out and climbed upstairs to the attic. She sat on her bed and stewed, forcing her panic down underneath her anger. Whatever she'd hoped freedom would look like for her, it was clear her father had other priorities. And if his fears meant making Charlotte a prisoner and Darcel her warden, apparently that wasn't too high a cost. But now, it wasn't just Charlotte he was holding back: if she couldn't get out into the world to finish the plans she and Nell had set in motion, Evie would be dragged off down South, a slave for life. Charlotte would never see her again, and never have the chance to make things right.

She set her hands on the quilted bedspread and dug her nails into it, clenching and unclenching her fists. She willed herself calm. There had to be a way around James's command. She couldn't be torn away from her friends and the important work they were doing—not now. And more than Evie's freedom was at stake—what about her own? After all Charlotte had seen and become part of, the thought of being housebound again was too much to bear.

As she sat on the bed, a soft knock came at the door. Her body stiffened until she heard the voice. "It's Darcel, can I come in?"

"What are you doing up here?" she asked, surprised.

"Just wanted a word," he said through the door. "May I?"

"Fine," she said.

He opened the door, a tentative half-smile on his face. She was a bit shocked; this was the first time she'd ever seen Darcel upstairs, and he looked wildly out of place standing there just inside the door-way.

"Looks like a new way of things around here, eh?" he said.

Charlotte nodded silently. Since he'd been hired on and started living with them a year ago, Darcel hardly seemed to set foot outside the kitchen except to serve food, shop, or sleep. He spoke little, and Charlotte didn't press him for small talk. Prickly as he was, though, Darcel clearly had well-developed powers of observation—after a few months, he must have noticed Charlotte's favorite foods, because he started giving her more generous portions whenever he made them. She wasn't much of a cook herself, so she didn't mind having him around, but she certainly hadn't planned on becoming his apprentice.

"Mr. Vaughn's right about one thing, no harm in learning your way around the kitchen and how to put together something good to eat," he said, as if he'd read her mind.

"Oh, is that what this is about?" Charlotte asked sarcastically.

Darcel let the question lie there unanswered. The man was no fool, always saying as little as possible to avoid letting on just how much he knew. After a pause, he spoke again as he backed out of the room. "Why don't you just take it easy the rest of the day, and we'll get started tomorrow morning with breakfast." He quietly shut the door behind him.

Charlotte spent the rest of her day in her room. She didn't feel like going downstairs for dinner and had no appetite anyway—her anger at her father had stolen it. James was nothing if not consistent. Once again he'd torn her away from the people who mattered most to her and set her down in some new place she never asked to go: this time it was the kitchen. And he did all this without so much as a backward glance. He never talked about their lives at White Oaks or about Evie, Daniel, Auntie Irene, or even Charlotte's mother—not even when they were completely alone. He just didn't seem to carry all that with him the way Charlotte did.

The hours passed slowly. After all the books and papers James had thrown away, there was nothing she wanted to read. The old books he'd assigned to her sat untouched on the corner of her desk. Sometime after sunset, his familiar knock sounded. Charlotte rose from the bed, grabbed the books from her desk, and went to open the door.

Before James could step into the room, she handed the books to him across the threshold.

"I don't think I'm in need of any more lessons from you." She shut the door again, watching his sad, resigned expression disappear behind a wall of wood.

———

Chapter 15

EVIE

———

EVIE'S NERVES HAD FRAYED TO THE POINT OF UNRAVELING. Last time she and Charlotte talked, Charlotte had promised to bring her some sign of progress toward getting Evie out of here—if she didn't deliver today, Evie was sure she'd lose her mind. As it was, she could hardly hear herself think with Kate chattering nonstop about Mr. Brooks and their wedding plans. In constant anticipation of news about her escape, Evie had become a coiled snake, ready to lash out at the slightest irritation, made oddly fearless by the idea that she wouldn't be here for much longer. When Kate started rambling about floral arrangements as Evie brushed her hair, Evie just set down the brush and walked away.

"You're all set, Miss. I've got chores before the market." Kate sputtered behind her, but Evie didn't even bother turning around. Instead, she hurried to put some distance between them and went down to draw fresh water for the washbasin. Afterward, she turned to sorting clothes for laundry, and even polishing the furniture in the downstairs library—anything to keep away from Kate. But as she worked, she'd contrive reasons to go into the hallway toward the back staircase, where she could listen for whether Ada, Peter, and Louise had come down yet for the trip to the market.

She was careful not to draw the attention of Kate and the rest of the family, but as the morning wore on and she kept up her frenetic back-and-forth, she could feel more eyes on her. Finally, around ten o'clock, Ada poked her head out of Cousin Maggie's room. "Time to get going."

At the market, Evie did her best to linger near the bakers' stalls where she and Charlotte were set to meet, returning there after each time Ada or Louise pulled her away to help them find and carry one thing or another—a bag of rice, cuts of beef, or heads of broccoli from the produce shelves.

When they finally left Evie alone for a moment, she kept close to the baker, pretending to browse the loaves of bread on the table. Ten minutes drained away, then half an hour, and then more while she loitered. As each minute passed with no sign of Charlotte, the hope seeped out of her, a slow bleed from an old wound that wouldn't close. Into that hole crawled a sour, queasy understanding as Evie trudged back to the wagon to ride home. Charlotte had failed her, forgotten her. She was on her own again.

That evening, Kate chattered on in the background of Evie's fog, with Evie making the usual supportive murmurs in return. But inside, it was like a light had gone out. She'd expected to feel a flicker of anger at Charlotte, but even that was missing. There was only a cold, bone-deep disappointment in herself—that she'd dared to think anything good was coming to her, or that anyone was coming for her. After all, every person who'd ever mattered in her life was gone now. They'd all left her in one way or another.

The only constant was Kate, the ever-present, tormenting sun around which Evie revolved, and would revolve and revolve, until the end of her days.

The comedown after her buildup of hope felt like a deep grief, and it must've shown on her face.

"Evie? Evie? You seem distracted," Kate said. "Didn't you hear me? We've got to start thinking about what I'll wear tomorrow night."

"Of course, Miss—your family's meeting Mr. Brooks's folks. How exciting."

"No, what's gotten into you? Mr. Brooks is taking me to see a show. Haven't you been listening?"

No, she had not. It was hard to hear over the sound of her own future shattering.

"Yes, sorry, Miss. I'd been thinking of another night—I know how much you love to be the hostess, that's all, and I was excited to help," Evie said, squeezing Kate's shoulders. "Must've gotten myself turned around."

Kate looked at her quizzically and then visibly shook off her questions. Curiosity about anyone else's state of mind simply wasn't in her nature.

Just then, the dinner bell rang. Kate sauntered downstairs, leaving Evie alone with her thoughts. With her gone, Evie sat down heavily at the vanity table and put her head in her hands, surrounded by Kate's cosmetics.

At dinner that night in the slaves' quarters, Evie sat sullen and quiet while the others around her ate, talked, and laughed. Ada sat beside her, and wordlessly slid her an extra slice of pie. Evie smiled weakly, took a polite single bite, and said nothing.

"I know you must be homesick, but it's not so bad here," Ada said. "If you come round some evening after dinner, sometimes we make music and even play cards if the notion takes us. Some fun and a little company might do you some good."

"I get along fine on my own," Evie said. She slid the plate of pie away and stood. "Good night, everyone."

Chapter 16

———

CHARLOTTE

———

IN THE DAYS AFTER HER FATHER'S EDICT, CHARLOTTE PLAYED THE part of Darcel's unwilling shadow. She abandoned her housework entirely, and instead spent hours in the sweltering kitchen, sweating beneath her uniform and saying little. James wanted wallpaper for a daughter, so that's what he was going to get.

When the following Tuesday had finally rolled around, she'd woken up feeling hopeful—Darcel would have to bring her along for his weekly grocery shopping at the market, and there she could slip away to meet with Evie and tell her the escape plan. But when they stepped out of the house that morning, instead of turning north toward Market Street, Darcel had headed east. Bewildered, Charlotte finally spoke. "Are you sure this is the right way?" she asked from behind him, trying not to sound panicked.

"Same way I go every week," he said, not bothering to turn around. "Come on." When they reached Second Street, Charlotte's hopes were dashed. Just ahead of her between Pine and Lombard, the redbrick headhouse and the sheds of Society Hill's small market came into view. All her worries about running into Darcel at the city's larger, more established market uptown had been for nothing—this must have been where he'd been shopping all along. It was all she could do to keep from bursting into tears—she wouldn't find Evie here. Thwarted, Charlotte lapsed back into silence as she followed behind her new companion.

———

IN THE WEEKS THAT followed, once she recovered from the disappointment of her market mix-up, Charlotte was still determined to reconnect with Evie and Nell. Gradually, she began to clock Darcel's every move, from how long he stepped away from the kitchen for his midday break—almost always twenty-three minutes—to the time of day he'd start baking bread for an evening's meal. In studying his habits, she hoped to discover some clue to escaping his watchful eye.

She tried everything she could think of to get away from him: She proposed they take days off from their unusual arrangement, she gave him books to read in the hope he'd become absorbed and forget about her. Once, she even claimed she had urgent errands to run related to some feminine problem. He'd scrunched up his nose at that last one but still wouldn't bite.

Charlotte could only imagine what Evie must be thinking since she'd disappeared on her. Still, her hope to make things right between them burned on. In quiet moments, Charlotte settled into her sewing corner upstairs, attached the buttons to Evie's dress, and finished the embroidery: an intertwined row of yellow marigolds sewn across the shoulders of the cape.

With another Tuesday looming, Charlotte knew Evie was likely to be back at Market Street looking for her, and she weighed her options. A new approach suddenly occurred to her: maybe the key wasn't getting away from Darcel but getting him to go where she wanted. But she'd need to be more engaging to make that happen.

That morning, she woke at first light and marched determinedly down to the kitchen. The room was already warm, and smelled of charred wood and spices. The sun was just barely peeking in from the back courtyard, letting wisps of light into the dim room. When she came in, Darcel was standing beside the hearth waiting for her with a spare apron in hand.

"You're up awfully early," he said.

"Wanted to try my hand at breakfast today," said Charlotte. "Isn't this when you usually begin?"

"Mm-hmm," Darcel replied. "We'll start with something simple, quick breakfast biscuits. Come and watch."

He took a bowl from the shelf and gathered all his supplies from the pantry. Charlotte stood by as he scooped and pinched and poured the snow-white ingredients into the bowl: flour, salt, baking powder, sugar. He never measured anything and spoke not a word as he worked. He knew by sight and feel just how much of everything went into the bowl. When he scooped out the flour, a light dusting settled onto his bronze-colored hands.

Charlotte strained to pick up his patterns, making mental notes— had he pinched the salt with two fingers or three? How many scoops of flour had it been? She needed to seem interested if she was going to win him over. But as she scanned for an opportune moment to bring up the market, the actual mechanics of his work sparked her curiosity. His focus and sureness reminded her of the way her father had looked carving away in his workshop when she was a little girl.

Darcel stirred everything together with a wooden spoon, then turned to Charlotte.

"Go to the icebox and take out the butter."

It seemed strange to worry about buttering the biscuits before they were even baked, and stranger still that Darcel was keeping butter in the icebox, where it would grow too cold and hard to spread. She hesitated.

Darcel shook his head. "You're here to learn, yes? Icebox. And bring the buttermilk too."

Charlotte shrugged and did as she was told. "You know, I've heard they have the best buttermilk in the city up on Market Street. You think we could try going there today?"

Darcel raised an eyebrow and ignored the question. He took down a smaller bowl from the cabinet, poured in some of the flour mixture, and slid it toward her. "Actually, I'll let you try it your way—take a little of this and mix it with your softened butter on the counter. Then we'll add the buttermilk."

Charlotte went to the butter dish and scooped up a generous helping. The spoon slid through the soft butter easily, and it stirred effortlessly into the flour mix in the little bowl. As she stirred, Charlotte glanced over at Darcel. He was chopping his icebox-hardened butter into small pieces and tossing it into his bowl with a spoon, carefully avoiding ever touching it with his hands. Once he'd poured in enough buttermilk to make a sticky dough, he pushed the bottle over to Charlotte and motioned for her to do the same.

"I'm just saying," she tried again, "it's nice sometimes to see the different things the city has to offer."

She watched him turn his bowl over onto a floured spot on the counter, roll out the dough and then fold it over again and again before cutting out several little round discs. Charlotte copied as best she could with the little bit of dough from her bowl, yielding two biscuits of her own. To her surprise, she found herself enjoying the process—working with her hands, whether sewing or cooking, at least gave her busy mind some respite from her worries.

Darcel scooped her two biscuits onto the baking sheet and slid them into the tin oven in the hearth along with his. While they baked, Darcel set some sausage to roast over the fire while he cleaned up the bowls and spoons. He didn't offer any direction, so Charlotte just hung back and watched.

He never turned around but began to speak. "That's what you're missing, then—seeing new things?"

"You could say that," Charlotte responded warily.

"I remember when this whole city was something new to me—nothing like where I come from. But I guess everyone finds their way eventually." He glanced over his shoulder at Charlotte. "I think we can stick with the Society Hill market today, as usual."

So, he'd heard her after all.

Some ten minutes later, he slid the baking pan out of the tin oven. In spite of herself, Charlotte rushed over to admire her accomplishment. There sat four tall, fluffy biscuits with steam rising from their lightly browned tops. Beside them were her creations: two nearly flat discs of hardened dough.

She turned to Darcel, frowning. He shrugged.

"Better to see with your own eyes than for me to tell you. You'll learn."

Darcel tossed her one of his own perfect biscuits and swept the rest into a basket to be set on the dining room table with the sausage.

"Mr. Vaughn'll be down soon," he said. He sounded cautious, like he was afraid the mention of James would ruffle Charlotte's feathers. "Once he's eaten, we'll head out for the day."

"It's really all right, Darcel, I can stay behind. Or maybe we can split up the shopping? I know you don't want me tagging along after you all day," she said. On their last few shopping trips, he'd insisted she stay within his view every minute.

"What I want or don't want makes no difference. Mr. Vaughn told me what to do so that's what I'm gonna do—that means teaching you and yes, having you tag along after me. Might as well just accept it. Seems to me it's all just meant to keep you safe."

Charlotte huffed. "Being kept under lock and key isn't the same thing as being safe, no matter how alike *he* thinks they are."

"Lock and key? Come on now, it's not so bad as all that—at least you've got decent company!" he said. He pointed at himself and smiled at his little joke. He was kind, if a little gruff. But Charlotte wouldn't be so easily prodded out of her sullenness.

She glared at him. "You know, just because he said something doesn't mean you have to do it. We aren't slaves."

"Believe me, I know how far we are from that," Darcel said. "But just the same, if I'm given a job to do, I'm doing it. That's that."

Her plans would have to keep waiting.

When they set out to do the household shopping later that morning, Charlotte tried to find some reservoir of patience within herself as she followed Darcel through the small market, watching him gather all they'd need for the week. She supposed being angry with him wouldn't solve her problems, and none of this was his fault anyway. Watching him work, she tried to exhale.

He carried no list. He just went from one merchant's stall to another, meat to vegetables to dry goods, poring over the wares and making his selections piecemeal along the way, as if he intuited what was needed and how it would come together. Charlotte observed in silence, taking in his technique—checking for freshness by examining the clarity of fish eyes and the color of their gills, and always choosing beef with smooth white fat rather than yellow. He moved fast and explained little, speaking only when it came time to haggle with the shopkeepers.

There was just one spot where Darcel lingered, and it was outside the market. He brought her to a store on Water Street, wedged between the docks where tall ships unloaded casks of rum and crates of coffee and spices from the Indies, day in and day out. Inside, a dark-skinned man stood at a counter surrounded by bottles and bottles of dried leaves, powders in shades of deep red, yellow, and rusty brown, and tiny round balls that looked like seeds. Charlotte didn't recognize much, but Darcel seemed right at home.

When they'd entered, he and the shopkeeper had nodded at each other. Darcel moved through the shelves methodically, picking up bottles one by one and opening them, wafting the scents toward his nose with his hand. Sometimes he nodded approvingly, other times he scrunched up his face and set the bottle down with a "hmmph." Charlotte drew closer when he lifted a bottle of red powder. Cinnamon, maybe? She wondered just what he was checking for when he sniffed so determinedly.

"May I?" she asked.

He nodded and she leaned in. Charlotte was surprised by the earthy, savory scent that filled her nostrils as she inhaled. Whatever it was, it wasn't cinnamon. But it was familiar. Darcel had been using it in his cooking back at the house.

"Paprika," he said. Her ignorance must've been written on her face.

"Paprika. Mmm. What are all these things, Darcel? I've never seen half of them before," Charlotte confessed.

"Spices, my girl, spices," he said proudly. "There's a wide world out there beyond salt, pepper, and garlic. My own parents taught me that, flavors and wisdom from back home."

"And where is home?"

"An island far south of here, it was Saint-Domingue when we left—now it's called Haiti." His voice was wistful, and the lines beside his eyes wrinkled as he smiled warmly, as if he could feel the sun on his deep-brown face.

This was the most Charlotte had ever heard Darcel say about himself, or about much of anything. To her surprise, he kept talking. He described Haiti with immense pride: a warm, lush green island, one now governed by free Black people who'd thrown off their masters and formed a nation of their own in the middle of the sea. But not everyone got the chance to stay and savor their victory. Amid the bloodshed of the revolution, thousands of white people fled to seek refuge in America, dragging their slaves along with them—Darcel and his family included. Though Philadelphia welcomed the white refugees, their continued presence had a condition: they had to free their slaves. Darcel had lived in the city as a free man ever since, and in the decades afterward his parents had died and his sister moved north.

"It's just me now," he said. He looked up from the spices he'd been examining, making eye contact with Charlotte. "You know a little about that, then, don't you?"

He was hard to read. It was impossible to sort out exactly what he knew, and with the talk of her family situation the conversation was headed into dangerous waters.

"I'm on my own, that's right." She picked up a bag of another spice and inhaled. "Do we have everything we need?"

Darcel squinted at the abrupt subject change, but he moved on quickly.

"Just let me pay for these and we can make our way back. Surprised to hear you're in a hurry to get back into the house." He laughed.

Charlotte chuckled. "Not that this hasn't been interesting, but all these scents are making me hungry."

Darcel paid for the spices and bade farewell to the shopkeeper with a silent nod.

"We'll be back here before long," Darcel said. "This shop always has the freshest spices. People say it's where all the finest chefs and caterers in the city come—Bogle, Jones, and Marion."

"Oh, is that what people say?" Charlotte asked, smiling.

Darcel laughed. "You're not the only one who gets out and talks to folks."

IN BETWEEN ALL THE cooking lessons and shopping, Charlotte eventually started attending to her housework again, though Darcel regularly checked to make sure she was where she should be. While she worked, pungent scents often wafted up to the attic and upstairs rooms, where she'd be busy pressing clothes or sweeping. She'd smell some of the familiar spices from the market, and the loaves of bread Darcel would bake and keep around for nibbling. But one rainy afternoon, strangely, the sweet, tangy scent of orange floated out into the parlor while she was mopping the floor.

She peeked into the kitchen and saw Darcel slide an orange cake out of the oven, set it aside, and furiously scribble something in a notebook on the counter. James hated oranges, so it couldn't be for him. Maybe it was a sweet treat just for her and Darcel to enjoy. She kept about her business the rest of the afternoon, looking forward to dinnertime and the promise of dessert. But when she returned to the kitchen that evening, the cake was nowhere to be seen.

She looked at Darcel, puzzled, undecided whether to say anything. He just looked back at her blankly. It was hard not to wonder if she'd imagined the whole thing.

She shrugged, and the two of them got to work making a simple dinner of rabbit stew over rice. Darcel set out the ingredients and reminded her how best to slice the carrots and chop the onions, then stood aside while she cooked mostly on her own. He jumped in only when it came time to add the seasonings. He pulled out the jars and bags they'd painstakingly chosen at the spice shop, lining them up on the kitchen counter. He brought over a few more from the pantry, those he'd already had in stock and used as staples: salt, pepper, dried garlic.

Charlotte stood by amused as he maneuvered himself into position in front of the pot. She smiled as he fanned the scent toward himself, contemplated, grabbed a bottle, and spooned varied amounts of the seasonings into the stew. So scientific. When they finished, they sat to taste the results of their work before serving James.

Darcel settled onto his stool and lowered his spoon into the bowl. Charlotte watched expectantly. He brought the soup to his mouth and paused, raising his eyes to look up at her and laugh. For all her reluctance, she was surprised to feel so concerned about having gotten the stew right, but the process actually reminded her a bit of sewing—bringing together all the different elements to create something not only useful but also pleasing, something more than the sum of its parts.

"Not bad, not bad," he said. "Perfectly seasoned."

"If you do say so yourself," Charlotte ribbed.

"Mr. Vaughn will be glad to have this, to see for himself how you're coming along," Darcel said warmly.

The smile went out of Charlotte's voice. "I'm not fussed about what he thinks."

Without turning around, Darcel cocked his head to the side. He walked the food out into the dining room without saying another word.

Charlotte sighed and pushed away the thought of her father. Standing beside the counter, she stretched her hands. They felt a little stiff from all her work in the kitchen, but the ache was almost satisfying—a reminder of an evening unexpectedly well spent.

Chapter 17

—

NELL

—

WEEKS HAD PASSED SINCE NELL HAD HEARD ANYTHING FROM Charlotte, and it was beginning to weigh on her. With no explanation, Charlotte had stopped showing up for their regular rendezvous at Washington Square Park. The first time she'd missed it, Nell had thought it was odd given all the plans they had in motion, but she gave her friend the benefit of the doubt and waited on the bench for an hour as people ambled by along the walking paths. The next week, Nell was more than a little embarrassed when Charlotte's absence was pointedly questioned at the Wheatley Association meeting.

"Where is she?" Lillian had asked. "I thought you two were working on a new reading to share with us for this week, though I assume you were taking the lead on that, Nell. Charlotte sometimes seemed a bit hesitant." At that, Nell's placid smile had tightened. That was the trouble with some of these social groups. It often wasn't entirely clear which members were truly accepted rather than just tolerated. Lillian, for one, had always been polite to Charlotte, but not without something icy in it. Now she reveled in her sudden absence, as she had when Nell's prior working-class friends had slowly drifted away.

Nell had thought things would be different with Charlotte. She'd been around for quite a while now, and they'd grown so close. Especially lately, their friendship had an energizing, purpose-driven quality to it. When Charlotte brought her into the effort to save Evie, it felt like Nell was finally becoming the woman she'd always strived to be—someone who made a real difference. She missed Charlotte, yes. But perhaps more than that, Nell missed who she was with Charlotte.

And for her to cut things off so abruptly felt strange, enough that Nell wondered whether there was something deeper going on than being scared off by Lillian and the others.

The third week of Charlotte's absence, Nell once again sat alone on a hard stone bench. In the park, the buds were just beginning to form on the sycamore trees, the scent of early spring in the air. She must've waited there an hour at least. No sign of Charlotte. Now Nell was beyond surprise, beyond hurt, beyond curiosity. Now she was worried. It was a perilous business they'd gotten themselves into, scheming to aid a would-be fugitive slave, and any number of things could have gone wrong. Charlotte's friend Evie might have been caught talking about their plans, or Charlotte herself could've been exposed and taken. In truth, it was possible the whole scheme had been uncovered, and that would mean danger for Nell and Alex as well unless Charlotte could manage to keep their arrangements a secret.

When they'd met at the *Pennsylvania Freeman*'s office and made the plans for Alex's colleague to spirit Evie away, Charlotte had been oddly subdued, as if she were saddened somehow by what should've been a triumph. And then she'd disappeared. Nell had pushed away the thought at the time, but now she wondered anew: What wasn't Charlotte telling her?

And then there was the small matter of Nell's own subterfuge. Charlotte might've disappeared, but that left Nell just as engaged to Alex as she'd been before, with no signs of a way out. Finally set loose on their long-wished-for wedding planning, her mother and Mrs. Marion were forging ahead like an unstoppable train, carrying Nell through all the trappings of bridal preparations just in time for the social season. The deeper into it they threw themselves, the guiltier Nell felt for dangling the cherished matrimonial dream in front of their mothers on a whim—and now with Charlotte gone, it all seemed to have been for nothing. Nell and Alex would have to tell their parents eventually, but neither was in a rush to do it—how did one find the right moment to break one's mother's heart? And in the face of their silence, onward their mothers rolled.

First on their agenda was the engagement party. When Nell and Alex had begged off on a time line for the wedding itself, their mothers decided an engagement celebration would be just the thing to tide them over. Any excuse for a party. Social events were the norm in their circles, and Nell didn't begrudge them that. It would be dancing and dinner, and Nell and Alex were set to the task of planning a menu from some of the classics in the Marions' catering repertoire. Mrs. Gardner and Mrs. Marion would brook no less than the best for the son and daughter of the community's finest families, and the Marions' culinary creations were undoubtedly the best.

The evening they'd set aside for menu planning, Nell arrived at the catering storefront to find the front dining room empty and dim. She called out when she stepped inside, and heard Alex respond from a distance.

"Back here!" he called. She followed the sound of his voice through the elegantly appointed dining room, down a short, narrow hallway that opened into a giant kitchen, which stretched the full length of the building. There were two brick ovens, one at each end of the room, and the air was hot and sweet—it smelled of chocolate. At the center of the kitchen, Alex stood stirring a pot on the cast-iron cookstove, leaning forward so that he could take in the aroma.

"I thought we were just going over the menu?" Nell said tentatively, taking off her cape and laying it aside.

"What fun is that without a tasting? Might as well get a few good meals out of this charade, right?"

Nell smiled. "Who am I to argue with such perfect logic?"

She grabbed an apron from the hook beside the counter and slipped it on. She reached back to tie it, but Alex rushed behind her to help and had already picked up the strings. "I've got it," he said, his fingers brushing hers. At his touch, she felt her face flush. Just a warm kitchen.

When she turned around, she saw that Alex had rolled his shirt-sleeves up to his elbows. It had been ages since she'd seen him looking so casual.

Nell settled onto a stool in front of the counter, and Alex went to grab the first course from the oven: deviled crab with fresh meat from the Chesapeake seasoned with onion, green pepper, paprika, and garlic, all baked on top of the crab's own shell. He and Nell each grabbed one off the plate. Eyes closed to savor the rich and briny taste, for just a moment Nell managed to forget her worries. But before long they were back again, and she set her fork down, a little resigned.

"Still worried about Charlotte?" Alex asked quietly. Things had been bad enough when Evie missed the rendezvous with Alex's associate, but Nell had no idea what to make of Charlotte's vanishing act. When she'd first told him about it, Alex had tried to remain cheerful. He said they'd just make a new plan and get it all sorted out. But as the days dragged on, Nell had become more and more withdrawn.

"Have you thought about going over to see her?" he asked. Nell felt her face scrunch up at the thought. Showing up at someone's home uninvited? Imagine.

As if he could read her mind, Alex went on. "I know it's not exactly mannerly, but we don't have to stay in the boxes we were born into. When it really matters, it's right to take a stand," he said, getting up to stir the chocolate sauce again. "You can't have forgotten that, you've taught it to me so well."

Nell looked up. "Have I?"

He nodded. "I'm . . . writing something," he said tentatively. "For the newspaper. I decided to take them up on the offer of a column, to write about what's happening with the vote and everything else."

That was surprising. And very public. The Marions were nearly as conservative as Nell's parents when it came to these matters. As caterers who served the most prominent citizens of the city, both Black and white, they were constrained by their success and kept their views quiet so as not to ruffle any feathers. Taking a stand in the pages of the newspaper was new territory—far more exposure than Alex's family might've liked. It made Nell nervous too.

"It's a bold stroke," she said slowly. "But aren't you worried about the reaction?"

"Other men have done it and things have turned out all right for them," he said.

Now he was being naïve. "You know perfectly well what happened to Mr. Purvis last fall, and it was just a few summers ago James Forten's son was nearly killed for doing far less than writing a public editorial," Nell said. The younger Mr. Forten's mere existence—young, Black, free, and the son of one of the wealthiest and most politically vocal men in the city—was enough provocation for a gang of white toughs to attack him: they'd been roaming the neighborhood just blocks from Nell's and Alex's homes during yet another riot, and when Robert Forten happened by, they saw a convenient figure on whom to take out their senseless anger. The incident had rocked the neighborhood and rattled Nell's parents badly. But apparently not Alex.

"It's a risk I'm willing to take. I can't be stifled into silence by fear and my father's business all my life," he said. "What, are you worried about me?"

Terribly so, yes, she thought to herself. He was her best friend. But she admired his courage.

She shook her head, resigned. "It sounds like there's no talking you out of this. So, why don't you tell me about it?" She leaned forward on the counter, grateful for the chance to think about something other than the fiasco with Charlotte.

Over the next three tasting samples—a creamy terrapin soup flavored with a generous splash of sherry, a light salad they rejected for the overabundance of radishes, and buttery sweet rolls with crisp crusts that steamed when they broke them open—Alex walked Nell through his editorial. He broke down his arguments and she fired back questions, suggested lines, and shared anecdotes from her reading to back up what he planned to say. Nell was completely engaged. This dance delighted her even more than the ones they'd shared at the ball.

"I should've asked for your help sooner, you're incredible," Alex said finally. "As sharp as you are, if there's anyone who can get to the bottom of what's going on with Charlotte, it's you."

"We'll see," said Nell. "Perhaps I can find some other way to sort all this out." She turned the page of the notepad where they'd been rating the courses. "Looks like we've got a few winners. Is it time for—?"

"Dessert!" he answered, motioning her over to the pot. He lifted the lid and the scent of chocolate overtook Nell's senses. "We'll drizzle this onto the ladyfingers when they've finished baking." He grabbed a spoon and dipped it in. "Here, taste," he said, holding it up to her mouth. Nell poked her lips out and dabbed them just at the tip of the spoon, careful not to let any drop. It was smooth and velvety.

"Do we have to drizzle it over anything? Maybe we can just eat it like soup," she said, savoring the lingering taste. "Your turn!" She took the spoon and dipped it again, then lifted it. Alex leaned forward with gusto, took the whole thing into his mouth and gulped it down. No surprise, he ended up with a smear of chocolate on the side of his mouth.

Nell shook her head and laughed. "Still as much of a mess as ever," she said. It felt like she'd spent half their lives straightening him up, as he was the chaos to her order. With the tip of her finger, she reached out to wipe away the chocolate. He looked into her eyes and smiled, taking her hand before she could pull it back. He leaned his face close to hers, and to Nell's surprise she found herself drawn in his direction, his breath sweet and warm, inviting her forward.

But just then, the bell rang up front to announce someone opening the door to the dining room.

"Alex, you here?" Mr. Marion called.

Jolted back to her senses, Nell stepped away. She glanced up at

Alex's face and wasn't sure if she was reading confusion at what had nearly happened, or disappointment that they'd been interrupted.

"Alex?" the voice called again.

"Back here, Pa," he said. Nell rushed to take off her apron and pick up her shawl.

"This was lovely," she said. "I think we're all squared away for the dinner, no?" She hurried toward the kitchen door.

"Nell, wait," Alex said in a hushed voice. But she had to get out of there.

"I'll catch up with you soon, and let you know how things go with Charlotte." She breezed into the dining room. "Nice to see you, Mr. Marion," she said, quickly kissing Alex's father on the cheek before rushing out onto the street.

At home, she tried to shake off what had happened—or almost happened. Her head had been swimming in the heat of the kitchen, and she'd just lost herself for a moment, that was all. She and Alex would probably laugh about it later, once they figured out how to untangle themselves from this fake engagement, especially since they didn't need the cover anymore. She'd meant to bring that up, but their conversation about the editorial had distracted her. Still, perhaps things would somehow work out with Charlotte, so it was best to hold on a little while longer. She and Alex could talk about breaking things off another day. In the meantime, she would focus on trying to figure out why her friend had disappeared.

As she went to hang up her dress, she winced. A smear of chocolate had found its way onto the back. She'd been so distracted she'd forgotten to wipe her finger before taking off the apron. Distraction and messiness—this was no time for either. Still, at the memory of the sweetness of the chocolate, and the moment, Nell couldn't help smiling.

THE NEXT MORNING AT BREAKFAST, Nell marched into the dining room and found her mother sipping coffee and reading a book while her father finished the last of his eggs before heading off to work. She cleared her throat.

"Mama, Papa, I need your help," she said. Her mother looked up, and her father set down his fork and cocked his head to the side. They were listening. The next words came out all in a rush, by design, so that they couldn't interrupt her to refuse.

"It's about my friend Miss Charlotte Walker, the young woman I've brought around the neighborhood sometimes. She's a member of the Wheatley Literary Association, too. A few weeks ago, she suddenly broke with me and I'm very concerned. I need to know more about her situation, especially if I'm going to continue keeping company with her. I'm not sure where to begin, but I think the wisest course would be to start with her employer. Will you help me?"

Her mother's eyes widened in shock, and her father let out a sharp "Ha!"

"You're asking us to start some kind of investigation into a local white man because your friend, his *maid,* stopped coming around? Am I understanding you correctly?" her mother asked skeptically.

"I don't know that it needs to be as formal as an *investigation,*" Nell said, "but would it be so much trouble for you to ask around? Perhaps find out if anyone knows him, or if any of his other housemaids have had trouble?"

"But who would we ask, dear? We don't know any housemaids."

The combination of patience and innocence in her mother's voice was maddening.

"Yes, Mama, I'm aware that you do not personally know any housemaids, apart from the one we employ. But perhaps some of your social contacts can help, or maybe someone has met the man himself. Charlotte tells me he's some sort of woodworker; I think he makes cabinets and other furniture," she said. She racked her mind for any details she could remember from the scraps Charlotte had shared with her. "His name is James Vaughn, and he and Charlotte arrived in the city going on four years ago. She said they came from out west—Lancaster, perhaps?"

"Even if we were to look into this man and find something out, what could possibly be done?" asked Mr. Gardner. "There's no sense in us involving ourselves in white folks' affairs, Nell. It sounds like nothing but trouble."

"This isn't white folks' affairs, it's about my friend. She's a young colored woman, the same as I am, about the furthest thing from a white man that she could be. Isn't there some value in trying to look after our own folks?" Nell pushed.

"We do! We contribute to the benevolent societies and volunteer at the fairs and such. We don't have to go around befriending everyone on top of that. You make us sound as if we've turned our backs on the poorest among us, and that's not fair, Nell," her mother said, sounding wounded.

Nell was exasperated. "There are limits to what you can do from a distance by tossing money at people, Mother."

"Nell." There was a note of warning in her mother's voice. She had overstepped. She didn't usually speak to her parents this way, but her anxiousness had started to overpower her composure. Still, she realized she had to apologize.

"I'm sorry, Mama. I don't mean to be unkind. Charlotte has been a good friend to me, and I just want to do right by her. Isn't that the sort of woman you raised me to be?"

"A little too well, it turns out," Mr. Gardner broke in.

"Perhaps," Nell retorted, half-smiling. "Just see what you can find out? I won't ask for anything beyond that." Her parents shrugged and nodded. With that, she gratefully settled into her seat to begin her own meal.

In the days afterward, life resumed its usual rhythms: meetings, teaching, and a busy spring social calendar, all while trying to keep a bit of distance from Alex. As for helping Evie, Charlotte had kept Nell frustratingly separate from her, so there was no way to reach out and help her directly. There was little Nell could do but wait.

———

Chapter 18

EVIE

———

IN APRIL, THE TREES AROUND PHILADELPHIA BURST INTO BLOOMS of pink and white, but the sudden brightness brought Evie no joy. In the creeping spring warmth, she felt the heat of the South reaching up to drag her back down. Unbidden, the stories of the brutal goings-on deep in the Carolinas she had heard from people passing through at White Oaks forced themselves to the front of her mind. An unforgiving sun, and slaves worked near unto death in the heat, under the whip, and punished something gruesome if they ever put a toe out of line. And the massahs down there, with even more of a taste for young Black girls' flesh than the ones in Maryland. No one batted an eyelash at the passels of high-yellow babies born from the tired, broken bodies of women put to more intimate work each night after the sun set.

But even with all her hopes of escape dashed, there was only so much sulking Evie could do. There was little room for her sadness, not when Kate and her whole extended family were abuzz with wedding plans. It was all her mistress could talk about, and every place she dragged Evie had something to do with the wedding, from the dressmaker to the print shop for invitations. It might've been easier to plan the wedding where it would happen—at the Jackson family's estate in Virginia—but Kate insisted on staying in Henry's sights as long as she could, the better to make sure he didn't slip her snare. And so her dress would be made in Philadelphia, with Evie ac-

companying her to fabric selection and fittings, making appropri-
ately excited noises as Kate stared at her with demanding eyes.

And then, of course, there were the visits from her fiancé. Henry
would take Kate out for carriage rides and shows at the theater.
Sometimes he came to the house for midday visits during breaks
from his office, "Just to see your lovely face," he'd always say to her.
Evie was always in the background of their romantic interludes, on
hand in case Kate needed something—a handkerchief, another glass
of lemonade, a bite from the kitchen. No one but Evie would do.

All that hovering gave Evie time to take the measure of the man
who meant to be her new massah. He often talked about life on his
beloved Willow Creek plantation, how he couldn't wait to get back
to the rolling hundred-acre fields, planted with row upon fluffy
white row of cotton, and happy darkies singing dawn to dusk as they
picked away. The place sounded huge and lonely all at once, with its
scores of slaves, each set apart and assigned to one duty or another:
field hands, drivers, seamstresses, blacksmiths, housemaids. At White
Oaks, there'd been so few of them that every slave had to do a bit of
everything, and could all fit around a single table for dinner in their
quarters.

The more Evie learned about Willow Creek, the more questions
she had. But her most pressing questions were about Henry himself.
If life under his thumb was going to be her future, Evie wanted to at
least go down with eyes wide open.

One evening after dinner, she decided to visit the small room off
the kitchen where Peter, Ada, and the others would talk and play
games. Evie settled into a chair quietly, unsure how to wriggle herself into the conversation. Everyone chattered on for a little while
before the voices died away and all eyes flitted over to her.

"Surprised to see you down here so late," said Ada. "Something
on your mind?"

"Just trying to figure out what I'm in for after this wedding, is
all," Evie said. She lowered her eyes to the tabletop. "What kind of
man this Brooks is, you know—if he's a bother around the quarters
at night."

The other women murmured "Mmmm" and nodded. Everyone understood what she was getting at. Peter shook his head.

"Ain't heard nothing like that," he said. "Me and his old driver used to talk sometimes, before the new one got swapped in, and the next one after that. Hard to keep track of 'em all, but the old one, Odysseus, said Brooks was all right as massahs go. Kept off the young girls at least, but left things to a hard-edged overseer down there who worked folks to the bone. Odysseus said he was glad to be clear of the place for a little while."

Evie settled back into her chair. It wasn't exactly good news, but it wasn't as bad as it might have been. She relaxed a little after that conversation, but it wasn't long until she had new reason to worry.

Later the same week, Henry came around for afternoon tea with Kate. There was a little chill in the parlor and Kate had sent Evie off to get her a shawl, but as she headed out of the room Evie caught Henry's eye on her. He stared at her a little longer than felt comfortable. "How old is she, anyhow?" he asked Kate under his breath.

Evie's blood ran cold. So much for Peter's word. Maybe there were some things a driver wouldn't pick up about another man. She took her time coming back from upstairs with the shawl, dropped it off, then left as fast as she could, not wanting to offer Henry any more viewing time than she had to.

But once he'd gone for the day, Kate was in an even better mood than usual. Evie couldn't figure why—Kate had grown up down South and wasn't so naïve that she wouldn't have taken the meaning of his interest in Evie. But she was positively giddy. Kate looked around the parlor to make sure none of her family were about, then patted the seat next to her on the couch. Evie looked around too, and sat.

"Henry's got exciting plans for you after the wedding, you know. We'll practically be new brides together!" She paused for dramatic effect. Puzzled, Evie leaned forward.

"He tells me there are some likely young bucks down there that'd make a good match for you—a few might even be handsome, in that rough, Black sort of way, and they're already popular with some of the other girls," Kate continued. "By Henry's lights, you're just the right age to start having little pickaninnies of your own, and he wants to set you straight to it. Our little ones will get to grow up side by side!"

Evie's mouth went dry. *Just the right age.* She was only sixteen years old. Her throat tightened, and she suddenly feared she'd choke. Distracted, Evie reached over to the end table, picked up the glass of iced tea Henry had left behind, and gulped half of it down. Kate reached out and snatched the glass, staring at Evie aghast.

"You know better than to use our crystal! What's gotten into you?" she exclaimed.

Evie stood up. "Sorry, Miss, just got so overcome with all the excitement." She forced a smile. "Can't imagine anything better than to share this stage of life with you."

Kate nodded, satisfied with Evie's self-correction. With that, she said she needed to rest and told Evie to run along and finish her work. The rest of the day, Evie moved through the house in a fog. It seemed these upcoming nuptials would be to everyone's profit except hers: Kate would marry herself into money, Henry would breed himself a valuable new generation of laborers, and Evie would be forced to pay for their happiness with her own body.

It was no more than any enslaved girl could expect out of life. Hardly anyone ever spoke about it, but it must've been what happened to Mama, to Carrie's mother, and probably would have happened to Carrie herself if she hadn't run off. But the notion that Black girls were worked over and used up just the same way in every generation, on every plantation—it was no comfort at all. An everyday horror was a horror just the same. That day, Evie decided she would never give herself over to it.

But with Charlotte having disappeared again, running off was too big a risk. She had no one to run to. Though that disappointment wasn't a complete surprise, it had cooled Evie on the wisdom of depending on someone else to solve her problems. But she could count on herself. If Charlotte wasn't around to get Evie clear of Kate, then getting Kate away from Henry and all his big plans would be the next best thing. There was nothing else for it—the wedding had to be stopped.

———

FOR ALL THAT KATE seemed a soft touch, there was no way Evie could get away with open rebellion. Anything that wounded Kate's sense of their friendship would bring retaliation—Evie had seen that a hundred times with Carrie at White Oaks, and had lived it herself. Speak to Kate too sharply or show a flash of disobedience and just like that, little privileges and small luxuries she usually offered would quietly dry up: sweet treats suddenly unavailable, a warm quilt taken away because it was supposedly needed in a different room. But the currency Kate clawed back most eagerly was time. It would suddenly become near impossible for Evie to get a moment to herself even to do housework, the better to keep her close to Kate and remind her of their intimacy. That's how she responded to backtalk or overstepping. For the bigger transgressions, there was always Cousin Frank, skulking around the town house with his cane in hand— a silent, silver-handled warning: *Behave, or else.*

No, this would need to be a subtler kind of sabotage. Evie should come off as bungling at worst, not ill-intentioned. Of course, wriggling Kate out of a desperately needed engagement in a discreet way would be a challenge. The surest card to play—exposing all of Kate's lies about her past—felt too dangerous to even consider.

Instead, Evie tested the waters with little things. First, she started fixing Kate's hair in unflattering ways, hiding away her rouge, nudging her toward dress colors that washed out her already pale skin and made her look every bit her age. Such was Kate's trust in Evie that she went along with all of it, once even thanking Evie for helping her adjust to northern fashion and the unfamiliar climate. Half the time, Evie hardly needed to do anything at all: many days the spring rain had wilted Kate into a drowned cat by the time she'd come in from her evening strolls with Henry. But for his part, Henry hardly seemed to notice his bride-to-be's waning good looks. He kept right on coming round, and the wedding plans forged ahead. Every so often Evie would feel Henry's greedy eyes on her and she could almost hear the coins piling up in his head as he imagined the profits her labor and her children would bring him. The man wouldn't be so easily put off.

When he next came to visit, Evie crept into the kitchen angling to catch up with his new driver. Odysseus had been gone for months, but the new one, Achilles, had looked friendly enough when Evie caught sight of him bringing the carriage around the last few times.

"Down here lurking again?" Ada said, popping her head into the room as she passed with arms full of laundry.

"I was hoping to run into Achilles, you seen him?"

Ada grinned. Evie pursed her lips, stifling a grin of her own. Whatever folks wanted to assume was fine by her. Ada pointed to the back door.

Outside, Achilles was leaning on the side of the house sipping from a ladle of water. He was tall and lank, with deep brown skin that reminded Evie of her brother. He was a good bit older, though—somewhere around thirty, she guessed.

"Guess we'll be seeing a lot more of each other," she said.

"Is that so?" asked Achilles. He put the ladle back into the water barrel.

"Can't see a way around it, what with the upcoming nuptials," said Evie. "Folks seem awful excited. It's mighty fast though. Makes you wonder if they've done their due learning about each other." She reached for the ladle and took a sip. Achilles eyed her curiously. This was the moment. If she could put a word into his ear about what Kate really was—a lying, penniless, disgraced widow—the truth might get back to Henry. Achilles didn't seem overly interested, but at least he was listening. She wound up to lay it all out.

"What I mean to say is—" Evie began, but he cut her off.

"If you're smart, you don't mean to say a thing about white folks' business. Best leave all that to them." He sounded resolved, and his tone didn't invite any more conversation. Evie's shoulders dropped.

Not such a willing audience after all. Evie sighed. She hung the ladle back over the side of the barrel and went inside.

———

Chapter 19

NELL

———

WITHIN DAYS OF ENLISTING HER PARENTS TO HELP FIGURE OUT what was going on with Charlotte, Nell started to grow impatient. Every afternoon, she'd march into the house after attending her meetings and make a beeline for the parlor, where she'd find her mother sewing some dainty handkerchief or lace doily. Her mother's placidness was an unwelcome contrast with her own increasingly frenzied worry.

Each time, Nell addressed her mother without preamble: "Well?"

And each time, her mother would look up serenely. "We're working on it, darling," she'd say. If Nell had been raised differently, she might have stomped a foot or even pounded a fist on the sideboard table in frustration. As it was, she merely exhaled the tiniest, sharpest puff of air, blowing a nonexistent hair off her forehead while she strained to keep an even tone.

"Of course. Thank you, Mama," she'd say.

Before long, though, it seemed Nell's mother had sensed her frustration.

"These matters can be so sensitive, you know," she'd said. "And sensitive matters can take a little bit of time, if handled properly." Handling things properly was everything to the Gardners.

Finally, when a week had passed since Nell's request, they had something to report.

"Come in here, Nell," her mother's voice rang out from the parlor.

Nell hurried to answer. "Yes, Mama?"

"Have a seat, dear, your father's found something out about Mr. Vaughn," she began. "A few things, in fact."

Settling into the sofa, Nell crossed her ankles and sat quietly to await her father's entrance. He would've heard her join her mother in the parlor, having no doubt planned this little conference well before executing it.

When he came into the room, he started talking before he even sat down.

"Well, as you told us, he's a woodworker. The word is that he makes some of the finest furniture in the city. His pieces are quite sought after; it seems the mark he puts on them—'JV' in script—is fast on its way to becoming a sign of one's social standing."

"That's lovely for him, I suppose, but what would any of that have to do with Charlotte?" Nell asked, impatient.

"I'm coming up to that," he said. "He's only just started making a name for himself in the city in the last four years or so. But it hasn't been all praise and sales. He put a foot wrong shortly after setting up his shop downtown."

Nell leaned forward, listening intently.

"He opened a workshop and straightaway put out an ad for apprentices and journeymen to work alongside him, learn the craft, and take on some of the workload. But for some reason he didn't think to specify in the advertisement that only white men should apply for the positions. When the time came, there were a half dozen young colored men lined up outside the workshop looking for an interview."

"Goodness gracious," said Mama as if she were hearing the story for the first time, though Papa had most assuredly told her the whole thing before this conversation started. Nell glanced at her mother and suppressed a smirk.

Her father went on. The line of Black boys waiting must've attracted the attention of some whites who'd come to seek the position, and a fight broke out. Vaughn broke things up and shooed the troublemakers off, but a few men, white men, stayed around for interviews and ended up getting hired. One of the Black boys did go back the next day to give it another shot, and Vaughn hired him on too. But he only lasted a week or so, until the white apprentices Vaughn had brought on raised complaints, and customers threatened to pull their orders. That wasn't the worst of the trouble though.

At the end of that week, the other apprentices waited around after the workday had finished until the Black boy was on his way home. They beat him so badly he was left with permanent scars on his face and a limp that still bothered him even years later. And for his trouble, Vaughn dismissed the boy on top of it.

Since then, Mr. Vaughn had been sending money to the young man's family. They lived just a few blocks away on Pine Street, Papa said. And when Vaughn began the hiring process all over again for new apprentices, his advertisement specified whites only. Hardly a surprise, but Nell still felt disappointed at hearing it.

She shook her head.

"Was his reputation that fragile?" she asked. Or his convictions, perhaps.

"That's the thing—he had no reputation to speak of. I couldn't find a single person who knew him before 1833. No customers, business partners, family members, nothing. It's as if James Vaughn appeared out of thin air all at once, fully formed and in possession of a business plan."

That was strange. Charlotte had said they moved to the city from Lancaster, and plenty of people traveled back and forth between the two cities for business regularly. How could no one have heard of him?

"In any event, since opening his shop on Second Street he's been steadily growing in profile, taking commissions from ever more prominent families, getting close to the deeper pockets in the lending industry. I hear that he's expanding the workshop to take over the lot next door, so he must be doing a brisk business," her father continued.

Nell paused to take it all in. She wasn't hearing anything that might tell her why her friend had suddenly disappeared, nothing to confirm or deny her worst fears. It was all just a lot of workshop and business talk, but what she needed were the details of his home life. That's where there might be some clue about what was going on with Charlotte.

"Is he married? Any children? Perhaps he's courting someone?" she asked.

Nell's mother raised an eyebrow. Even if her father's tale had raised concerns about the man, she was veering into unseemly territory by prying into such intimate details about a white man she'd never met. Her father shrugged.

"As far as I know, he lives alone," he said. "Except for your friend, of course."

Silence followed as Nell and her parents looked at one another uncomfortably. A white man living alone with a young Black woman, one pressed into service as his maid and, perhaps, something more. It was a story as familiar in free Philadelphia as it was in the slaveholding South, enough that an unwelcome notion crept to the forefront of Nell's mind even as she strained not to assume the worst. She'd heard and read enough to know that while some talked of love and what was voluntary in these affairs, more often they were something to be endured, survived. Was that why Charlotte was suddenly being shut away at home? Had Mr. Vaughn begun to fear that too much time outside the house might turn her head? Or was she hiding something?

Still, it was hard to square the suspicion that Vaughn might not be such a kind gentleman with the way people said he looked after his former apprentice's family, even if it was his own missteps that caused their hardship. One didn't make that sort of choice in this city without having at least some semblance of right versus wrong. But perhaps, as for so many other men, his good morals didn't extend to his dealings with young women.

"I understand your disappointment, but perhaps it's for the best your friend is maintaining her privacy right now. That frees you to shift your attentions to more appropriate company, and to your own wedding," her mother said, as if she could hear Nell's thoughts. "It can be a very. . . . delicate time for a young woman in her situation."

Nell's hand flew to her mouth at her mother's suggestion. It was too awful to even imagine, that Charlotte might be carrying her employer's child unwillingly, and hiding in shame behind closed doors to conceal it. She shuddered—Nell didn't want to believe the worst, but Charlotte's discomfort any time she spoke about the man was obvious. It had been clear from the beginning that something was amiss between the two of them, and if it wasn't this then Nell hadn't the faintest idea what else it could have been. But she was going to find out.

THE FOLLOWING MORNING, Nell sat on a bench in Washington Square silently arguing with herself. She had every intention of marching over to Charlotte's house to get to the bottom of all this, but the trouble was that the house wasn't Charlotte's home—not really. Although she lived there, it was mainly her place of work, and as such not a place where she was supposed to be accepting visitors. That much had been clear the day Nell first met her.

It had been a little less than a year ago now, back in the sticky heat of July. The women's Antislavery Society had one of their petition drives going, and Nell was out canvassing door to door all over the city with a few other ladies. They walked from Cedar Ward, where their abolitionist message was met with some interest, over to Society Hill, where polite dismissals were more common. A few women answered their own doors to callers, but mostly it was a mix of Black and Irish housemaids coming to answer when Nell and her white comrade Lucy rapped on the doors. When they'd arrived at Charlotte's place—a sturdy, large, and well-kept row home with a green door—Nell had admired the neat little rosebushes out front in full bloom. They knocked, waited, and almost walked away in the time it took for someone to answer. When the door finally opened, Nell had been delighted to meet a woman near her own age, friendly, and dressed in a uniform and apron. She'd seemed nervous, as if she rarely spoke to other people. Still, something about the woman's spark had drawn her in. Nell struck up a conversation, while Lucy all but pulled at her sleeve to get things moving along.

Charlotte never did sign the petition that day—she was cagey about why—but Nell walked away feeling she'd gotten something much better than a signature. What started as a conversation with a reluctant petition prospect blossomed into an invitation to coffee as Lucy looked on aghast, and soon Nell and Charlotte were thick as thieves. Until now.

Nell wasn't ready to give up on Charlotte yet. If her friend needed help, Nell was going to be there for her whether she asked or not. With her mind made up, Nell found her way over to Charlotte's doorstep once again. She knocked. After a few moments, a short and dark-skinned man arrived at the door.

"Yes?" he said.

"Good afternoon, sir, my name is Nell Gardner. I'm here to see Charlotte. Is she available?"

"She expecting you?" he asked. His accent had a pleasant lilt; it sounded almost French to Nell's ear.

"I don't think so, but I hope she'll be pleased to see me," she said.

He paused, thinking. "Well, as it is, Miss Charlotte's indisposed at the moment—elbow deep in some bread dough back in the kitchen."

"I'm happy to wait," Nell offered.

"No, I don't think she'd want that. You'd best be on your way."

It was difficult not to be taken aback by his rudeness. Nell stood rooted to the spot on the front step and tried to peer discreetly over the man's shoulder into the house. She couldn't see anyone.

"Do tell her Nell stopped by to see her, please. Perhaps I can come back another time," she said.

"It'd be best if you kept your distance, Miss, Charlotte's very busy tending to her job these days, and she can't hold with too much distraction. You understand." He shut the door.

It was hard to imagine Charlotte would hide in the back of the house and let this man speak for her. Something was obviously wrong, but Nell had crossed enough social boundaries for one day and was too polite to press further. She turned and left, casting one last, worried glance over her shoulder.

Chapter 20

———

CHARLOTTE

———

With James's all-important dinner party only a few weeks away, Charlotte and Darcel were feeling the pressure to get the house ready and firm up the meal plan. James had laid the preparations at their feet, after all. In the kitchen one morning, Charlotte's mind turned to the party while she and Darcel were crushing currants to make a jam for the bread they were baking.

"I've got some ideas for the dinner party menu!" she said to Darcel.

"I'll bet you do," he replied, laughing. Just yesterday one of Charlotte's "ideas" had been to craft a sauce to go over their pork chops and make it out of garlic and chocolate ("they both taste good on their own!" she'd argued). The week before that, her grand experiment was to make a spicy cake using some fresh peppers they'd picked up at the market. Feeling the heat in their mouths after taking a bite, Charlotte and Darcel had laughed for ten minutes with tears streaming out of their eyes. She'd suggested serving James just one slice, but Darcel had pulled her back on that. He was good-natured in the face of her exploratory approach to recipe development and didn't pry too much into the root of her anger with James, which she appreciated. While she was eager to take advantage of this dinner party to try her hand at some dishes, she knew they'd have to be a little closer to the mainstream than some of the wilder combinations she'd been dreaming up alongside Darcel.

"I've asked Mr. Vaughn about the party a couple of times, to see if there's something in particular he wants to serve folks, but he keeps putting me off," Darcel said. "You're right, though, we're getting pretty close now and if we're gonna have all we need, we have to set the menu pretty soon."

"Maybe I can nudge him," Charlotte volunteered.

"You sure? It's been prickly with you two," Darcel said. She couldn't argue with that. While things had always been quiet between her and her father, the silences now were far more pointed. Though she was making the best of her situation and had grown to enjoy Darcel's company, she still couldn't forgive James for ruining all her plans with Nell and Evie. Her anger hadn't cooled, and the two of them often passed in the hallway like ships in the night, with him murmuring a stilted greeting and Charlotte ignoring him. Even though he'd torn her away from her own life, she had no interest in trying to wedge herself back into a small corner of his.

Still, there was work to be done, so Charlotte couldn't shut him out entirely.

"Well, we need to know, don't we? And how much pricklier could it get?" she said.

She wiped her hands on her apron, covering it with flour, then balled it up and tossed it onto the chair beside the kitchen door. It was early yet, and James hadn't left for the workshop. Like every morning, he was rushing around the dining table without sitting, grabbing quick bites of breakfast before running out for the day. She stepped in, gingerly.

"Morning," she said. He looked over at her in surprise.

"Good morning, Charlotte! How are you?"

She wasn't interested in small talk. "Just fine. I wanted to check with you about the dinner party."

Hearing her businesslike tone, his face fell. "Oh, I see. What about it?"

"Darcel and I are trying to nail down the menu, and we need the details from you: how many folks it'll be, what you want to serve, and all that. You must've decided by now," she said.

"Oh, yes, I can see why you'd— Hmm." He paused. "The thing is, with so many people coming and this being such an important affair for me, businesswise, I thought I'd better leave it in the hands of professionals. That is, I've decided to bring in a caterer. So that you and Darcel can have the night off."

"Is that right?" Charlotte said. Of course he would do this. All the better to cement his image as an enterprising man about town.

"Yes. The caterers will cook and bring in a few extra hands to help serve. It makes everything much easier, don't you think?"

"Doesn't seem to much matter what I think, does it?" Charlotte said. "I'll let Darcel know." With that, she turned on her heel and headed back into the kitchen.

Darcel was standing there right beside the door, looking stung. He'd heard everything.

"Sorry about that," Charlotte said. "I don't understand him sometimes. But those guests will be missing out with you not doing the cooking."

Darcel shook his head. "A night off, eh?" He sucked his teeth. "And who would these caterers even be? If my food's good enough for him to eat every day, how is it not good enough for his little party?"

"Anything to impress the white folks," Charlotte said, shrugging. Darcel raised an eyebrow. "The *other* white folks, I mean. All that's left for us is to get out of the way." That was a familiar enough feeling. But Darcel seemed to take the news hard.

"I know you'd been looking forward to planning for it," she ventured. "I was too. Had you told Mr. Vaughn you wanted to . . . ?"

"Mmmph," Darcel grunted, brushing flour off the apron stretched over his round belly. "No sense trying to tell him anything, you know that better than anyone. Come on, get your apron back on and let's get this bread into the oven." He picked up his rolling pin. "The sooner we get done the sooner we can get out of here and do our shopping."

A little fresh air and walking would do them good, and maybe take Darcel's mind off what he'd plainly received as an insult. Later that morning, he was quiet while they walked along Spruce Street as the familiar calls of the sidewalk saleswomen filled Charlotte's ears.

"Pepper pot, smokin' hot! Get your pepper pot soup here," one woman called, waving her ladle in the air. Her huge heavy-bottomed pot stood steaming at her feet on the sidewalk. She wore a brown-and-red head wrap and a fringed calico cape over her shoulders. She pointed to Charlotte. "You, Miss? Best pepper pot in the city!"

Charlotte turned to Darcel. "How about it? It'll fill us up at least, so we can keep shopping." Darcel looked skeptical. "My treat," Charlotte tempted.

He shrugged. "Why not?"

They walked over and Charlotte handed the woman seven cents. In return, she gave each of them a spoon and wooden bowl, then ladled in the steaming hot stew, careful not to spill a drop. In their bowls, beef tripe, potatoes, kale greens, and onions swam in a rich beef stock fragrant with all the kinds of spices Darcel had been teaching Charlotte about.

They thanked the woman and stepped aside to dig in. Darcel took the first bite, and grinned. "Now, that's flavor for you!" He dipped a little bow to the soup woman, who winked back.

"See? I bet you're glad you listened to your daughter!" she said, smiling. Charlotte and Darcel looked at each other and laughed, and neither bothered correcting her. In truth, Charlotte half-wished what she'd said was true. Spending time with Darcel felt almost like having a real father again—one who proudly looked like her and walked alongside her. She stood next to him happily and ate.

"How's your soup, Charlotte—taste anything you know?" he asked.

And the delight of it was, she did. Bringing the spoon to her mouth, she recognized thyme, paprika, garlic, marjoram, and heaps of pepper—black and cayenne both. Her mouth tingled from the heat, but she kept eating. It was delicious.

"There now," she said to Darcel as they were finishing up. "Who needs a fancy caterer when we've got this? I bet we could do this."

"Ha! We ought to give it a try," Darcel said, laughing.

"Sounds good to me," said Charlotte. They handed their bowls back to the woman along with their thanks and started walking again.

THAT WEEKEND, DARCEL LET Charlotte borrow a few of his books—mostly cookbooks, along with a few novels and volumes of poetry. With those and the books Nell had loaned her before James had shut her inside, Charlotte could at least keep herself entertained. She was reading in her attic room when James came up and asked her to join him on a trip to the caterers' storefront. She balked, not wanting to betray Darcel, but James wouldn't take no for an answer.

"Why don't you change into one of your church dresses? Maybe the yellow one you did up so nicely," he said. "This will be good for you, you can learn more about running a household and managing events, to go along with your cooking." None of that interested her, but he never did trouble himself much about her interests.

When they set out a few minutes later, Charlotte grew more nervous with every block as they headed closer to the rougher areas near the city limits. They weren't far from Society Hill or even from Nell's pleasantly prim neighborhood, but Philadelphia was slippery that way—changing shape from one block to the next, peace and prosperity melting into squalor and menace in just a few minutes' walk. Below South Street, she'd been insulted or outright propositioned on the sidewalk enough times to make her wary. She kept a few steps behind James, taking in the strange glances he attracted as an elegant white man out of his element. Maybe if people were focused on him, they'd leave her alone.

When they arrived at the storefront, she was grateful to realize it wasn't below South Street but *on* it, so they wouldn't need to cross the city's official southern border. James paused in front of the building. It was a simple two-story shop with a sign in large script: MARION'S.

Charlotte smiled to herself, overjoyed at her incredible luck.

Without knowing it, James had brought her exactly where she needed to be.

The line below Alex's family name read DINING ROOM AND PUBLIC WAITER, telling passersby that not only could they eat inside, but if the food and experience were to their liking, they could bring the same luxury and good taste into their own homes—if they could pay twenty dollars a plate. Charlotte wasn't surprised that James had sprung at this chance to burnish his image; hosts who could afford to hire fashionable Black caterers like Charles Marion and Robert Bogle were the envy of their friends and business associates. But James insisted on tying some larger lesson to his posturing.

"This is the sort of example I want you to learn from," he said, looking reverently at the sign over the entrance. "Never mind about all the political agitating that colored folks are doing in the city; this is where the real prospects lie for raising ourselves up. Hard work, and building something of your own to sustain you without drawing ire. That's what every Black Philadelphian ought to be working toward. It's what I've done."

"Oh?" Charlotte said evenly. "Are you a Black Philadelphian today?"

James shot her a look. "At least listen to Mr. Marion and me while we go over the plans. I want to make sure everything's perfect—and you might learn a thing or two."

At the door to the building, Charlotte was thrilled to see a familiar face. Alex introduced himself to both James and Charlotte as if he'd never met either of them. He carried himself seriously, but a smile played at the corners of his mouth.

Inside there were shelves all around laden with elegant dishware and linens, and dozens of well-polished wooden chairs stacked along one wall. Off to the side, there was even a full-length dining table, with a cleverly disguised expansion leaf in the middle. James must love this, Charlotte thought. It reminded her of the dining tables he'd made back at White Oaks. His largest was a tasteful, perfectly polished table much like this one, for Massah and Missus, of course.

But quietly, he'd gathered up scrap wood over several months and made a replica that the slaves kept down in their quarters for big meals with Evie and her mother and brother, and the two other families who lived and worked alongside them all those years. Their table was a little more rough-hewn and couldn't be polished as often. But it was no less smooth, no less finely constructed. James took pride in his work, that much was clear to everyone. And sharing that work seemed to be the best—the only—way he knew to express his care.

Near a smaller table in the middle of the dining area, Charles Marion was already waiting. He was an impeccably dressed, straight-backed man with skin the color of honey, just a few shades darker than James but unmistakably Black. He was no more than an inch or two taller than Charlotte, but the sheer elegance of his presence made him seem larger. Charlotte looked from Charles to Alex, and back again. The son's face was an echo of the father's more distinguished one.

Alex and Charlotte sat together at a nearby table as Charles and James talked through the details of the catering arrangements.

"Well, this is a happy surprise," Alex said quietly. "Where have you been? Nell's been worried sick." He paused and looked down at his hands. "She's been so sad."

Charlotte wanted to believe him, but she had been nursing doubts for weeks. Though she was the one who'd disappeared, Charlotte was wounded Nell hadn't tried to get back in touch. Maybe she'd realized lower-class friends like Charlotte were more trouble than they were worth, especially after her poor showings at the Wheatley Association and then at the Antislavery Society meeting.

Charlotte looked at Alex. "Well, at least she's had you, hasn't she? Her fiancé?"

"Ha," Alex laughed, cocking his head to the side. James looked over and they both went quiet until his attention turned back to their discussion. Alex shrugged. "I do what I can for her, but she keeps me at arm's length lately."

Charlotte nodded. Not surprising. Nell was nothing if not single-minded about her work. "Then let me at least send you back to her with some good news. I can't explain now, but tell her I haven't abandoned our plans. I'll be in touch when I can, but I need you both to keep working on a way out for Evie."

"That isn't much to go on. Nell will want more."

"It's all I can tell you," Charlotte said.

It might have been easiest to just send Nell directly to Evie, but there was no way to be sure of what Evie would or wouldn't tell her. Unwieldy as it was, Charlotte would have to keep juggling. If only she could get clear of the house.

"Charlotte, are you listening?" James said. "Please come over here and make a note of how much table space we'll need for each place setting. I want you to hear how Mr. Marion will arrange for all the right dishes and portions."

Charlotte got up and joined them. With her father insisting on her attention, she didn't get the chance to say any more to Alex. The most she could do was send him a pleading look as they left. He nodded—he'd get the message to Nell.

On the walk home, James brimmed with excitement about the plans he'd made.

"This dinner party will change everything for us, you'll see," he said. He was in such a good mood, Charlotte wondered again if she ought to tell him about Evie after all. But when she thought about the way he'd reacted to the abolitionist pamphlets in her bag, it was clear to her he'd want nothing to do with it. She kept quiet.

When they got back to the house, he ushered Charlotte into his office, apparently so he could continue offering his unwanted life advice.

"You ought to start thinking about what you can make of yourself, now that you've seen some of the world," he said, leaning against his desk. Charlotte stood in front of the chair. She wouldn't sit, since she didn't intend to stay. She didn't want to talk, but it seemed he was going to keep poking at her all day until he got some kind of response. He wasn't going to like it.

"I was already making something of myself, just not the way you want," she said. "There's more to the world than business."

"I see. I suppose you think the only people doing any good are the ones holding all the abolitionist meetings, making speeches, and publishing pamphlets." He said it so quietly, so resentfully, it almost seemed he was talking more to himself than to her. Charlotte raised her eyebrows in surprise but didn't bother to answer. He wasn't entirely off base about what she thought.

"You're wrong, you know. The lot of you," he went on. "You don't hear the things whites say amongst themselves, when they're sure no one disagreeable is listening. Some of them are sympathetic to slaves, in the abstract. But it doesn't go past that, and more than anything else they crave order. But what people like your abolitionist friends are up to? This giant meeting hall they've constructed for their cause? Nothing but trouble will come of it. The harder you all push, the more they resist. The brazenness of it all stands to do far more harm than good to the cause of freedom."

Charlotte was taken aback. That was the most she'd ever heard her father say about abolition. He had always seemed to be nonpolitical, not aligned with any cause, preferring instead to sidestep tough issues by disappearing into whiteness, where none of it was his problem anymore.

Her heart beat faster as she took in his words. What right did he have to say how other Black people in the city ought to fight for freedom, for fair treatment, when he'd abandoned them—her—so completely?

"You think because you hear white folks talking amongst themselves you've got some kind of special insight?" Charlotte said. "We all know *exactly* what they think—we couldn't have survived otherwise. And just because some of them are skittish doesn't mean our cause is any less right," she said through clenched teeth. "Have you forgotten what our lives were like at White Oaks?"

"I could never," her father said, aghast.

"Then how can you stand by while people like us—our family, our friends—are left behind in that muck? How can you do nothing?" she cried.

James stood up straight and walked out into the parlor, and waved his arm toward every wood-paneled wall, every velvet curtain, every piece of crystal carefully displayed on the sideboard. "You call this nothing? I risked *everything* to get you away from there and bring us both to freedom, and look what I've built since. The comfortable life you enjoy, the same life that gave you the time to run around the city with your literary club instead of working yourself to the bone for some indifferent white family—that's what I've *done*. For you."

Charlotte shook her head. "What you've done is build a house of cards that doubles as a prison," she said. "What kind of freedom is that, when you've got to pretend to be white and all I get to be is another piece of furniture in here so you can live *your* dreams out there? At least abolitionists are trying to make real freedom possible for *all* of us."

James sat down, looking weary.

"You don't know how vulnerable you'd be if I were just another Black slave who ran away to Philadelphia, or worse yet, still back at White Oaks. Maybe I can't set the whole of our people free, but I can take care of us. Take care of *you*. For me, that's enough."

But it wasn't, not for Charlotte. What was most infuriating was how he kept insisting he'd done all this for her. She knew plain selfishness when she saw it, and nothing he said could change all she'd watched him do. Charlotte was determined to be better than that. Whatever it took, she'd get the plans for Evie back in motion.

Chapter 21

———

NELL

———

EVEN WITH CHARLOTTE HAVING GONE SILENT, NELL COULDN'T get the mysterious Evie's predicament out of her mind. It just wasn't her nature to let this sort of thing go. As the days wore on, she racked her brain, turning the problem over and over, seemingly to no avail. What could be done if her only connection to the person she wanted to help had been severed?

With plans for the Pennsylvania Hall opening in full swing, and everything with Charlotte having unraveled, Nell was grateful for a quiet afternoon with Sarah to clear her head. They took tea at the Douglasses' home on Locust Street, a house grander even than Nell's, with mahogany double-doors out front and enough space for Sarah's mother to run her hatmaking shop out of a side wing with a separate entrance. Nell and her own mother had bought their bonnets and churchgoing hats from Grace Bustill Douglass for as long as she could remember. Inside the main house, the parlor had the well-lived-in feel of a family that'd been synonymous with Black Philadelphia for decades.

Sarah poured Nell a cup of bergamot-infused tea from the family's painted-china teapot. But even the bright citrus scent couldn't cure Nell's distraction.

"Is everything all right with you, Nell?" Sarah asked. "You've seemed a little preoccupied lately."

"Preoccupied" was putting it mildly. First all her plans with

Charlotte had fallen apart, and then there was whatever was going on between her and Alex. Nell's life was becoming uncharacteristically messy, and she had no idea how to put everything back in order. She weakly tried to smile, unsure how to answer Sarah without incriminating herself—about what, she didn't even know.

"I'm sure it's just wedding planning keeping you busy, no?" Sarah said, stirring sugar into her own steaming cup.

"Everything just happened so fast," said Nell. "I feel like I'm still catching up with it all."

"Fast? You and Alex have known each other for ages! It can hardly have been a surprise."

"Not exactly, no. Of course, Alex is such a good man, and I'm not blind," admitted Nell, thinking back to the sight of him staring at her across the counter of the Marions' catering kitchen. Sarah smiled and raised her eyebrows in silent agreement. "But I think I just . . . had other plans for myself," Nell continued.

Sarah nodded. "He is a catch, it's true. And so are you! But if all this isn't what you want, you must know it isn't too late to change your mind," she said gently.

That was precisely the trouble—Nell realized she *was* changing her mind, just not in the way she'd expected. And nothing unnerved her more than deviating from her own carefully laid plans. If she were to get married, who would she be then? She hesitated.

"What if it's become what I want?" Nell finally asked quietly. It was a relief to say out loud what she had been struggling to admit to herself, let alone anyone else. But one other question still lingered on her mind. She leaned forward. "Would you think less of me for it? For marrying?"

"My goodness, no!" Sarah exclaimed, putting down her cup. "I don't regret my choices at all, but I know my path isn't the only one for a woman who wants to do some good in the world." At thirty years old and unmarried, Sarah was well into old maid territory— but she was also one of the best-loved and most respected women in the city. Unencumbered with running a household or chasing after children, or any of the other things marriage weighed women down with, she was free to champion causes, organize, and concentrate on abolition work—all the things Nell cherished, right along with her independence.

Before she'd gotten Alex tangled up in her latest scheme, Nell had assumed she'd live out the same story, with Sarah and she as elder and younger spinster sisters-in-arms. Now she was the one who was tangled up. But she didn't have to stay that way. Even with Sarah's reassurance, she knew the best thing for everyone—the safest thing—would be to end the engagement. After all, there was no longer any need for it.

As they finished their tea, Sarah looked her in the eyes. "Whatever you decide, all anyone can ask is that you're honest—with him, and with yourself. Do that much, and I know everything will turn out all right."

LATER THAT WEEK, ALEX caught Nell walking out of the house on the way to Pennsylvania Hall, and she took her chance. Before he could even say a word, she spoke. "I've been thinking, now that things have fallen off with Charlotte, it may finally be time for us to come clean with our parents, and end this engagement before anyone's too badly hurt." She could've sworn she saw him flinch at her pronouncement, but just as quickly, his face switched back to his usual even expression. Nell paused, and took a deep breath before saying the rest. "I won't deny that it feels like there could be something more between us, Alex, and you know how much I care for you—"

"Nell—" he interjected, placing a hand on her shoulder. But she plowed onward.

"Please let me finish. What I want to say is that even if my work with Charlotte hasn't amounted to much, it's reminded me how important the work is—and I've always known I can't do it without my autonomy. Being a wife, and then a mother—my whole world would shrink down to one house, when there are so many more lives

I can touch if I try. I can't marry you. I can't marry *anyone*. I've always known that, and you've heard me say so for years now. So, might we just agree to stick with our original plan? We'll cancel the engagement party, and then quietly let everyone know we've broken things off?"

Alex listened patiently and looked an odd mix of wounded and distracted. As she finished, he drew his hand back from her shoulder. "I'm not here to talk about our engagement," he said, staring down at his feet. "I have a message for you, from Charlotte. She showed up at the catering shop this morning."

That stopped Nell short. Alex told her everything, from describing the man Charlotte had arrived with to what she'd told him: that the plans to free Evie were still on. At the end, he gave her a weak smile. "See? You can't throw me over quite so easily." There was something hollow in the way he laughed as he said it.

"This is wonderful news!" Nell exclaimed. She peppered him with questions about Charlotte's well-being, but he didn't have many details to offer. Nell wondered if he'd seen any sign that she might be pregnant, but her sense of propriety wouldn't let her ask about such an unseemly subject. She supposed hearing Charlotte looked "fine" would have to be reassurance enough for the moment. There was work to be done.

"This means we can dive back into planning," said Nell.

"There's one hitch, though, I'm sorry to say," Alex said. "The man who was going to help us, the landscaper with the Vigilant Association—he's been arrested. He was found out for being involved with another escape."

"How awful!" Nell left unsaid that perhaps it was for the best that Evie hadn't ended up in his care after all. What they were trying to do carried real risks, and this city never let them forget it for long. Still, Charlotte was back in touch—that, at least, was cause for hope.

"It's a setback, but I'm sure we can find another way," Alex said.

"Of course we can," said Nell. Seeing how determined he was to help her, Nell suddenly felt awful for having pushed him away. "And, Alex, I didn't mean to—"

"Don't worry about it," he interrupted, waving away her chance to speak. "What matters here is the work. Back to business, just like you said."

FOR THE NEXT ANTISLAVERY Society meeting, in early May, the women gathered at Sarah's schoolhouse in the evening to discuss plans for yet another petition drive. These had occupied much of the society's time over the last few years, along with fundraising and fair planning. The group regularly drafted ringing antislavery statements, circulated them around town for signatures, and shipped them off to Congress. As women, they had no other way to make their voices heard on matters of federal policy. Still, Nell's faith in their effectiveness was flagging; the congressmen had gotten so tired of being buried under reams of paper that they'd passed a gag rule that automatically tabled all antislavery petitions without discussion, in the hope that would stop the avalanche. But the group's leadership, particularly the white officers, clung to the practice as a method of shifting public opinion, and so it continued.

Of course, where Evie was concerned, Nell had something far more provocative in mind than a strongly worded statement. As the meeting went on, she kept finding her eye drawn to Hetty, remembering how eager she'd been to join the proposed committee on direct action to aid fugitives, and the advice she'd given about the Vigilant Association. Maybe Hetty was the person Nell needed to talk to now. She had to know something about arranging an escape, after all, since she'd engineered one for herself.

Once petitioning plans were squared away, talk turned to settling the meeting schedule for the national Women's Antislavery Convention, which would coincide with the opening of Pennsylvania Hall on May 14. With less than two weeks to go, the excitement was growing. The hall opening promised a grand meeting of the minds, a space to refine and debate the very ideas that bound together abolitionists around the country and to work out how to put them into practice. Increasingly, that practice—the *doing* of abolition—was where Nell wanted to put her efforts. And that kept bringing her around to Hetty. Silently, Nell wondered why Hetty didn't offer herself up as a speaker, or why someone in the society's leadership didn't bother trying to recruit her for the job. With her life experience, Hetty could enlighten the crowd not only on the harsh realities of slavery but on what freedom really felt and sounded and tasted like, and where it fell short. Why not put her forward, rather than Angelina Grimke? Even as a staunch ally to the cause, Miss Grimke had lived through slavery as a beneficiary, not a victim—someone like Hetty could offer all the same insights, and more.

And that was to say nothing of Hetty's sheer audacity. Not just for running away from her masters—it was easy enough to understand the impulse to do that. But also for being brave enough to insert herself into *this* circle. High-minded as Philadelphia's upper class might be on abolition, they weren't so different from any other upper class when it came to mixing and mingling with those below their station. Nell knew that better than anyone, from the way her parents and friends scoffed and sniffed at her newly made acquaintances like Charlotte. Even if an outsider managed to maneuver herself into an official space like this, she couldn't miss the signals that the welcome was conditional, and limited: tea invitations not offered, sewing circles kept tightly closed, cotillions and balls with opaque rituals unintelligible to the uninitiated and uninvited. As much as Nell tried to model stretching good works across the full span of her life—political *and* social—for most women like her, interaction with their lessers began and ended with the work. And that was the wasps' nest Hetty had voluntarily stuck her hand into, all to help others achieve the same freedom she now enjoyed. She might well be Evie's best hope.

After the meeting, Nell was mingling with her colleagues when she noticed Hetty at the front of the room—in that moment, she decided not to let the opportunity slip away. Seeing Hetty lingering near the tea and cookies, deep in conversation with Lucy Stewart, Nell stood aside and waited for an opening. But what had looked like a conversation at first glance was, upon further inspection, Hetty being cornered and interrogated about her background and life story.

"What exactly made you run?" Lucy asked.

"Well, I—"

"What was it like?" Lucy could scarcely get one question out before she interjected again. "You absolutely *must* come and speak with my sewing circle. You would be perfect for it; we would all learn so much. And would you consider—"

Nell cut in. "Begging your pardon, Miss Stewart, I think I heard Miss Mott looking for you a moment ago. Something about the leaflet plans for next week . . . ?" Nell trailed off, but that was enough. Lucy frowned and walked away in a huff, not bothering to excuse herself. "Honestly," she muttered, "every time I think we've decided on a printer, this interminable process . . ."

Hetty smirked. There was a glint of gratitude in her eyes.

"She can be tricky to disentangle from," Nell said. "Fortunately I've known her long enough to know just which thread to pull."

"Ha! My plan was just to smack her over the head and run off, so you're a step ahead'a me," Hetty said. "My bag of tricks for getting clear of white folks only got but a few tools in it."

Nell smiled, and Hetty laughed deeply.

"What brings you my way?" Hetty asked.

"Honestly, Miss Reckless, I'm an admirer of yours and was hoping to talk with you more. I've found myself in a bit of a . . . situation, and I wondered if you might be the best person to point the way out of it," Nell said. She surprised herself with her own candor.

"Huh. I can't think what kind of situation you'd be in that I'd know much about, but I'll see what I can do. And call me Hetty, please."

"I'd be glad to, Hetty!" Nell replied. "Perhaps we can find a time in the coming week? Thursday? We can meet at Franklin Square Park."

"Why not here? Sarah would let us use the space, I'm sure," Hetty said.

Nell leaned in more closely. "Ordinarily I would, but I think this conversation calls for more discretion, away from prying ears. Do you mind?"

"I take your meaning," Hetty said. "Thursday then, eleven o'clock."

"That's perfect."

Hetty nodded and took her leave. Nell breathed a sigh of relief.

Chapter 22

———

CHARLOTTE

———

With the weeks rolling on, Charlotte wondered anxiously if there was a way to get a message to Evie as she'd been able to with Nell. Under Darcel's watchful eye, there were only a few places she was allowed to go, and in any case, it was impossible to know who she could trust.

The city grew tenser by the day, and not only on account of the upcoming antislavery conference at Pennsylvania Hall. Charlotte discovered that Darcel hid copies of *The Pennsylvania Freeman* in the pantry, where James wouldn't see them—he liked to keep up with the goings-on, he explained to her, since he often wondered whether Black folks in America would ever rise up the way they had in his country. So far, no Black revolution appeared to be on the horizon, but there were plenty of political rumblings spread across the news-paper's pages. The worst of it was the Pennsylvania legislature forging ahead with its plans to strip Black men of the vote—"petty nonsense," Darcel called it. The reaction in the Black press had been strong and steady.

Even after years in the city, the politics sometimes mystified Charlotte. It was strange to think Black men ever had the vote at all—they might be up North but they were still Black, and no one let them forget it. But to allow the right to vote for years and then take the trouble to snatch it away? White folks were nothing if not changeable, and the changes rarely amounted to good news for Black people up here or down South. A columnist in the *Freeman* had strident words for the legislature:

> As colored men we've more than proven our value to this nation, and as a people we've more than demonstrated our moral worthiness. Expulsion can't be the only solution to the intractable color problem in this state—expulsion from the franchised populace, no doubt to be followed by expulsion from this nation to colonize foreign shores. For our troubles here, and our desert, the colored men of this state are owed more than freedom—we're owed equality.

The column went on to quote the words of Robert Purvis, who'd continued publicly advocating against the new law even after the violent reaction to his speech in the fall. In the months since, Charlotte had seen him around the city, often walking arm in arm with a Black woman who must be his wife. At the sight of him, Charlotte couldn't help but wonder if James had ever shown that kind of warm affection to her own mother.

The column writer's pen name was unfamiliar—Marius Allen, of Philadelphia—but read like an echo of a name she'd heard before: Alexander Marion. Charlotte smiled. At least her friends were keeping busy while she was locked away. She slid the newspaper back into the pantry.

As she and Darcel milled around the kitchen, checking the cupboards to make a shopping list, Darcel was unusually chatty. "Looks like we're running low on allspice. One of my favorites; my mother used to bake this rum-soaked cake laced with it. I still remember how my mouth would tingle."

"Mm-hmm," Charlotte answered absentmindedly while she rummaged through the cabinet beside the cutting boards.

"Me and my big brother, and little sister, we'd bother Mère about making it every chance we got, but she really only made it on special days—around Easter and such."

"Uh-huh," Charlotte said, not lifting her head. But as she listened, the beginning of a plan presented itself. If he was in such a nostalgic mood today, maybe she could turn that to her advantage. "Well, why don't you show me how to make it?"

"Mmmph. Suppose I could. If you think you can handle it," Darcel replied, wiggling his eyebrows at her playfully.

"I'm game if you are," said Charlotte. Then, she baited the hook. "I had a delicious one from a baker in the Market Street sheds once. You think your version will measure up?"

Darcel scoffed. "Ha! You think some up North baker can stand against an authentic Caribbean spice-and-rum cake? Go on with you!"

"How about we find out? Make a contest of it," she proposed.

For a second, Darcel looked skeptical, but his competitive spirit got the best of him. "All right, let's go," he said.

When they arrived at the market, Charlotte contrived a reason to separate. It was a Tuesday morning, and she clung to the hope that Evie might be there, and she could finally set things right and help her, somehow.

"I'll pick up the cake from the baker, why don't you go see what kind of meat they've got for sale? I'll catch up with you!" she called. By the time she'd said the last words she was already in motion, calling to Darcel over shoppers' heads. Still, she'd seen the look on his face before she rushed off: he'd considered objecting, but decided against it. In fact, she could have sworn she saw a little smile. Charlotte wondered why he was suddenly willing to let her wander off. Maybe she'd won him over at last.

Freed from Darcel's watch for a few minutes, she made a beeline to the baker's stall beside the market's Third Street entrance. There was no sign of Evie. Charlotte was disappointed, but knew she shouldn't have dared to hope—she'd been out of touch nearly two months. Of course Evie would just assume she'd abandoned her. But as she stood looking around, dejected, Charlotte's eye fell on the baker himself. Back in the winter, he'd been willing to move some of his goods aside to let Nell and the rest of the women's Antislavery Society set up their table for the fair, so it seemed reasonable to think

he was sympathetic with the abolitionists' cause, or at least not outright hostile. That, and he'd always been friendly on the occasions
Charlotte came around to buy pastries. Without much else to go on,
she had little to lose by leaving a message with him. She leaned in
close as she set the spice cake on the counter.

"There's a young Black woman who comes through here sometimes with a few other house servants, Evie, a friend of mine." Charlotte described how she looked, then continued. "I've lost track of
her lately, but if you see her come by, could you please tell her something for me?"

The baker's eyes widened. He nodded silently.

"Tell her I haven't given up, and she shouldn't either. I don't know
when I'll be able to get back here, but if she needs to send word to
me, I'm at seventy-one Fourth Street in Society Hill."

She paid for the cake and took off in search of Darcel.

"ALL YOUR BIG PLANS come together at the market?" Darcel asked
after a quiet walk home.

Charlotte froze, nearly dropping the cake. "What?" She turned
around.

He looked at her with that knowing expression, then shrugged.
"You don't have to take everything on all by yourself, you know."

She was struck by his candor. But even if he was right, it felt impossible for Charlotte to ask for anyone's help without revealing
more about herself than she wanted. The curious thing about Darcel, though, was that she was never quite sure just how much he already knew.

"I don't know what you mean," she said. "And anyway, I haven't
got anyone to help me take things on. Not anymore."

"Guess I don't count for much?" he asked gently. She hadn't
meant to offend him, but he spoke again before she could say so. "I
know a girl your age wants to be around other young folks like you,
any fool can tell that. If you just try talking to your—to Mr. Vaughn,
maybe you can get him to see things your way?"

Charlotte's ears perked up at Darcel's near-slip.

"Let's just get the food on the table, mm?" she said.

After dinner that night, Charlotte lingered in the kitchen. She didn't usually help much with the dishes, but she needed the distraction to calm her nerves. It would take a lot of luck for her message to find its way to Evie, but she was at a loss for what to do but wait.

Darcel stood as mostly silent company, passing her plates, pots, and utensils to dry after he rinsed them off. Her mind wandered with the repetitive motion. Before she knew what had happened, they were finished and it was nearly dark outside. Darcel stepped away from the sink, and Charlotte walked around in the waning light, gathering up linens for the next day's washing. When she picked up the potholder next to the icebox, underneath it she found the notebook she'd seen Darcel scribbling in.

She looked over her shoulder. Had he gone upstairs? She peeked through the pantry and found him sitting at the dining table polishing the silverware. Still trying to get ahead for the dinner party, even after James had shoved him aside.

With Darcel safely occupied, Charlotte gave in to her curiosity and started flipping through the notebook's pages. It was full of recipes. Big, complicated recipes. Soup for a dozen people, soufflés, and what could only be the orange cake she'd seen a few weeks ago: 4 cups of flour, 1 cup of sugar, sliced oranges, and a honey glaze.

"See something you like?"

She startled and turned around, looking sheepish. Darcel was behind her, shaking his head. "Minding your own affairs isn't a talent of yours, is it?" he said. But he didn't seem too angry, more embarrassed really.

"What is this?" she asked, her interest overwhelming her remorse for snooping. "You haven't been teaching me any of these recipes. Where'd you get them?"

"They're all mine. I'm working on building out my repertoire," he said.

"Repertoire, eh? Well, look at you. But it all seems like a bit much for just the three of us."

"Who says it's just for us?"

She shrugged and handed him the notebook, still waiting for an explanation. Darcel sighed, and smiled.

"Nothing wrong with having ambitions, right? Plenty of other men are doing well as chefs, caterers, and the like. Why not try my own hand?"

Of course. Charlotte thought back to those times at the shops when he seemed to be carrying more than they needed, and the afternoons he spent hours tinkering in the kitchen, only for the food never to materialize. He must've been paying for extra ingredients from his own pocket, practicing, and building up a plan.

"You've been at this awhile," she said. It wasn't a question.

He nodded. In his deep brown eyes, Charlotte saw the brightness of hard-won pride.

"Come, sit. Tell me all about it," she said.

They sat at the dining table side by side, polishing forks and knives and spoons, and Darcel laid out his whole dream as Charlotte listened: how he'd build a strong base of recipes, grow his reputation with a few small private dinners at first, then strike out on his own with a storefront. Charlotte understood now why he'd been so disappointed not to cook for James's dinner party; that would've been a prime chance to start making a name for himself. But he had his plans well in hand now, and it all sounded so promising. It was true, there was nothing wrong with imagining a life outside the four walls of this row house, and here was someone who understood that.

"What about you, Charlotte?" asked Darcel. "You must have plans of your own, something you want. Don't think I don't notice all your scheming."

Charlotte smiled sheepishly. Maybe she was less clever than she'd thought. She took a deep breath.

"I'm just trying to work toward something better for myself, and the people I love, same as you," she began.

Darcel set down the fork he'd been polishing and was still. "I'm listening."

In some way, that was all she'd been waiting for someone to say.

As the moon rose and shone into the dim dining room, Charlotte told Darcel the winding story of her life: how she'd been a slave in Maryland until she'd run away to the North, leaving behind love and family. Carefully, Charlotte left James's role out of her narrative, but explained that once she got to Philadelphia, she hadn't known what to do with herself until she'd met Nell and seen all that was possible for Black people in this city. Since then, all she knew was that she wanted out of this house, and a chance to make a life of her own without all the baggage and pity that came with being a runaway. Maybe become a seamstress, or a dressmaker—anything but what she was. But then Evie showed up, and just like that, Charlotte's past was staring her in the face.

"So, I started working with the abolitionists, making friends, and trying to help Evie get free too without making a mess of all I was building, and it was working. Until Mr. Vaughn ruined everything," she said.

"Mr. Vaughn?" Darcel said slowly. The skepticism in his voice was unmistakable, inviting her to let go of the one truth she'd been holding back.

Charlotte sighed. He already knew, didn't he? And even if he didn't, he deserved to. After all their hours together, she knew her secret would be safe in Darcel's hands. "My father," she said at last.

Darcel nodded and patted her on the hand. "It's not hard to see. There's more of him in you than you know," he said. Somehow, she felt he wasn't just talking about her looks.

"Maybe so," Charlotte said, "but there's still a lot he doesn't understand, and even more he won't risk. But I owe this to Evie. If I could just have a chance to tie up some loose ends . . ."

"Don't tell me anything more," he said. She froze. "The less I know about it, the better for when Mr. Vaughn starts asking questions. Do what you need to do—he won't hear a word from me."

She smiled gratefully. It was getting late, but she felt so much lighter now. Lighter, and exhausted. She had stood and started upstairs for bed when Darcel called after her.

"They didn't forget about you, you know—your friends. One

came by looking for you a few weeks ago, a young woman. Very fancy, and very determined." Charlotte laughed. *Nell*.

"It may be she can handle more of the truth than you think," Darcel added.

Charlotte continued up to the attic. She was glad Nell hadn't completely forsaken her, but she wasn't ready to tell her everything and become just another needy runaway in her friend's eyes. Just as she'd told Darcel, she wanted better for herself than that. But that didn't mean she couldn't still work with Nell to finish what they'd started with Evie. She decided she had to visit Nell at home. It was time to get back to work.

Chapter 23

EVIE

FOR A KNOT THAT HADN'T EVEN BEEN TIED YET, THE ONE THAT linked Kate and Mr. Brooks had turned out to be impossible to untangle. Evie hadn't made a stitch of progress in spoiling their engagement, and she was starting to lose sleep over it. In the dark early hours of the morning, she'd sneak out of her room, pace, twiddle her thumbs, and even wander the halls, racking her brain for something, anything else to try.

In the meantime, Kate kept Evie's days and nights occupied with endless jabbering about the city's social season and the preparations for her wedding. One evening, as Kate returned from the engagement party of a family friend, Evie wound herself up to launch into her usual show of pretended excitement. Kate swept into the bedroom and held her hands out to the sides, signaling Evie to start the undressing process. "I'm so exhausted," she sighed.

"Was it a nice party, Miss?" Evie asked.

"Oh, it was very interesting, so many nice people. New people, and a few I've met before," she said, trailing off.

"And Mr. Brooks? Did he have a nice time?"

"He surely did. Made some business connections and had the pleasure of introducing me around to the whole crowd. I could tell how proud he was to have me on his arm." Now she'd really get going. Evie mentally settled in as she unlaced the back of Kate's corset.

"I wish we could have a party like that," she said, pouting. "But Henry doesn't want all that fuss. He's a very private man, you know. But a proud one! You should've heard him, Evie. 'Allow me to introduce my beautiful fiancée,' and 'Oh, Mr. So-and-So, have you had the pleasure of meeting my wonderful wife-to-be?' and on and on," she cooed.

"I can just imagine," Evie replied. She was well used to this kind of gushing and had a ready supply of responses that gave Kate the appearance of the engaged audience she wanted but freed up Evie's mind for her own private concerns. And just now, her main concern was finding a new way to put Mr. Brooks off Kate.

"He was just so excited. I can understand why, of course; he may be wealthy but he's newer money and my family name is truly a thing of value for him—for his profile and all of that, I mean," Kate went on.

"Yes, of course, Miss, such a proud lineage," Evie responded, pulling the dress off over Kate's head.

"But I know that's not all of it. He truly cares for me; I can feel it. It shows in the little ways, you know."

Evie did not know. "Mm-hmm, the little things can tell so much."

"It's endearing, really, how much he seems to be looking forward to getting married. We talked about it tonight, you know. The wedding. Just about all the details are finalized. I've always known I'd make a blushing June bride," she said, giggling.

Evie let the "blushing bride" comment lie there a moment. Every time Kate said something else that erased the fact of her marriage to Massah Murphy, Evie was brought up short. It wasn't her place to remind the woman she'd been married before, or warn her what would happen if Henry found out she wasn't the unmarried maiden of the Jackson family, however much the "little things" made her think he was in this for love and not status. But maybe a simple slip would be all it took to help him see the honeypot he'd stumbled into. Though Kate insisted Evie forget that she rightly ought to be called "Missus Murphy" now, widowed or not, Evie could hardly be blamed for struggling to keep her mistress's lies straight. And would

Henry still want her if he knew she'd already given away the precious "family name" he was so drawn to? Maybe if she called Kate by her married name with Henry in earshot—*accidentally, of course*—that might be enough to get the wheels in his head turning so he'd dig deeper into Kate's background. It was a huge risk, but Evie was running out of options.

As Kate ran on, Evie turned her attention to planning. She didn't have much time, and her plan would need the right moment. The sooner Mr. Brooks could be gotten rid of, the better.

"We met so many nice folks tonight, I wonder if any of them might be someone Henry will want to invite for our big day, though it is getting late for that," Kate said. She mentioned he was coming by the next day to go over their guest list.

Tomorrow it was then.

WHEN MR. BROOKS ARRIVED the next morning, the downstairs maid seated him in the parlor as usual, and Evie escorted Kate downstairs. This was her moment. She brought Kate to the door of the parlor, showed her into the room, and said in a stage whisper, "Mr. Brooks is here for you, *Missus Murphy.*"

Kate froze and shot her a glare. Evie pantomimed an exaggerated apology, making sure she was in full view of Brooks through the doorway, and then corrected herself: "Begging your pardon, Miss Jackson." Then she disappeared around the corner. She hoped that would be enough to plant a seed. How could a man reach his stature in business without thinking to ask more questions before he entered a deal?

Evie strained to listen from outside the parlor and was thrilled to hear the confused suspicion in Henry's voice when he spoke. "What did your girl just say?" he asked. "She called you—" he began again, but before he could repeat the name Kate had hoped never to hear again, she broke in.

"Oh, don't mind her, the silly thing," she said with a hollow, unconvincing giggle. "Evie was just thinking of someone else, I'm sure." She was trying to sound casual, but Evie could hear the little tremor in her voice as she stumbled for an explanation.

"Who else? She's only ever in your service," said Henry.

"Well, I—that is, she, um . . ." Kate stammered. Finally, she landed on an excuse. "What I mean to say is, a family friend of ours by the name of Missus Murphy visited yesterday, and Evie was helping her a bit while I was out. She must still be on her mind!"

"Oh, all right, I see," he said. Evie could hear a note of lingering skepticism in Henry's response, but it didn't sound like he was going to press the matter any further. Quickly, Kate turned the conversation toward their wedding.

"Shall we get to work on finalizing the guest list, dear?" she asked, sounding hopeful.

"Of course, darling," Henry said. "Now, will we need to send a wedding invitation to this Missus Murphy?" Evie's ears perked up.

"No, she's not a terribly close family friend," Kate said, with frustration mounting in her voice. "Let's move on, all right?"

Henry seemed to accept that, and the two turned to talking about other potential guests. Dejected, Evie slunk away to go about her chores. Short of cornering Henry and laying out Kate's entire history to him—an idea too crazy to entertain—she'd used nearly every weapon in her arsenal. And there was sure to be a cost. Evie spent the rest of the day on edge. Kate wasn't one to let a slip like that pass unremarked.

Later, she overheard Kate talking with her cousin upstairs.

"I just don't know what's gotten into her. To make a mistake like that in front of Henry," Kate said. She sounded confused, at least, not angry. That was safer. But Cousin Maggie was far less forgiving.

"You can't afford that kind of foolishness, Katherine. Things are on the verge of turning out so well for you, you've got to keep all your ducks in a row. Henry is too new to Southern society for his reputation to survive being made a fool of. He'd set you aside in an instant if he knew the truth about your first marriage—he won't stand for a scandal," she said. "If your girl is going to cause trouble, at the very least you ought to send Frank to have a word with her—he'll straighten that behavior right out."

Kate murmured that she simply couldn't.

"Then you've got to get rid of her until you're safely wed," Maggie continued. "Isn't she about due to be sent back down South anyhow? It's been more than five months; you've only got a couple weeks before—"

Kate cut her off sharply. "I know. I'll send her down soon, I just need her for this next dinner party." She sighed. "I do so hate to be without her. You'll let me borrow one of your maids until I head down for the wedding?"

"Of course. Good girl."

Evie stood stock-still. What was she being sent back down South for? Kate needed her, she always said she did. Evie couldn't imagine being sent away unless there was some truly pressing need for it. Or was this a punishment? Evie plodded back to her room, Kate's words ringing in her ears.

That night, Kate returned to the bedroom, changed into her nightgown and robe, and settled into her vanity chair for Evie to take down her hair. She yawned, and Evie stifled a yawn of her own in response.

"It's so late, Miss. I'll hurry so you can get to bed," Evie suggested.

"It's been such a difficult, exhausting day," Kate said pointedly. "I just know I'll be sore tomorrow from the tension. In fact, Evie, would you be a dear and draw me a warm bath? I'm so tired, but it'll be worth it to try and fend off the pains," Kate said.

"Of course, Miss," Evie replied through gritted teeth. Her back and shoulders seized up in anticipation as she thought of all the trips up and down to the kitchen for water.

"I'll have it ready in no time, you just rest," Evie said.

"You're so good to me," Kate said, smiling, resting her hand on top of Evie's. It was soft, almost childlike from decades of idleness, and so unlike Evie's callused hands, which were rough and scarred from years of scrubbing, stitching, and carrying. As Evie headed out of the room, Kate nonchalantly kept talking. "Perhaps when we get to Virginia, I can find you some time to visit with your mother."

Mama? Evie froze at the mention of her. The day her mother had been sold, no one had said where she was headed; she was just loaded onto a wagon and driven off, with only enough time to give Evie's hand one last squeeze. She'd stared at her daughter as the coach drove away, and once more Evie saw the tracks running down Mama's face, the same silent river of tears she'd woken up to many nights in their cabin. In that last moment, Evie had sobbed and cried out for her. Only Daniel had held her back from running after the wagon, not knowing it'd be his own wagon Evie watched ride away just a month later. *Mama.* To be with her again. But down South. What was Kate saying? Evie turned around.

"Miss?"

"She'll be at the wedding, of course, attending to my sister-in-law." So that was where she'd gone. Sold to Kate's brother, to be a housemaid and seamstress to his wife. "I might be able to spare you for a little while to visit with her, if we're not having any more *trouble,*" she said again, leaning on the last word. Evie took her meaning well enough. Stay in line, go down South, and I'll toss you this scrap.

"Of course, Miss," she said. "Thank you, Miss. Let me get the bath going."

Outside the door of Kate's room, out of her sight, Evie's back lost its straightness. She trudged down the stairs, bent under the weight of the heavy pitcher for filling the tub, and she hadn't even put in the water. Up and down, down and up she went, sweating under the weight and heat of the water that was near to boiling when she took it out of the pot in the hearth. By the last few trips, Kate had already climbed into the tub and lay there luxuriating while Evie poured the steaming water over her back.

As the water flowed onto Kate, the embers of rage that had smoldered inside Evie were snuffed out under the deluge. The old, familiar numbness came back, that empty, burned-out sensation that had overtaken her after Kate sold Mama and Daniel. To Kate, all of them were nothing more than pawns to be shuffled around or knocked off the chessboard of her life whenever it suited her. That was the essential, wearying truth of Evie's life, and it had been a foolish little girl's dream to imagine she could do anything about it.

That night, she slumped heavily down onto her bed and slept deeply.

Chapter 24

———

CHARLOTTE

———

CHARLOTTE WALKED BRISKLY DOWN LOMBARD STREET, DETER-mined to make it to Nell's house first thing in the morning before she ran the risk of missing her, especially because she was showing up uninvited. Or maybe unwelcome. After the way Charlotte had disappeared, it was hard to imagine Nell would be warmly disposed toward her.

But alongside her nervousness, Charlotte sheepishly admitted to herself she was excited to visit Nell at home. She'd seen the fine neighborhood the Gardner family lived in before, right outside the eastern edge of Society Hill. As she neared Nell's street, the spaces between densely packed row houses opened up, as if giving one another room to breathe more comfortably. Crowding would be too unrefined. It was a Black neighborhood, of course, but Nell's smart freestanding brick house was in one of the more well-to-do parts, not far from the homes of some of the city's better-known Black aristocrats. Their enclave was wealthy, politically engaged, and well connected.

Charlotte had been given a taste of their lifestyle with the Wheatley Association and she could admit that sometimes it felt a little frivolous—women sipping tea in a plush library and talking about literature. But that life also felt wide open, luxurious, and more than a little powerful—it felt free. That was Nell's world, and Charlotte was grateful to have been part of it.

She arrived and walked slowly up the front path. The windows were outfitted with mint-green shutters, and plush curtains framed the insides of the windows, richly colored and heavy. She tapped the knocker gently, hoping it would be loud enough for someone inside to hear, but not to wake the whole house. Mercifully, it was Nell who opened the door.

"What a nice surprise," she said evenly. All subtlety and grace, but without her usual warmth.

Nell beckoned her into the parlor, where light flooded in through the windows that stretched from the floor up to the high ceiling. Charlotte suddenly felt small and exposed. Politely, Nell offered Charlotte a seat on the rolled-arm sofa, then sat in a chair opposite her and crossed her arms. She looked wary.

"I'm sorry for leaving things like I did," Charlotte said. She opened and closed her hands at her sides.

"Oh? After you had me turned away, I thought that—" She sounded hurt, and Charlotte rushed to interrupt her and explain what she could.

"I didn't mean to— I didn't even know you'd come," Charlotte said. "None of this was my choice, but I'm here now."

Nell leaned forward, and her tone softened. "Are you in some kind of trouble?" she asked carefully. Charlotte could've sworn she saw Nell glance at her belly. "Whatever it is, I can help you."

Some part of Charlotte wanted to just tell her everything and stop trying to live in between one life and another, the old and what she so desperately wanted to be the new. But seeing Nell sitting there, her face awash with concern, Charlotte couldn't get the words out.

"You don't have to worry about me, I'm just fine," she said.

"I wish you'd just tell me what's going on," Nell said, beginning to sound frustrated. "If you trusted me enough to come to me with Evie's situation, don't I at least deserve that much?"

In her mind, Charlotte latched on to the mention of Evie's name, and wondered how to shift the conversation—and Nell's attention—

back toward freeing her, and away from prying into Charlotte's problems. Even more uncomfortable than Nell's curiosity was the look of benevolent compassion shining from her eyes as she pressed her questions—that was exactly what Charlotte had been avoiding. She didn't want Nell's pity, she wanted her friendship, and her respect—as an equal. In that moment, she realized the best way to get those things was to focus on their shared aim of helping Evie. At the very least, the realities of what they were trying to do could help Charlotte explain why she'd disappeared in the first place, and why she remained so guarded even now.

"I think I got nervous about all of it, the danger, with abolitionists being jailed and ruined. I wasn't sure I was ready, and I balked, and I'm sorry," she said.

Nell nodded sadly. "You were right to be worried for yourself, I'm afraid," she said. "Alex's associate, the man we were supposed to work with, was arrested and thrown in jail a few weeks ago."

Charlotte's heart sank. They were right back where they'd started.

"But I don't want to give up on figuring this out," she said, shaking her head determinedly. "I made Evie a promise."

"Have you been in touch with her?" Nell asked. "How much time do we have before she's sent away?"

Charlotte shrugged. That was the trouble. Without being able to contact Evie, there was no way of knowing what kind of plan might be workable, or if she even wanted their help anymore. There'd been no sign of her at the market since Charlotte had been back. Maybe she'd let Evie down one time too many. But they needed to consider every available option.

"What about the Antislavery Society? We could go back and start with your committee, and work our way from there," said Charlotte. "How long can a proposal and committee deliberation really take?"

Nell smiled wanly. "Longer than any of us has time for, I'd imagine. But there's something else: I've arranged to talk with Hetty Reckless in case she's able to offer any suggestions. We're set to meet tomorrow. If anyone will know what to do, it's her," said Nell.

———

THE NEXT DAY, WITH Darcel once again turning a blind eye as she left the house, Charlotte met with Nell and Hetty in Franklin Square Park, just across the street from Pennsylvania Hall. With construction finished, the building looked majestic and bright, and seemed to gleam with possibility. In recent days, the building had begun to host light traffic as the groups prepared for the conventions. Meeting rooms, shops, and even the newspaper office were all up and running, but the beautiful weather made the park a more appealing prospect. As they sat on the benches amid the bright green lawns, they took in the flowers opening all around. Hetty came in through an opening in the wrought-iron fence. Charlotte watched her, fascinated—she was dressed in a simple blue-and-white cotton dress with few adornments, but the confidence in her stride made her look like she owned the park.

"Hetty, you remember my dearest friend, Charlotte," Nell said as Hetty joined them on the bench. "I know you're a busy woman, so I'll come straight to the point. There's a young girl in town, a slave, who wants to escape from her owner. For months, we've been trying and failing to find a way to get her out, and we've run out of ideas. As I was just telling Charlotte, I cannot imagine a better person than you to help us decide what to do next."

Hetty laughed. "You got the right woman, that's true. Thing is, you're thinking about this wrong—can't be that you go in and pull her out. That'll just cause a stir and risk you getting picked up yourself. No, you've got to help her figure out when it's safe for her to run out *herself,* and make sure she's got somewhere safe to go right away."

"There are many safe houses in town, or just outside the city limits—I know that much," said Nell.

Hetty leaned in and whispered, "Of course there are. I own one of 'em. Isn't that why you came to me?"

Charlotte and Nell looked at each other. They'd had no idea. Hetty had always seemed to share their way of thinking about the world, they'd seen that at the Antislavery Society meeting. But her safe house was news to them. Wonderful news.

"Close your mouths before the flies get in," Hetty said, laughing. "You'll have to forgive my not mentioning it sooner, but I take my time getting to know folks before telling *all* my business. Can't be too careful."

Charlotte composed herself, and Nell found her voice again. "Of course, we completely understand. But, Miss Reckless, would you consider—"

"Absolutely. That's what the house is there for, isn't it? Your friend can head straight for my place on Rodman Street, I'll look after her."

Nell and Charlotte fell all over themselves to thank her, but Hetty shushed them.

"She can come to me, but that's just a start. If her massah lives here in the city, she can't hang around too long," said Hetty.

"No, we'll need to get her out of town and headed north, the sooner the better," said Charlotte. She sat for a moment and tapped her chin. As she thought, her eyes wandered across the street. Trickles of people both Black and white were coming in and out of Pennsylvania Hall. On the first floor, the outlines of books suggested themselves through the windows, while men outside climbed ladders to hang signs and streamers for next week's conventions.

Charlotte stood up in excitement. "Of course! The opening. Abolitionists from Boston, New York, maybe even Canada, all coming here for exactly this cause, and then turning right around to head back north."

"Now you're thinking," Hetty said. "We line up the right folks, give your friend the date to run, and she'll be clear of here in no time."

Still seated on the bench, Nell beamed up at Charlotte. "It's brilliant," she said, her face alight.

Charlotte paced back and forth to think through the logistics. "It's too late to write letters, people are already on their way," she said, "so we'll just have to talk with them when they get here."

"In the meantime, we can gather up supplies for Evie—clothes, food to eat on the road, and so on," said Nell, following Charlotte's train of thought.

"And payment—we can pay the person for their trouble," Charlotte added.

Nell turned to Hetty. "Is that customary?"

"Couldn't hurt," she replied.

"Good," Charlotte said. "We can't tell you how grateful we are, Hetty. It'll be a weight off my shoulders to get my friend away from this awful woman."

Nell glanced at Charlotte. Feeling questioning eyes upon her, Charlotte cleared her throat and corrected herself. "I mean, I can only imagine what it's been like for her." She had to be more careful.

"Mmmph. I can do more than imagine," Hetty said. "And you got nothing to thank me for, you're the ones who figured out what to do."

That afternoon, Charlotte made the walk back home to Society Hill with renewed energy. With their plans set, all that remained was to let Evie know when she should plan to run. Charlotte prayed she hadn't given up entirely.

Up in her room, Charlotte put the finishing touches on the dress she'd been sewing for Evie and packaged it up neatly in a bag that'd be easy for her to carry on her journey north. Charlotte couldn't give back all Evie had lost, but she could at least send her off with a reminder of what they'd been to each other. It wasn't much, but it was more than nothing.

Chapter 25

NELL

WITH THE PLANS ALL SQUARED AWAY, NELL COULDN'T WAIT TO tell Alex what they'd achieved. He was at least partially to thank for it, after all. He'd delivered Charlotte's message at just the right moment, and now they'd finally made solid—no, superb—arrangements to spirit Evie away to freedom.

After leaving Charlotte and Hetty, Nell popped over to the Marions' before even stopping at home and knocked. When the Marions' maid, India, opened the door, her eyes went wide.

"Why, Miss Nell! It's been a while; we weren't expecting you." Her eyes shifted from side to side.

"I'm just here for a short visit with Mr. Alex. Is he at home?"

Before India could answer, Mrs. Marion called out from somewhere in the house: "Whoever it is, please send them away." Her voice sounded ragged, and it was unlike her to shout across the house. Something was wrong.

"Forgive me," Nell said before leaning into the doorway and calling out. "Mrs. Marion, it's just me, Nell. Is everything all right?"

After a deep sigh, Mrs. Marion called to India to let Nell in.

Mrs. Marion came to the parlor door. Her eyes were puffy, and Nell could see she'd put on powder to mask the dark circles underneath. Still, she was as straight-backed as ever. She took Nell's arm.

"I'm sorry, he wouldn't let me send for you," she said. Her words were jumbled, and Nell couldn't quite make sense of what she was being told, only that Alex seemingly had not wanted her involved. As she spoke, Mrs. Marion walked Nell through the house and to the back door. "He's out there, see for yourself," she said.

Alex was sitting out in the courtyard poring over a newspaper spread out on the small round wicker table.

"Alex, your fiancée is here," said Mrs. Marion.

He turned to them, and Nell gasped. His face was swollen and bruised, marked with deep purple and blue splotches on each side. One eye was blackened, and his lip was split, with a dark scab just beginning to form over the angry red cut.

Nell rushed forward and put a hand up to his cheek. Alex flinched and started to smile, then stopped abruptly—it looked like he'd nearly reopened the wound on his bottom lip.

"What on earth happened to you?" asked Nell.

"It was my newspaper column," he said, wincing at the pain. The day after it ran, he'd been coming out of the catering shop after closing it down for the evening when a bunch of white men accosted him on the street. His pen name apparently wasn't as subtle as he'd thought. The men roughed him up, ranting about how Blacks should never have had the vote in the first place. "'You people should be glad that's all you're losing,'" one of them had said. Alex's father and a few other men on the block were able to chase them off, but not soon enough. Alex lay bleeding on the pavement with a cracked rib and a face so swollen they could hardly recognize him.

"The column," Nell said, staring at him. The same one she'd inspired him to write, that she'd pushed him to make more strident, more forceful—more of everything that she should've known would result in exactly this. Black people in the city hardly had to do anything at all to stir up whites' anger, so writing something like that was practically calling it down on Alex's head. She should've known better. And now here she was, staring into the broken and bleeding face of this man, her oldest friend and her—what? Coconspirator? Fiancé? It was too much to bear.

"I'm so sorry, Alex. We shouldn't have— Maybe we should've

been more careful," she said, fighting back tears. This was all her fault. She should never have encouraged him to stick his neck out like this. Guilt and terror at the thought of losing Alex swirled in her belly, making her queasy. How could she have been so reckless?

"Sometimes doing the right thing is more important than doing what's safest," he said. "I know I don't have to explain that to you."

Of course not. Alex was just like her, in his way—and if Nell hadn't seen it before, there was no looking away from it now. Still, she felt sick at the thought of all she'd dragged him into, and of what might've happened if the other men hadn't gotten to him in time. What if he'd been alone and under attack, and she'd come here only to find that the worst had happened—her mind recoiled from the thought like a hand from a flame.

"Will you be all right?" she asked. "Your parents must be beside themselves."

He nodded. "Ma and Pa both want me to leave all the newspaper work alone and concentrate on the catering business instead, at least for a little while. The politics are just too volatile right now, they're saying. As if there's ever been a time when they weren't." That was Alex's parents: tied up financially and socially with white folks, and always careful not to rock the boat. She stared at him and shook her head. "But if you didn't know about all this, what's brought you over here?" he asked. "Is there news? Tell me."

She forced a smile. If he was in good enough spirits to ask for a distraction, perhaps he wasn't in such bad shape after all. Feeling as though she'd been holding her breath since first seeing his face, Nell exhaled.

"I'd come to tell you that Charlotte and I have figured out arrangements for Evie's situation, so at least that's one less thing for you to worry about."

Alex straightened up in his seat. "It's no trouble, I'm happy I was able to help."

"Of course, and I'm so grateful to you," she said. "But now that things are nearly settled, it really is time for us to call off our engagement," she said. Her voice quavered, but she went on. "Your parents have had enough of a shock for one day, so we can find a way to tell them later. But at least things can go back to the way they were."

Alex looked at her closely, keeping his eyes on hers. "Can they?"

"They have to," she said, standing up and smoothing her dress. She sounded more certain than she felt. Knowing how she'd come undone at the thought of him in danger, Nell realized it was exactly this sort of distraction that had put her off marriage in the first place—there was too much important work to be done. But didn't Alex understand all that? The work was the whole reason he was attacked, after all. Nell shook her head, pushing the thought away.

Alex exhaled, resigned. "Of course. You know your own mind, and it's not for me to try and change it. But I'm always here to help, if you need me—you and Charlotte."

She turned around and bent down to give him a kiss on the unbruised cheek. "You're a wonderful friend, Alex."

The walk across the street to her own house felt long, and it was an effort to keep from turning back. Upstairs in her room, she blinked quickly in the hope of drying her eyes. She was determined no tears should fall, though her eyes were full.

She sat down at her desk and dove into plans for the hall opening and the conference. No distractions.

Chapter 26

EVIE

FOR THE NEXT FEW DAYS, EVIE HAUNTED THE TOWN HOUSE ALMOST entirely in silence. She was both there and not there, remained but was already gone, going through the motions of her life not at peace but too hopeless to change anything. And with the chance to see Mama again dangling in front of her, did she even want to try? Day in, day out, she brushed Kate's hair, laid out her clothes, listened to her chatter, and waited to be shipped off. At first, Ada had tried talking to Evie, asking her if she was all right, and what had gone wrong, and if she could help. But after a few days of being met only with silent brush-offs and vacant stares, she'd given up, and now gave Evie a wide berth when they passed each other in the hallways. *Maybe giving up is catching,* Evie thought dimly. It was a wonder she hadn't caught it herself before now.

In truth, it was safer. Trying to make any more trouble for Kate would only risk bringing more punishments. Sending Evie down South wasn't the only thing Kate could do, after all, or have done to her. Though the ladies of the town house never lifted a hand to lay down a beating themselves, they never once lifted a hand to stop one either. Kate and Maggie clung tightly to their fig leaves of innocence, but Evie and every other person enslaved in the house saw the truth of it well enough, and knew there was no crossing the women for free. The bill always came due.

Since deciding to send Evie away, Kate had grown quieter too, though she still kept Evie close. Her essential neediness wouldn't permit anything else. If she noticed Evie's downcast mood, she never spoke a word about it, and she didn't let up on her silly little demands either. A couple of days before Evie was to leave, Kate whined how she'd been missing the spice cakes Evie used to bring her from the market and insisted she go and get some to keep her sweet tooth satisfied while Evie was away.

Evie no more wanted to go to the market than she wanted to be sent to Virginia. Since Charlotte had abandoned her, she'd been avoiding the place as best she could. It was an unwelcome reminder of how foolish she'd been to trust someone else to help her. How naïve she'd been to hope. But this time Kate wouldn't be put off, and she sent Evie out with sickly sweet words singing the praises of her own generosity.

"We take such good care of each other, don't we, sweet girl?" she'd said. "Go along and enjoy the fresh air at the market, and then you'll have your trip to look forward to, and the wedding."

Kate watched Evie, waiting for gratitude, but Evie could barely muster a wan smile. Inside, she felt torn up but resigned. At least she'd be with Mama soon.

That morning, there was a warm spring breeze blowing in through the windows of Kate's sitting room. Evie dressed herself lightly in a simple gray muslin frock with cap sleeves that exposed her arms. Over her shoulders she tied a worn old fringe shawl. The smell of breakfast rolls and bacon wafted up from downstairs, but she had no appetite—she hadn't for days.

In the kitchen's side room near the slave quarters, Peter and Louise sat waiting until it was time to leave for the market. With so much to do around the house, they always planned to head out early so that they could be back in time to fix lunch for themselves and whatever white folks might still be lounging in the parlor or library in the middle of the day.

Ada was the last to come down. "Y'all know Miss Maggie. Sorry," she said, shrugging. Her mistress needed a lot of maintenance in the morning, which meant Ada spent the first several hours of each day tending to her thinning hair and helping her choose just the right wig, while shuttling back and forth between upstairs and the kitchen every time Maggie requested something different to eat. Bring her a biscuit with honey, no, she wants jam today; wait, sausage now, and how about some poached eggs? It wasn't even 9:00 and it was plain Ada had been run ragged.

It was just a short ride to the market, and Evie was grateful for it. All she wanted was to go in silence, get the cakes, and go back to the house. But as they arrived under the market sheds and waded into the crowd, Evie couldn't fight the tiny flicker of hope that had her scanning people's faces in case she chanced upon Charlotte. But it was no use. The crowd was a crush of strangers, and not one of them there to help her or even spare her a kind word. At least Charlotte knew enough to be too ashamed to show her face here anymore, Evie thought bitterly.

The group walked together until Evie came to the bakery stall near Third Street, where she'd pick up Kate's cake. Peter and Ada went off in another direction, toward the stalls where they could buy household items like soap and lamp oil. Ada waved as she walked off, tossing Evie a quick smile. She could only summon a blank stare in return. What was the point in being friendly anyway, when in two days she'd be gone?

In the baker's stall, she listlessly rummaged through the tables of deep brown bread loaves and yellow cakes until she found the spice cake Kate had wanted. There was only one today. Kate would be disappointed. Evie took some satisfaction in that. She picked up the one and got in line to pay.

When she finally reached the front of the line, she set the cake on the counter and reached into her purse. When she looked up and handed the money over, she found the baker staring at her curiously.

"Yes?" she said.

The baker quickly glanced from side to side, then—as he accepted her payment—leaned forward and whispered, "Evie?" Evie's eyes went wide, and she nodded. The baker went on. "Your friend asked me to look for you, said you might come back around. I can get word to her, if you need."

Evie took a step back. Was this some kind of trick? Or could it be that Charlotte hadn't forgotten about her after all? She turned it over in her mind, fighting to beat back the faint hopes that were now pushing themselves forward.

The baker cleared his throat, and Evie snapped out of her momentary reverie.

"Where is she?" she asked. Maybe there was still a chance. Maybe she didn't have to go down South after all.

"Seventy-one Fourth Street in Society Hill, that's where she said to send the message," said the baker. "Anything you want me to tell her?" He had a pencil and paper at the ready.

"No," Evie said. "I'll tell her myself." Seventy-one Fourth Street. The market was on Third, so that wouldn't be far at all. As soon as Evie got clear of the market's crowd, she could make a run for it. Free. *But Mama.*

Just as she set down the cake and stepped away from the bakery counter, there was a hand on her shoulder. Her throat tightened and her shoulders tensed up practically to her ears.

"Don't you need that?" said Ada. Evie turned, and Ada pointed to the spice cake she'd left on the counter. "It's the whole reason you came!"

"Oh!" Evie tried to laugh casually. "I must've gotten distracted; thought I saw somebody I knew." She picked up the cake and sidled back into the bakery line, with Ada by her side. Though she'd already paid, standing in line again would give her a moment to think. All the while, she was looking over Ada's shoulder for a pathway out.

She strained to keep sight of the crowd around them while Ada chatted away. Evie barely heard her. Silently, she prayed Peter and Louise didn't show up too—they'd make it impossible to get away. After a moment, Peter reappeared and started toward them, and before she could stop herself, she yelped, "No!"

"Lord!" Ada said, looking at her quizzically. The reply jolted Evie back to the conversation. "Never heard somebody so against picking up an extra loaf of sourdough bread. Wouldn't even cost that much, and we could keep it for ourselves in the kitchen, but if you don't like it . . ." She shook her head.

"Sorry, I must've heard you wrong," Evie said, pulling herself together. She paused to think. "An extra loaf sounds good, but this isn't the right bakery for sourdough, is it? If you want to run to the other stall to buy one, I'll meet you over there once I've finished here."

Ada looked a little suspicious but agreed. "Sure," she said.

"Be right over," said Evie. Ada walked off, but Evie hesitated. She ached to get back to her mother, but Mama herself had said it—she'd have done anything to keep from going back down to the deep South. However much Mama would want to see Evie, she wouldn't want that for her daughter either. No, if Evie saw her again, it had to be as a free woman, on her own terms. Not Kate's.

This was her moment.

As soon as Ada was out of sight, Evie hurried off in the other direction, peeking into every stall and kiosk and around every aisle corner before continuing on, desperate to stay clear of everyone from the Jackson house. It wouldn't be long before Ada, Peter, and Louise realized she was gone, so if she was going to get away, it had to be now. She turned for one more look and caught sight of the backs of their heads. They were looking every which way to find her. A pang of guilt seized her at the sight of them, and a wave of nausea rose up in her throat. Here she was, having decided in a snap to do to someone else exactly what Charlotte had done to her—leave them behind without a word.

But this was no time to sit in her self-reproach—she needed to move. She scanned the market's crowd to find an exit. The instant she saw an opening, she hurried out from the stalls and onto the beckoning streets.

EVEN WITH CHARLOTTE'S ADDRESS in hand, Evie was in trouble. She didn't know her way around the city, and as she kept moving she feared she'd get lost. Evie rushed along the cobblestone streets, nervously glancing from the huge buildings to the crowds of people as she tried to find her way. In her hurry, she nearly stumbled into a man pushing along a food cart and shouting about fresh oysters. The sharp, briny smell of seafood hit her nose and she took a step back, right into the path of a well-dressed brown-skinned man with a bright yellow handkerchief peeking out of his pocket who was striding at a determined clip. "Pardon!" he huffed, as Evie mumbled an apology.

To get her bearings, she moved to the edge of the sidewalk. The scene was a jumble of paths she might take—she could go anywhere she wanted, but she had no idea which way was right. The sudden freedom of movement was both thrilling and utterly disorienting.

Nearly everything looked unfamiliar to her, but then she remembered that when she'd gone on errands with the other house slaves and they headed south from Market Street, there were suddenly a great many more people who looked like them. With no other clue to guide her, she stepped back into the crowd's flow and started walking south. As she rushed on, denser main roads gave way to quieter side streets of charming brick row houses with flowers in the window boxes, and she started to breathe a little more easily. Across the street, walking in the other direction was a pair of older women with golden brown skin that set off the peach of their new-looking frocks. They moved down the street arm in arm, laughing and talking with their heads close together. If all this was the look of freedom, it must be something indeed.

But as much as she'd have loved to keep wandering this pretty neighborhood, taking in the sights and the fresh air, Evie knew she had to get off the street and out of sight. She needed help. When another finely dressed young Black woman came passing by, Evie reached out to touch her shoulder. "Excuse me, Miss?"

The girl frowned at her and yanked her shoulder out of reach. "*Excuse* me," she said, and kept walking. So much for standing together, Evie thought. She tried again, this time with a woman who looked about her mother's age, who was just stepping out of a nearby fabric shop. "Begging your pardon, ma'am?"

The woman looked up from her bag, which she'd been rifling

through as if she'd forgotten something inside. "Hello there. What can I do for you?"

"Well, um, I'm in town to stay with a friend and I've just lost my way," Evie said. The woman held her gaze, and Evie took in the stateliness of her figure. Suddenly Evie felt aware of her own drab, muted gray dress with dangling threads along the sides, and her worn shawl. She didn't know how believable her quick lie was, but she felt safe even as the woman looked at her with visible skepticism.

"What's your name, baby?" the woman asked kindly, squeezing Evie's shoulder.

"Evie, ma'am."

"Well, Evie, I can get you on your way," she said. After a pause, she began again. "But first, do you want to tell me what's really going on here?"

Evie pressed her lips together and looked down at the ground.

"Here, come with me," the woman said. She maneuvered Evie toward a bench halfway down the block in front of a tavern. The two sat down, Evie smoothing her wrinkled dress over her knees. The woman leaned in close and spoke in a voice almost too low to hear. "We get all kinds of folks coming into the neighborhood, you know. Coming into, or hiding in, or passing through. All kinds."

That sounded well and good but Evie didn't know what it had to do with giving her directions. She nodded slowly.

"What I'm telling you is, most folks around here are happy to help someone if they know who and what they're helping," the woman said. Then, more quietly, "Not all of us started off free."

Evie looked up and right into the woman's face. Slowly, she turned to look at all the other Black people walking the streets: shopkeepers, women with their babies, laboring men with the grime of a hard day's work on their plain clothes, and businessmen in their well-tailored suits. Any of them could have begun just where she was now. She turned back to the woman, feeling a hint of hope.

"What gave me away?"

"Lost, carrying almost nothing, and frightened eyes," the woman said, smiling. "It wasn't too big a leap."

Evie nodded. "I ran from a house near the river, and I'm trying to find my way to the home of a friend, but I barely know the area," said Evie. "She lives in Society Hill, seventy-one Fourth Street."

"Society Hill, eh? Those are some nice places," the woman said. "Is your friend expecting you?"

"I won't be too much of a surprise," Evie said. The woman peered at her curiously for a moment but didn't pry. Evie wasn't in the mood to explain much. Out in the street she felt exposed, as if the others from the Jacksons' house were going to come around the corner and find her any minute. She scanned the street for familiar faces, just in case.

"All right, well, let's not sit out in the open air for too long," the woman said, reading Evie's mind. "I'll take you most of the way there—you aren't too far."

The two walked on until the sea of faces on the sidewalks shifted from brown to mostly white in hue. What had been welcoming smiles and hello-how-do-you-dos now transformed to questioning looks, or complete indifference. The midmorning sun was shining on them, but Evie felt cold.

When they came to the corner of a street with trees covered in cherry blossoms, their petals carpeting the sidewalks, the woman stopped. "This is where I'll leave you," she said. "Turn down this street, and keep walking until you see a house with the number seventy-one on it. You can read numbers, can't you?"

Evie nodded.

"Good. You'll be all right now; you're dressed like a housemaid so nobody'll bother you. Go on."

With that, Evie turned down the street and slowly walked toward Charlotte's house. As she passed a bin on the street, she tossed Kate's spice cake into the trash.

Chapter 27

———

CHARLOTTE

———

OUTSIDE THE WALLS OF THE ROW HOUSE, THE CITY STREETS called to Charlotte. For days now, Philadelphia had swelled with new energy. Just through the windows, new faces passed by on the streets of Society Hill. Abolitionists from Boston, New York, and all the northern centers of politics and free thought had gathered in the homes of Philadelphia friends to eat, drink, celebrate, and prepare. Pennsylvania Hall was officially open, and Charlotte was missing it.

With only a day left before James's dinner party, there was a crush of chores to finish and Charlotte had no choice but to do them. She was trapped. Darcel would have been glad enough to let her go where she pleased—things had been much better between them since their talk—but no. The problem, as ever, was James. He was determined that everything be perfect: the furniture freshly polished, the rugs beaten. He even opened and shut windows on every floor trying to get the temperature just right. Worst of all, he'd taken to leaving his workshop and coming home unannounced at odd times to check how preparations were going. With no way to predict his movements, Charlotte couldn't risk leaving. She'd have to trust Nell to see their plan through and make arrangements at the hall for Evie to leave town. But the task of getting word to Evie had fallen to Charlotte, and she was utterly at a loss. As she dusted and polished and scrubbed, she turned the problem over and over in her mind, and the walls of the house pressed in closer.

On the first morning of the conventions, Charlotte's frustration at being trapped threatened to boil over. It must've shown on her face, because Darcel suggested she take a break from cleaning and relax. "Rushing around fretting and forcing things won't help you," he said. "Mind doesn't work that way. Let yourself breathe; a solution will come to you."

Charlotte didn't really believe that, but what else could she do? She went to the kitchen and made herself a cup of hot tea. She wrapped both her hands around the cup, enjoying its warmth, and settled herself into a chair at the little table in the corner where Darcel took his meals. Even when no one was cooking, it was always warm in the kitchen, and in the last few weeks it had become a comfortable, almost peaceful part of the house for Charlotte. But before she had a chance to take a sip, there was a sharp knock on the front door. She set down her cup and went to answer.

"Yes, may I help you?" said Charlotte as she pulled the door open.

"I hope so, Carrie," came the reply. Evie stood there on the doorstep, hands on her hips. Before she could say another word, Charlotte yanked her inside and shut the door behind them. After a swift peek out the window to make sure no one had seen them, Charlotte hugged Evie tightly and then stepped back to look at her. Darcel had been more right than he knew: a solution had come to Charlotte all right. And with it, a host of new problems.

Still, she tried to speak as gently as she could.

"How did you get here? Where does Kate think you are right now?" asked Charlotte.

"At the market with the others. She probably doesn't even know I'm gone yet," Evie said. "I couldn't stay; she was talking about sending me away in two days. I didn't know what I was going to do, but then I got your message."

Yes, a message about how to contact her, not to show up on her doorstep! But there was nothing to be done about that now. Evie was here. She looked at Charlotte with expectant eyes. There would be time for more questions, but first Evie needed to be out of sight of the windows. As Charlotte drew her farther into the house, Evie looked around.

"You all seem to be doing well for yourselves," she said. Her voice was cold. "Where's Uncle Jack?"

Charlotte had forgotten how Evie used to look up to her father. He had doted on the little girl at White Oaks the only way he knew how, carving her wooden dolls to match the ones he made for Charlotte. But the man Evie remembered did not live in this house. Uncle Jack might have welcomed her, but James Vaughn was someone else entirely, and Charlotte had long since stopped trusting him to look after anyone but himself.

"He may be back soon, but he can't know you're here," said Charlotte. "He's the reason I haven't been able to get to the market to see you. After he found some abolitionist papers in my bag, he pretty much locked me in here. He'd want nothing to do with this, and we should oblige him." Evie looked doubtful, but Charlotte didn't have time to convince her. James could show up at any moment, and the conversation about how Evie had appeared in their hallway was one Charlotte did not want to have.

"Let's get you upstairs and out of sight, then we can figure out what we'll do about you," Charlotte said, pulling Evie toward the back staircase.

"Do about me?" Evie huffed. "If I'm such a pest, why'd you leave your address for me with the baker?"

"I'd meant you could get *word* to me here, and we could set a day to meet and make a plan," Charlotte said. "Glad as I am to see you, *this* is not a plan. This is no safe house, Evie—we're going to have a dining room full of people tomorrow!"

Evie crossed her arms and stood firm at the bottom of the stairs. "How would I have gotten word to you? I can't exactly write you a letter!" she said, sounding angry. "You know what? Never mind. Just point me to the nearest train station and I'll be out of your hair."

Charlotte's breath quickened, and it took all her self-control not to yank Evie up the stairs by her arm. She spoke in a harsh whisper.

"Don't be ridiculous, I'll look after you. But you have to come with me *now*." She led Evie up to the attic on tiptoes.

"If you hear anyone coming up, get under the bed or tuck yourself into the armoire as quick as you can," she said when they arrived upstairs. "Otherwise, you can sit out here in my room, but you'll need to keep quiet. Can you do that?"

Evie nodded, stepping farther into the room and looking around.

"You're safe here." Charlotte wrapped a light wool blanket around Evie's shoulders. She knew her friend must be tired after all she had been through. She'd probably been running on pure nerves since she took off.

Evie looked up at her. "Carrie, I—"

But before she could finish her thought, Charlotte headed for the door. "I need to go downstairs to attend to my chores now," she said. "We wouldn't want anyone to think something's wrong. I'll be back to check on you."

Downstairs, Charlotte found herself strangely relieved to get back to work. Dusting and sweeping were simple enough to reckon with; being in such close quarters with Evie again threatened to overwhelm her. But Darcel had said once, she didn't have to take everything on alone. She set aside the broom and headed back to the kitchen.

"Who was at the door?" he asked.

She told him, and he just shook his head. "Well, looks like all your plans got moved up," he said. Then, after a long pause: "If you need to go find your friends to help, I'll cover for you."

That was exactly what she needed. Stashing Evie in the attic and exposing them all to arrest or worse was decidedly not part of the plan, especially since she could've been seen or followed on her way to the house. There was no doubt Kate would come looking for her, and she'd find a lot more than she bargained for if she made it to 71 Fourth Street. No, Evie had to be moved to an actual safe house right away, and that meant Charlotte needed to find Nell and Hetty.

She thanked Darcel and told him that she wouldn't be gone long; Nell's house was just a few blocks away down Lombard Street—she'd hurry there, update her, and come straight home. Darcel nodded, and Charlotte rushed upstairs to grab a shawl before leaving.

"I've got to run," she told Evie as she rummaged through the armoire. "Nell and I had already arranged a safe house for you in the city, I just need to alert her and Hetty, and when it's dark, we can get you out of here and on your way."

She started for the door again, but Evie's voice stopped her in her tracks. "And that's what you want. For me to be out of the way," she said quietly.

Charlotte turned around to face her. "What? Evie, how can you say something like that? I've missed you every day since my father brought me here."

"Then why won't you talk to me?" Evie answered. Her voice was small, as if her tiredness had finally crowded out her anger. "You've run away from me every chance you got since I came. You're doing it right now."

The truth in Evie's words pricked at Charlotte's guilt. Evie had meant something to her once, and still did, yet all this time she'd been holding her at arm's length, treating her like a problem to be solved. It was easier that way, to try to keep Charlotte's old life at White Oaks a safe distance from the new one she was clawing and scratching to build here. But Charlotte knew it was more than that. She turned away from Evie in shame.

"What could I possibly say to you?" Charlotte asked. Her eyes burned, but she fought to hold back the tears. "You've lost everyone you had because we left, and nothing I can say will ever make up for that. And God only knows what's happened to Auntie Irene, and to Daniel, because of my father and me. I don't even know where to start except to say that I'm sorry. I'm so, so sorry. I never asked to leave White Oaks. But I couldn't stay."

She sat down suddenly on the side of the bed and wept. Still, she didn't dare ask forgiveness. She couldn't. After a moment, Evie came over and sat beside her.

"I couldn't stay where I was either," Evie said. "Even though Kate said I could see Mama again if I went down South, and I wanted to.

I *want* to. I miss her something awful. But then I got your message, and saw my chance to get away, and I just—"

"Took it," they said together.

"I ran, and left the other house slaves behind at the market. Leaving them felt so wrong, and I barely knew them," Evie said, hanging her head sadly. "You left me and didn't say a word, and we grew up together. I waited for you for months, and cried for you. Why didn't you come back for me?"

"I didn't know how. Even now, I can barely figure how to have you here and keep myself safe at the same time. It feels impossible," Charlotte said, her shoulders drooping. "Why can't there be a way to have freedom and our families too?"

Evie sat silent for a moment, then asked tentatively: "Could *we* have been family someday? For real, I mean? Daniel took it hard when you left, you know. Real hard."

Charlotte felt a blush creeping up the sides of her face and nodded.

"There was something between us—I never got a chance to tell you," she admitted. "I barely know what it was—it was so new, and strange in its way. Now I don't know if I'll feel anything like it ever again." She hung her head.

Evie didn't say anything, but she took Charlotte's hand. They sat together in the quiet for a moment, until Charlotte let go to wipe away the tears that had run down her cheeks.

"Let me get you free and somewhere safe, it's the least I can do. I promised to help you, and I will," she said. Evie nodded, and Charlotte stood, picked up her shawl, and started for the attic door. "I'll come back for you as soon as I can."

But just as Charlotte opened the door, James's footsteps echoed in the foyer downstairs.

"Charlotte? Charlotte!" he called.

She turned back to Evie and held up a finger. Finding Nell and Hetty would have to wait.

Charlotte tossed the shawl onto her bed and hurried downstairs.

"How are the preparations coming?" he asked, peeking into the parlor. "Things don't look too different around here."

"We're getting there, little by little."

"Well let's hurry please, we've only got another day. I'll stay home now to help out until the party, that should move things along."

Charlotte's body tensed up. With him around the house all day there'd be no getting out to tell Nell what was going on—no getting out at all. It was going to be a long night, and an even longer day.

SHE SPENT THE NEXT few hours cleaning, all while straining to hear if any noises came from upstairs. Fortunately, Evie didn't draw any notice.

After dinner, Charlotte straightened up the pantry while Darcel put the rest of the food away, and she made her way toward the stairs with a pair of rolls wrapped in a napkin, wary of taking anything more and drawing attention to herself. As she walked by the dining room, she was surprised to see James in there going over the dining table with a flannel rag and another coat of polish. It was his own recipe, a mix of white wax, rose pink, and linseed oil. The smell was overpowering, but the wood shone beautifully. She tried tiptoeing by, but he looked up.

"You don't often take up a midnight snack," he said. She shrugged theatrically and kept walking, but he called after her. "Will you give me a hand?"

Evie must be starving upstairs. But Charlotte sighed and set the rolls on the sideboard. James tossed her a silk handkerchief so that she could smooth after he'd polished. She started at the opposite end of the dining table, working quickly and silently in the hope of getting upstairs as soon as she could. But he was in a reflective mood.

"It looks like you've been learning a lot from Darcel," he began.

"Mm-hmm."

"Have you been enjoying the process, at least?" he asked. Charlotte shot him a glare. "I know it didn't start off on the best foot. I just—sometimes I don't know what to do. I'm only trying to keep us safe."

Charlotte nodded. She wasn't sure what he wanted her to say. In the silence, he kept talking.

"But I see how seriously you've been taking it, and how you've done as I asked," he said, moving his way down the length of the table. "I know it's been a long few years. I just needed to be sure you were mature enough not to upend all this." He was only a few chairs away now.

Charlotte looked up from her polishing. "I am. I'm not a girl anymore."

He shrugged. "To me, you may always be," he said. "But after tomorrow night, once things are squared away with my business, maybe we can talk about doing things differently. There may be room for you to get out more and spend your time how you'd like, if you can promise to stay out of trouble."

Charlotte swallowed hard, but the guilt had made her mouth go dry. She knew just the kind of trouble he meant—the kind that was upstairs, waiting for something to eat.

How strange: just as James had finally thought to reach for her, Charlotte had stepped over the threshold out of his grasp—or maybe Evie had pulled her across. Months before, this might've been a different conversation. She loved him, at the root of things, but the promise he wanted was one she couldn't make, not anymore—she'd already given her promise to Evie. She finished polishing her side of the table and set down her rag.

"I've got to get up to bed," she said, grabbing the rolls from the sideboard. As she turned to leave, she softened. "I hope tomorrow goes how you want." He offered a small smile in return, and Charlotte headed back upstairs.

She crept into the room with the rolls, and Evie took them gratefully, relishing them with the appetite of someone who'd been on a long, hard journey. Evie looked up with a small smile when she was finished, and Charlotte reached over to gently brush the crumbs from the side of her face.

"It looks like at least we'll have another day together," she said. "There's no way to leave until after this dinner party."

"I can hold on one more day," Evie said. "At least I'm not with Kate, right?"

They laughed quietly together. But it was late, and both of them were exhausted. Charlotte gathered up her blankets and her own pillow and laid them on the floor beside the bed for Evie, on the side farthest from the door. Evie lay down heavily, and Charlotte tucked herself into bed. She was a little chilly under just a sheet, but grateful to have her friend's company. She hung her arm down over the side of the bed, as she always had when Evie had slept over in her cabin at White Oaks. After a moment, Evie's hand, now so much larger than a little girl's, closed around Charlotte's little finger.

THE GRAND OPENING OF PENNSYLVANIA HALL WAS UNDER WAY, but so far, the complexion of the proceedings was a stark mismatch with the content. A full day's events already done, and so far, not a single Black speaker had graced the grand stage of what many in the city had started calling the "Abolition Hall." The opening had attracted a crowd of hostile onlookers who'd begun grumbling outside as soon as the conventions began, but for all their fears that the hall threatened to upend the racial order, the pro-slavery toughs might have been downright pleased with what was going on behind the building's enormous columned façade. For Nell, the speaker slate was just another reminder of how out of step many white abolitionists had fallen with the very people they claimed to be saving.

On the first day, thousands had gathered at the hall only to be welcomed with tepid opening remarks by the founder of the Philadelphia Antislavery Society. He seemed to argue for gradual abolition in the remaining slave states, possibly giving enslavers years or even decades to warm up to the notion of not buying, selling, or hunting down Black people. What was more, he warned against immediatists taking "intemperate measures" to advance the cause of freedom—like scheming to smuggle fugitives out of the state, perhaps? His lack of urgency was galling, and Nell wasn't the only one who thought so. She saw Hetty clench her jaw and roll her eyes more than once during the speech. But the man wasn't that much of an outlier. Nell had been contending with the same lack of urgency in the women's Antislavery Society for months. At the time, it had seemed ill-mannered how Charlotte tried to shove them toward more action, but increasingly, Nell understood her frustration.

And then there were the protesters. When Nell returned on Tuesday morning for the conference's second day, she entered the building warily. The outside had already taken a beating: on the Haines Street side, one of the brand-new windows was boarded up. Rumor was that an agitator had hurled a brick through it the evening before, and the façade sported fresh dents and scratches from even more onlookers throwing rocks both day and night.

Still, though some at the conference had disappointed her, the inside of the hall was everything Nell had hoped for in a meeting space. On the first floor, the shelves of the abolitionist bookstore were lined with passionate, well-argued books, tracts, and pamphlets to sway wavering hearts toward the cause. Across the entryway, a produce store sold goods made only with nonenslaved labor, a commercial testament to the hall's guiding principles. Then there were the new offices of *The Pennsylvania Freeman* in the basement. For a moment, Nell wondered if Alex was down there working on the special conference edition of the paper or if he'd taken his parents' advice and quit. She hadn't spoken to him since she'd broken things off, but the distance hadn't settled her feelings as much as she'd hoped—she still worried about him. Often throughout the day he would take over her thoughts, even when she was surrounded by the bustle and energy of the crowd at the hall.

In the Grand Saloon upstairs, thousands packed in to take their seats in the carved wooden chairs with plush blue silk cushions. Nell took heart. Even as pro-slavery agitators and others in the city insisted the abolitionist cause was dangerously unpopular, it was clear there was real strength in their numbers. On the stage, a rose-adorned arch featured the motto VIRTUE, LIBERTY, AND INDEPENDENCE. At least *inside* the hall those values animated the crowd.

To start the second day of the opening celebration and conventions, William Lloyd Garrison, the firebrand white abolitionist from

New England, took the podium unexpectedly in the Grand Saloon. He cut an imposing figure between the stage's two enormous Ionic columns, and the crowd looked up at him, spellbound as he spoke. He was easily the most famous man at the opening, and arguably one of the most radical—he insisted that immediate and total abolition of slavery was the only moral course; not gradual abolition or, even worse, shipping former slaves off to a colony in Africa. He spoke out against the conventions' all-white speaker slates and verbally lashed the gradualists and colonizationists who'd spoken the day before. What good did their timid, measured calls for abolition do for the Black people being denied freedom *now*?

His words stirred such a passion in the crowd that the convention organizers arranged a debate for the following morning, welcoming all comers—immediatists, gradualists, colonizationists, and slavers alike—to rhetorically have it out. Nell was wary. Refuting the gradualists was all well and good, but inviting the slavers was hardly necessary. Why were white people always so willing to entertain debates that treated Black people's humanity as a radical idea?

The question of abolitionist strategy was no mere hypothetical issue for Nell. She had real work to do, starting with arranging Evie's passage out of the city, and then figuring out how to shift the women's Antislavery Society away from its safe, narrowing focuses and get to the real work of freeing Black people, keeping them safe, and enriching their lives. That afternoon, Nell went into the first session of the Antislavery Convention of American Women with a fire in her belly, determined to press her case. With women gathered from all over the country, she hoped the fresh perspectives might push the Philadelphia branch of the Female Antislavery Societies to take a stronger stand.

She strode into the first-floor session hall just as the meeting was gaveled to order and started speaking before even sitting down.

"We need to discuss formalizing my committee to explore how we can aid fugitive slaves more directly," she said without preamble.

The Philadelphia women's Antislavery Society president, Sarah

Pugh, who was leading the proceedings, stared at her icily, unblinking. She spoke slowly and deliberately.

"If you'll kindly sit down and keep your outbursts to a minimum, Miss Gardner, we're here to discuss the agenda for the rest of the week's proceedings, not to get into any substantive matters," she said.

"Very well, then we need to discuss discussing it," Nell retorted. Some of Charlotte's directness had rubbed off on her in the last few months. And if Sarah Pugh insisted on observing the formality of a meeting-before-the-meetings, Nell could play that game too. She settled into her seat.

With the session called to order, the women debated a range of topics: how abolition societies should engage with churches that condoned slavery, whether slaves' right to self-defense comported with the women's nonviolent values, and more. Each was put to a vote, and those topics the group approved were added to the agendas to be discussed at the week's remaining meetings.

The women spent most of the afternoon turning over the question of whether men should be allowed to attend any speeches the women's convention hosted. Renowned abolitionist crusaders like the newly married Angelina Grimke Weld were slated to speak the next day, and likely to draw eager crowds. Nell thought they should welcome anyone who wanted to hear her—at least Miss Grimke Weld would interrupt the parade of male speakers that had dominated the opening week so far, though she wouldn't change the whiteness. But after hours of discussion, the taboo against women speaking in front of mixed-gender audiences proved too strong. The group would let men attend Miss Grimke Weld's speech, but they'd strip away the Philadelphia Female Antislavery Society's official imprimatur as hosts to duck the controversy.

With the convention exhausted after going many rounds over the issue, the president sought to adjourn for the day.

"Excuse me," Nell interjected. "We've forgotten to take up the matter I raised earlier."

Miss Pugh's mouth was a straight line. "Of course, forgive me." She turned to the wider group. "We'll put it to a vote: Shall this group convene an open discussion about violating state and federal laws to hide and transport runaway slaves?"

"Wait just a moment," Nell objected. That phrasing was grossly unfair—though not exactly inaccurate. But before Nell could finish her thought, the president plowed onward.

"All in favor say 'aye,' all against, 'nay,'" she boomed.

The nays came in an avalanche, burying Nell's hopes to radicalize the Antislavery Society for the sake of Evie and every other runaway in immediate danger. Still, her defeat wasn't total. Nell heard a scattering of bold ayes in the crowd, mostly from other Black women, and a handful of more rebellious whites. She had a few allies, at least.

"The nays have it," said Miss Pugh. "Adjourned."

As the room emptied out, Nell, frustrated, was packing up her belongings to head home when she felt a tap on her shoulder. She turned around, and Hetty was standing there with a white woman who smiled primly.

"Nell, this is Miss Mary Smythe, she's joining us here from New York. I think you'll find her amenable to our way of thinking," said Hetty.

Mary spoke in a low voice. "Miss Reckless has told me about your particular need, and I'm ready to help."

Nell looked at Hetty, wide-eyed. "While Mary's here in the city she's staying in the home of a friend of mine," said Hetty. "When she leaves at the end of this week, she can take your friend back up to New York in her carriage and no one will be the wiser."

"We'll look after her there," Mary added. "Clothes, food, a place to stay, whatever she needs until she gets on her feet or decides to keep moving north."

The end of the week then. Nell and Charlotte would have until then to get word to Evie and connect her with this new ally. Though Charlotte had said she'd be busy with housework for the first few days of the opening, she was expected to join Nell tomorrow, and they could strategize from there while taking in the rest of the conventions. Even with Evie squared away, there would still be plenty more work to do nudging their fellow abolitionists toward more immediate action. Mr. Garrison wasn't the only one with something to say on that score.

Nell strode out of the hall feeling hopeful. Even the curious, angry-looking gawkers milling around near the building didn't dampen her spirits. Amid the familiar faces coming in and out of the building, she nodded a greeting to Mr. Purvis as he helped his wife out of their carriage. Many of the city's most powerful residents were on the side of right, and that was reason enough not to despair.

But as Nell passed one of the lampposts on Sixth Street, the spring went out of her step. Fixed to the pole at eye level was a placard with its message scratched out in stark black lettering.

Whereas a convention for the avowed purpose of effecting the immediate abolition of slavery in the Union is now in session in this city, all citizens who entertain a proper respect for the right of property and the preservation of the Constitution of the United States must interfere, forcibly if they must, to prevent the violation of all we have heretofore held sacred. All persons so disposed should assemble at the Pennsylvania Hall to-morrow morning, May 16, at 11 o'clock, and demand the immediate dispersion of said convention. Signed, Several Citizens.

Nell walked on, and the city held its breath.

———

Chapter 29

CHARLOTTE

———

THE DAY OF JAMES'S TRIUMPH HAD FINALLY ARRIVED. EVENING was coming on quickly, and the house stood ready to welcome its invaders. In the dining room, the dark cherrywood table hosted an elaborate floral centerpiece and runner. The freshly polished, ornately carved chairs all sat atop a finely woven rug with a detailed paisley pattern. In the corner of the room, the sideboard stood ready to be laid out with food. In the foyer the side tables were topped with lace doilies and vases of fresh flowers. For those, James had allowed Charlotte to leave the house. The flower shop was just up the block, so he could keep an eye on her from a window.

He had been a nuisance all day, following after Charlotte as she did her chores, making sure everything was tidied up exactly to his specifications. She did most of the work, but he was treading behind her, fussing with the details, rearranging the knickknacks on a side table and wiping down doorknobs. His promises of change the evening before notwithstanding, in the light of day he was back in far more irritating form. But his working her nerves wasn't enough to distract Charlotte from her panic. A house full of guests was one thing, but the unexpected guest in the attic had disoriented her completely.

All day, she braced for a knock at the front door to bring the whole scheme tumbling down. Would it be the police who showed up and threw her in jail for stealing Evie? Would Kate show up herself with slave catchers to drag all three of them—Charlotte, Evie, and James too—back to White Oaks? Or maybe James would just take a notion to visit the attic, find Evie, and send her back to Kate himself. There was no end to the ways everything might go wrong. As much practice as Charlotte had with pretending, bluffing her way through the party in a mask of servile normalcy still felt near impossible. She willed herself to look and act calm. *Just get through tonight, and we can move Evie to the safe house, where she belongs.*

At least Darcel was doing his part to lighten the mood. When Charlotte finally finished preparing the front of the house to her father's satisfaction, she went back to the kitchen.

"What else do we need to do?" she asked.

"You mean besides hush up and get out of the way?" Darcel retorted. Charlotte snorted with laughter. Darcel was still smarting over James's decision to bring in caterers, and he wasn't above mockery to take out some of the sting.

"Come on, let's straighten up in here before they arrive," said Charlotte.

Together, they wiped down every surface in the kitchen, from the countertops to the cabinet doors. Next, they cleared space. The way Charlotte had heard it at the Marions', caterers brought in their own more sophisticated versions of everything and would have no use for most of the items already in the kitchen. That meant taking Darcel's prized knife block and sharpener and carefully tucking them into a cupboard, and moving the flour, sugar, and salt canisters off the countertop and into the pantry.

As they shuffled through the kitchen, Darcel muttered to himself in what sounded like a mix of English and French, his accent as pronounced as ever. Charlotte moved silently.

After what felt like no time at all, the clock struck five and right on the last chime, a sharp knock came at the side door.

"Nice to see you again, Miss Charlotte," Charles Marion said over the threshold, his voice smooth. "Is Mr. Vaughn available?"

"Of course, come in, I'll let him know you're here," Charlotte said. As the rest of his staff stayed outside, unloading the supplies from their carriage, Charlotte escorted Charles to wait in the parlor while she went to fetch James.

Upstairs, he took a moment to answer her knock, so she spoke through the bedroom door. "The caterers are here. Mr. Marion's waiting for you in the parlor." She was about to go back downstairs when the door opened.

Standing before her was a man transformed. James wore a formal evening coat and britches with rich accents throughout: sterling silver buttons on his jacket, and a silver watch chain hanging from the pocket on his right breast.

What was most striking wasn't his outfit, though. It was his face. The powdery scent wafting off him was overpowering. He was almost completely clean-shaven, and had made himself up to look even whiter than usual. That was no mean feat, considering how pale he already was from carefully avoiding the spring sun. It was subtle, not the sort of thing one would notice if they didn't see him every day. That, and his hair. Living with James her whole life, Charlotte knew by now that his hair was the most dangerous part of his entire charade. If it got too long, his loose, deep brown curls frizzed in a way that invited second glances, ones that lingered as people tried to figure out exactly who and what they were looking at. He'd have none of that tonight. The hair was trimmed and firmly slicked down. Behind James, the vanity table sat in disarray—every lid opened, brushes and puffs askew.

"How do I look?" Anxiety and excitement were written all over his powdered face.

"Oh, you look just so," she said. Per his instructions, Charlotte was unadorned in comparison, dressed in her plainest dark brown dress with her hair pulled back into a neat braid, which she covered with a small maid's cap. She had no reason to look especially nice tonight, just presentable enough to open the door and take coats when people arrived, then disappear entirely.

"Coming down?"

James cleared his throat and smoothed his suit jacket, then fell in step behind Charlotte as she headed down to the parlor.

"Nice to see you again, Charles," said James, extending a hand to Mr. Marion.

"Likewise, Mr. Vaughn. We've brought everything we need, I just wanted to check in with you and ensure there were no special instructions beyond what we discussed already."

"None at all, you have my complete confidence. I could not be more thrilled to showcase your renowned cookery at our party this evening," said James.

"You're far too kind, sir. I hope to live up to your lofty expectations."

The two laughed genially, formally. Charlotte merely stood by, momentarily forgotten, until James gestured her way.

"Charles, Charlotte helps Darcel out in the kitchen sometimes, and knows the house better than anyone," he said, beaming at her with something well short of fatherly pride. "She'll help you find everything you need."

She led him back. Darcel stood at the doorway of the pantry with his hands clasped behind him in a facsimile of a butler's formal stance. Charles extended a hand.

"Charles Marion. How do you do?"

"Nice to have you here with us, Charles," said Darcel with plain insincerity. "Darcel Boudier."

Charles smiled and leaned in close.

"Ah, Darcel—Mr. Boudier. What island do you come to us from? Or was it your folks?"

Darcel's look of surprise melted into a beaming smile at the question.

"Saint-Domingue! Left when I was just a boy. Are you—?"

"No, my family's been in the States for a few generations now, but I get around," said Charles. "I'm sure I've got plenty to learn from you this evening; chefs from the islands are some of the best there are."

Charlotte stifled the urge to laugh. Darcel was at war with himself. Any fool could see he was being charmed, but he seemed to be deciding that he didn't mind it all that much.

For the next ten minutes, Charlotte trailed along as Darcel walked Charles through the kitchen, pantry, and dining room while they traded stories about their culinary victories and their most complicated dishes. She wasn't sure they remembered she was even there, but soon Charles turned to her and said, "Pardon me, Miss, would you be so kind as to go and let our servers know I'm ready for them to come in?"

By the time Charlotte got outside, all three of the young men were loitering near the side door, arms full of trays of food and fine china, just waiting for the word. There Alex stood—he was dressed in his finest, but something about his face looked strange. As she peered at him more closely, Charlotte could've sworn she saw the fading shadow of a black eye, badly concealed under face powder. She wondered what could've happened to him and wanted to ask if he was all right. And apart from that, she was practically bursting to tell him about Evie. But as she led all the men inside and offered them the same tour Darcel had given Charles, Alex hung back with the others, frustratingly just out of her reach.

After showing them around, Charlotte deposited the whole catering crew back in the kitchen so they could begin their work while she and Darcel prepared to slowly fade into the background of their own home. They watched from the side hall as the caterers picked up the runner Charlotte had laid on the table and replaced it with two tablecloths of their own, a smooth red fabric and a white lace overlay, perfectly centered. Next, they laid out their own set of china, complete with soup bowls, entrée and salad plates, crystal goblets, and more silverware at each place setting than Charlotte had ever seen in her life. Alex walked around the table with a small measuring stick to make sure the spacing between place settings was precisely even.

As the sun went down, Charles and Darcel retreated to the kitchen, and from the dining room Charlotte could hear them chatting like old friends as the scent of what smelled like seafood soup wafted through the doorway. There came a tap on her shoulder.

"Maybe you can help me to smooth out this tablecloth," Alex said when she turned around. The other waiters had stepped away.

Charlotte looked at him, then at the already perfectly smooth tablecloth, then back at him again. "Of course," she answered brightly, then lowered her voice as she spoke again. "But what on earth happened to your face?"

"Oh, this?" he said, gesturing at his eye and trying to sound casual. "It turns out my editorial wasn't very popular in some circles."

Charlotte gasped and shook her head sadly. "Oh, Alex, I'm so sorry."

"It's all right. I'm back on my feet now, and undeterred as ever," he said, waving away her concern. "Is this why you've looked so worried since we arrived? I assumed it wasn't just about the dinner party."

"No, not just that. Evie took off from her mistress's house," Charlotte murmured, pretending to flatten the tablecloth with her hand in case someone wandered in. "She's here. Upstairs."

Alex started to look upward, but Charlotte yanked the tablecloth, trying to signal him not to draw any attention in that direction. Instead, he stumbled forward against the table in surprise, and its legs scraped loudly across the floor.

"Everything all right in there?" Darcel called from the kitchen.

"We're fine!" Alex called back. Then he spoke again more quietly, pulling the table back into place with a small smile. "Sorry," he said to Charlotte. "But what's the problem? This is good news, right? She's out, so the hard part's over."

"Not over, just different," said Charlotte. "We can't get her out of town until the end of the conference in a few days. Kate's likely to come looking for her before then, and she was supposed to be at a safe house, not here. Who knows what kind of trail she left?"

"Trail? I don't expect they'll send hounds after her through the city streets. We just need to hold on for a few days," he said. "We"— that was easy for him to say. He wasn't the one with a fugitive in his attic.

She watched with disappointment as Alex walked back into the kitchen.

Guests would be arriving any moment. Charlotte took a deep

breath and headed to her place in the side hallway, ready to receive the arrivals and take their coats.

By 7:15, the knocks on the door were coming fast and furious. A husband-and-wife couple here, an older and very businesslike man there. James stood in the foyer beaming at people as he greeted them, paying Charlotte no mind whatsoever. She started off annoyed by the whole procession, but eventually it became rote and almost hypnotic, lulling her into calm despite the potential powder keg upstairs. Charlotte went through the motions countless times: take a coat, walk it back to the closet, hang it up, and repeat.

As she worked, she watched her father out of the corner of her eye. With the evening in full swing, he stepped fully into his persona: James Vaughn, artisan carpenter and sophisticated business owner all wrapped up into one. And of course, white. White, white, white, from the way he'd powdered his face and slicked down his hair to the strange reedy tenor in his voice as he welcomed people and talked to them. It was the first time Charlotte had seen this version of him in full bloom, and she found it embarrassing to watch.

But the guests were enthralled. One person after another exclaimed over what a grand discovery they'd made in his work, and how they longed to have a *JV* original in their very own homes. It appeared Mr. Wilcox and his monied interests had successfully greased James's induction into the upper crust, just as he'd wished.

At about forty-five minutes past the hour, the final guests came straggling along, a little more than fashionably late. Charlotte opened the door for them. She saw two couples, the first an older man with graying hair and his much younger, red-haired wife. But it was the second pair that stopped Charlotte's heart.

There, in the doorway just a few inches away from Charlotte's outstretched fingers, stood an elegant man with jet-black hair, and his companion: a brown-haired white woman with a pinched face and gray eyes like deep filthy pools. She locked eyes with Charlotte and her mouth fell open in shock. Charlotte very nearly dropped the coat the man was handing her as he stepped over the threshold.

"Excuse me!" he said as she fumbled. At the sound of his voice, the woman regained her composure and spoke before Charlotte could say a word. It was Kate.

"It's all right, dear, let's hurry inside. We're already late. Here," she said, handing over her coat. She looked more unkempt than Charlotte remembered. Without Evie around to tend to her hair and dressing, she must have been on her own or in unfamiliar hands. But if Kate was feeling at all unsteady, it barely showed.

"The parlor is this way?" she asked, gesturing to the left and peering intently into the room. Charlotte managed a weak nod, and Kate and her companion breezed in to join the other guests.

Charlotte's heartbeat thundered in her ears as she struggled to understand what was happening, and she fought the urge to scream. While she headed toward the closet, she felt the air being squeezed out of her chest. Her body moved as if through tar. After she hung up their coats, she stood frozen, at a loss for what to do next.

It had been a full four years since she'd laid eyes on Kate, and in truth she didn't think about the woman very often. No, when Charlotte looked back on her time at White Oaks, she had not the slightest regret for leaving Kate behind, though she was sure her needy ex-mistress would have imagined otherwise. It had been Evie, Auntie Irene, and sweet Daniel that she missed—the family she'd come so close to being a part of, only to have her father rip her away from them on a whim. And all for what? So they could be hunted down and dragged back after a too-short taste of something like freedom?

She had to warn James. He'd been mingling with guests in the parlor, but as it got close to dinnertime, he'd disappeared into the kitchen. He had no idea what was waiting for him outside its warm, cozy confines.

As Charlotte hurried down the side hall, she felt a breeze. How fast was she moving? Was she running? Dazedly, she realized that in her shock she'd left the front door open. Wind was rushing into the house, rustling the flower petals in the vases.

She went back and shut the door, almost slamming it. Some guests stopped to stare before turning back to their conversations. The only look that lingered was Kate's. They locked eyes again, with

Kate looking strangely sad, as if there was some woundedness mixed in with whatever else she was feeling. Charlotte couldn't understand what Kate was doing. If she was here to take them, why join the party?

Before Charlotte could get into the kitchen, her father rushed out.

"What was that? Did you slam the door?" he hissed. He didn't stop moving even as he spoke to her.

"Not on purpose," Charlotte said quickly. "Wait, please, I need to talk to you!" She tried to hurry after him but feared she'd come into view of the people in the parlor again. She stopped short before crossing the doorway, even as James kept moving.

"Whatever it is can wait, I've got guests." Before she could pull him back, he stepped into the parlor. He put a jovial tone back into his voice as he addressed the group.

"My apologies for the wait, but we're making sure everything is shipshape. I hope you brought your appetites!"

Wilcox piped up in the background. "And your wallets and purses!" Everyone tittered with laughter at that, and Wilcox, who was already in his cups, pressed on. "Mr. Vaughn's star is on the rise, and you need only look around at the beautiful pieces here in the house to see why. You won't want to leave without one of your own, and it's my hope that many of you will want to invest even beyond that."

Striking a note of false modesty, James interjected. "All right, Ethan, let's not lay it on too thick now," he said, laughing. "But please, come on through, everyone, we're just about ready to be served." He gestured from the parlor into the dining room. Mr. Marion stood at the dining room door, welcoming each guest in with a graceful sweep of his hand.

Frozen to her spot, peeking around the doorframe, Charlotte watched the whole scene unfold like two carriages colliding. The guests walked by in clumps, and then, suddenly, James saw Kate and the laughter died in his throat.

James stared into her face, speechless with horror, and she stared back. Mr. Wilcox must've seen the strange tableau too. He hurried to James's side to introduce his guests: Mr. Henry Brooks and his fiancée, Miss Kate Jackson. Miss? *Jackson?*

Kate stared at James and extended a hand, her face a perfect mask of polite indifference. "Pleased to make your acquaintance, Mr. Vaughn," she said. Her extended hand invited him to kiss it. He looked baffled. Charlotte could see him working out the angles of the situation in his head as he quickly recovered and took her hand. He hesitated a moment before placing a polite peck on the back.

"Charmed, I'm sure," he said.

Kate's smile didn't reach her eyes. From Charlotte's vantage, it was a warning.

"Kate has been visiting in the city these last few months," said Mr. Brooks. "Though I hope she'll be a more regular fixture in the future, at my side." With mock casualness, Kate tilted her left hand so the light from the chandelier caught the jewel in her ring.

"Yes, it's such an interesting place, though it surely is different from the life I knew back in Virginia," said Kate, laughing.

Virginia? For all Charlotte had tried to forget about White Oaks, there was one thing she knew for certain: it was in Maryland. Apparently James wasn't the only one who'd invented a whole new past. Evie had mentioned Kate was engaged, but this was one wrinkle she'd left out.

With the guests filing into the dining room, Charlotte retreated to the kitchen and ran headlong into Alex, who was standing there with a tray of warm cloths diners could use to wipe their hands before the meal. A few sloshed to the floor, and he and Charlotte bumped heads as they both knelt to pick them up. When she met his eye, he stared back at her with concern.

"You all right?"

She shrugged helplessly. Where to begin? But Alex couldn't wait long for an answer.

Charlotte lingered in the pantry as the evening went on, peeking out into the dining room with panicked, morbid curiosity. Seeing Kate with this new suitor was strange. He was a far cry from the old

man she'd been hitched to at White Oaks, and it was hard to miss
how every other minute Kate gazed at him adoringly.

Soon, everyone was seated. The dinner was the portrait of James's
dreams, turned to a nightmare: a sea of wealthy white faces around
his precious cherrywood table, welcoming him into their society at
last. Except by some misadventure, he'd invited the very woman
who could destroy his life.

Charlotte listened with a mix of shock and pity as he stumbled
over his words during the first course, trying to describe his all-
important workshop expansion. Once he even mixed up the names
of two different chair styles he carved, one of which had become
among his most sought-after pieces. His eyes darted around the table
but studiously avoided where Kate and her companion were sitting,
as if by not meeting her gaze he could make her disappear from his
presence. As James faltered, it fell to the increasingly lubricated Mr.
Wilcox to make his business case.

Having lived on the Murphy plantation nearly all her life, Charlotte knew a drunken white man when she saw one. The glassy eyes,
the flush of red in the cheeks, the way the words slid over one another and stuck together like he was talking with a mouthful of
maple syrup. Still, even as far gone as Wilcox seemed to be, the other
guests found his act charming. They were eating out of his hand; so
much the better for James.

Charlotte remained in the pantry doorway, transfixed. She automatically moved out of the caterers' way as they came through with
each course. One set down a plate in front of James, bearing a fillet
of flounder drizzled with a brandy-colored fish sauce. With the food
on the table, guests chatted and swapped stories. Henry Brooks's was
a familiar one: he was a son of the South who'd made his fortune first
in cotton planting and now owned textile mills that stretched up
even into the North. When the dinner conversation turned to the
subject of all the building going on in the city, it wasn't long before
the guests started chatting about Pennsylvania Hall. With the official
opening under way and apparently causing a stir in town, everyone

seemed to have an opinion on it. That included Henry, who—though not native to Philadelphia—had plenty to say about local goings-on.

"It's brave of you to set down roots in a city like this, Mr. Vaughn," he said. "I'm afraid I've nearly had my fill of it, with all the division being sown by abolitionist types and their provocations, like this building. It's a damn shame the wild ideas they're putting into the darkies' heads."

The caterers' backs stiffened at that, and Alex cut an angry glance in Henry's direction. Around the table, there were nods and uncomfortable murmurs.

"You're so right, Henry," said Kate, glancing at James. "It's knowing these types of folks are up here that tempts so many slaves into running off, shirking their responsibilities at home to chase after heaven knows what. I cannot tell you how many perfectly good slaves I've seen ruined by this sort of thing."

Charlotte's heartbeat picked up. Kate was talking about her, and James—and wanted them to know it. But then why hadn't she exposed him yet, and exposed this whole dinner—this whole life—for the charade it was? Charlotte racked her brain trying to figure out why Kate was behaving so strangely, until the worst possibility pushed itself forward in her mind: that Kate was simply preserving her good manners by not making a scene, before coming back to snatch them in the dead of night. As the conversation kept unfolding in its terrible normalcy, Charlotte began to sweat under her uniform.

"People ought to just live and let live, I say—not spend so much time worried about Southern folks' way of life," Henry said, nodding. "Eh, Vaughn? Don't you agree?"

In the pause that followed, Charlotte imagined a thousand different things James might say—even wished for a few. But the next voice she heard was Wilcox's.

"I tell you what, with all this building going on, it seems to me more folks are going to be in the market for fine furnishings!"

Nervous, grateful laughter broke out around the table as Wilcox

steered the conversation back to safer waters. But James was still rattled. He'd hardly touched his fish, and the caterers were clearing
people's plates for the next course: veal, roasted beets, English peas,
and fingerling potatoes covered with an aromatic gravy. James had
done at least one thing right for the evening when he hired the Marions to cater dinner: it was clear they knew their business.

"Tell me, Mr. Vaughn, have you any family nearby?" asked another guest. "It's hard to imagine a successful tradesman like yourself
getting by all on his own." Kate looked off into the distance.

"Oh, I do fine on my own," James said. "I suppose I've become
set in my ways over the years."

"Not all by yourself, of course, James! He's got himself an excel-
lent cook, and a little Negro maid who keeps house for him. Otherwise, though, yes, quite the lonesome bachelor!" crowed Wilcox.
James forced a laugh, but his face had somehow turned even whiter.
Wilcox, too far gone to read any cues from his panicked business
partner, plowed on.

"Best of all, at the workshop James's got himself a full fleet of
helpers too. Things have really turned around since that unpleasant-
ness a few years ago." Several guests awkwardly cleared their throats.
Wilcox hiccuped. "That is, there's always room for growth, looking
to the future."

James nodded again, and forced out an unenthusiastic "Quite
right." Just in time, another guest jumped into the conversation and
pulled the focus from a relieved James. But even with the attention
away from him, he looked like he was going to be sick.

The caterers cleared the table once more, and dessert soon followed: a sticky sweet raspberry sponge cake, warm from the oven
and topped with Parmesan ice cream—one of the Marions' decadent
signature dishes. Seeing it go by, Charlotte inhaled sharply. Without
realizing it, she'd been lulled into calm as everyone stayed in their
seats at the table. But dessert meant they'd soon go back into the parlor for drinks, conversation, and more mingling. With everyone
moving freely, Kate might say anything, do anything.

As the cake slices were set on the table, the blood rushed away from Charlotte's head. She tried to steady herself against the counter in the pantry, but silently, slowly, she lost her grip. Before she could hit the floor, a pair of wiry, strong arms caught her.

"Hang on there," Alex said, with a note of alarm. "Here, come with me." He helped her shuffle back into the kitchen, where she slid down against the wall beside the doorway.

With the hard floor underneath her, Charlotte felt grounded enough to catch her breath. She felt the smooth, reassuring wall against her back and focused her eyes on the wooden front of the kitchen counter, streaked with stray lines of flour from the evening's cooking. Blood was still rushing in her ears, but Alex's voice pierced through.

"Are you all right? Charlotte? Charlotte!"

"What?"

"I asked if you're all right," he repeated. "What happened out there?"

She shook her head, as much in response to his question as to try to force herself fully into the present. Collecting herself, Charlotte remembered the small matter of the fugitive in the attic. She needed to get Evie out of the house before Kate could take her, but with the evening winding down, their chance was on the verge of evaporating. There was only one solution.

"Alex, you have to take Evie with you," she said.

He looked at her like she'd lost her mind, but then Charlotte stood up and pulled him to the pantry door. She pointed into the dining room toward Kate. "That woman—she's Evie's mistress. She's found us. Found her, I mean. I don't know what she's playing at right now, but we have to get Evie out of here before she goes looking for her," Charlotte said.

"How can you know that's Evie's mistress?"

This wasn't the moment to tell Alex her whole sordid history. Instead, Charlotte reached for a lie, and her mind grabbed hold of Kate's jewelry. "That huge emerald ring she's wearing, Evie told me about it. How many of those can there be in the world?" She paused, wondering if he even believed her. Probably safest to move on. "Can you take Evie out with you and get her someplace safe?"

He considered for a moment and nodded. "My father will know what to do."

And so it was settled. Dazed but decided, Charlotte made her way upstairs.

Chapter 30

———

EVIE

———

THE NOISE FROM THE PARTY CARRIED ALL THE WAY TO THE ATTIC. Evie couldn't make out particular words or voices in the din, but the clinking of crystal and china, the uproars of laughter—those came through clear enough. Must be some kind of life Uncle Jack had built here, rich and at ease enough to entertain in such style. And it wasn't just downstairs that made clear how different this house was from the old cabins at White Oaks.

Alone in Carrie's room, Evie took the measure of the place. The space was small, an echo of her room at the Jacksons' town house, except that this room at least had a window. But all around, there were little touches that made it feel lived in, like a haven for Carrie or even like a home: the frayed blue quilt draped over the bottom half of the bed, a handful of dried purple flowers on the nightstand, and all the books piled high on the desk, looking like they'd tumble down at the slightest touch.

So very many books. Evie stood beside the desk, picking them up and turning them over in her hands, flipping through the pages and peering at the lettering on the spines. She couldn't make heads or tails of any of it, of course, and found herself wondering how Carrie had become so well read. Then she remembered, not Carrie now— Charlotte.

She'd heard that here in the North there were schools where Black women and men could learn different ways of making a living, and also be taught the basics of arithmetic and reading. Maybe Charlotte spent her days here doing that, going to school and learning to read so that now she was the kind of person with books in her room.

One thing was plain, Charlotte wasn't spending the time cleaning. Though Evie had said nothing about it, on the way upstairs she'd taken note of just how dusty the house and the attic were, like they'd been neglected for months or even years. So yes, maybe school. Evie wouldn't put it past Uncle Jack to arrange that for her, especially since it seemed the two of them were living pretty high here in the city.

Maybe school was where Charlotte had met this woman she was so convinced could help Evie escape, this Nell. As she sat there waiting for Charlotte to come back upstairs as the party went on, irritation and suspicion washed over Evie. She wanted to believe what Charlotte had said—that she'd missed her and only wanted to help. But with Charlotte's fancy new home and all her books to read and these new friends of hers who were supposedly so smart, and so powerful, what use could Charlotte have for her abandoned little play-sister?

At least Charlotte had promised she wouldn't have to go back to Kate. That alone was worth all this trouble. High above the streets in the close, stuffy attic, Evie felt strangely light and free, with no one there, no one expecting anything from her, no Kate weighing her down with the sheer mass of her bottomless need.

That sense of being unburdened stayed with Evie, though on some level she understood the burden she had now put on Charlotte and puzzled over the strange way she seemed to be carrying it. The oddest part was that she hadn't told Uncle Jack about any of it.

Evie pulled her legs in tighter, looking around the room. Where was Uncle Jack now? She fought the temptation to go downstairs and peek in on the party, to see this strange new creature Charlotte said her father had turned into. That morning, Evie had asked Charlotte straight out why she hadn't confided in him. She'd flinched a little at the question, or maybe at the sound of her father's old name—Evie couldn't tell. So many of their interactions were guess-work now instead of the easy, familiar grooves that used to run be-tween them. Their loss was the work of four years and hundreds of miles.

But Charlotte had sighed and turned to look Evie in the eye. "He calls himself James now," she said. After a pause, she continued. "Honestly, I can't say for sure whether he'd be glad to see you or not, whether he'd try to help or . . . I don't even know what."

"What do you mean? You're telling me he's got something against slaves running away from folks? That's rich," Evie had said, incredu-lous.

Charlotte had shrugged, and when she spoke there was a note of sadness in her voice. "I don't know how to explain it, exactly, but he's moved beyond all that. Or he thinks he has. I don't know that he'd even see himself as one of us anymore, or you as the same as him. Everything he does now is with an eye toward passing for white and building up his business. That's what this dinner is all about. He's actually getting to be pretty well known."

For someone sharing the story of her own father's success, Char-lotte hadn't had even the barest hint of pride in her voice. She had sounded weary, and disappointed.

In the hours since, Evie had gone rifling through Charlotte's desk and armoire, looking for something to do. She didn't find much be-yond a set of brightly colored dresses, Charlotte's sewing kit, pack-ages and magazines, some yarn, and a pair of her knitting needles. Evie was sitting in the corner halfheartedly starting a pair of socks when Charlotte came back through the door.

"Sounds like folks are enjoying themselves down there," Evie said. She knew she sounded grumpy.

Charlotte was in a hurry. "You've got to come downstairs with me, now—Kate's here."

Evie stood and dropped the needles, backing away from the door until she hit the wall at the far end of the attic, and there was no-where left for her to go.

"I'm not going down there," she said, struggling not to scream. "I can't go back to her! You promised!"

Charlotte gasped and took a step back. "I wouldn't do that. How could you think I would do that?" All the rush had gone out of her voice. She sounded hurt.

Evie folded her arms and looked at the ground. "I knew it, I knew you didn't want me here." She felt small, and suddenly very alone. How could she have believed Charlotte would actually take care of her? Still, how could Charlotte dare to bring Kate here to her and James's own house? Wasn't it as dangerous for them as it was for Evie?

But Charlotte shook her head firmly. "No. No. It's not that—" A burst of laughter from downstairs cut her off, and Charlotte snapped to attention again. "Evie, please, there's no time. Just let me get you out of here, and we can talk more later. We'll take the back stairs so Kate doesn't see you. My friend is going to take you somewhere safe, but we don't have a lot of time. Please, come on."

She seemed to have no end of friends in this town.

"Just me? Shouldn't you leave too?" Evie asked, wary.

Charlotte looked tempted but shook her head.

"No, she's already seen me. I've got to stay and hash things out with my father, and Darcel. But I'll come for you," she said. Evie looked at her skeptically. "I will."

Evie still hesitated. She wanted to trust Charlotte, but she knew Charlotte had every reason to want Evie gone. Even so, in that moment the only way out was to do as she was told and hope Charlotte would keep her word—otherwise Evie might as well just march downstairs and turn herself over to Kate right then.

Charlotte was just getting ready to step out of the room when she turned around like she'd forgotten something. She grabbed a bag holding a package wrapped in brown paper and handed it to Evie. "Take this, please."

Reluctantly, Evie tucked the bag under her arm, gripping it carefully so the paper didn't make a sound as she followed Charlotte out of the attic. They tiptoed down the back stairs, and at the bottom there was a young man with reddish brown hair waiting for them with a pushcart that held a few pieces of china.

"Get in," he said.

Evie hesitated. "It's all right," said Charlotte. "This is Alex. We can trust him. You'll be safe now."

"But what about you?"

"I'll be just fine. I'll come and find you tomorrow," Charlotte said abruptly. Evie went quiet. It was clear Charlotte wanted to cut her off before she said too much, and Evie felt her frustration and suspicion rising. "Alex, will you get a message to Nell for me and tell her what's happened?"

"Of course," he said. Evie squeezed herself into the pushcart, tucking her knees up to her chest and folding her head forward. When she was settled, she heard Alex whistle to another of the caterers. She felt them roll the cart through the kitchen and out a back door. Inside the cart, the sound of the wheels bumping over the cobblestone was impossibly loud, and the constant thumps set Evie's teeth rattling. After a moment, she felt herself be lifted into the back of a carriage, and soon they drove off.

She was rumbled and bumped through the streets for several blocks, until at last they came to a stop. She managed to peek out of the cart. It was hard to see, but it looked like they were at a storefront or some sort of business. In the glow of the moon, there was a sign above the door, but she couldn't read it.

Around back, Evie climbed out of the cart and Alex gestured for her to stay quiet. He brought Evie around to the side of the carriage and helped her in while his father explained they were taking her to their house, where she'd be safe. Unsure what else to do, Evie simply said "Thank you" and rode along in silence. As they moved through the city, she pressed herself back against the plush carriage seat, well away from the window. It was dark, but after the night she'd had so far, she didn't want to take any chances.

When the carriage finally came to a stop, Alex opened the door and stuck his head out to make sure no one was watching. "All clear," he said. "Come quickly."

He helped Evie down, and in an instant rushed her into the large, looming house. Quietly, he guided her upstairs.

ONCE AGAIN, EVIE FOUND herself tucked away in an unfamiliar room in an unfamiliar house. The moonlight streamed in through the window of the upstairs room she'd been brought to, shining onto the door of the crawl space Evie was told to retreat into if trouble came knocking. Alex had given her a candle, which she set on the table beside the bed, where she now sat with her hands folded in her lap. Unable to sleep, she looked around, taking in the room: the plush crimson-colored curtains and the carved four-poster bed with a deep-blue canopy that looked and smelled freshly laundered.

Alex's parents and brother soon appeared. They treated her gingerly, carrying up warm tea and a plateful of food.

After setting her up in there, for the most part they left her on her own, but said to ring the bell if she needed anything. This was the sort of place that had bells to be rung, and with Black folks doing the ringing instead of just the stepping-to. The catering business clearly kept the Marion family in the kind of comfort Evie had only seen belong to slave owners; in fact, the place was even more finely appointed than the Jacksons' town house across the city. That made Evie smile. She might have gone just a few blocks, but she was worlds away from Kate's family house now.

But even safe as she was, as the night continued, Evie's panic curdled, growing sharper and more sour by the minute. Left alone and waiting yet again, she tried and failed to force aside the thought that maybe Charlotte and James had gone on to save themselves and simply forgotten about her. The one person she could be sure wouldn't forget about her was Kate.

As she tried to calm down, Evie sat on the edge of the bed with the package from Charlotte in her lap and opened it. Inside was a beautiful pale blue dress the color of Evie's favorite irises at White

Oaks, with embroidery on the sleeves in the same yellow as the marigolds Charlotte had always worn in her hair.

She ran a hand over the fabric and stitching—Charlotte's own work, hours and days of it, all for her. Thoughts of their garden came rushing back: little hands in the dirt, flowers in their hair, bright pops of color in the spring sunshine. She'd been remembered after all.

But was this gift an apology, or a goodbye?

Chapter 31

CHARLOTTE

As the party wound down in the parlor, James and Kate saw their mutual charade through to the end, mingling within each other's orbits but carefully avoiding direct contact—two magnets with the same charge, repelling each other. Once Evie was safely out of the house, Charlotte had gone back to the side hallway to keep watching the whole strange dance, until finally Kate and Henry decided to leave. At the front door, she handed them back their coats without a word. Kate seemed to look through her, and just as quickly, they were gone.

The remaining guests would have to get their own coats. Charlotte had had enough. Upstairs, she peeled off her uniform, balled it up, and threw it into a corner of the attic. Everything to do with this night she wanted as far away from her as she could get it. But voices wafted up from the parlor; the party was still going on—James was still going on, somehow. Charlotte changed into a nightgown, pulled the blanket off her bed, spread it out on the floor, and lay down. She needed to feel hard floor beneath her tonight, to be rooted in a sense of place, otherwise her mind would pull her back to White Oaks. She wouldn't let it. And come to that, she wouldn't let Kate do it either.

Charlotte stared up at the ceiling for what felt like hours until she heard the last guest leave, and the door shut behind them. The night had gone late, and there could be only a few hours until dawn now.

She heard glasses clinking as Darcel and James gathered up the remnants of the last guests' drinks from the parlor. Her father would come up soon, no doubt, before retreating to his own bedroom and—what? Collapsing from the sheer panic and adrenaline? Smugly admiring himself in the mirror for having gotten away with it all?

The way Kate had behaved, someone who didn't know them would've had no idea she and James had ever set eyes on each other before. But Charlotte had seen Kate's wide-eyed horror at the start of the evening, then watched it quickly subside as she resumed her role as a carefree, sociable Southern belle. Kate's emotional swings were more than legible to Charlotte—they were the rhythm by which she'd lived the first fifteen years of her life.

But why? Why hadn't Kate given them away?

Charlotte went over every detail of the night in her head. The catch in Kate's voice when she was "introduced" to James. The way she'd immediately scanned the room, undoubtedly looking for Evie. Then there were her opulent clothes, nicer than anything she'd ever worn at White Oaks, and her man. That man. The way she'd clung to Henry, slipped her arm through his and refused to unlock him for even a moment until they'd been seated for dinner. In all her years at White Oaks, Charlotte had never seen Kate hold fast to Massah Murphy with that much determination, or that much affection. Not once.

People said she had been young when she'd wed Massah Murphy, no more than twenty-two years old. Many had wondered why the two of them never had any children but figured it was just down to old Murphy's age and ill health. He'd had a fondness for his own tobacco, fine wines, and rich foods, and brooked no limits when it came to indulging himself. No one was terribly surprised when he'd keeled over and died one night at the dinner table, and Kate herself didn't seem too heartbroken about it either. Now here she was in a new city, acting the blushing bride-to-be of some rich young man like the whole thing had never happened.

As Charlotte lay awake on the floor replaying the evening in her mind, sure enough she heard her father's footsteps and then a knock on her door. What usually was a gentle rapping was now insistent. He walked right in. Startled, Charlotte stood up and didn't wait for him to speak. She'd had a terrifying night, and her stress and anger boiled over at the sight of his hangdog face lit by her window's dawn light.

"You *had* to invite all those people, didn't you?" she said, feeling her nostrils flare. "After everything you did to keep me from exposing us, it was *you* who invited Kate to our doorstep!"

James sighed. "Wilcox made the guest list," he said. "Her name— it was different. And she behaved so strangely tonight. As if none of our lives before had ever happened." He wrinkled his forehead and stood there thinking. As much confusion as there was in his voice, there also seemed to be curiosity. Calmer, Charlotte slowly sat down on her bed and listened.

"Perhaps she doesn't want to make trouble for me. For us," he said, correcting himself. "Maybe we can make some kind of deal and she'll leave us in peace. But what could we offer?"

Charlotte glanced at the doorway behind him, suddenly grateful she'd gotten Evie out of the house when she did.

"We've got no business trying to haggle with Kate," she said. "We ought to just leave her alone."

James shook his head, as if something Charlotte said had woken him up. "No, of course, you're right. It would be foolish to make ourselves vulnerable to her. We cannot stay here. We have to go, right away." The finality in his voice was undercut with sadness, but he seemed resigned.

Charlotte stood up in alarm. She wouldn't be so easily shuffled off into the night.

"No, wait—I didn't mean we should run," she said. "There's plenty of middle ground between making deals with her and abandoning our lives here."

"No," said James. "I'll wind up my affairs at the workshop tonight and gather up what money I can from there. I don't know how long it'll take her to hire slave catchers, but we should leave as soon as possible. Pack our things while I'm gone, no more than we can easily carry, and we'll go north right away."

He was tripping over the words and could hardly get them out fast enough. His own speech was feeding his rising fear. Charlotte held up a hand to interrupt.

"And Darcel?" she said.

"What about him?" asked James.

"Shouldn't we do something to make sure he stays safe? They'll assume he helped us," she said. But James didn't seem concerned about their cook.

"Darcel will be paid out for his work and his troubles and then some, I won't leave the man adrift," James said, waving his hand.

Money. Never anything more than that. Paying him out his wages was hardly the point. To Charlotte, Darcel had become more than a fellow servant these last few months, and here was her father, ready to leave him with the blame for their choices.

"We'll leave as soon as I return from the workshop," he repeated.

Charlotte said nothing as he walked out. It wasn't worth arguing, not yet anyway. If Alex did as Charlotte had asked, Nell would come to the house first thing and they'd be able to sort things out for Evie, at least. That still left the matter of Charlotte's own freedom, which now hung in the balance along with everyone else's.

But with Evie set to be spirited away, and James ready to run, Charlotte had no idea where she fit into her own life anymore. And that wasn't a question anyone else could answer for her.

Chapter 32

———

NELL

———

Nell had been fast asleep when Beth-Anne knocked on her door to tell her Alex was downstairs. She'd glanced at the clock—12:30 a.m. Beth-Anne didn't say what he wanted, she only smiled and shrugged when a bewildered Nell asked why she'd let him in at all.

"Who am I to stand in the way of young love?"

Oh, for heaven's sake. As quietly as she could, Nell pulled on her blue-chiffon dressing gown over her nightclothes and unwrapped her hair, letting the cottony soft coils she usually pinned up fall lightly onto her shoulders.

Alex was waiting for her at the back door, just inside the kitchen, leaning against the wall. He straightened up when he saw her, and Nell's skin tingled as his eyes swept over the unusual way she'd appeared—all undone. For a moment, he just stared, unable to find words.

"Yes?" Nell prompted. "Alex, what is it? It's the middle of the night!"

That seemed to snap him out of it. "It's Charlotte, and Evie. Her mistress found them and showed up at the house tonight during Mr. Vaughn's dinner party. We were able to smuggle Evie out in a catering cart, but Charlotte's badly shaken and didn't know what to do next. She asked for you."

Nell put a hand over her mouth. What had Evie been doing there in the first place? That wasn't their plan. Something must've gone wrong.

"I'll go to her first thing. Where is Evie now?"

"We're getting her settled at our house, she'll be safe."

"We?" Nell repeated. Who else had been brought into this mess?

Alex took a deep breath. "My father and I. We have a safe room for runaways. He's my connection to the Vigilant Association—he knows everything. He has for some time."

Nell's mouth fell agape for a moment before she remembered herself. More and more, it felt like Nell knew far less than she thought she did. All this time she'd assumed she and Alex both needed their cover story, one as much as the other, since their parents were so conservative. It turned out the Marions weren't conservative at all. They were discreet.

"But then, does he know about us? Our engagement?" she asked.

Alex nodded.

"Then why on earth did you go along with it for so long?" she asked, incredulous.

"Because you needed me."

It was true. From the beginning, he'd done whatever she asked, and followed her lead—never getting in the way of her work, or her independence, but standing beside her and supporting it, all because that's what she needed.

In the late night's haze, the idea of how Alex might fit into her life after all—as more than a friend—seemed to come more clearly into focus. She took a deep breath and stepped toward him. "Alex—" she began.

But before she could speak her piece, Beth-Anne's stage whisper cut in from the next room: "Better hurry this up before your parents or your brother hear you stirring, Miss Nell."

Nell sighed, and laughed quietly. Always another interruption—with all the intrigue and emergency in their lives lately, it seemed impossible to slow down long enough to take stock of what their

engagement might really mean. Still, whatever was between her and
Alex had kept for this many years; she supposed it could wait a little
while longer.

"Coming," she whispered back to Beth-Anne. She turned to
Alex, took his hand, and gave it a squeeze. It was warm, and strong.
"Thank you for all of this, truly."

He doffed his nonexistent hat at her and was gone. The warmth
of his hand lingered in hers.

THE NEXT MORNING, WHEN Nell arrived at the row house, Charlotte
welcomed her in with a ragged voice and sunken eyes. She hadn't
slept all night—her uniform was a mess of wrinkles, and her hair
wasn't in its usual neat bun.

"Alex told me everything," Nell said, putting her arms around
Charlotte's shoulders. "How can I help?"

Charlotte took a deep breath, as if she was winding up to explain,
but just then the man from the other day—their cook, Nell guessed—
came into view at the back of the house, calling for her.

When he spotted Nell, he stopped short. "You again?" By the
friendly twinkle in his eye, Nell gathered he wasn't terribly surprised
to see her.

"I'm not so easily put off," she said with a smile. She turned to
Charlotte. "Why don't we go outside and talk things through?"
Some fresh air might do her friend some good.

Charlotte and Nell stepped out into the warm spring morning
and ambled down the block, headed nowhere in particular. Before
Charlotte could speak, Nell jumped straight to business; at a time
like this, her decisiveness was the best help she could offer.

"You needn't worry about Evie, she's quite safe with the Marions,
at least for a short while. But she cannot stay here in the city, not
with her mistress looking for her. Why don't we go down to the hall
today and see if we can move up our plans for her to leave town?
Think of it, Charlotte, she's nearly free already."

Charlotte looked at Nell wearily and nodded. "I'm lucky to have you on our side," she said. It seemed something more was weighing on her mind, but she only stared at the ground and kept walking. "Let's circle the block one more time. You were right, the fresh air is making me feel better."

As they moved down the sidewalk, Nell felt the unsettling sensation of a pair of eyes on her back. She stopped short, and Charlotte nearly tripped from the abrupt stop. Nell looked around, but there was nothing to see beyond women sitting at the windows of their row house parlors, watching the day go by. She tried to shake off the feeling.

They walked on in companionable silence for another block. Before long, Nell heard a third set of footfalls behind them, moving in step with their pace. Her shoulders tensed as she fought the urge to break into a run. Charlotte looped her arm through Nell's and drew her close.

"You hear that?" she asked.

Nell nodded. "Probably just someone going the same way as us, is all."

She was trying to convince herself as much as Charlotte.

"Let's turn back onto the main drag at the next block, get ourselves around more people," said Charlotte.

But before they could reach the next intersection, a pair of hands yanked Nell's shoulders from behind, breaking her away from Charlotte. Nell yelped in surprise, but too late for anyone to hear—whoever it was had already clapped a hand over her mouth. As Nell was dragged backward, she looked from left to right in search of Charlotte, who had disappeared. Maybe she'd gotten away. Maybe she'd be able get help—her cook, or Mr. Vaughn, someone. Anyone.

Nell couldn't see the face of the man dragging her along from behind, toward what she didn't know. She could only feel her feet scraping against the sidewalk as she desperately scrambled to regain her footing. But the man's arms were squeezed tight around her rib cage, with his fingernails digging into her flesh. She scratched and grabbed at his hands trying to pry herself loose, but his grip was so tight that the air was being crushed out of her lungs.

The man didn't release his hold on her until they turned in to a narrow alleyway, where he picked her up and tossed her into the back of a large wagon. She hit the wagon floor with a thud, and the man pulled her arms behind her back, sharply wrenching her shoulder. Before she could move away, he tightened a rope around her wrists, tied a cloth over her mouth, and threw a burlap blanket onto her head. There was no more seeing the street, or anything else.

As the wagon lurched forward, Nell struggled to breathe in the close, stale air under the blanket. It smelled of hay and chewing tobacco. Her mind grasped at straws, searching for any scrap of a reason why someone would assault her this way. Had her involvement with the Antislavery Society made her a target? Was it something to do with Charlotte and Evie?

Desperate for answers, she strained to hear what the men were saying at the front of the wagon as they rolled down the road.

"That was easier'n it shoulda been," one said with a drawl that made clear he was from somewhere down South.

"Well, they said there'd be a lighter-skinned one and a darker one—Carrie and Evie, the Jacksons called 'em. And we followed the lighter one right from her house, so it's for sure she's who we want," he said.

All right, so these men thought she was Evie. But who on earth was Carrie? As she racked her brain, someone reached out from beside her in the wagon, squeezing her hand. *Charlotte?* The friendly presence was a relief, but not nearly enough to assuage Nell's terror. For all she'd read about free Black people being snatched off the street in this city, she never truly imagined it would happen to her. Now she lay defenseless and aching, with every bump in the road making the coarse rope scrape against her skin and jarring the hurting places where the man's brutality had bruised her. Worse than the pain, a sense of helpless dread bore down on her body like lead.

With every inch the wagon rolled along the road, hauling her off to only heaven knew where, her panic rose. She wanted nothing so much as to go home to her family, where it was safe. But who could say she'd ever see home again? She wasn't sure what plans these coarse men had in store, but she knew with bone-deep certainty they wouldn't be anything good. Beneath the blanket, the air felt too thick to take in as Nell imagined her parents' worry, and with it their anger—she hadn't listened to them, and now look what she'd gotten herself into. Terror and shame crashed over her. She couldn't catch her breath, and before long, she was pulled under, and all went dark.

Chapter 33

CHARLOTTE

BENEATH A BLANKET AS THE WAGON ROLLED DOWN THE STREET, Charlotte clutched at whatever shreds of calm she could grasp. From the instant she heard the men's hideously familiar drawl, every nerve in her body awakened with alarm, a million tiny pinpricks underneath her skin. Her side was rubbed raw as she bumped and scraped against the hard bottom of the wagon. Panicked, she struggled to catch her breath.

Worse still, she felt utterly alone. Poor Nell's hand had gone slack in hers shortly after the wagon started moving—she'd likely fainted. Charlotte would've welcomed relief from consciousness herself, but the swirl of worst possible outcomes wouldn't let her mind rest. There was no mystery what was going on here: Kate had found her—the only question was how far these slave catchers would take her: to the town house Evie had run from, or all the way back to Maryland? For a moment, she considered taking her chances jumping out of the wagon and running, but she thought better of it—she couldn't leave Nell, not now.

But she didn't have much longer to stew in her fear; after a few city blocks and a handful of twists and turns, the wagon slowed down. With her arms lashed painfully behind her back, Charlotte wiggled herself to the edge of the blanket and lifted it with her head to steal a glance at their surroundings. Stretching out behind them was a narrow cobblestone road with three-story townhomes lining the sidewalks, each of them two lots wide—a testament to their owners' wealth. The roofs were obscured by huge old trees. By the look of it, they were still inside the city, but she couldn't guess just where. In the air, she smelled hints of silt and sulfur, a clue they weren't too far from the banks of the river.

The wagon made one more slow turn and then rolled forward a few yards before coming to a stop. It creaked and shifted as the men climbed down in front, and then their footsteps came around the side and grew closer, closer.

"Leave them," one voice said. "I'll go in and tell Mr. Jackson we've arrived. He'll know what the family wants done with them."

The second one grunted in response. His feet crunched on the gravel as he walked up to the house. The man who stayed behind paced around the wagon aimlessly. Under the blankets, Charlotte felt Nell stir and squeezed her hand.

"Everything will be all right now," she whispered, desperately willing herself to sound calm for her friend. "They didn't mean to take you—tell them you're not Evie and they'll let you go home," she said. They'd have other plans for Charlotte, no doubt, but there was no sense worrying Nell about that now.

But Nell was stubborn. Her head was still under the blanket, but her sharp "No" came through clear as a bell.

Charlotte grabbed her hand back as if she'd been burnt. "Nell, please—there's no need for you to get caught up in this!"

"We don't even know what *this* is," Nell retorted. *If only that were true.*

More crunching gravel. The other man was back. "Let's go," said the gruff voice. "They want them in the library. Sooner we dump these two the sooner we get paid."

One of them ripped the blanket off Charlotte's head, yanking out a tuft of her hair. The other uncovered Nell and then shoved them both unceremoniously out of the wagon and into a long alleyway. Bypassing the house's front door, the men dragged Nell and Charlotte around to a side entrance, untied their hands, and knocked softly.

The door opened right away, and a young white man stepped out. He looked Charlotte and Nell up and down like he was inspecting goods at the market. Under his gaze, Charlotte's skin crawled. She knew that impatient, appraising stare all too well, and felt sick to her stomach at the thought of what he'd do with her—*to* her—the minute he got the chance.

But as he stepped closer—enough for Charlotte to smell his sour breath—and squinted first into her face, then Nell's, his interested look hardened into fury. Splotches of red rose up under the skin on his neck.

"You damned fools!" he shouted, enraged. "Did you just grab the first pair of colored wenches you saw on the street?"

The two men murmured indignantly to each other, until one spoke out in a thick Southern accent.

"Now wait a minute! We know our business, and these here are the two colored girls Miss Jackson was looking for," he said. He jabbed a finger at Charlotte. "We snatched *her* up as soon as she stepped outside with the other one. We used the address Miss Jackson gave us!"

"Like hell you did," the man in the doorway said. He raised his cane and pointed it. "Neither one of these is Miss Jackson's maid. And did you hear either answer to the name of Carrie?"

The two kidnappers shuffled their feet and looked at the ground. Charlotte, too, stared down into the dust, avoiding Nell's eye.

"I thought as much," said the man with the cane. "Leave them, and get out of here. I'll sort this out myself." He stepped inside and grabbed a small bag, dumped out half the contents into one hand, then tossed the bag at the men with the other. The bag jingled and rustled with the mingled sounds of coins and folded money. "For your trouble, that's half the price we agreed upon." He stepped forward and pulled Charlotte and Nell into the house.

The two men stood at the threshold, one of them opening the bag to rifle through it.

"I'll thank you to count that elsewhere," the young man huffed.

"Should we still come back for the transport down South then?" one of the men asked. Charlotte's mouth went dry.

The young man didn't bother to answer the question—he scoffed and shut the door firmly in the kidnappers' shocked faces.

"You two will come with me," he said. Nell's body visibly stiffened, and her eyes went wide with panic. She was frozen to the spot until the man started shoving both women down a dim back hallway. Charlotte didn't resist. This wasn't her first experience with rough treatment—not by a long way—but now she'd dragged a dear friend into it, and the poor woman hardly even knew why it was happening. Nell looked over at her, but Charlotte could barely meet her eye.

There was no point in trying to bolt out the same door they came in; there was every chance they'd run into the kidnappers again if they did. With no idea where the other exits might be, there was nothing to do but to follow the young man. Charlotte heard someone call him Frank.

As they stepped from the hall into the parlor, light flooded Charlotte's eyes. The signs of wealth were everywhere. Velvet curtains lined the parlor windows, and a plush royal-purple couch formed the focal point of the room—a clothier had once told Charlotte that fabric dyed that shade cost a fortune since the color came from the crushed remains of a rare seashell. On the side tables were painted vases the likes of which she'd never seen, and delicate porcelain figurines of women in elaborate gowns.

As she looked around, Charlotte wondered whether it really was Kate who'd ordered those men to snatch them up. As much as she and Massah Murphy had tried to put on airs at their run-down plantation, they'd never had much money or many nice things—surely nothing so grand as this place.

Frank pushed Charlotte and Nell farther along, into a library with built-in shelves stuffed with books.

"Sit," he said, like he was talking to a pair of unruly dogs. Nell sat and pulled Charlotte's arm until she sat too.

"Good," Frank muttered. "Not much you two can get up to in here." He walked out of the room and shut the double doors behind him. The turn of the lock thundered in Charlotte's ears.

Alone at last, she and Nell were finally free to talk.

Nell took hold of her hands. "What is happening?" she asked in a panicked whisper. "Do you know where we are? Who are these people?"

"They must be looking for Evie," Charlotte said. *And looking for me too.* There was no keeping that from Nell now, but she still couldn't get the words out. Nell's brow was furrowed and her eyes were darting all around, like she feared she'd be knocked out and snatched again at any moment. Her breathing was shallow.

"Someone will come looking for us, won't they? Someone will notice we're gone, before they can take us . . ." Nell said, trailing off as if she was too afraid to finish the thought.

Charlotte nodded vaguely, looking at their surroundings, thinking about how they'd been treated like animals, all because of who and what she was. Nell deserved to know the truth about why she was caught up in this mess.

"I'm so sorry for all this," Charlotte said.

"It's not your fault, slave catchers make these kinds of mistakes all the time," Nell reminded Charlotte, nodding to herself—maybe turning this into an opportunity to teach her friend made her feel more in control. "It's what makes them so dangerous."

"But it isn't all a mistake." Charlotte took a deep breath. Now or never. "They're looking for me too. Evie and I were once slaves on the same plantation, and Kate was mistress to both of us. My father took me and ran a few years ago, and that's how I got to the city. I've been trying to leave all that behind, and so has he—but we can't. It just follows you everywhere, like a mark that can't be washed off."

The words came out all in a rush. She put her head in her hands, unable to bear looking Nell in the face.

"Your father?" Nell asked quietly.

"Mr. Vaughn. He's passing—that's how we got this far."

"I see," Nell said. Her quietness made Charlotte feel worse. "Well then, he'll know where to find us and why, so that's something."

Charlotte swallowed hard.

"He knows some of it, but not the Evie part," Charlotte said. Nell inhaled sharply and stood up. She took a few deep breaths, then rounded to face Charlotte again.

"You haven't told him? Is there anyone at all you've been honest with?" Nell asked. In her voice, Charlotte heard not only surprise but a sharp edge of judgment. Nell was aghast, and her composure had finally slipped.

How could Charlotte make someone like Nell understand her mistrust of her own father? Nell's family seemed normal enough—tight-knit and happy, from all Charlotte remembered ever hearing about them. The gulf between Charlotte and James might be beyond what Nell could conceive of. Still, now that she'd started, Charlotte couldn't fight off the urge to keep explaining, keep unburdening herself. She began again slowly.

"I don't think my father would mean Evie any harm," said Charlotte. "But I couldn't be sure he would help her either, not at the risk of being exposed. Since we've been here, keeping up the life he's built has been all that matters to him. He thinks it makes us safer. That's what he told me, anyway. I just thought it'd be better for everyone if I handled this on my own."

"Well, that hasn't turned out very well, has it?" Nell said. Her voice was cold.

Charlotte shrugged. "I don't know what he could have done for her. Helping runaways and defying the law aren't the kinds of things he gets involved with."

"But doesn't he? I mean, how else did the two of you arrive here if not by him deciding to *be* a runaway himself and defy your masters and the law?" Nell interjected.

"That was different. Once he saw how easy it was to just . . . cross over, and leave all the troubles of being a slave and a colored man behind, he's never been the same. He's looked after me in his way. But . . . I don't know him, Nell. Not anymore."

As much of a stranger as he was to her now, how could she trust him? But as Charlotte considered all her own lies that had brought them into this situation, it dawned on her that maybe Nell was asking herself the same question about Charlotte.

"I'm so sorry to have gotten you mixed up in all this, but I promise you it'll be all right," Charlotte said, resting a hand on Nell's shoulder to try to steady her. Nell pulled away. Maybe she didn't believe her. How could she, since Charlotte had so foolishly made sure Nell didn't really know anything about her?

In truth, Charlotte had no idea what they were going to do, and there wasn't much time to figure it out. They'd heard Frank earlier— they were going to be shipped off down South, and soon. She took a few deep breaths and scanned the room, looking for any clues about the house, who else lived here, and how to get out. When she stood up to scout around, Nell startled.

"What are you doing? He told us to sit!"

"He's gone now. Maybe something in here can help us figure out how to get away." Charlotte moved from shelf to shelf, inspecting the books and knickknacks. She wasn't at all sure what she was looking for.

"Charlotte, stop," Nell whispered to her from the couch. Charlotte didn't answer, determined as she was to keep poking around.

Then came another voice.

"Is that what you're calling yourself now, Carrie?"

Charlotte whipped around. She hadn't heard the door open, but there stood Kate, staring at her intently. Charlotte drew herself up to her full height, such as it was, and met Kate's gaze. She didn't move from where she stood, and Kate's face softened.

"It's been so very long," Kate said, all syrupy Southern politeness. "And who's this?" she asked, gesturing at Nell. Still, Charlotte made no reply. Nell looked at her, and then at Kate.

"I'm a friend of Charlotte's, Miss," she said tentatively. Before she could go on, Charlotte jumped in.

"She's no concern of yours. I'm guessing you were looking for someone else when you had those two men grab us off the street?"

"Not at all. After I ran into you last night and realized you were here in the city, it was you that I wanted to be reunited with. I've missed your company and your good work," Kate said. She was trying her hardest to sound calm, unruffled, but the cracks in her breathy voice gave away her unease. Her smile was insincere, and Charlotte knew she was lying.

Kate had never been very bright, so it was no surprise that the men she'd hired weren't particularly smart either. They were sent to do a simple task, and instead the pair of thugs had snatched the daughter of one of the most prominent Black families in Philadelphia. It would have been funny, if it wasn't really happening.

"Everything will be all right now," said Kate. "Once I'm wed, you and Evie will accompany me and Mr. Brooks down to South Carolina. Things will be just as they were."

Standing in front of Kate all these years later, Charlotte felt some of the old fear rising in her as she wondered exactly what the woman was up to. Could she be so deluded as to think Charlotte would go with her quietly? And then there was Nell, an innocent who was no part of this at all—what was Kate planning for her? Worried as she was, Charlotte wouldn't give Kate the satisfaction of showing any distress, and certainly not the warmth she was so desperate for. This was not White Oaks, and Charlotte was now no more a slave than she was a little girl. Here in Philadelphia, she was a free woman, and owed this plantation mistress no more deference than any stranger on the street.

"I'm not going anywhere with you," Charlotte said, catching herself before she added a respectful "Missus." She would not be observing the formalities.

Kate stepped back, looking like she'd been slapped across the face. "It's true what they say about all the freedom talk in this city, it's ruined you. You've got no call to speak to me that way; I've always been good to you." She dabbed at her eyes. "But I can at least keep Evie from being spoiled like you. Tell me where she is, won't you? She must want to come home."

"Evie? Haven't seen her," Charlotte said. "Isn't she back at White Oaks with the rest of her family?" Charlotte made her face look open and curious, like she was baffled why Kate would ask her about this at all.

"You know perfectly well she's not. You and Jack are hiding her somewhere, and until she's returned to me you and your friend aren't going anywhere," Kate spat.

Ah, so Charlotte and Nell were collateral. But Charlotte had had enough of being shuffled around like property to last her a lifetime. As ever, Kate's blithe use of everyone else's lives for her own ends was infuriating. But Charlotte didn't have to quietly absorb it anymore. Without thinking, she lashed out in the way she figured would hurt Kate most.

"Does your fiancé know you've hired white trash to commit mistaken kidnappings for you? What would he have to say about that?" Before Charlotte could say another word, Kate stepped toward her and slapped her. At the sharp smack of Kate's palm connecting with Charlotte's face, Nell flinched and stifled a gasp. Charlotte put up a hand to cradle her stinging cheek.

"Tell me where Evie is," Kate said, her voice quavering.

"I got nothing to tell," Charlotte said. "And even if I did, Nell's got nothing to do with this. You'll only stir up trouble for yourself if you don't let her go—her family will notice she's missing, and they're powerful in this city."

Nell looked at Charlotte and furiously shook her head. But Charlotte went on.

"You don't need both of us, Kate. Let her go, and we can sort the rest out on our own."

Kate scoffed. The notion of a powerful Black family was completely foreign to someone like her. But underneath her derision, the wheels of worry were clearly starting to turn. Without a word, Kate left the room.

Nell grabbed Charlotte by the shoulders and whispered, "What on earth are you doing?"

"I'm trying to get you out of here," she said. "If it wasn't for me, you'd be safe at home with your family right now."

Before Nell could say anything more, Frank came back in. "You two are going out back. There's laundry to be done, piled up since the other girl ran off."

He marched them past the back stairs into a small room off the narrow courtyard, where a large cauldron had been set to boil, with a tub, a washing board, and a misshapen glob of lye soap beside it.

Charlotte looked at him, looked at the pot, and crossed her arms. She'd done the last of anyone's laundry.

"Well?" Frank said. Nell flinched but took a step closer to Charlotte and stood still. Frank stared back at the two of them, his disbelief hardening into anger as they refused to move. "I said get to it!" He picked up his cane, and shoved Nell in the shoulder so sharply that she fell to the ground. He took a step closer and raised the cane again, but Charlotte got in between them. Before he could strike, Nell's voice came from behind her: "Please, it's all right. We'll get to work." She stood up, brushing the dust from the dirty floor off her skirts. "Won't we, Charlotte?" She looked at her pointedly.

Wanting to spare her friend any more violence, Charlotte walked over to the cauldron and dropped in a few of the garments that had been lying on the table. She began to stir. Nell sat down by the washing bin and board, ready to receive them.

"Good," Frank said. "You'd both better learn your places, and quick. I don't care what puffed-up colored family this wench is from," he said, jabbing his cane toward Nell again. "The men who escorted you here would be glad to sell a soft young thing like her on the open market, and pocket the profit—you keep acting up, and I may just oblige." With that, he went back inside.

For the next several hours, Charlotte and Nell worked side by side, in silence. They were damp with sweat and steam from the boiling water, and they grew wearier by the minute. As Charlotte's body moved through the motions with the familiarity of an entire life's work, the shame bubbled up in her. She glanced aside at Nell, poor

Nell, fumbling her way through the scrubbing, scraping her delicate and uncalloused hands against the board, trying to wipe away the few stray tears that escaped her eyes before Charlotte could see them. She didn't belong here. Charlotte didn't know what to say, and she had no tears to add to her friend's—not within Kate's sight.

When it came time to hang the clothes on the line, she stood beside Nell and put her hands over hers, showing her how to work the clips. When all was finished, they sat down on a stone in the little clearing beside the clotheslines and exhaled. The sun was setting. Nell broke the silence.

"I wish you'd trusted me enough to tell me everything." Even with all that had happened, her voice held no anger anymore—only sadness. "I would've helped you. I'd have been glad to."

Of course, Charlotte knew that. That was the whole problem.

"I didn't want to be one more person you reached down to help. I wanted to stand beside you." Instead, she'd dragged Nell down with her, into the dirt. "I thought I could make all this work somehow, but I don't know how to be your Charlotte and Evie's Carrie all at once. My father may be that kind of chameleon, but I'm not."

"No one's asking you to be," Nell said gently.

Charlotte shook her head. "Once Evie was safely out of town, I'd hoped everything would just go back to the way it was. We could've done so much more together, with the Wheatley Association, and maybe I could've helped out at your school. And my dressmaking . . ." she said, staring at the ground. "But that's all done with. The important thing now is for you to get out of here, at least. This isn't your fight."

Nell stood up, suddenly agitated. "For heaven's sake, it *is* my fight. It's *all* of ours. Don't you see that? Not understanding that is how we ended up where we are. But if we don't learn to trust each other—slave, fugitive, or freeborn—not a single one of us is safe."

Charlotte stared up at her. For all Nell didn't know about clothes washing, she knew a little something about the world they were moving through; Charlotte had just been too blinded by Nell's finery to see her wisdom, and her strength. She nodded.

"Now, you know far more about these slavers and running away than I ever will, because you've lived it. And I know this city," said Nell. "I bet between the two of us, we can find a way to get out of here. What do you say?"

Charlotte took Nell's hand and stood up with her. "All right, you and me then," she said. "We've got to get Evie out of town before Kate finds her, or my father gets wind of what's going on and goes looking for her himself."

"Wouldn't she be safe with him?"

"I wish I could believe that, but I'm afraid he'd try to trade her just to get me back. Either we're all free or no one is, like you said. Pennsylvania Hall is still our best bet."

Nell nodded. Together, the two of them scoured every inch of the courtyard for any means of escape, a passage out, anything. But their captors knew enough not to set such valuable goods where they'd easily slip their grasp—the courtyard had one way in, and one way out: the door to the house. Charlotte and Nell might as well have been in a cage.

As the sky darkened and the moon rose, Frank came for them. "Inside," he said. He led them down a corridor past the kitchen; at the end of the hallway an older maid stood waiting for them. Her shoulders were stooped, and her right eye was swollen nearly shut, with the eyelid discolored to a deep purple. Near her temple, a small gash had crusted over with dried blood. At the sight of her, Charlotte and Nell glanced at each other and grimaced—it seemed Nell wasn't the only one who'd suffered Frank's wrath after Evie took off.

"Ada, set them up in you and Louise's room," Frank ordered. "Don't worry yourself about clearing too much space for them though, they won't be here long."

Nell's face went ashen, and Charlotte swallowed hard. They both took Frank's meaning—it would be only days, or maybe hours, before they'd be tied up again and shipped down South, stripped away from anyone who knew them, in chains for the rest of their lives. With every step she was forced to take within the walls of the Jacksons' house, Charlotte felt herself losing control of everything she had—her life, her body, and maybe even her mind. Enslaved again, inch by inch.

With all she'd endured already, she felt a gnawing certainty that she wouldn't survive being a slave again. Knowing how she'd be worked, and used, and hurt, broken in body and spirit—it awakened a fear so primal that Charlotte could barely hold on to a complete thought—only a single word: *No!*

But her silent protest didn't, couldn't, register. This was a slaver's house, and she had no choices here. Behind Ada and Nell, Charlotte climbed the stairs of the slave quarters, dimly trudging farther from free air with every step.

Chapter 34

EVIE

E VIE HAD LOST COUNT OF HOW MANY HOURS HAD PASSED SINCE
she'd gotten to the Marions' house, but she did notice the late
afternoon shadows stretching across the wood floors. The day had
dragged on with no word of Charlotte, no matter how many times
she rang the bell and asked. Having started the day at a low simmer,
Evie's worry was beginning to boil over. She couldn't decide what
was worse: if Charlotte had left her behind on purpose again, or if
she hadn't. While she worked it over in her mind, a commotion
downstairs announced someone's arrival. Maybe whoever was at
the door would have some answers. Evie went to the top of the
staircase to listen.

As she strained to hear, she could barely make out the conversation, but she heard enough to know a woman was crying and a man
was demanding to speak to Alex about his daughter. Her ears also
picked up a name, "Nell." Of course. These could only be the parents of Charlotte's friend. If they were at the house and she wasn't,
something must have gone badly wrong. And all because Evie had
decided to run.

She sat and listened as long as she could, curling herself up into a
tight ball in the corner of the hallway atop the stairs. She wanted to
hide from these people, and the blame they'd surely heap on her
head. But what else could she have done? Let Kate send her away
down South and use her up till she was dead, or sell her off? Evie was

just as much worth worrying over as Nell and Charlotte. And they were probably fine anyhow. No one could say for sure they didn't just lose track of time at some meeting or another. That's what these free, rich Black folks liked to do up here, wasn't it? Go to meetings?

Evie fumed, trying to stoke the embers of her own resentment to drown out her worry and her guilt. But it was no use. She could see how much Charlotte had risked for her—there was no way her friend would just give up on the whole plan when they were so close. But Nell was a stranger to Evie and owed her nothing.

After nearly an hour, the weeping and rushed talking downstairs weren't letting up, and neither would Evie's conscience. Kate must have taken Nell, and Charlotte too—now both women were suffering thanks to Evie's choices. She had to go and explain herself, to account for all that had happened—it was the right thing to do. But when she tiptoed down to the parlor and peeked through the open door, she hesitated a moment.

Finally, she cleared her throat. Both the Marions and Nell's family turned and stared, lapsing into silence as they searched her face for answers. She stepped forward, fumbling for the right thing to say to Nell's parents and the young man standing beside them, who must've been Nell's brother.

"I don't think Kate will hurt your girl," she began, regretting it instantly. The woman who'd been crying—Nell's mother, no doubt—looked back at Evie, and her face showed both disbelief and suspicion. "If that's where they are, I mean," Evie mumbled. "Nell won't be harmed." Evie wasn't so sure she could say the same for Charlotte.

Nell's father shook his head sadly. "Harm has degrees, I'm afraid," he said.

Evie stood there feeling she ought to say something else—but what? I'm sorry? I'm grateful? Nothing seemed to fit. She went quiet and moved to the side of the room. If Kate had snatched Charlotte, she'd probably be coming for Evie any moment, and who knew what her plans would be for Uncle Jack. As Evie watched the Marions and

Gardners talk among themselves, she could see they were terrified, yet still so far removed from the life Evie had run from. She'd never felt more out of place. As she fought the urge to bolt out the front door, to go find Uncle Jack and warn him, or maybe just to get away from here, the realization that there seemed to be no other safe place in this city kept her rooted to the spot. That, and if she disappeared now, she couldn't help get Charlotte back, and might never see her again. She would wait. Always, more waiting.

Across the room, Mr. Marion put a reassuring hand on Nell's father's shoulder. The Gardners could stay until Nell was safely returned, he said. Everyone settled back into their chairs, side by side, with Mrs. Gardner staring at some fixed point on the wall and pressing her hands together, interlacing her fingers and taking them apart again, over and over. Evie glanced at Alex. He was looking at the floor. He was as mixed up in all this as she was, really, but so far he wasn't saying much.

With every minute that passed with no news, and no sign of Nell and Charlotte, extended what had already been a long day as the dreadful certainty fixed itself in the air—they were in serious danger, and might never be found.

At loose ends, Evie could think of only one way to occupy herself: to get up every few minutes, walk over to the sideboard, and take a sip of water. She could feel her muscles tightening as the late afternoon crawled by, all while Nell's parents sat talking quietly and trying to keep calm. But they weren't the only ones whose daughter had disappeared.

Sometime after sundown, a knock came at the door, and with it, the sound of a familiar voice. "Are Mr. and Mrs. Gardner here? The maid next door told me Nell's parents were at this house. I'm looking for her, and my housemaid." Mid-pace, Evie set down her water glass and ran into the front entryway.

The man standing at the door looked nothing like she remembered. Gone were the threadbare, sawdust-covered breeches and leather carpenter's apron he'd always worn around White Oaks, with the sheen of hard work's sweat always on his brow. Instead, before her was a face-powdered gentleman in a silk waistcoat with brass buttons and slicked-down hair. But his eyes—those were the same.

"Uncle Jack?" she said.

His mouth fell open. "Evie? What are you doing here? Where is Charlotte?"

The questions tumbled out one after another as he walked over to embrace her. She hesitated, not letting him pull her close. He softened his voice and stepped back, putting up his hands to make clear he meant her no harm. Another man came in just behind him, one with a stern-looking, slightly lined face and deep-brown skin. He stood quietly behind James, a stark contrast to his paleness, but the man's eyes darted around the room with the same look of worry and hope—whoever he was, he was looking for Charlotte too.

James looked to Mr. Marion. "You remember my cook, Darcel," he said. Evie stared at him. He must've known she'd been at their house all along, especially with Charlotte bringing up extra food.

"He told me Charlotte and Nell went out together earlier today. When Charlotte didn't come home, I thought I might try here before assuming the worst—Darcel gave me Nell's name; he said Charlotte had mentioned she lived around here. What's happened?"

Alex stepped forward. "Both Charlotte and Nell have gone missing. Nell went to see Charlotte at your house this morning, and no one has seen either of them since."

Evie spoke up. "Kate must've taken them, looking for me."

"Why would she be looking for you at my house? How on earth did you get here?" James asked. Evie raised an eyebrow and glanced at Darcel, who kept his face blank and looked away. Whatever he knew, he'd told James only the bare minimum.

As the group moved from the foyer into the parlor, Evie told James how Kate had brought her north, and how Evie had found Charlotte and asked for her help to escape before finally just running off.

"I don't know what I thought was gonna happen. I just—I needed to get away from Kate. You know what she's like. I thought if I could just get out of the house, it would be all right." She paused, and swallowed. "But all I did is make everything worse."

"There's a lot of that going around," said James, hanging his head.

Mr. Gardner interrupted their self-pity. "Well, something must be done. We can't just sit here while this woman is doing heaven knows what to my daughter." He turned to Alex. "And why would slave catchers be anywhere near Nell? She's never been a slave a day in her life!"

"They must've seen her with Charlotte and assumed she was Evie, and just decided to take both of them," Alex said.

"And what exactly do we know about this Charlotte who's got her mixed up in all this?" Mr. Gardner asked.

"I've known her all my life, sir," interjected Evie. "We worked on the same plantation together down in Maryland." James went wide-eyed. Evie made eye contact with him and held his gaze, unflinching. She didn't need his permission to say the rest, and she wasn't asking for it.

"I found her here, at the market, and she and Nell were good enough to try and help me. And Alex too. That's all. Your daughter's a good woman, Mr. Gardner. Her and Charlotte both."

Out of the corner of her eye, Evie saw James blinking back tears. Mr. Gardner looked at him. "I can see you must care a great deal for Charlotte," he said carefully. His voice was cold.

"More than anyone in the world," James said. Both Mrs. Marion's and Mrs. Gardner's mouths twisted like they tasted something sour. Quickly, James must've realized what they were thinking and rushed to clear things up. "She's my daughter."

To that, Mr. Gardner seemed to have no words in reply. He raised an eyebrow and then glanced over to Alex, as if he might hold the key to whatever strange confession was unfolding here. Alex shrugged, and James spoke up.

"It isn't quite what you're thinking. I'm not— That is, I know what I look like, but I'm a colored man same as you. Me and Charlotte ran from a plantation in Maryland some four years ago now, and I guess it's finally catching up to us. To me." He sighed. "I'm so sorry your Nell got dragged into all this. But it is a simple case of mistaken identity, Mr. Gardner. Rest assured, we'll get everyone back where they're supposed to be."

Evie's muscles tensed. Going back where *she* was supposed to be wasn't going to happen. Mr. Gardner didn't find James's words very comforting either. He clenched and unclenched his fists, and took a deep breath. He shook his head like he was trying to rid himself of what he'd just heard. He was appalled. He seemed to give up trying to respond politely to James and instead turned to Alex and spoke through gritted teeth.

"Did you know about all of this?"

"Only bits and pieces, sir," Alex said.

"How could you have gotten Nell mixed up in all of this? You're planning to marry her, you ought to protect her!"

Mr. Marion stepped forward to answer, but Alex stopped his father. He could speak for himself.

"I've always looked out for her, every step of the way. But," he said, pausing to swallow, "we were never really getting married. She just didn't want you to know what was going on."

Mrs. Gardner gasped, and Mr. Gardner just shook his head. Evie was skeptical. Whatever Alex said, she wasn't so sure their engagement was as fake as he claimed. She'd seen him pacing the floors all day long—he was terrified for her.

Even as everyone seemed focused on laying blame, for Evie it was plain enough that what they *should* be worrying about was how to get Nell and Charlotte back. An answer presented itself to her as she looked around and took the full measure of the assembled group and all their fine things: the Gardners' elegance, the Marions' grand home, even Uncle Jack and his carefully designed appearance, from his precisely combed hair to his spotless and well-made clothing. The solution was staring her in the face—it was the one thing nearly every adult in the room had in common, the one thing Kate wanted but didn't have: money. Evie leaned forward and spoke up.

"I think I know how to fix this," she said. "Kate's been broke since Massah Murphy passed, that's what this whole engagement is about. I bet she'd gladly accept a payment in exchange for Carrie and me, and hush all this up. It looks like your money has solved most of your other problems, Uncle Jack. Why not this one?"

He looked doubtful. "You're suggesting I just offer to pay Kate and her family for the slaves they've lost—for what I've 'stolen'—and they'll agree to be done with it?"

"I can't tell you if they'll agree or not, but have you got a better idea?" Evie sat back and crossed her arms.

He considered for a moment, then shook his head.

"And the offer needs to include your silence," Evie said. "The one thing Kate can't abide is if her fiancé finds out about all this, or anything to do with White Oaks really. Far as he knows, there's no such place, no Massah Murphy, none of it."

James's eyes widened. "That must be why she was behaving so strangely at my dinner party," he said. "As if she didn't know us at all."

Evie nodded. She had marveled at how easily Kate had decided to erase every trace of her old life. And she wasn't alone in that—between Kate, Carrie, and Uncle Jack, everyone was eager to put White Oaks behind them, out of their minds and even out of their pasts. The inconvenience, for all of them, was Evie.

Nell's brother suddenly spoke up. "Forget the money, why not just threaten to expose the woman if she doesn't give Nell and Charlotte back?" the young man offered.

"George Gardner!" shouted his father, sounding appalled. "What you're describing is *blackmail*. If we jump straight to breaking the law to resolve this, all of us could end up in worse danger than we started—Nell and Charlotte included!"

James nodded thoughtfully. "That's right. If this can be resolved peaceably, that's best. Kate can have my silence and as much of my money as I can pull together if that gets my daughter and yours back," he said.

"Darcel, will you wait here in case there's any news? I'll go to see my business partner and find out what I can borrow in a hurry." Darcel nodded, and James stood to leave.

"But, Mr. Vaughn, surely we can all put in together and have enough to pay this woman, if you'd just wait a moment—" said Mr. Marion.

"No," James interrupted. "This is my daughter, and my own mess. I'll see to it." And with that, he was out the door, looking relieved to have a reason to pull himself out of the whole uncomfortable scene.

Evie couldn't blame him. With all she had lost, and the losses she'd caused since, she felt ready to get away from it all too.

THOUGH NELL WAS TRAPPED WITHIN A NIGHTMARE, AT LEAST the servants in the Jacksons' town house were kind. She clung to that thought like a life raft as Ada led her and Charlotte upstairs to their quarters, even as she felt miles opening up between her and her family, and her safe, genteel life. She'd heard what Frank said about a transport down South—and her blood ran cold at the thought: this wasn't their final stop, and Nell knew the kinds of horrors that lay beyond Pennsylvania's southern border. Unless she and Charlotte could get out of here, Nell was staring at a future so far away and fearsome that she could scarcely let herself imagine it.

But first, she'd have to get through the night. Ada brought Nell and Charlotte into a room with two simple pallets laid out on a rough-hewn wood floor. "Might could find you two some straw mats or some such, if you give me a bit of time," she said.

Nell forced a warm smile. "You're so kind, thank you." Her manners, at least, still felt familiar—safe.

At the sound of her voice, Ada cocked her head to the side. "Where you from, anyhow? You don't sound like nobody's slave."

"Not too far from here, my family's lived in the city for generations now. I just got . . . swept up in things, I suppose."

Charlotte rested a comforting hand on her shoulder, and from the corner of her eye, Nell watched her. In some ways she hardly knew this woman, but now it seemed they had no one to rely on but each other. She supposed she couldn't begrudge Charlotte her fabricated life story—it wasn't like Nell herself hadn't dabbled in spinning convenient tales lately to smooth out all their plans. Now she might never have the chance to unburden herself and be honest with her parents. And then there was Alex. Perhaps the biggest lie she'd told to him—and to herself—was that she could ignore the way she felt about him. But none of that mattered anymore. Now, the only thing she felt was fear, and wherever Alex and her parents were, they were surely as afraid as she was. Would they come for her? Could they find out where she was? There was nothing to do but ready herself for the night, and hope.

But just as she and Charlotte began to get settled in Ada's room, a tinkling bell rang out from the hallway. Charlotte stood stock-still and stared at Ada, but she didn't jump to. It rang again not a second later; whoever was at the other end was clearly impatient.

"That'll be Miss Kate for you," Ada said, nodding at Charlotte. "Best get on up there or Frank'll be at you again, most like."

Charlotte sighed heavily and turned to Nell. "I won't be gone long, I promise," she said, squeezing her shoulder. "Ada, will you look after her?"

"Of course. Go on. Kate's room is up on the third floor, second door on the right after you come to the landing."

Left behind by the only person she knew in the house, Nell couldn't sleep a wink. Her body ached in a way she'd never felt before and begged to be dragged down into the depths of sleep—rest, or maybe just an escape from this waking nightmare. But it wouldn't come, and she lay staring up at the moon out the window, wildly wondering if perhaps there wasn't some way to climb through and— what exactly? Shimmy down the side of the house, scraping her hands and knees on bricks before tumbling to the ground? Maybe twisting an ankle and hobbling her way home through the dark and dangerous streets of the city—her own city, yes. But this house, this way of living, was some other world within it, and Nell wasn't made for it. Of course, no one ever was.

With Ada's and Louise's soft snoring in her ear, she tossed and turned, trying to find a comfortable position as she waited for day. Even through the straw mat, she could feel the unyielding hardness of the floor. Louise had kindly offered to let Nell take her bed for the night, especially after hearing who she was and how she'd come to be there, and Ada had agreed. "Wouldn't be right for you to sleep on no hard floor—you been through enough for one day," she'd said. But Nell had insisted—she couldn't bear the thought of taking even some small comfort from these women who already had far less than she did. Or used to have. Would she ever get back to her home, her family, her things? A soft bed was the furthest thing from her mind now. Mostly she thought of her mother, and imagined her staring up at the same moon, tears streaming down her face, sick with not knowing where her daughter was, or if she'd ever come back. Nell felt the same sickness rising up in her chest, but she swallowed hard, forcing it back down.

Hours passed, and Nell grew increasingly alarmed when Charlotte didn't return. She rubbed her hands, sat up, and finally stood and paced in circles as quietly as she could, until Ada grunted and rolled over, and Nell felt she had to lay back down. She didn't want to be any trouble to them. The night crawled onward, and she sat with her knees drawn in, the straw from the mat making her legs itch. She carefully spread out her skirts to act as a barrier, but it didn't help, she itched all the same. Ada had offered her a night shift to change into, but Nell had turned that down too. Somehow, she felt if she kept her own clothes on, it'd be less like this was happening to her—less like Frank, Kate, and the others could turn her into something other than what she was. Awake in the dark, she waited for dawn with dread.

Chapter 36

———

CHARLOTTE

———

A̲s̲ ̲s̲h̲e̲ ̲b̲i̲t̲t̲e̲r̲l̲y̲ ̲s̲h̲u̲f̲f̲l̲e̲d̲ ̲u̲p̲s̲t̲a̲i̲r̲s̲ ̲t̲o̲ ̲a̲n̲s̲w̲e̲r̲ ̲K̲a̲t̲e̲'̲s̲ ̲s̲u̲m̲m̲o̲n̲s̲, Charlotte took in more of the house's finery. Must be true what folks always said, Kate's family was far richer than Massah Murphy ever was—the woman must've been exactly as much of a fool as she seemed to take up with that old man and leave this kind of wealth behind for sad little White Oaks. She had often lamented the decision to Charlotte: Kate had been young, and her family always teased her for being plain compared to her comely older sisters. As she came of age, she'd watched them marry handsome, wealthy men from the finest families while she languished and looked to become an old maid. So when Murphy had come sniffing around at a county barbecue, lavishing her with attention and selling dreams about how his tobacco plantation would soon make him rich, she'd jumped at the first and only proposal she expected to receive. She'd lived to regret it.

But in the years since he died, it looked like Kate had learned enough about cunning and patience to turn things around with this new man of hers, who was everything Murphy had promised but never became. What giant plantation did this Mr. Brooks own that Kate would ship Charlotte off to when all this was said and done? She'd disappear into rows of cotton, or cavernous hallways in some far-off big house, swallowed up and never seen again.

When Charlotte arrived at the bedroom door, it was ajar, and

Kate was sitting there at her vanity surrounded by all the same oils and rouges and perfumes. The familiar, sickly sweet smells wafted over to Charlotte even as far as the doorway, and instinctively she took a step back—back away from White Oaks, back away from wherever Kate aimed to send her next.

"Come now, brush out my hair, Carrie," Kate said without turning around. Charlotte took another step back, away from that name. Kate, fool that she was, could read only fear in Charlotte's reluctance—not rebellion. "Oh honestly, you know you have nothing to fear from me. Come in and talk a little while you brush, I so want to make things right between us."

"And Nell?" Charlotte asked. "That's what needs to be made right. Let her go."

Kate turned around. "You needn't worry about your friend, she'll be looked after."

Looked after in the slave quarters? What must Nell be thinking right now, if she could even think at all?

With nowhere else to go, Charlotte stepped into Kate's room.

"It's good to have you close again," Kate said in that familiar sing-songy voice. "Come, now."

Charlotte stood stock-still where she was, not breaking eye contact with Kate in the mirror.

Kate turned around and reached out a hand. "Is all this really necessary, Carrie? We were close once, you and I."

Charlotte shook her head slowly. Without Nell here needing protecting, there was no good reason to do a thing Kate said. Instead, Charlotte pulled out a chair from the small round table and sat. Kate's muted outrage was plain on her face. Still, Charlotte said nothing.

"I know you're probably angry with me because of the things your father told you, but you have to understand I had no good options back then," said Kate. "I would've found some way to see you, to get you back."

Charlotte leaned forward. Bold of Kate to assume her father had ever told her much of anything, but then Kate never had kept up with the ins and outs of her slaves' family relationships.

"Get me back from where?"

"From my brother, after I sold you to him," said Kate. She looked confused. "I know Jack must've overheard us discussing it and run off because of it; the two of you disappeared the same night we signed the papers. It would only have been for a little while, until I was back on my feet financially."

Charlotte sat back silently. James had never mentioned a word of this, not the night they took off nor in all the quiet, awkward years since. Given no truth to work with, Charlotte had filled in the blanks based on what she knew of her father and what she'd seen every day since: that they had run so he could make a better life for himself, and her life was just a casualty of his ambition.

But everyone at White Oaks had known what kind of man Kate's brother was, a deadly mix of lustful and brutal. On his plantation down in Virginia, there were more than a few golden-skinned babies running around, their Black mothers slogging through the fields with bent, scarred backs and haunted eyes.

Her father hadn't run to build himself up. He'd run to save her.

As Kate prattled on in her ear, Charlotte stared at the floor and sifted through every moment, every act of the last four years. James had dragged her to her freedom with one hand, only to hold her back from it with the other. He'd kept her hidden away, and maybe it *was* half to keep her safe, yes, but there was no doubt it had become more in service of his own ends. He'd torn her away from the family she'd known, from Auntie Irene, Evie, and Daniel, but brought her here to this city—one that showed her new worlds, and new people.

The freedom he'd given her was a raw, rough chunk of wood, but what she'd carved out of it was her own—a life stitched together from the scraps of her own curiosity and boldness, and this city, and the skills she'd brought with her. She weighed all James had done for her against all he'd done *to* her. The scales didn't quite balance, but it wasn't the brick and feather she'd held in her mind for so long either. It was like she could see him whole now. As she turned it over in her mind, Kate blathered on, self-absorbed as ever.

"Even after you disappeared, I still held on to Evie for you, for both of us," she said. "Selling off Irene and Daniel was enough to make up the difference, sad as it was. But once Evie is back, and we all move down South, things will be better—even better than they were, I promise. Henry will look after us all, and you'll forgive me in time, I know it." She grudgingly picked up the brush and started working out her own tangles, as Charlotte looked on. "What this city does to people—it's a real shame. We'll get far away from here, and we can move on with our lives. I'll marry, you and Evie will have each other again, and the two of you can even find young bucks of your own and have little babies like Henry said. We can all just go on."

She was half-talking to herself. At last, Charlotte broke in.

"How you want us to go on, and how *we* want to go on are two different things. And no matter how far from this city you take me, I won't forget it." With that, Charlotte stood up and started for the door.

"No, you won't be returning to the slave quarters," Kate said. "I can't have you stirring up anyone else with your wild ideas about running away. You'll spend the night in there." She pointed to a small room tucked away across the bedchamber. Charlotte didn't bother arguing—she'd need to pick her battles if she and Nell were going to come out of this safely. Wearily, she stepped into the tiny room. The effect was jarring. This had been Evie's room, there was no missing that. The air itself and the sheets on the thin-mattressed pallet still bore her scent: the light breath of rosewater she put in her hair, the handmade soap she'd always use, that she mixed with a touch of rose oil. The oil was the same little token Kate had given to Charlotte when she was her housemaid, a castoff from her own collection that the girls were expected to gratefully accept. Charlotte had never worn it, and now the scent grated on her, dragging her mind back to a place she didn't want to go.

Once again, Charlotte's whole world was collapsed into one selfish woman's bedroom, managing her insignificant feelings and needs. For the first time in a long time, Charlotte was utterly alone, with everyone taken from her—or had she lost them all by her own dishonesty? Save Darcel, there wasn't one single person in her life she'd told the whole truth to until she was finally caught. She'd been too busy trying to control how people saw her and to make sure Evie's dream of freedom didn't disrupt who and what Charlotte wanted to be now. She thought of her father. Maybe she wasn't as unlike him as she'd believed. And now she might never see him again, or Evie. Her eyes filled, and she blinked back tears.

As Charlotte turned over all her failures and losses in the darkness, again and again her mind returned to Daniel. If what Kate said about selling her was true, there would have been no future for them even if James hadn't taken Charlotte and run. The plans they'd made, the twisted branch ring Daniel had slid onto her finger as a promise— it was all built on sand, washed away by the brutal truth: they were slaves. They barely belonged to themselves, so how could they promise themselves to each other? She'd always lived and loved at the mercy of someone else's plan, whether it be a sale or an escape. And now here she was, at Kate's mercy again.

At the thought of once again being ripped away from a life she was just beginning, the embers of anger inside Charlotte burned. What would Kate do with her tomorrow? Dawn was only a few hours away, and Charlotte was too incensed to sleep. She sat on the edge of the bed, her knees drawn in—a prisoner awaiting her punishment.

Chapter 37

———

NELL

———

AFTER WHAT FELT LIKE AN ETERNITY, THE NIGHT CRAWLED TO a close, the sky turning from blue-black to a predawn purple. With the light peeking into the slave quarters, both Ada and Louise stirred. They stood and stretched, and Nell heard their bones crack as they pulled on their uniforms for the day.

"You all right?" Ada asked.

Nell nodded and forced a small smile.

"Come on down with us, we'll get you something to eat before I have to get up to Miss Maggie, and I'm sure all this'll get sorted out directly."

Nell stood, and found she needed to stretch too—the cold of the hard floor had forced its way into her bones, and she was stiff. Down in the little room off the kitchen, Louise set her up with a cup of hot coffee and a simple oat porridge. Nell ate slowly; she didn't have much appetite, and the strong coffee only set her jangled nerves even more on edge. Before long, the bells in the hallway started ringing, and one person after another jumped to—off to dress the mistress, to bring massah his breakfast, to start the day's scrubbing and tidying in the bedrooms once the white folks left them. The bells rang, and they all disappeared—just as Charlotte had the night before.

And where was she now? What had been done with her? And what would be done with Nell? Her thoughts raced, consumed with questions about what would happen next but terrified to learn the answers. The bell rang one more time, and she jumped—now Ada, the last servant who'd been left with her, stood to leave. "That'll be Miss Maggie, I'll come back and check on you when I can." Nell looked at her with sympathy as she walked off—overnight, the purple of Ada's swollen eye had faded to an ugly yellow that looked sickly against her brown skin. Left alone at the table, Nell carefully touched her own shoulder. With the jolt of pain that followed, Nell knew she'd gained a bruise of her own to match poor Ada's.

When footsteps sounded in the hallway a moment later, she only half looked up, assuming it was Ada returning for something she'd forgotten. Instead, looming in the doorway was Frank, his cane in one hand.

"You. Come," he said. Warily, she stood and followed him down the hallway, keeping as far back from him as she could. He didn't say a word to her, only muttered to himself—"Ridiculous. We'll be well rid of her."

Of whom? Nell or Charlotte? When they reached the library, he stopped walking, grabbed Nell and pushed her inside, and slammed the door behind her. There, she found Charlotte waiting, and rushed toward her. Charlotte didn't look any better rested than Nell was.

"Why didn't you come back last night? Where were you?"

"Kate sent for me and wouldn't let me come back down," said Charlotte.

"My God, we have to get out of here!" Nell said, horrified. "I'm going to talk to them—tell them about my family, we've got money. Maybe they'll . . ."

Before she could finish her sentence, Frank came back into the room. "That's enough," he said. He yanked Nell away from Charlotte so hard she feared her arm would come out of its socket.

"Stop!" Charlotte shouted. Nell reached out for her, but Frank kept pulling, painfully, until she was outside blinking in the bright morning sunlight. He forced her to the curb, and shoved her into a carriage, with his rough hands on her back nearly knocking the wind out of her.

"More trouble than she's worth, this one," he grumbled to the driver.

As the carriage started moving, Nell scrambled to look behind her, only to see Charlotte get tossed into a second carriage loaded with bags. It pulled off in the opposite direction, and soon was out of sight.

ONCE AGAIN BEING BUMPED along city roads with no earthly idea where she was being taken, Nell tried to remain calm even as she trembled in her seat. Was this it? Was she being sent south? She pressed her ruined hands together to steady herself, only to be startled once again by the sight of them, peeling and sore from the heat of the washwater, the scrubbing, and the harsh lye soap yesterday.

The carriage hadn't been driving long, perhaps a dozen blocks, when it came to a sudden stop. The driver climbed down from his seat, reached into the carriage, and hoisted her out by the waist, his fingers digging into her sides. He set her down roughly on the ground, then climbed back up and drove off, leaving her in the middle of the street. In the cloud of dirt kicked up by the carriage's wheels, Nell coughed and her eyes burned.

When the dust cleared, she looked around. In the light of the early morning sun, she barely recognized the brick homes of her own neighborhood. The same streets she'd lived on her entire life looked different, warped and foreign somehow, now that she'd been what felt like a world away. On aching feet, she walked slowly to her front door, brushing off her dress and adjusting her hair as she went.

Beth-Anne answered the door. "Miss Nell, it's you! Thank the Lord Almighty," she said, hugging her tightly. "Are you all right? Everyone's worried sick, been up all night."

Disoriented and unsteady, Nell stepped past her into the foyer. As she looked up the staircase for her family, her stomach came up her throat. She doubled over and was sick on the tiled floor.

"Sit down, Miss, let me get you some water," said Beth-Anne, rushing to her side to rub her back.

Nell shook her head. "Where is everyone?"

"They're next door, at the Marions', been there all night," said Beth-Anne.

Then that's where Nell needed to be. She apologized to Beth-Anne for the mess, wiped her mouth, and headed over. The walk felt impossibly long. As she fought to keep steady with each step, all she'd seen and felt flashed through the cracks in her composure. Utterly powerless, treated like less than nothing, and her body no more than a soulless vessel for thankless work, or an animal to be beaten when it was disobedient. A single day and night of living that reality, and Nell felt like she was carrying the shattered pieces of herself across the street in a silk purse. Charlotte and Evie had endured all that and worse, for years.

She knocked on the Marions' door with her aching hand and winced, less from pain than from shame. She felt so foolish. As much as she'd thought she'd known, as much as she'd believed she had to teach Charlotte, a world of horrors had opened up to show Nell she hardly knew anything at all.

Alex opened the door. He grabbed both of Nell's hands and stared at her, then embraced her tightly. "Thank God," he said, pulling her into the house. Behind him, she heard the others in the house gasp and exclaim at the sight of her.

Back with her family, and safe at last, Nell was flooded with relief. Though her body was stiff and sore, she softened in Alex's arms. She'd very nearly been pulled away from him for good, just as Charlotte and Evie had been stolen away from the people they loved, and like countless other slaves whose names she'd never know. Before, she'd taken for granted what it meant to be free to choose—stay or go, fall in love or stand on her own, marry or not. Even in her haze, Nell wondered if she ought to get on with exercising that freedom, finally—and wondered where the man whose strong, familiar arms surrounded her might fit into it all.

But she hardly had a moment to think before her parents rushed to her side, pulling her from Alex's embrace into their own. "Oh, Nell, Nell!" her father cried. "We're so relieved to have you back!"

"What happened to you? Are you hurt?" asked her mother, sounding joyful and worried all at once. Both parents fussed over her, searching for any signs of injury. Nell's mother lifted her daughter's hands and looked at them, then covered her mouth in shock. Nell gently pulled them back. She knew she must look a fright, but even as shaken as she was, there were far more pressing concerns.

"Please, I'm all right. I'm not the one we need to be concerned about now," said Nell. "Is Evie here?" Alex stood aside and glanced over his shoulder to the foot of the stairs. There she was.

Nell took in the full measure of the girl, eyes sweeping first over her hair and face, then down across the unassuming gray dress she'd borrowed from Charlotte, to her bare feet, then up to her face again. Evie stood stock-still and stared, looking Nell over in return.

Nell smiled warmly and came closer to her.

"I'm Nell, a friend of Charlotte's," she said gently. Recognition flashed across Evie's face. "She'll be glad you're safe, at least."

"But why isn't she with you?" Evie asked.

Charlotte's father's cook, who'd been standing aside and saying little, added his own questions before Nell could answer.

"Has she been hurt? Is she safe?" he asked, his voice worried.

"No, she's not safe, I'm sorry to say, but neither of us was too badly harmed." Nell paused and considered whether it was worthwhile to say how they'd been put to work and how little Nell herself had fought against any of it. That part seemed more embarrassing than the fact of having been kidnapped at all. As everyone gathered around her, Nell pushed past the others to enter the parlor and lowered herself onto the sofa. Her brother, George, who'd been standing by as their parents attended to Nell, wrapped a blanket around her from behind. She leaned back gratefully. She was more exhausted than she'd realized, and it felt good to be somewhere familiar. But rescuing Charlotte had to come before her own comfort.

Nell explained how they'd been separated all night and sent off in two different directions come morning. Though Nell had been released, she was sure that they had other plans for Charlotte.

"I'm terribly afraid they may be taking her down South," she said. "That's what the man said he planned to do, before he let me go."

"We've got to find her before she leaves the city, then, and ransom her back," said Darcel. "Mr. Vaughn went to get the money from his business partner, but he's been gone all night."

"Why on earth would he waste time doing that? We have plenty of money between our families, if he'd only asked——" Nell huffed.

"Too proud for that," Evie interjected, shaking her head. "That's Uncle Jack for you."

"Well, we can't just wait around for him," Nell said. "We have to do something, go back and get her or——"

Nell's parents had kept in the background of the conversation thus far, but they had heard enough. "Go *back*? Haven't you put us through enough already?" her mother interjected, eyes wide with fear.

Nell sighed. She'd hardly gone and gotten kidnapped by slave catchers on purpose. She opened her mouth to speak, but her mother held up a finger. "Don't. Don't you get clever with me. The only reason this happened in the first place was because you were some-where you ought not have been, with someone you ought not have been with. You're better than this—we've told you and told you."

"Mother. I'm *not* better than this. None of us are better than this." Nell stood up, letting the blanket drop to the floor. "You're deceiv-ing yourself if you think that at the end of the day I'm anything more than just another colored woman to these people—one to be worked, or used, or sold away at will. *That* is why I was snatched off the street. It's why they couldn't tell me apart from a runaway slave girl."

Evie huffed and cleared her throat. Abashed, Nell quickly mouthed a silent apology.

Nell's father sighed. "Do you think you're saying something we haven't heard before? That we don't know? But the way they see us isn't who we are. How we've raised you should be enough to tell you that. All we want is for you to be safe, and well taken care of."

"You should want more than that," Nell said. "What's my safety worth if it can be snatched away in a second because of the way I look—if *I* can be snatched away in a second—and thousands of others in this city, walking the same streets, can have no hope of safety at all?"

Her parents' narrowness was infuriating.

"We're not going to keep going around in these circles with you, especially after everything you've put us through tonight," her mother said. "But—"

Oh, for heaven's sake. What would it be now?

"But we know how brave you must've been to come through it, and to find your way home," her father cut in.

That was unexpected, kind, and wrong.

"No, I was terrified," Nell said. "*Charlotte* was brave. She looked after me, kept me calm, and made sure I got home to you even if it meant she'd have to face whatever was coming all alone. I owe her everything. And so do you, Evie. We owe it to her to see this through. All of it."

But even as she raised her voice, Nell felt the adrenaline seeping out of her body, sapping her strength. She slumped back down onto the couch.

A moment later, as she sat and tried to take deep breaths, through the parlor doors she saw a fair-skinned man come into the foyer. He was tall, brown-haired, and a little familiar looking around the eyes. This could only be James. But he wasn't the proud man Evie had just referred to. There was no stride to him at all. His shoulders sagged and his feet barely lifted off the ground, giving him a shuffling kind of gait that made him look more like a chained ghost than a living man. He seemed utterly defeated.

Evie rushed past Nell to meet him.

"Uncle Jack?" she asked tentatively, as he stepped inside. "Did you get the money?"

But he only shook his head. "I couldn't. Mr. Wilcox wouldn't see me," James said. He sounded confused and fearful. "I know he was there, I know it. He always works late into the night, but his clerk wouldn't let me into the office. The way he looked at me—he knows something, I'm sure of it," he trailed off.

He looked almost on the verge of tears, as his whole carefully constructed life seemed to be unraveling and his livelihood along with it. Most of the others averted their eyes out of politeness, but Nell and Evie stared at him with pity. He'd gone to all that trouble and been humiliated, and for nothing.

But when James noticed Nell on the couch, he suddenly perked up.

"You, are you Nell?" he said, hurrying into the parlor. Nell nodded. "Is Charlotte—?"

"She's not with me, I'm sorry," Nell said before he could finish his question. "They let me go, but not her—I saw a carriage pull away with her in it, but I haven't any idea where they'd have gone."

At that, James staggered to a chair and sat down heavily.

Though he seemed broken up about his own failure, it hardly mattered anymore: with Charlotte already being carted out of town, it was likely too late to buy her back anyhow. They'd have to find another way. Nell settled back onto her seat on the couch, preparing to think it through. But her parents seemed to read her mind and had other ideas.

"Nell, I understand you're worried about your friend, but I think we've done all we can for the moment," said her father. "Let's please get you home and cleaned up before we think about next steps."

She couldn't muster the energy to resist. The whole situation had taxed her nearly beyond her limits, and she'd need to collect herself if they were going to figure out how to help Charlotte. As she walked out the door with her mother and father, she felt Alex's eyes on her but tried not to look back. There never seemed to be enough time to sort things out between them.

At home, her mother came into her room and helped Nell undress. Her body ached, whether from the tension or just from the little bit of physical labor—more than she'd ever done in her life—she couldn't tell. Her mother's hands were gentle, unbuttoning her dress, taking down her hair. She stood behind Nell and nudged for her to lift her arms so her shift could come off more easily over her head. It was then that she finally spoke again.

"I wish you would've trusted your father and me enough to be honest with us about what you were involved in," she began quietly. "We may not be as radical as some, but we would've kept your secrets—we'd never put you or your friend in harm's way. Surely you know that."

"But you would've tried to stop me," Nell said. "Somehow, that seemed worse."

"And Alex didn't?" her mother asked. "That's why you went to him for help?"

Nell nodded. Her mother sighed and shook her head. "He told us everything, you know. Maybe it's for the best you two won't be married. I don't know that we can forgive his not keeping you safe in all this," she said.

At that, Nell turned around. "None of this is his fault, you can't blame him," she said, her voice rising. "He's been with me every step, and any danger I wound up in wasn't because of him! I don't want this to be a reason for our families to fall out."

"I don't want that either, but it isn't as if we're joining our families together anymore—maybe taking some space from each other for a little while wouldn't be so bad." Her mother stared intently at Nell. "Would it?"

She could tell that her mother was trying to get to the truth, but Nell hardly knew how to answer her. She only knew she was exhausted, and sick to death of being afraid. She pulled on a fresh dress and sat down on her bed for a moment to rest. It was soft and warm; Beth-Anne must have heated the sheets with a hot-water pan. But she permitted herself only a few minutes' indulgence. Charlotte needed her, and there was no time to waste.

Chapter 38

———

CHARLOTTE

———

BY THE TIME SHE FOUND HERSELF TOSSED INTO A CARRIAGE outside the Jacksons' town house, Charlotte had already made the decision to run. The only question was when. Just a few minutes after ripping Nell away from her, Frank had shoved Charlotte out onto the front porch and picked up his suitcases as they went. There was an enclosed carriage waiting for them with a driver in the front, and a bench seat outside at the back. Frank pushed Charlotte's wrists together and tied a ribbon tightly around them. It dug uncomfortably into her skin. He hoisted her up and shoved her onto the bench—the notion of sharing a carriage ride with a slave girl was apparently too far beneath his dignity, even if avoiding it meant Charlotte would be out of his sight. But he left her with a warning before he stepped into the carriage: "You'd better not make any trouble, girl. If I hear a single sound out of you, you'll pay for it."

Silently, Charlotte prayed that he and Kate had come to their senses and let Nell go home—maybe she'd even still be able to help Evie. But in the meantime, the only person Charlotte could save was herself. During the night, she had fretted over how she'd gotten here and whether she'd ever get back to her friends. As the hours had worn on, she'd imagined tiptoeing out of the room and making a run for it while Kate slept, bolting out the same door Frank had dragged her in through and running down the street with the cool night air rushing in her face. But she decided it was no use. There was too much ground to cover between upstairs and down—someone would've caught her. Still, she'd been determined to find a way out, and the scene she saw at dawn had only steeled her resolve.

Kate had stirred at first light, and for nearly half an hour Charlotte had watched from the door of Evie's tiny room as Kate tried and failed to dress herself. She huffed and grunted, hopelessly struggling to pull on her own dress and tie her own stays behind her back. Before long, she gave up and stuck her head out into the hallway, her undone hair looking like an oriole's nest. "Maggie! Maggie! I need your girl to come in and help me!"

In a moment, Ada came in. The swelling on her eye had calmed somewhat, but the cut on her temple still looked an angry red. Things here were the same as they were at White Oaks, the same as everywhere: runaways ran, and the slaves left behind suffered the consequences.

"Dress me, Ada," Kate had said, gesturing at the pile of clothes on the floor. Charlotte stared as Ada went to work, primping and tying, brushing Kate's hair and making her ready for the day. Ada was silent, her weary eyes focused on her work, but through it all, Kate kept chattering at the woman, trying to make eye contact and get her to engage. The whole scene had unfolded in front of Charlotte as if she was peering into a looking glass and watching her own life as it had been for all those years at White Oaks, and as Kate insisted it would be again.

Before sending Charlotte downstairs, Kate had turned to her. "I expected better from you, Carrie. I didn't blame you for going with your father when he stole you away—what else could you have done? But I've never known you to be this way yourself, defiant and conniving. If you won't tell me where Evie is, there's nothing for us to discuss here. You can go back down South. You'll leave this morning, and Frank will accompany you. But we'll see each other again before too long. I can only pray by then, you'll have returned to yourself." Kate's eyes had welled up as she waved Charlotte off. But Charlotte couldn't even muster irritation at Kate's maudlin display, and she had no tears of her own—only terror, knowing what was to come.

Now, as the carriage threatened to roll her back to a life of hard, bitter work and unending servitude, Charlotte balanced herself on the seat and stared into the distance. Just as Evie and even James had been brave enough to reach out and grab their freedom, it was time for Charlotte to claim her own. No matter what Kate said, the South had seen the last of her. Whatever the risk, she simply had to try to escape.

The carriage started moving, with Frank closed inside and Charlotte sitting out back facing opposite the carriage's direction. As they drove away from the house, the sun shone right into Charlotte's face. They were headed west, away from the Delaware River. The streets were still waking up, but as the carriage approached the center of the city, shops were opening, sidewalk peddlers were setting up their wares, and men and women hurried down the dusty roads, off to factories to make clothes, workshops to bend metal, and homes to scrub floors. Charlotte looked from side to side as people rushed by. She tried her best to read the street signs, then paused to try to figure out where exactly she was. It was easier to tell without a blanket over her head, at least.

By the look of things, the carriage was headed toward the train depot on Vine and Broad streets. To get there from the town house, they'd have to travel down Arch Street, not too far from Pennsylvania Hall. Charlotte decided that was where she would make her move. With the opening conventions under way there would be plenty of people around—people who might be inclined to help.

As they got deeper into the center of town, the once-bare light poles and awnings looked different. Square paper placards with large, dark lettering seemed to be everywhere. Charlotte strained to read them: she was stunned to see that they called for people to "interfere, forcibly" with the hall opening. On looking closer, she realized the placards were dated the day before.

But Charlotte didn't have to wonder whether rioters had succeeded in stopping the conventions; the thickening crowds moving up Sixth Street proved they hadn't. Hundreds of men and women rode along in carriages and open-topped wagons, while mixed groups of Black and white folks walked side by side on the cobble-stone. A few pairs of white and Black women walked briskly up Sixth, arm in arm, toward Race Street. Between keeping company with each other and their businesslike pace, they could only be headed to the Women's Antislavery Convention. Whatever the mob had tried to do, it hadn't worked. The opening events were continu-ing into their fourth day—May 17—and Charlotte's safe harbor was just blocks away, if only she could get there.

As Charlotte scanned the crowd in search of a familiar face—or even just a friendly one—she puzzled over how she might call some attention to herself. In most parts of the city there would've been no point in making a scene—the city was as much South as it was North, and almost no one would've troubled themselves to help a Black woman in distress. But this close to Pennsylvania Hall, during this week, the odds were much better—there was nowhere else she'd be around so many people who might be willing to come to her aid, but her chance slipped farther away with every block she was carried past Sixth Street.

Without any good options, she reached down and tore off a large piece of her underskirt. The seams of the fabric popped apart. Tak-ing the cloth strip in hand, she stretched her tied hands to feel around the outside of the carriage for something to tie it to. There was a small hoop above the bench she sat on, a few inches over her head. She knotted the fabric around it and fluffed out the wings into a great white bow to make it easier for passersby to see. To draw even more attention, Charlotte clasped her hands together and raised them up just beneath the bow. In her pose, she was the supplicant—the chained and pleading slave woman stitched and printed onto aboli-tionist tracts, pamphlets, and even handkerchiefs and blankets throughout the free North. Nell had pressed more than a few of those materials into Charlotte's hands since they'd known each other, and they'd sold many at the holiday fair. The image wasn't one Char-lotte liked, but to anyone in the antislavery movement, her awkward position might look familiar enough to tell them she was in exactly the kind of trouble they most abhorred.

Charlotte held that posture uncomfortably for several shaky blocks and attracted more than a few puzzled looks along the way. She was undeterred—this was no time to be bashful. Finally, once the carriage crossed Eighth Street, a welcome face caught her eye: Hetty Reckless.

She was walking alongside another woman, a younger one, with fair olive-hued skin and dark brown hair that cascaded around her shoulders in loose waves. Her looks put Charlotte in the mind of her father. Charlotte made eye contact, and Hetty and the young woman stared back at her, eyes darting from Charlotte's posed body to the bow tied onto the carriage, then back to Charlotte again. Charlotte wanted to shout to them but couldn't risk Frank hearing her. Instead, without making a sound, she simply mouthed "Help" as clearly as she could. For a moment, the woman looked confused, but Hetty whispered something in her ear and she nodded as if a notion had suddenly come to her.

In an instant, the two rushed up the sidewalk to get ahead of the carriage. There, the younger woman stepped into the street to cross. Curiosity shook Charlotte out of her pose, and she craned her neck around to see what was going on in front of the carriage. She watched as, quite theatrically, the woman lifted a hand to her head and said "Oh! My goodness!" before fainting dead away in the middle of the road.

The carriage jerked to a stop, along with all the other traffic. Charlotte was thrown back, bumping into the rear of the carriage. A few horses tripped at the sudden stop, rattling shocked passengers. Distracted by the commotion, passersby on the crowded sidewalk ran into one another, yelping as their heads smacked together.

Frank poked his head out and prodded the driver with his cane. "What the devil is going on out there? Why have we stopped?" Other men had jumped down from their horses and exited their carriages and wagons to attend to the young woman on the road, but Frank apparently had no such gentlemanly impulses. He looked around and, satisfied that there would be only a short hitch in his plans, ducked back inside.

Amid all the commotion, Hetty appeared suddenly behind the carriage and extended her hand to help Charlotte down.

"Come with me, quick." She led Charlotte a block back toward Sixth Street, weaving through the stalled carriages, wagons, and men on horseback to put as much distance between them and Frank as possible in just a few seconds. When they reached the next intersection, Hetty dragged Charlotte down a side street and then ducked with her into an alleyway.

The two of them paused to catch their breath, and Hetty untied Charlotte's hands.

"Thank you, you have no idea what you've just saved me from," said Charlotte.

"I think I can guess," Hetty said, laughing. "Let's get you up to the hall—if it's like yesterday, the crowd there will be thick enough to hide you completely." Gratefully, Charlotte fell in step behind Hetty. As they walked, she fought off the urge to look over her shoulder. The packed city streets would have to give her cover. Forward, only forward.

Chapter 39

EVIE

IN THE MARIONS' PARLOR, EVIE SAT DOWN BESIDE DARCEL AS everyone waited for Nell to return so that they could do something— anything. By now, everyone had talked themselves out. As they sat in the quiet that stretched into midmorning, the Marions' house- maid brought in food and coffee. "Keep your strength up," she'd said quietly before disappearing into the back of the house. But no one had any appetite, and the fruit she'd left on the sideboard sat un- touched.

Before long, Nell marched back into the house and planted her- self in a seat beside Evie. She took charge right away.

"All right, we need to get Charlotte back," Nell pronounced. "Evie, do you know the route that Frank would take south? Perhaps one of the other servants in the house would've said something to you?" Nell asked.

Evie looked up, feeling guilty at the mention of the others—Ada, Louise, even gruff Peter. She'd rushed away from them at the market with hardly a second thought, but now uncomfortable questions were swirling in her head. Could she have brought them with her somehow? Why hadn't she even tried? And worst of all, in abandon- ing them, what horrors had she left them to?

"Did you see the others? Are they all right?" she asked, distracted. "They were good folks, and I was sorry to leave the ones I still knew."

"Still knew?" Nell asked.

"Well, with Kate's family members coming and going every few months, the staff changed a lot—sometimes they'd even send slaves back to the family's main plantation in Virginia and bring up new ones to take their places," Evie explained. "It was hard to get too comfortable with any one of them. I don't know why they did it."

"Maybe to keep them from learning too much about the city and trying to escape?" James said quietly, looking pointedly at Evie.

Nell shook her head. "That may be part of it, yes. But it's because of the law. When slaves visit Pennsylvania with their owners, they don't automatically become free—not right away. That only happens if they stay too long," she said. "It's a compromise with the slavers who vacation and do business here, a way to keep them coming in without having to fear losing any of their precious property. It's shameful, really, and—"

James interjected before Nell could continue her speech.

"How long is 'too long'?"

"Six months, I believe," said Nell. She'd read about it in the abolitionist papers, she explained—slavers had been using the loophole to bring their slaves back and forth with them to "free" Philadelphia for decades. There were even whispers that President George Washington himself had taken advantage of an earlier version of the law back when the city served as the nation's temporary capital.

James cut right to the heart of the matter.

"So that means Charlotte is legally free, then? And me too?" he asked. "We've been here much longer than six months."

"That's right," Nell said. "If Kate tries to take either of you back south with her, she'll be breaking Pennsylvania's law against kidnapping—she's got no legal claim to you after so many years. And you, Evie—how long have you been here?"

"Me? I haven't kept count of the days, and I couldn't tell you exactly when we came up. But I remember Christmas didn't come around until I'd already been here a month or so."

"November, then. The middle or the end of it. You're so close to your freedom—no more than a couple of days, if that," Nell said.

"Maybe so," Evie said. She sat quietly for a moment and took that in. And as she did the math in her head, her thoughts turned to Ada: How long had it been since Maggie last took her back to Virginia? She might be free and not even know it—Evie couldn't be sure, and she felt another pang of guilt at having left her. But for the moment, she needed to focus on the person in the most danger. "I can't think about that now. We've got to get Charlotte back, like you said. Kate must be panicked, and I'm scared of what she'll do."

Nell inhaled sharply. "Would she hurt her?"

"No," said Evie. "But she would try to keep her and pay no mind to whatever the law says about kidnapping or six months."

James leaned forward. "And all she wants is to have Evie back? Like some sort of trade?" he asked. Evie shifted in her seat. She didn't like the feel of his question.

"What she wants is immaterial. No one is trading anyone," Nell said, in a tone that brooked no argument. "And those orders come straight from Charlotte. We'll find another way."

"We may have legal recourse here since Charlotte is a free woman," Mr. Marion interjected. "If we can get to her before she's crossed out of Pennsylvania, there may be a chance. But we can't press our case alone—we ought to have reinforcements from the Vigilant Association to plan how to go about it. Would you be amenable to that, Mr. Vaughn?"

He stared at the floor, not answering.

"Everyone will be at Pennsylvania Hall today," Alex said. "We can find them there."

"And Evie and I will join you," Nell said. "That way we can at least get you safely out of Kate's reach, Evie, and the other abolitionists there can help us figure out how to get Charlotte back."

Evie nodded and looked to James for some sign he was on board. "Uncle Jack?"

Still, he said nothing. He looked conflicted, and Evie suspected she knew why. His plan to pay for Charlotte's return would've settled matters quietly—privately. But that plan had failed, and now Evie wondered if all their remaining options seemed too public, too unlikely to work, or both. In truth, Evie didn't know how much hope she should place in the abolitionists either. She turned to Nell.

"What can they really do for us at some meeting?" Evie asked. "It's all just a lot of talking."

"We have our ways," Alex said, stepping forward.

"Please, Evie, I promised Charlotte I'd look after you and I'm as good as my word," Nell said. "Let's go. We lose nothing by trying."

As they departed, Mr. Marion invited James and Darcel to stay at the house and wait for any news, and Darcel nodded quietly on their behalf.

Nell and Evie left James sitting in the parlor, head in hands.

PENNSYLVANIA HALL DWARFED ANY building Evie had ever seen in her life. It towered over the street with its gleaming white columns, and stretched farther back than she could see from the corner. But what shocked her most was how Nell and Alex strode into the place with such confidence, as Evie followed behind them in silent awe. In the crowds outside, there were more than a few hard stares from white faces as they arrived and entered the building, but inside seemed to be some kind of sanctuary where Black and white people mingled freely. A few white women smiled and nodded greetings to Nell, while a mixed group of Black and white men came by and shook Alex's hand, asking if he was headed down to the newspaper office.

Other women were beginning to gather, and one came by and gave Evie the once-over. "Another new friend, Nell?"

Evie didn't like her tone.

"Nice to see you, Lillian." Nell was all cool politeness. "This is Evie, and she knows more about the matters under discussion today than anyone else you're likely to have the privilege of meeting."

Evie smirked. Lillian looked like a dog who'd been bopped on the nose with a newspaper. "Pleased to meet you," Lillian said in a pinched voice. "I'll see you both inside." She walked off. Were these the sorts of people Charlotte had been spending her time with?

"Just what is it you all do here?" Evie asked.

"I suppose you could say we're about the business of freedom—discussing it, working toward it, reshaping what it looks like," Nell said. She talked about the meetings they had, and all the little nooks and crannies the building held, from shops selling goods produced only by nonslave labor to the newspaper offices, and of course the rooms where the conventions were under way. "Truly, there's no safer place for you in the entire city than here," said Nell.

"I'm not so sure about that," Alex said, glancing warily out the front windows at the crowd they'd just walked through. Evie followed his gaze and wondered.

"I wouldn't be too concerned," Nell said. "It seems like the conventions have managed to go on without too much trouble so far, so I'm sure everything will be all right. But let's get out of the entryway."

As Nell led them along, Evie hurried to catch up and walk next to her.

"You and Carrie spend a lot of time here?"

Nell looked confused for a second, then must've understood. Evie kept forgetting Carrie called herself something else now.

"Not yet since it's so new, but I hope we will. There's so much work to be done," Nell said. She and Evie stopped and stood in the hallway outside one of the meeting rooms. "We can wait here," Nell told her. The Women's Antislavery Convention was set to gather there ahead of the afternoon's planned keynote, and the women Nell had made arrangements with would be there any minute, along with the others.

Evie gazed up at the soaring ceiling and grand staircase. "I can see why Carrie likes this sort of place. Where we grew up felt so small you could hardly breathe," she said.

Nell smiled and took her by the hands. "I'm glad you're here. Though I wish we'd met under better circumstances," she said.

Evie shrugged. "Seems like this is the only way we'd ever be in the

same place, honestly. Carrie told me a bit about you, you know, before I had to leave for the Marions'. It's like you were the first person
she thought of when I showed up," she said. Evie knew she ought to
be grateful, but the outsize space Nell took up in Charlotte's new life
just made her feel pushed aside. Nell didn't seem to see it that way,
though.

"I'm afraid I haven't really lived up to her high esteem," she said,
her eyes downcast. "And I know I'm not the most important thing to
her. She's made some mistakes in how she's handled things up until
now, but Charlotte's never once stopped trying to get you free—not
even when her father all but locked her away at home."

Evie listened as Nell pled Charlotte's case and found it hard to
argue with her. Since she'd found Charlotte again, Evie was closer to
being free than she'd ever been before. Not only that, but she'd
glimpsed full, rich lives among her own people—Black people ac-
countable just to themselves and not to some whining missus or
hateful massah. Quietly, Evie admitted it to herself: if she'd been
brought here and shown all this, she wouldn't have tried to go back
to White Oaks to rescue anyone either. She'd breathed free air now
and never wanted to feel the earthy musk of the plantation fields or
the stale air of some massah's big house in her lungs again.

She stood beside Nell and tried to blend in.

Chapter 40

CHARLOTTE

CHARLOTTE RUSHED UP RACE STREET, PANTING AS SHE WEAVED through the crowds and tried to keep pace with Hetty's unyielding dash toward Pennsylvania Hall. When the building's soaring bright white columns and the freshly paved pathway leading up to the main door came into full view, Charlotte breathed a sigh of relief. Get inside, and she'd be safe—that's all she had to do.

But hundreds of people were gathered around the hall, and at the sight of their scowls, Charlotte suddenly felt like she'd been thrown back into that terrifying mob at Mr. Purvis's speech. Alarmed, she slowed her walk, hesitating to get any closer. "Come on!" shouted Hetty. But it was hard to hear her over the din. On either side of the pathway to the door, white men of all ages were red-faced and screaming at passing attendees. "No race mixing, amalgamation is abomination!" "Shame on you!" "Respect the Constitution, respect property rights!" All those signs calling for people to "interfere" with the opening had done their work after all.

Charlotte leaned closer to Hetty, frightened by the bile and rage that surrounded them on all sides. She kept her arms down, clutching at her skirts.

"Don't pay them no mind, they've been at this for days," Hetty shouted. "We just keep on doing what we need to do."

The building's front door was propped open to let people in for the conventions. But a pair of men was stopping everyone at the threshold.

"What group are you with?" they were asking.

As she and Hetty waited their turn to get inside, Charlotte heard the array of answers. This one was with the Pennsylvania Abolitionist Society. That one represented the Massachusetts Antislavery Society. And here was a member of the Ladies' New York City Antislavery Society—Charlotte eyed that woman skeptically, remembering how Nell had told her the New York society didn't admit Black members.

When they reached the entrance, Hetty told the men they were with the Philadelphia Female Antislavery Society and there for the women's convention. The men waved them in and handed them programs that listed the day's planned events.

"Nell may be here. Me and her had made some arrangements for your other friend, but she never showed up yesterday," Hetty said, carefully avoiding saying Evie's name. "We can all catch up this afternoon." Charlotte scanned the crowd. She desperately wanted to believe Nell had made it back all right. And if she had, maybe she'd be here with Evie. But whatever else happened, Charlotte already owed Hetty her life.

"Hetty—" she began. Hetty put up her hand.

"You don't have to explain anything to me, I know better than to ask. You're safe now," she said.

Charlotte exhaled. "A long story for another time," she said.

"But I'll tell you," said Hetty, "you ought to hang around here awhile to make sure the man who had you isn't still looking for you in the streets. Give it a few hours, and at the end of the day some of us can walk you home."

Home. Where was that? Charlotte had been dragged from White Oaks to Society Hill to Kate's family town house, but there was nowhere in particular she could say she truly belonged. Except maybe here. For all she'd tried to scrape and scratch out some kind of freedom that felt like her own, maybe a grand hall filled with people dedicated to liberty was the closest thing she'd find to a place that was really for her.

But where were her people now? They'd have no way of knowing she was safe. Nell would be worried sick, and Evie would be terrified. And then there was her father. Being more than preoccupied with the matter of her own kidnapping, until that moment Charlotte hadn't yet thought about what kind of danger James must be in. If Kate was willing to have her and Nell snatched off the street, how much worse would she do to the man who started this whole mess in the first place?

Charlotte pressed in with the crowd, working out her next move. She wasn't alone, at least. Thousands were packed into the hall, all gathered around the single purpose of ending slavery. And according to the posted schedule, the women's convention was set to reconvene in just thirty minutes in the Grand Saloon upstairs. That was as likely a place as any to reconnect with everyone. She attracted a few stares as she moved through the crowd and realized how disheveled she must look. After ducking into a women's lounge to smooth her hair and brush the road's dirt from the bottom of her dress, she started toward the Grand Saloon.

As she worked her way up the wide staircase, she could hear the insistent throngs outside keeping up their harassment. Men pounded on the exteriors of the windows and doors, shouting and cursing, until the racket became too loud to ignore. The majestic walls standing between the conventioneers and the crowd outside seemed too thin to keep them apart. In Charlotte's ears, shrill screams about race mixing competed with hoarse shouts about Blacks unfairly taking jobs from hardworking white men, and bitter complaints about all the trouble the fugitive slaves kept stirring up with Pennsylvania's Southern neighbors.

Listening to those last pointed remarks, Charlotte felt exposed. The old gnawing fear curled back up inside her, crowding out the fleeting peace she'd been feeling at the idea of this place as a sanctuary. Even among so many well-intentioned people, her defenselessness was never far from her mind. She kept climbing.

The Grand Saloon bustled with scores of people gathered beneath its gleaming gold-inscribed arch. At the center of a magnificently painted sunflower that filled the enormous domed ceiling, a mirror reflected the crowd below. In it, Charlotte caught sight of a familiar tuft of red-brown hair atop someone's head: Alex. And with him, thank God, was Nell, standing with Evie right by her side. Just as Charlotte lowered her eyes, they saw her. All at once, the three young women rushed together and embraced.

Charlotte stepped back and looked Evie over to make sure she was all right.

"We're a long way from White Oaks, eh?" Evie said.

Charlotte laughed. "And staying that way." She turned to Nell, taking her by her hands. They were still reddened and raw looking. "And you, are you all right? I'm so sorry."

Nell curled up her hands and put them at her sides, hiding them in the folds of her skirt.

"We're all safe now, that's what matters," she said. "How did you get away?"

Charlotte told Evie and Nell about the carriage ride through the city, her plan, and how finally it was Hetty who came to her rescue.

"And I got plenty of rescuin' to spare." Hetty, smiling broadly, had come over as Charlotte told the story, placing a warm, protective hand on Charlotte's shoulder. "This your friend?" She gestured at Evie. Charlotte and Nell nodded.

"Glad to see you here, dear, but you all will need to make her a touch less obvious if this is going to work." Evie was still in the housemaid's uniform she'd borrowed from Charlotte, which was conspicuous enough, but that wasn't the only trouble. It was her hair. Still in two pigtail braids, her style stuck out like a sore thumb among all the elaborately coiffed women—Black and white—who'd gathered for the convention.

"Miss Smythe will be back this evening, we can hand her off then. In the meantime, get this girl disguised," said Hetty. But even with Evie squared away, Charlotte couldn't relax. Whatever they did, Kate was still out there somewhere, ready to come back for any of them—Evie, James, Charlotte herself—at any time. She leaned back in her chair and folded her arms, irritated by the tension that wouldn't leave her shoulders.

With the women's convention about to resume, it was time for any lingering men to clear the room. Alex recognized his cue and stood, gathering up his notebook and pen. "I'm headed home to get some rest, but I'll see you all back here later; my editor wants me to cover the remarks tonight." On his way out, he looked up at the stage and grinned. "It's a shame you three can't take the podium yourselves; you've got quite a story to tell."

Charlotte looked around the hall. The women were legion, united by their opposition to slavery but representing a mishmash of conflicting interests beyond that. Imagine telling this wide-ranging coalition everything that had brought Charlotte and her friends to this moment: a girl smuggled here by a white-passing fugitive, a slave plotting to destroy a white woman's marriage before it started, and a supposedly respectable young woman spearheading an illegal scheme to smuggle a runaway out of town. Captivating as a speech like that might be, every last person involved would be ruined by it.

Charlotte sat up straight in her seat. Of course. The answer had been staring her in the face all day, shouting at her even: the crowds. With so many people in town who loudly, publicly opposed Kate's entire way of life, Charlotte, Evie, and Nell's story was a scandal just waiting to be dragged into the light of day. And yes, their reputations would suffer, but Kate's house of cards would come tumbling down in the bargain. Who in this mass could resist the sordid tale of a liar and kidnapper? It was the only sure way to guarantee that Evie was safe forever, and that Kate left them all alone for good. The truth would be what kept them free.

Or at least the threat of it.

"I need paper!" Charlotte said. "And Alex." Nell got up and hurried after him. Meanwhile, Hetty led Charlotte to a table on the side of the room, pushed aside the decorative bolt of blue silk that had been laid on top, and offered her a seat. There, Charlotte wrote out her story: how she'd grown up on Murphy's White Oaks plantation, how she'd arrived in Philadelphia to start a new life with her father and then run into Evie, and how Kate had snatched her and Nell— two free Black women—off the street, threatened them, and illegally put them to work. It was the nightmare of every free Black person in the city, she knew, and the unfairness of it would also resonate with white allies gathered at the hall. Not least, the scandal would upend all of Kate's plans.

When Charlotte was finished, she beckoned over her friends.

"Alex, can you take a copy of this down to the newspaper office and set it in type?" she asked. "We'll show Kate what the costs will be if she chooses to keep chasing us."

"I'd be glad to," he said. After what Kate had done to Nell, he looked downright pleased. "It'll take a few hours, but I'll have it ready by tonight."

He started to hurry away, but Nell reached out for his hand and squeezed it. "I know you must be tired. Thank you," she said, looking him straight in the eyes. He smiled in return and was off. As soon as he was gone, Charlotte caught Nell's eye and raised her eyebrows. Nell smiled sheepishly and turned away.

With Alex's work in motion, Charlotte began to feel at least a little bit more secure, and less vulnerable to Kate's dangerous whims. But somehow, that didn't feel like enough. Owning up on paper to all she'd been through had been a relief. In pouring out her hurts, her losses, her fears, and her hopes, Charlotte found that her experience was worth more than a scheme to blackmail an enslaver. The story she'd written down was true, it was hers, and she needed to tell it. If the women at this convention were going to dedicate their lives to ending slavery, they ought to hear from women in the thick of it. And with the truth told openly, without any more lies or shame, maybe Charlotte could begin to knit all the pieces of herself into a livable whole: a former slave, yes, but also a daughter, a sister, a friend, and a young woman with dreams and ambitions of her own.

When the presiding officer opened the meeting, Charlotte stepped out from behind the desk and raised her hand, signaling for permission to speak. After a moment's grumbling from the president and the crowd about this highly irregular intervention, Hetty sighed impatiently, stood up beside Charlotte, and led both her and Evie to the front of the room. With a single withering look from Hetty, the president moved aside.

Hetty turned to Charlotte and winked. Gratefully, Charlotte smiled back and stepped up to the podium. She looked out at the room. With nearly a hundred delegates in attendance, every seat was taken and some women were left to stand at the back of the room. With a mix of white and Black faces staring up at her, some looking skeptical or annoyed, others merely curious, Charlotte cleared her throat.

"This week is all about freedom, and how we're willing to fight for it. As you well know, that's a fight that's come to our very doorstep, even in this city. In my case, a fight that I've brought here with me." She took a deep breath and held nothing back. "I myself am a runaway. Just this week, my former mistress found me here in the city and tried to drag me back down South, back into chains, along with my dear friend Evie." She nudged Evie forward. "Another young woman whose life she's stolen and pressed into her service. But we're more than just what some plantation mistress made of us.

"I've only just begun to feel what it is to live and walk freely here in Philadelphia, to claim a life and destiny of my own—some of you have even become part of that. Evie deserves the chance to do the same, and so does every other man, woman, and child trapped in the brutal system of slavery. That system may strip us of nearly all our choices and hopes, yes—but not of the humanity we share in common with everyone in this room. So today, we're here not only as fellow members but as supplicants. We ask you not just to safeguard *our* hard-won freedom but to do whatever it takes—no matter what the law says—to win that same freedom for all."

Charlotte exhaled. As soon as she finished speaking, Hetty came to her side. "I can always tell a fellow self-emancipator," she said warmly. A titter of nervous laughter in the room broke some of the tension. Hetty put an arm around Charlotte's shoulders. "We'll look after you."

Before Charlotte could leave the podium, dozens of women rose from their seats and rushed to the front of the room. Suddenly, Charlotte and Evie found themselves encircled as delegates both Black and white lauded their courage in escaping, and in speaking out. Some had been touched deeply by Charlotte's words and had tears in their eyes as they thanked her for stepping forward the way she had. After a few moments, a few of the Black delegates took Charlotte's and Evie's hands and asked to pray with them.

Before Charlotte bowed her head, she saw Nell standing outside the circle, simply watching, her face etched with relief, and respect. Charlotte couldn't say if Nell had forgiven her for all the lies she'd told, or whether she'd soon trust her again, but that look was worth something. Even if the two of them had to start over again to really know each other, they'd begin on even ground.

After Charlotte's speech, the more formal remarks began, and there was still plenty more business for the convention to attend to. She, Evie, and Nell settled back into their seats. From where she sat, Charlotte couldn't see the people gathered beyond the building's doors, but she could still hear them.

As the afternoon wore on, the convention passed resolutions and made new fundraising plans. More than once, out of the corner of her eye Charlotte caught Nell shaking her head and grumbling. "We aren't going to fundraise our way to abolition," she muttered. "Direct action has to be met with direct action." Watching her, Charlotte wondered how much longer the women's Antislavery Society would be able to count Nell as a member after what she'd gone through.

In truth, the whipped-up crowd outside made it all but impossible to forget just how pressing these issues were. With every hour that passed, the mob grew more aggressive, shouting threats and slurs through the windows and pushing against the doors, trying to get inside. Three women from the convention went out to plead for calm and quiet, to no avail.

When the afternoon meetings finally concluded, one of the building managers nervously circulated among the departing women.

"Ladies, everyone, please—as you leave, use the exit that leads you out the back of the building. Take the main staircase down and turn left, you'll find the back door there," he said in a shaky voice. As he scanned the room, he looked over at where white Antislavery Society members like Lucretia Mott and Sarah Pugh were talking with Black ones, including Hetty and Nell, and visibly winced. "And please consider separating yourselves, by color I mean—we don't want to anger the crowd out there any further!"

Several of the ladies scoffed and continued their conversations for a few minutes more. But eventually, the Grand Saloon emptied out. Downstairs, a few undeterred women started toward the front door. The crowd outside roared, and a building manager tried to redirect the women toward the back. They would not be moved.

"We won't shrink away that easy," Hetty called out.

"Indeed not, ladies. We won't let a little appearance of danger deter us," Lucretia agreed. "Come," she said, reaching out an arm to Hetty. "We'll go out together, and keep close."

The manager looked at them aghast.

"That's exactly what's got them all riled up in the first place!" He threw up his hands as the pair continued walking toward the front door, Hetty's deep brown arm threaded through Lucretia's plaster-white one.

The front door swung open. The crowd's shouts thundered into the building, echoing off the high ceilings. At the sight of the crush of humanity just over the threshold, their reddened faces twisted with anger, Charlotte's heart leapt into her throat. She fought off a wild urge to run after Hetty and Lucretia and drag them back inside by the backs of their dresses.

The two women weren't heedless of the danger—they flinched a little at the sight of what lay outside the doors. But, as if moved aside by their will, the crowd opened a path just wide enough for them to go through. Men formed a wall of hatred on either side, shouting and cursing. But Lucretia and Hetty kept going forward.

Made brave by their courage, Charlotte stood up straighter. She took Evie's arm and stepped through the large front door. Over her shoulder she could see Nell following close behind, arm in arm with another of the white Antislavery Society members.

As they got into the thick of the crowd, the shouts and hisses grew louder and closer. "Amalgamation! Abomination!" Evie clung more tightly to her.

"Eyes ahead, just keep walking," Charlotte said.

In this roiling sea of barely suppressed violence, the rest of the world felt far away. Charlotte could conceive of nothing but herself and Evie, moving through the crowd deliberately, gingerly, desperate not to provoke anyone.

When they finally made it safely across the street, Charlotte turned back to survey what was happening. She wondered if the rest of the building would be evacuated—Alex was still downstairs in the newspaper office working on the task she'd set him to.

"Shouldn't we go back in to find Alex?" Nell asked, as if she'd read Charlotte's mind.

"I'm not sure—but, as long as he stays inside, he should be safe, I think," Charlotte said. In truth, she was worried, but it was too great a risk to turn back and try to wade through that crowd again—the men had begun to surround the building, and by then were even pressing toward the back door. "We should keep moving."

Charlotte looked around, squinting and peering down side streets, then turned back to look more closely at the crowd. Nell did the same.

"I don't see any policemen, or anything that looks like the kind of civilian militia they'd usually raise for a mob like this," said Nell. "Maybe things will settle down by tonight's meetings."

But as the last few people strode out of the hall, the screaming from the horde only intensified.

BACK IN NELL'S NEIGHBORHOOD, curtains were pushed aside up and down the street, with faces looking curiously out the windows at the little cohort assembled on the Marions' doorstep. Almost no other people were outside, and even ten blocks away from Pennsylvania

Hall, they still felt perilously close to the mob. When Mr. Marion opened the door to Nell, Evie, and Charlotte, he looked over their shoulders as he welcomed them inside, scanning for his son, or any sign of danger.

"We've had visitors coming by all day telling us what's going on downtown. There have been signs posted that drew the mob together and riled them up. It may be a difficult night," Mr. Marion said. "Did you see Alex?"

"He's still at the hall, just finishing a small project at the newspaper, but I'm sure he'll be along soon," Nell said.

"Hopefully things will calm down. We'll have to bring Evie back for the evening programs to meet with her transport out of town," Charlotte said.

"Carrie? Carrie? Is that you?" Her father's voice rang out from the parlor. He rushed into the entry hallway, pulled her in close, and squeezed her tightly. Charlotte stood stiff, with her arms at her sides. Eyes darting around the room as her father held her, she scanned the faces of her friends, who had averted their eyes politely—all except Darcel, who stood just behind James's shoulder and beamed at her, relieved.

She cleared her throat and gently pulled away, trying to put some space between herself and James.

"It's all right, I'm all right." She spoke to him as she would a child. "There's no need for all that."

James stepped back and searched her face. "What happened? I'd been trying to figure out how to get you back, and I hadn't given up. I was waiting here to sort out what to do next. I wouldn't have left without you, you must know that." His voice rose at the end, making a question of his words. Then at last, he asked, "Why didn't you tell me about Evie?"

Charlotte finally softened, her shoulders slumping as the tension went out of them. She shrugged.

"I think you know the answer to that," she said. Evie looked at the floor.

"What matters is that we're all here now," Charlotte went on. "Kate tried to send me south, but I ran."

At that, James's usually stern mouth stretched out in a small smile and he stood up a little straighter. Charlotte could've sworn she saw his chest inflate a half inch. Maybe they had something in common after all. Encouraged, she went on, regaling him and the others with the tale of how she found help on the street, then managed to make her way to the hall. As far as she knew, Charlotte explained, Frank had no idea where she was—she'd disappeared into the crowd.

"He and Kate won't leave us alone though, not without a reason. That's why I've written an article to expose everything about her," said Charlotte. "Alex is getting it ready to print right this minute."

James's jaw visibly tightened. She might've guessed he wouldn't like that part. He took her aside, out of everyone else's hearing. His voice was low.

"Print what you will, but please leave me out of it," he said.

Charlotte shook her head. He always seemed to find new reservoirs of ways to disappoint her. Couldn't he see how different their lives could be—how much better—if only he'd own up to who he really was? "After all this, you're still worried about protecting this lie you've built?" she said.

"I built it for you."

"I know that now," she said. "Kate told me everything."

James exhaled, and he looked into her face, searching for understanding. "I was sure you wouldn't want to leave White Oaks, but there was nothing else to be done," he explained. He'd overheard the whole sordid scheme one night in the big house after Massah Murphy died. It turned out the man had been deep in debt, barely keeping the plantation afloat on credit. For the last few years, all the slaves had suffered the pangs of their dwindling food rations, even as Murphy slowly sold them off while tobacco overgrew the fields and soon withered away with not enough hands to harvest it. He'd always sworn he'd turn things around somehow. But when he died, the jig was up, all the bills came due, and reality crashed down on widowed

Kate's delicate little head. She saw the problem, then looked around at the plantation's few slaves left—mostly old men, women, and children—and figured a way to turn a quick profit and get herself out from under the worst of it. She would sell them off, as fast as she could.

The future she had planned for Carrie was particularly bleak. James had heard Kate talking to her brother, and he had expressed a particular interest in taking Carrie off Kate's hands, for a fair price of course. The moment he heard Kate strike the bargain, James's mind was made up, he explained: he would take her and run north to freedom, away from the kind of men who thought to purchase little girls so they could work them into an early grave and do God only knew what to them in the meantime. Not to *his* daughter.

The rest, Charlotte already knew.

"I wish you'd told me the truth," she said. "Everything could have been different. Maybe I wouldn't have been so angry with you."

"I'd rather you were angry with me than blame yourself for our leaving, or have to imagine for even a single second what Kate's brother wanted with you," he said, averting his eyes uncomfortably. "I just wanted to put it all behind us—talking about it wouldn't have helped. And none of that matters now. All that matters is that we stay safe."

Charlotte shook her head. Even after all these years, he still couldn't see how much had been lost in the name of safety. He'd saved them both from the worst of slavery, yes, but at the cost of the truth—and there was no joy, no peace, no real community in a life built on lies. She wasn't willing to live that way anymore, even if he was.

She stared at him, but his jaw was set. He wasn't ready, and there would be no forcing him.

"We'll keep your name out of the article, should it come to that," Charlotte said, sighing. "Hopefully it won't." She went back to rejoin the others across the Marions' parlor.

Darcel looked at her with sympathy. He'd been watching her talk with James on the other side of the room and could probably guess how the conversation had gone.

"You all right?" he asked. Charlotte just shrugged, and Darcel nodded with understanding. What was there to say? "Well, if everything's settled here, I'll head back to the house to make sure all is well," said Darcel. "You stay safe, eh?"

He started for the door. Charlotte followed, and before he could step outside, she hugged Darcel tightly. He laughed, but didn't resist. From the corner of her eye, she saw James glance over, looking a little wounded. But there was nothing she or Darcel could do for him now.

Though her father was mired in his old ways, Charlotte needed to focus on the present, and that meant preparing Evie for what came next. While Charlotte had been talking to James, Nell had taken Evie across the street to get her ready to leave town. Directed by Beth-Anne, Charlotte found them upstairs in Nell's room. It was more than three times the size of Charlotte's attic, and flooded with light just like the rest of the Gardners' house. At the center of the room, a four-poster bed with a lace canopy was covered in colorful pillows. She wondered, if she'd grown up this comfortably, would she be half as willing to risk it for other people's troubles as Nell?

When Charlotte arrived, Evie was just stepping out of the dressing room in the iris-blue dress Charlotte had sewn for her. It fit perfectly, with the brilliant hue bringing out all the brightness in her deep brown skin. The marigold-yellow-embroidered cape was elegantly draped over her shoulders. Charlotte exhaled. She'd messed up a lot in the last few months, but at least she'd gotten this one thing right.

Evie sat down at the vanity table, and together Nell and Charlotte undid her braids. They worked silently, the three of them worn out from the last days' trials. Nell and Charlotte trimmed and oiled Evie's hair, parting it in the center and braiding it into a crown that encircled her head. Nell placed a silk flower at the right side as the final touch. As they finished, Evie reached up and took hold of Nell's right hand, and Charlotte's left. "Thank you both. For everything," she said.

She was a young woman transformed, no trace of a runaway visible anywhere on her, and no more of a little girl either. Nell and Charlotte stepped back. In the mirror, they smiled at their handiwork, and at one another.

Chapter 41

———

NELL

———

IF ONE AVOIDED ALL THE PLACES IN THIS CITY WHERE AN ANGRY mob had once stirred, there'd be hardly any place to go. The South Street Corridor, Washington Square Park, the muddy streets along the river, Independence Hall, even the quiet and tree-lined stretch of Lombard Street Nell called home. Riotous crowds were Philadelphia's weather. They gathered and stormed, swept over the streets and dispersed, always threatening to gather again. For as long as Nell could remember, they'd rumbled in the background of her city's politics and its unevenly distributed freedoms, but she never saw them as a reason not to go outside, or a reason not to do the work. This night would be no different.

The evening programs at Pennsylvania Hall were set to resume at six o'clock, and the time to walk back over was fast approaching. There had been no sign of Alex yet, so they could only assume he was still there in the bowels of the building, typesetting Charlotte's exposé of the woman who would reenslave her. Mr. and Mrs. Marion had grown more anxious by the hour, with Alex's father pacing back and forth and his mother seeming to stitch the same square inch of her needlework once and again all afternoon. Their younger son sat silently beside Mrs. Marion, staring at the floor.

Nell worried for Alex but tried to keep her focus on the tasks in front of them: bringing Evie to the people who would guide her safely north, and continuing the conference in the hope that some-day escapes like hers would never be needed again.

Around half past five, Charlotte, Nell, and Evie prepared to leave. Evie said her farewells and thank-yous, and exchanged an oddly stiff hug with the man she still insistently referred to as Uncle Jack, who had stayed to see her off.

"That's quite a disguise you have there," James said to Evie as they stepped apart.

"Not half as good as yours," she retorted.

As the three young women headed for the door, Mr. and Mrs. Marion came toward them.

"We're coming with you," Mr. Marion said. Nell's parents agreed, and followed, and finally James moved toward the door as well.

"We can't have you girls wandering the streets by yourselves," he said.

They made no objections, since there was safety in greater num-bers. With Nell's and Alex's younger brothers both electing to stay behind and guard the houses, the rest of the group stepped out into the evening. As she left the warmth and soft light of the Marions' parlor, Nell's skin vibrated in the cool twilight air—the atmosphere was kinetic, a tightly wound coil on the verge of springing again. The neighborhood wasn't quiet, exactly. It was ready.

But as they walked north toward Race Street, the uneasy peace dissipated more with each block. Nearer to the hall, the telltale sounds of the mob echoed: cheers mixed with shouted curses, the scuffle of thousands of feet against cobblestone, and always, a desper-ate voice or two hopelessly calling for order. For the prudent, the familiar sounds rang out as a warning to stay home and wait for the storm to pass. But the foolhardy walked straight toward the trouble. Nell led the group on.

As they approached Sixth Street, streams of men passed by them, all headed in the same direction they were—some driven by mere curiosity, others with more menacing looks on their faces. The closer they got, the slower Mrs. Gardner walked, until she finally stopped short and grabbed her daughter's arm.

"Nell, maybe we should turn back, I don't like the look of this."

"It'll be all right, Mama, they look tougher than they are. They've been at this all day and everything's been fine," Nell said. She tried to sound assured, but she could hear the shake in her own voice, betraying her. Her mother's fears were understandable, and Nell was nearly out of bravery herself after the days she'd just had. But what she might lack in raw nerve, Nell more than made up for in industriousness. There was important work to be done at Pennsylvania Hall, work for which she'd helped lay the very foundations, and she would see it through. That's all there was to it. Besides, once they were back inside the building among like-minded people, they would all be safe.

Nell led the group around to the Haines Street entrance at the back of the building, where the crowd wasn't so thick. A few of the onlookers seemed willing to stand aside at a white man's behest, so James cleared a path for them and Charlotte and Nell walked up to the door. Nell pulled the handle, expecting it to give way. Instead, it slammed back an inch and caught, back an inch and caught, over and over as she kept yanking. A familiar sinking feeling descended into her stomach. Like countless other meeting halls she'd tried to pry open in the last year, it was locked.

With Charlotte at her side and the crowd at her back, Nell's mind went blank and she could think of nothing more to do than keep pulling at the door. They had to get inside to Hetty, to Mary. To Alex.

James stepped behind Nell. "It's not going to open," he said, looking around. The only other way in was the front door. He led the group around the building, and when they reached the main entrance, the building manager was standing at the front door alongside the mayor. He was trying to shush the crowd and call for order. Nell and the others strained to hear.

"This evening's proceedings have been suspended," he yelled through cupped hands.

Nell, Evie, and Charlotte looked at one another. There would be no programming tonight, no meeting with Hetty, and no getting Evie out of town.

The mob had won. Still, the restive feeling that its work was not yet done lingered in the air.

The building manager stepped aside and let the mayor address the crowd. He spoke, but the clamor had grown so loud that it was impossible to hear what he said. Before long, he gave up. The two men rushed away from the door and disappeared from view.

Nell looked around her in every direction. With men and women streaming in from side streets, the mob had grown to a crowd of thousands. It was all around them, a swarm of enraged white faces, screaming with spittle flying, their ire trained on the building that represented all that was unacceptable to them: freedom of speech, freedom for women, and most intolerable of all, freedom for Black people.

Scanning the scene, her panic rising, Nell realized there were still no watchmen anywhere around. She wasn't alone in that observation.

"Are there no police here? The fire chief? Anyone?" shouted her mother.

Mr. Marion gazed at the crowd and shook his head. "It looks like the last of the authorities left with the mayor."

Just then, the street started to go dark. Someone was extinguishing the gas streetlamps that had been lighting the growing darkness. Left in the dim glow of the half-moon, the mob quickly went to work. Nell and the others struggled to get away from the building as the rioters pushed forward. As they crossed the street, Nell saw a crush of stevedores crash straight into the hall's front door, using a wooden beam as a battering ram. Bang, bang, again and again they rammed until the wood of the door split. Given an opening, the crowd rushed in with crowbars and axes.

Nell watched transfixed, looking in through the windows as the mob ransacked the building. Men tossed broken pieces of the hall's polished cherrywood and walnut benches out the front door and ran out waving the axes they must've used to chop them apart. Others hauled armfuls of books out and threw them into a pile. Broken glass rained down onto the street from the second floor as the rioters overtook the Grand Saloon and destroyed it from the inside out, hurling the room's decorations out the windows to be ripped by the jagged glass in the panes. In the night wind, the torn blue silk billowed like a flag announcing the mob's coarse victory.

Speechless and dazed, Nell stared, worried that she might be sick again. All the abolitionists' work, all that the Philadelphia Female Antislavery Society had gathered, recruited, debated, and fundraised for, torn apart. And where was Alex? Had he gotten out?

As the chaos unfolded, Mr. Marion rushed forward.

"My son, my son is in there——" he said, trying to push his way through the mob. A white man elbowed him square in the face and he staggered to the ground. The man spat on him before Nell's father and James could lift him and drag him to safety.

"We have to go. Alex may be lost and the rest of us will be too if we don't move," James said.

"No," Charlotte yelled. "We can't just leave people behind!" She glared at her father, but underneath her anger Nell could see her guilt. The only reason Alex had stayed was that she'd asked him for help.

Behind Charlotte, Mrs. Marion choked back sobs. Nell went to her side to comfort her, but inside she silently panicked. She'd tried so hard to push Alex away, and now he could be killed all because he'd been so willing to do anything she asked. She would never see him again—never get a chance to tell him how she felt.

Without thinking, she broke away from Mrs. Marion and ran toward the front door. Behind her, her mother shouted to her, the cries of "Nell, stop! Come back!" nearly drowned out by the work of the mob. But she wouldn't stop—she couldn't. Doggedly, she pushed her way past men who clawed at her and tore at her dress; as she got closer to the door, the heat rose. She was nearly halfway there when she felt a pair of arms grab her by the waist and carry her backward. It was her father.

"Nell, you can't— We have to get away from here," he shouted. She tried to twist herself loose, but he wouldn't let her go. As he dragged her back to the group, the others were scanning the side streets to see which was clearest. The riot was out of control. They had to make a run for it. Just then, a blaze of orange and blue flame rushed out from the hall's front door and windows. The heat blasted their faces and the acrid smell of burning wood and plaster filled their nostrils. Behind them, shrill cheers poured out from the windows of buildings across the street. Nell looked up—white women were watching from their homes, applauding and waving handkerchiefs as the flames rose and licked the night sky. She turned and stared back at the hall. Within moments, it was engulfed.

"Everyone!" James called. "Let's go!"

The group took off running down the street, going around the back of the building. As they passed, the back door opened and more of the mob rushed past them to watch and cheer closer to the heat of the flames. But pushing against the crowd, a lone figure was hurrying out toward the street with two large rectangular plates in his arms. Nell stopped and squinted. The flames from the upper floors of the building flickered and lit up the man's face—it was Alex.

The others saw him too, and Mr. Marion and Nell's father hurried to his side, each grabbing one of the heavy printing plates he was carrying. As they lifted the weight from him, Alex nearly fell to the ground before James caught him and helped him walk safely away from the building and into the street.

Relief washing over her, Nell rushed toward Alex, threw her arms around him, and kissed him square on the mouth. As she remembered herself and backed away, he smiled broadly at her, his face half covered in dust and soot.

"Is this all I had to do to get your attention?" he asked.

Nell laughed. "You already had it," she admitted, brushing soot off his face. Standing there in his arms, she exhaled for what felt like the first time in days.

Meanwhile, their parents stared wide-eyed, and her mother's momentary confusion melted into a look of triumph. "Mm-hmm," she said in a satisfied voice and crossed her arms—she and Mrs. Marion had been right about the engagement all along, even if their daughter and son had only just realized it.

As Nell and Alex stood savoring the moment they'd finally found, an ember from the blazing hall landed on Nell's sleeve, singeing its way through a layer of the fabric before burning out. The barely felt threat of the scald on her skin was enough to jolt her back to the perilous scene around them.

"We'd better keep moving," she said.

"Back home?" Mrs. Marion asked.

"No, Mama. They've come through our neighborhood more than once before; we shouldn't be on the streets when they come to tear it up again," Alex said. Seeming to anticipate her worry about her younger son and the Gardners', he went on. "George and Theodore will be all right. They know to stay inside and away from the windows."

James stepped forward.

"You'll all be safe at our house," he said. "No one will be troubling anyone in Society Hill."

Charlotte looked at him in surprise, then agreed. "He's right," she said. "And we've got room enough for everybody until this all blows over."

As everyone nodded in agreement and started to walk away, Evie stood by, looking crestfallen—her escape plan was in tatters, and Nell could see she was scared. "Your house?" Evie asked Charlotte. "What about Kate? She'll come looking for me again!"

"With all this going on, I don't think she'll bother us tonight," Charlotte said. "And even if she does, what can she do to us?"

Nell shifted uncomfortably on her feet and rubbed her aching shoulder; the spot where Kate's cousin had shoved her throbbed painfully. The question of what else might be done to them wasn't one she especially wanted answered, but there was no better place than Charlotte's house for them to go now. After all, the one place in the city Nell had believed would be safe was up in flames.

Keeping close to one another, the group hurried toward the house, chased by the embers and the wind blowing the heat of the fire at their backs. Nell took Alex's arm—she wouldn't lose him again.

As they walked, the women pulled their shawls up and the men forced their hat brims down against anyone who might try to see their faces. They did their best to keep to the shadows since the night was ablaze with pockets of light: the moon, the streetlights, candles in windows, and that otherworldly blue glow from Pennsylvania Hall as the gas from the building's modern lamps drove up the ferocity of the flames.

They moved fast. But even from blocks away, they heard a deafening creaking sound followed by a crash. An enormous cheer went up, and the group turned back to look. The roof of Pennsylvania Hall had caved in, opening its once-elegant halls to the air as the orange and blue flames roared, smoke billowing out into the night sky.

Nell groaned, and the tears she'd held back for days finally flowed.

Chapter 42

————

EVIE

————

SOCIETY HILL'S STREETS WERE EMPTY OF PEOPLE, AND EVERY window was dark. As Evie and the others rounded the corner and approached James and Charlotte's row house, two figures came into view. A man stood resolutely at their front door, while the woman beside him tried to move him away, desperately pulling at his coat. Evie squinted in the dark, straining to see who they might be, but their shapes were familiar enough to set her heart racing. Closer, a familiar singsong whine floated through the darkness.

"Henry, please, darling. This is hardly necessary, can't we just—?"

"It is absolutely necessary. If this man has stolen from you, I plan to hold him to account. I can't very well call myself a Southern gentleman if I won't even defend my wife-to-be's rights in property."

Evie stopped dead, then backed away without even thinking. Charlotte must have seen them in the doorway too, but she took a deep breath and kept walking right toward the house.

Now Evie was the one yanking on someone's sleeve. "We can't let them see us!"

"Why? What's the difference now?" Charlotte said. "It'll be all right." She guided Evie toward the house alongside her.

As they neared the threshold, James came up from behind, then walked past them straight up to the front door. With a tinny note in his voice, he welcomed the unwanted visitors and stretched out a hand to Henry.

"Let's not have a scene in front of the neighbors," he muttered, almost too quietly to be heard.

Henry left James's hand hanging there. Instead, he gestured toward the door, a silent demand to be let in. Beside him, Kate's eyes darted fearfully from one man to the other.

Behind Evie and Charlotte, the rest hung back, unsure whether they ought to follow.

"What's going on?" Mr. Gardner asked. Nell whispered an answer into her father's ear.

Charlotte took Evie's hand and shepherded her and everyone else forward. "It's nothing to worry about. Let's all go inside," she said.

For Evie, the urge to bolt was overwhelming, but she let herself be moved into the house, floating on the current of Charlotte's bravery. Besides, Kate looked panicked and uncertain, and seeing her fear stiffened Evie's spine. Kate was not in control here.

Charlotte settled everyone into the parlor while Henry, Kate, and James moved through and stepped into James's office.

As James started to shut his office door, Evie and Charlotte looked at each other, their determination feeding off their shared anger at Kate. Together, they pushed their way into the room, and left the door open so everyone in the parlor could listen too. There would be no more whites-only decisions about their lives, choices made for them that they could only hope to overhear. If this was going to be settled, Evie would see to it herself.

Inside the office, the glow from James's desk lamp lit up his pale, exhausted face along with Kate's and Henry's. Kate had dark circles under her eyes, and her hair was a disheveled mass of limp curls half pinned up. Turned out she hadn't been lying all those years; she really did need Evie. *Well, too bad about that.*

Standing with his arms crossed and looking stern, Henry turned to James.

"Why you would choose to hide a fugitive slave is none of my concern—I can only assume you're one of the abolitionists this town is crawling with," he said. His mouth twisted with disgust, the very word *abolitionist* sour on his tongue. "My sole concern is that you have stolen from my fiancée."

James looked at him puzzled, and then at Kate. He spoke slowly. "You can only . . . assume . . . ?"

Evie shook her head in disbelief. Kate still hadn't told Henry the whole truth! Everywhere Evie went, it was nothing but people playing out these same tired charades. How they managed not to wear themselves out, she'd never know.

"Look," Henry interjected. "Your politics don't concern me. You're a businessman, so I'm sure you'd prefer to handle this quietly. That's a desire I share. Give the girl back and let's wash our hands of the whole matter."

Charlotte and Evie glanced at each other. It wasn't entirely clear which one of them he was talking about. But it didn't matter.

"*The girl* is not going anywhere," Charlotte said. Looking startled by the outburst, James put up a hand to try to quiet her, but it was no use. "You have no rights here, and neither does she," she said, turning to Kate. "Evie's been in this state six months—she's free by law and doesn't belong to you anymore, as if she ever really did."

Henry didn't bother to address her. Instead, he turned to James. "I'll thank you to get your maid under control." Evie glanced at Uncle Jack, waiting for the correction—not his housemaid, his daughter. Charlotte was watching him too. But he said nothing.

As the exchange unfolded, Kate stood by looking like she hoped to be swallowed up by the floor. But with the tension rising, she laid a hand on Henry's shoulder.

"I told you, we don't need to do this. I'm sure there are other ladies' maids at Willow Creek—I can do without Evie," she said. "Can't we just be on our way?"

Before she could move toward the door, Charlotte stepped in front of her. Evie smiled at Kate's helplessness. Finally, her enslaver got a taste of what Evie had dealt with her whole life—it wasn't so grand, not being in charge of your own comings and goings, was it?

"What's the hurry?" Charlotte asked. "You seemed pressed

enough for Evie's and my company just yesterday." She looked at Henry, then cast a knowing glance back at Kate. "Do you want to tell him, or should I?"

"Tell me what?"

"None of this matters, Henry," Kate said. The note of desperation in her voice rang out clear and true. "Let's go. Please."

"Oh, by all means, go," Charlotte continued. "I just thought you'd be interested to know, Mr. Brooks, that your bride to be is no spring rose. She was married before, to Elias Murphy in Maryland. That's where she knows us from. Owned me and my father both, in fact, not just Evie. That, and she's committed the crime of kidnapping—not just me, but another free woman too." She pointed out the door at Nell, who was standing in the parlor pretending not to eavesdrop.

"She owned you . . . and your father?" He narrowed his eyes and looked from James to Charlotte, then back again. James avoided his gaze.

"Henry, please. Let's go," Kate said, tugging once more on his coat. "This is ridiculous."

"Which part, Missus?" Evie said, drawing out the "Missus" as if she said it all the time. In Henry's face, there was a flash of understanding—he was no doubt thinking back to the other day. Evie's "slip" in calling Kate "Missus Murphy" had been no slip at all.

Emboldened, Evie went on. "Seems to me what's ridiculous is a half-dried-up widow pretending a whole marriage never happened just to hitch her way back into some money," she said. Kate glared at her, a look that was both angry and wounded, like she'd been betrayed by a friend. Evie shrugged. She had no more patience for Kate's one-sided notion of loyalty, where Evie had to serve her needs and keep her secrets all while Kate schemed to wring every last use out of her and punish her when she didn't play the perfect servant. Let Kate stand alone for once, with no slave girl to lean on. There wasn't much to her, it was plain to see now. And Mr. Brooks was seeing it too.

Charlotte stepped forward. "Ask anyone down in Anne Arundel County, Maryland, if you don't believe us. And we'll take all this public, come to that." She motioned for Alex. He came in and handed Kate a copy of the draft newspaper article they'd prepared at the hall.

"That story can run in this week's special edition of *The Pennsylvania Freeman,* and probably get picked up by every other newspaper in the city, not to mention the society gossip rags," said Charlotte. "I'm sure they'll be very interested to hear a story of kidnapping, Southern slavers, and fraud, especially after tonight. Good luck duping anyone else into marrying you after that. Or you can leave us in peace, and no one ever needs to hear about any of this again. We can print the story or not. The choice is yours."

Kate read the article silently, her face a mix of fear and fatigue. Henry, for his part, looked disgusted by the whole mess. He read a few lines over her shoulder, then snatched the paper and set it down on James's desk.

"That is quite enough. Your cousin Frank certainly left out a few details when he suggested we'd find Evie here, didn't he, Katherine?" His voice was cold. "You and I will discuss this privately; there's no need for a spectacle."

"I— But what about my—" she stammered. Now exposed, she reached out for the familiar—for Evie, though it was a mystery whether Kate wanted her back for good or only long enough to punish her for causing so much trouble.

Before Evie could move, Charlotte had stepped in front of her. In an instant Nell and her parents came into the room and stood behind Evie, joined by Darcel and the Marions. There was a flash of understanding in Henry's eyes as he stared at them. Surrounding Evie were more than enough prominent, well-respected members of Philadelphia society—Black though they were—to turn this whole episode into a public scandal. Maybe better than anyone else, Evie knew Kate wasn't worth it. She stood her ground and prayed Mr. Brooks could now see for himself that his fiancée had no honor worth defending.

Finally, resolved, he stiffly offered his arm to Kate.

"We have no further business here," he said. "I'll see you home, Katherine, and that will be that. Shall we?"

What little fight there had ever been in Kate was all used up. Defeated, she took his arm and they walked silently out of the office, through the parlor, and out the front door.

Once the door closed behind them, Nell sat down and crossed her arms with satisfaction. "Well, good riddance to them," she said.

She put on a brave face, but there was still a little quiver in her shoulders. One didn't shake off being kidnapped by slave catchers that easily. Evie offered her a hand, and Charlotte sat down beside Nell.

"You don't have to worry, I don't think Kate and her man will be bothering us anymore," Charlotte said.

Everyone smiled at the thought, but Evie caught a glimpse of Uncle Jack's face out of the corner of her eye. He didn't look so sure.

Chapter 43

———

CHARLOTTE

———

D AY BROKE, QUIET AND WARM. THE DAWN LIGHT STREAMED IN through the parlor window, brushing Charlotte's eyelids, and she awoke. She rubbed the ache in her neck and silently reminded herself never to sleep leaning against a wall again. Everyone else was still dozing where they'd sat the night before: James in a chair in the corner of the room, Evie curled up on the floor underneath a blanket beside Charlotte, and the Gardners and Marions on the long red sofa at the room's center. On the two-seater, Nell and Alex sat close together, her head on his shoulder. Looked like it wouldn't be such a long engagement after all.

The only person missing was Darcel. For a moment, Charlotte wondered if he'd retreated to his room as the night had worn on, but the buttery scent wafting in the air told a different tale.

Sure enough, when she got back to the kitchen, there he was keeping a close eye on one batch of biscuits in the oven while rolling out and stamping another, each cutout a nearly perfect match with its brothers.

He turned around. "You just gon' stand there?"

As Charlotte worked her way through their familiar side-by-side motions, some of the tension left her shoulders. There was plenty to be said about the night they'd had, but Darcel was all companionable gruff silence until, after a few minutes, he cleared his throat. "You been paying attention these last few months? Maybe you're ready to do all this on your own?"

"I think I could manage," Charlotte said warily. "Why?"

"Mr. Marion's invited me to work with him, learn the catering business—I think I'm going to take him up on it. But only if you'll be all right."

Charlotte grinned broadly. "Well, well, well," she said, by way of congratulations. "I'll get by. Just make me one promise?"

"Anything."

"Bring by one of your spice cakes every once in a while, will you?"

Darcel smiled. "With pleasure."

While they finished preparing breakfast, Charlotte could hear folks waking and moving around in the front of the house. In the dining room, Nell and Evie whirred around the table laying out place settings for breakfast. Evie took charge of the silverware, and Nell kept stealing glances at her while she worked, apparently surprised the young slave girl knew which fork went where. Charlotte shook her head and smiled. They all had things to learn, it seemed.

Once the food was served, the whole group ate together in easy quiet. Mr. Marion spread Darcel's homemade jam onto a freshly broken and steaming biscuit and took a bite. He nodded at Darcel, receiving a half smile in return. The rest of the group passed the bread basket around and poured themselves juice and coffee. As the others ate, Charlotte drank in the unusual sight in her dining room: a collection of brown faces of varying shades, all at home with one another. Something just shy of a family, or maybe something more.

There were empty chairs, but James stood aside in the corner.

"Come and sit down," Charlotte said to him. He stared at the table for a moment, then shook his head. He wasn't hungry, he claimed.

No one dared break the spell of a peaceful morning by bringing up the horrors they'd lived through the night before—the mob, the flames. Hardest to forget was the rage in the eyes of their fellow Philadelphians, their reddened white faces ablaze with hatred as they did their awful work. Daylight held them at bay now, but only just. Every hour that brought dusk closer was another hour closer to what might be another inferno. And where would this family be safe then?

"You're all welcome to remain here for the next few days," James said, breaking the quiet. No one needed him to say why.

"That's kind of you, Mr. Vaughn," Mr. Gardner answered, "and we're very grateful for your hospitality, but we'll be just fine at home. We look after one another in our neighborhood—we always have." He rose from the table, gesturing at Nell and her mother.

Nell stayed in her chair and reached for Charlotte's hand. Her palms were still rough from scrubbing Kate's laundry, and there was a dampness on her skin—the film of sweat betrayed how badly her nerves had been rattled by the last few days, and most likely still were. She needed to rest but would never admit it.

"We should be heading home now, dear, and the Marions should too," Mrs. Gardner prodded. "George and Theodore will be worried, I'm sure."

Charlotte nodded at her friend, squeezed her hand, and let it go. *It's all right.* Granted that silent permission, Nell relented.

"I suppose I could stop in at home and freshen up," she said. Then, turning to Charlotte and Evie, she said, "But where should we meet to head over to today's convention meetings?"

Charlotte stifled a laugh. Alex grinned and put his head down, trying and failing to hide his own chuckling. Nell would be Nell.

Before Mrs. Gardner could respond, Mr. Gardner tightened his grip on his wife's shoulders. She shook her head silently, making her private peace with the situation. Meanwhile, Mr. Gardner regarded his daughter with something that looked very much like pride. Unable to stop herself, Charlotte glanced at James.

His lips were pursed, and he stood up stiffly.

"It sounds like everyone's plans are made. I've got some affairs to attend to myself, if you'll excuse me. Stay as long as you like," he said after a beat. "Darcel, you'll look after them?"

"Sure will," he said.

Business, always business. James was into his coat and out the door in an instant. As he walked off, Charlotte invited everyone to sit back down and stay awhile. They lingered over coffee, making light conversation.

Finally, Charlotte, Nell, and Evie came together to firm up their plans—there was still the matter of Evie's freedom to attend to. They'd meet at eleven o'clock in Franklin Square. With Pennsylvania Hall reduced to ash and rubble, the women's antislavery societies would have to meet somewhere for the rest of the convention, but there was no way of knowing which venues—if any—would have them now. So, they'd gather in the shadow of the wreckage, and work their way through the city from there.

As breakfast wound down, Evie went up to the attic to rest. Nell and Alex lingered with Charlotte for a bit, talking over the table. "Quite a column I'll have for the next edition of the newspaper," Alex said as he headed toward the door with the printing plates under his arm. "And you're sure you don't want to go ahead and print the story about Kate? It'll take some time to get the old print-ing press set back up at the Arch Street office, but we can make it work if that's what you want."

Charlotte shook her head. "I'm true to my word—don't print it. She left us in peace, so the best thing we can do now is move on," she said. "But I won't forget what you risked for us, Alex."

And neither would Nell, from the way she'd been holding tight to him since the night before. Standing beside Alex, she nodded in agreement with Charlotte.

"She's right, we should let it be," Nell said. "Besides, I'm sure my parents would be grateful not to draw any more attention to all this than is strictly necessary. We'll hold on to the draft though—just in case."

With that, they were gone, and before long, just Charlotte and Darcel were left cleaning up the table in companionable silence.

With Kate no longer haunting Charlotte and James, an uncertain future stretched out ahead. There was no more need for their cha-rade. Without that, what was left between them? Reluctantly, an answer stepped out of a shadowy corner of her mind. Perhaps that same answer was what had driven James from the house. Distractedly, she piled plates on top of one another and poured the dregs of nearly finished coffee cups into the sink.

She could feel Darcel's eyes on her back.

"Just go talk to him," he said. "I've got things in hand here."

Her shoulders dropped and she sighed. She left her "thank you" unspoken and walked out.

By the time she made it to Second Street, the sun had climbed high enough in the sky that it shone right into her eyes as she turned the corner to the workshop. For a split second, she couldn't see it. But when the bright blindness lifted, the whole sorry scene came into view. There, where her father's carpentry workshop had once stood was a smoking pile of rubble. The morning air was warm, but Charlotte shivered at the sight, pulling her shawl tighter around her shoulders. How many of these charred ruins was she going to see today?

James was there in the wreck, lifting fragments of wood beams and pushing bricks aside. He seemed to be searching for something in the pile, which looked like it had only just stopped smoldering.

"Get out of there!" Charlotte shouted, rushing to him. She reached over what used to be the threshold and yanked him out by the sleeve. His once-white shirt had gone nearly black with ash.

"What on earth are you doing?" she demanded. The smoke curled its way into her nostrils, billowed down her throat, and Charlotte stifled the urge to gag. Her eyes watered. The strange thing was, the smell was familiar—the smoldering wood and char, it brought her back to the night before, and to White Oaks, wood chips burning in the stove in the outside kitchen in the summer. At last, some part of her deep down floated back to the day the cabin had burned with her mother inside, a half-remembered impression given new, solid form by the sight of her father here, dazed and broken.

"I'm just trying to see what I can salvage," he said. His voice was weary and small.

"James . . ." she began, placing a hand on his shoulder. At the sound of his name, he flinched.

"Please don't. I'm still your father."

She stared at him sadly. It seemed neither of them knew what that actually meant anymore. Charlotte just nodded.

"Kate is obviously behind this. It couldn't be anyone else," he said. "She's ruined me."

"There were lots of men roaming the streets last night with a mind for this kind of damage, you can't be sure she—"

"Every other shop on the street is still standing, Carrie. I know you're not that naïve."

"No," she said slowly. "I'm not. And it's Charlotte now." After all that had happened, she was ready to let go of who she'd been at White Oaks at last, but she would still find a way to look after the people who mattered to her. No new name would make her leave Evie behind again.

"Very well, Charlotte," said James. "But we both know what this means. We can't stay in this city. I've no livelihood left to sustain us, and something far worse will be coming for me once word gets around even further. My business partner may already know. We've got to keep heading north, start over . . ."

She listened as his voice trailed off. He was already lost in the plans for where to run next, and how, and what new life and new self he'd begin there. But Charlotte was beyond all that now.

"I *have* started over. And maybe you don't have to leave to do it too—come back to the house," she said, reaching out a hand.

"I don't think I belong there anymore," he said, shaking his head. He sighed wearily. "But maybe you do."

She nodded. Perhaps he could see her after all.

"I'll be safe here, with everyone. And we'll look after Evie," she said. "You'll have to do this next part on your own, Papa."

The last word was a mercy, and a farewell. He stared at her, his face a strange mix of pride and grief.

"The deed to the house is in the safe in my office, with anything else you'll need—money, papers, it's all there. You won't want for anything," he said. "I'll collect my things tonight and go. I don't know when, but I'll see you again."

Charlotte reached out and squeezed his hand, then took a step back over the charred threshold. As she walked away, she turned and cast one last look at the workshop and the ruined man standing amid the wreck.

And then, she turned a corner. The farther she walked, the lighter her steps became.

WHEN SHE ARRIVED BACK at the house midmorning, Charlotte climbed the stairs to the attic. The door was wide open. Evie was sitting on the bed, her dress torn. Without thinking, Charlotte found herself looking forward to mending it, maybe making her another. She glanced at Mae's card sitting on her desk—when things settled, an apprenticeship with the dressmaker would be just the ticket.

Beneath the sunlight streaming in from the little window, Evie was staring intently at a book she held in her lap.

"I can't make out a word of it," she said, furrowing her brow.

Charlotte sat down beside her. "You can learn, you know," she said. "I did—he taught me. And there are schools set up to get you straightened right out."

"Schools up North, you mean," Evie said. "Where you're sending me?"

Charlotte stared at her for a moment. Now that Evie was finally free of Kate, Charlotte couldn't tell whether she'd expected her to be excited or grateful or what. She mostly looked sad, and a little tired.

Charlotte thought back to the last time they'd parted ways without knowing if they would ever lay eyes on each other again. What would she have said to Evie then, had she been given a choice?

"On second thought, I'll teach you myself. If you'll let me," Charlotte offered. Evie looked up at her, surprise and wariness lurking behind her dark eyes.

"I want you to stay here, with me," Charlotte continued, taking Evie's hand in her own. "We're free, Evie—you and me both, and I don't want to leave you behind again. I won't."

"I would've been the one leaving, anyhow," Evie retorted. Her words were sharp, but the barest hint of a smile curled on her lips.

"I guess you would. I'm asking you then—don't leave me. This is as good a place as any for us to start over, and neither of us has to do it alone."

Evie squinted at her skeptically but took a deep breath and clasped Charlotte's hand.

"One more thing," Charlotte said. "At Kate's, I tried to find out what she'd done with Daniel, but there was nothing. I don't know where to look next."

Evie nodded. "We'll think of something," she said. "Now I know there are plenty of folks here to help us. We'll find him."

AT ELEVEN O'CLOCK, THEY went over to the corner of Sixth and Race to reconvene with the rest of the convention. The acrid smell of burnt wood and plaster lingered in the air. Where the majestic hall had once stood there was now only a smoking ruin, a blackened shell of the building that had briefly housed so many unfulfilled promises.

There, Charlotte and Evie found Nell standing beside Hetty, preparing to lead everyone to the schoolhouse for the day's meetings.

"There you are, Charlotte," Hetty said as they walked up beside her. "We were just talking—it may be time to think about taking our committee plans outside the society, maybe starting a group of our own to work more directly with fugitives."

"No argument from me," Charlotte said, smiling at Nell and Hetty.

"And on the same subject," Nell said, turning to Evie, "are you ready for the next leg of your journey?"

"There's been a change of plans," Charlotte interjected. "Evie's going to stay here with me—with us."

Evie locked eyes with Nell, giving her a look that was half expectation and half challenge. "That's right. There's a lot more folks looking to get free, and it sure seems like you all could use some help," said Evie, turning her eyes toward what was left of the hall. "Maybe if I join up, I can do some good."

Nell smiled broadly, a twinkle in her eyes at the recognition of a kindred spirit. "I certainly wouldn't bet against you."

The wind blew the smoke and ashes from the hall over their heads, nudging them onward, away from what had been lost. They walked down to the schoolhouse. Inside, they sat side by side in children's desks, the earliest arrivals to a meeting some said was now too dangerous to hold. But the enslavers, kidnappers, and Southern sympathizers hadn't stopped, so neither would they.

Other women began to arrive as Evie, Charlotte, and Nell huddled in close, with pencils and notepads splayed out before them to sketch out their battle plans.

"All right then," Charlotte said. "Let's get to work."

AUTHOR'S NOTE

THE INSPIRATION FOR THIS STORY CAME TO ME ONE AFTERNOON in October 2018, when I was sitting in my office listening to show tunes as the workday wound down. As the *Les Misérables* song "Who Am I?" played through my speakers, I listened to the fugitive convict Jean Valjean agonize over his decision to assume a new identity in a new city in order to hide his past. The song comes just before he becomes a father figure to the young orphan girl Cosette, and in it he sings about the fear of being sent back to prison and "condemned . . . to slavery" if the truth about his criminal past ever came out.

Though the lyric about slavery was meant to reference the hardships of prison labor, I was struck with an idea: What if the story had been set in the United States instead of France, and both he and his daughter were running from actual chattel slavery? And what if the story were told not from Valjean's perspective but instead centered on a character like Cosette, who was constrained by her father's overprotectiveness and understandable paranoia? From that admittedly unusual kernel of an idea, the characters of Charlotte and James—and their central conflict—were born. Earlier the same year, I'd stepped away from my career as a lawyer to return to journalism and had also been thinking about trying my hand at fiction, so when this idea hit me just a few weeks before National Novel Writing Month, I took it as a sign and decided to shape the story into a book.

THERE WAS NEVER ANY doubt in my mind that Philadelphia would be the ideal setting. At the time, I'd been working in the city for more than a year, and as I dove into research, I was fortunate to have access to the University of Pennsylvania's library system. There, I learned that between the Revolutionary War and the Civil War, Philadelphia was home to the largest and arguably most politically active free Black community in the northern United States. As I imagined what Charlotte's life might've been like and the circles of people she'd have been caught between as both a free Black woman and a fugitive slave, the characters of Nell and Evie emerged, offering windows into two very different echelons of nineteenth-century Black society.

By 1830 there were fifteen thousand Black people living in Philadelphia, mostly concentrated near what is now Center City. The community was as diverse as it was large, in terms of both socioeconomic status and its inhabitants' relationships to slavery. Among the free Black population, there were the poor unemployed, working-class domestics and dockworkers, washerwomen, and also a small cohort of upper-middle-class and wealthy Black families like the Purvises, the Fortens, and the Douglasses—the inspiration for the fictional Gardners and Marions. Such families thrived as real estate magnates, businessmen, milliners, caterers, and more. Indeed, the Marions' catering business was inspired by real-life Black caterers like Robert Bogle, Thomas Dorsey, and Peter Augustine, who pioneered that business in the nineteenth century. During this period, a range of terms were used to describe African Americans, including "colored," "black," and "Negro," which appear in dialogue in this novel, while in narration, I elected to use the modern term "Black."

Although most Black people living in Philadelphia were free by the 1830s, the ways they came by that status varied widely. Some had been born free, others had been emancipated over time by the state's Act for the Gradual Abolition of Slavery. Passed by the Pennsylvania legislature in 1780, the law didn't free anyone who was enslaved at the time of passage. Rather, it converted the future children of enslaved mothers into indentured servants who'd be emancipated only after serving their mother's enslavers for twenty-eight years. Afterward, their own children would be born free. By the early 1800s, Philadelphia also had a sizable population of refugees from the Haitian Revolution who'd been brought over with their enslavers in the 1790s. Learning that inspired me to create the character of Darcel. Last, the city played host to enslaved nonresidents, like Evie, who could be brought into the state by traveling slave owners under a loophole in the 1780 Act: the six-month rule.

I first learned of this accommodationist rule on my lunch break one afternoon when I went to visit the President's House historical site on Market Street. There, visitors can view the foundations of the house George Washington lived in during his presidency, when Philadelphia was the nation's capital, and where he kept nine enslaved Black people in his service. Given my background in law, the legal mechanics of exactly how and why he was able to hold slaves for so many years in a so-called free state piqued my curiosity, so I added that question to my research agenda. What I discovered ultimately became part of Evie's story, and those of the others enslaved by the Jackson family.

The 1780 Act gradually phased out slavery in Pennsylvania and banned the importation of slaves; however, it included some carefully designed loopholes and exceptions. Chief among them was this six-month rule, also known as the "sojourner law," which allowed slaveholders who were visiting ("sojourning") or passing through the state to bring slaves with them and keep them enslaved, provided they didn't stay in Pennsylvania longer than six months. Almost immediately after the legislation passed, slaveholders who were in Pennsylvania for extended periods started taking advantage of the loophole by sending enslaved Black people on brief trips out of state just before six months elapsed, and then bringing them back, essentially resetting the clock on their freedom. To the legislature's credit, it passed an amendment in 1788 to forbid such abuses. Nevertheless, many enslavers—including Washington—quietly disobeyed the amended law, just as the Jackson family does in this novel when they periodically send slaves back to Virginia.

In any case, the 1788 amendment otherwise left the six-month law untouched, meaning that seasonal travelers, businessmen, and visitors were still well within their rights to keep slaves with them in Philadelphia, as Kate does with Evie. It wasn't until 1847 that the legislature passed a law that freed any enslaved Black person the moment he or she set foot on Pennsylvania soil. But until then, slavery was ever present, with fugitives escaping into the city and Southerners bringing enslaved people in and out at will and chasing runaways into the state. Even free Black people weren't safe from being snatched up by slave catchers, much the way Nell is kidnapped near the end of the novel. That danger ultimately led to the creation of the Philadelphia Vigilant Association, a real-life organization that was headed up by Robert Purvis and other Black men and supplemented by a female auxiliary, which Hetty Reckless helped to found in 1838. The association provided clothing, travel assistance, and hiding places to fugitive slaves and also worked to protect both free and fugitive Black people from slave catchers. Its work was foundational to what would eventually come to be called the Underground Railroad. In fact, the Purvis family's house at Ninth and Lombard streets—the same neighborhood as Nell's and Alex's fictional homes—was known to be a station on the Underground Railroad until the 1840s.

Over all, in the early nineteenth century, Philadelphia was a hub for the abolitionist cause, and Black women like Nell were central to the movement and to the building of Pennsylvania Hall. Sarah Mapps Douglass; Harriet Purvis, wife of Robert Purvis; Margaretta and Sarah Forten; and Hetty Reckless were among the Black founding members of the real-life Philadelphia Female Anti-Slavery Society (PFASS), which played a major role in fundraising to support the building's construction—helping to collect more than forty thousand dollars in a year. As a mixed-race group of Black and white women, PFASS was considered one of the more progressive abolitionist groups in the country, since some (like the Ladies' New York City Anti-Slavery Society, for example) didn't admit Black members. Still, despite the interracial cooperation, historians have noted that there was some disagreement within PFASS about the organization's priorities. While many white members were focused mostly on the political work of abolition—hosting public speeches to change hearts and minds, advocating for legal reform, and so on—some Black members wanted to direct more resources toward community-level work, such as education initiatives for Black people within the city, and protecting and providing for fugitive slaves. By the 1850s, most Black members had fallen away from PFASS in part because of this conflict, the early seeds of which are dramatized in Nell's story.

Nell's and Charlotte's political awakenings through literature also accurately reflect the history. Many of the Black members in PFASS cut their political teeth in literary clubs, and while the Wheatley Literary Association was created for this story, Black women's literary clubs in Philadelphia like the Minerva Literary Association and the Edgeworth Literary Association thrived during this period. These clubs were gateways to abolitionist literature, with some of the members also writing and submitting newspaper articles about racial justice issues of the day, as Sarah Mapps Douglass was known to do.

But as much as Philadelphia was a wellspring of abolitionist organizing in the nineteenth century, during the 1830s and 1840s it was also roiled by frequent riots stemming from anti-Black racial resentment and backlash against those very same abolitionists, as well as prejudice against and among immigrants. While the riot that opens the novel was imagined for this story, it's meant to stand in for similar incidents during this period, including major riots in 1834 and 1842 that specifically targeted Black Philadelphians. And while this particular riot wasn't real, Robert Purvis's advocacy against the Pennsylvania legislature's plan to strip Black men of the vote was true to life: he was a vocal critic of the plan and wrote a widely distributed pamphlet arguing against it called *Appeal of Forty Thousand Citizens, Threatened with Disfranchisement, to the People of Pennsylvania.*

Of course, the riot that looms largest in this novel—the burning of Pennsylvania Hall—is indeed a sad historical truth. When I first learned this story, it seemed incredible that I'd never heard it before: a meeting hall built by a mixed-race coalition of Black and white abolitionists during one of the most volatile and riotous periods in the city's history, and then destroyed within days of opening seems too outrageous to have been left out of the history books. As historical events go, you'd be hard-pressed to find one that paints a more stark picture of the divide between the city's lofty founding ideals and its harsh reality. I hewed closely to the facts when describing the building itself and the riot that destroyed it while taking a few liberties to include my fictional characters. The riot ultimately lasted another two nights after the fire, and other places in the city were damaged as well, including the Shelter for Colored Orphans, which Nell visits in an early chapter. After the riots, abolitionists let the ruined shell of the building stand for years as a martyr to their cause. All that remains now is a historical marker at Sixth and Haines streets.

At its core, *All We Were Promised* is rooted in the social vibrancy, activism, political engagement, and diversity of Philadelphia's Black community. In telling this story, I hoped not only to resurrect the fascinating history of Pennsylvania Hall but also to shine a light on the often-overlooked agency and ingenuity of the Black women and men who helped shape Philadelphia and the abolitionist movement during the critical pre–Civil War period of American history.

ACKNOWLEDGMENTS

I'M GRATEFUL FOR THE WORK OF THE MANY HISTORIANS WHOSE books provided the foundations for this story, including *A Fragile Freedom* and *Never Caught* by Erica Armstrong Dunbar; *They Were Her Property* by Stephanie Jones-Rogers; *All Bound Up Together* and *Vanguard* by Martha S. Jones; *We Are Your Sisters: Black Women in the Nineteenth Century,* edited by Dorothy Sterling; *The Elite of Our People* and *Between Slavery and Freedom* by Julie Winch; *Forging Freedom* by Gary B. Nash; *The Abolitionist Sisterhood,* edited by Jean Fagan Yellin and John C. Van Horne; *Black Women Abolitionists* by Shirley J. Yee; *Pennsylvania Hall* by Beverly C. Tomek; and many more, along with several online sources, including the Encyclopedia of Greater Philadelphia, a project of the Mid-Atlantic Regional Center for the Humanities (MARCH) at Rutgers University–Camden.

I was fortunate to have the opportunity to revise and polish this novel as part of the inaugural cohort of the Black Creatives Revisions Workshop program run by We Need Diverse Books, a nonprofit dedicated to promoting diversity in publishing. Thank you to WNDB, the Black Creatives Fund team, Breanna J. McDaniel, and D. Ann Williams, who offered me invaluable guidance, support, community, and insight as I shaped and reshaped this book.

To my amazing agent, Jamie Carr, thank you for your vision, your partnership, and all your encouragement to breathe more life and joy into this story. It's made all the difference, and I'm so grateful to have you in my corner.

I'm deeply indebted to my extraordinary, eagle-eyed editor, Susanna Porter, who has been everything an author could hope for—patient, exacting, knowledgeable, and deeply invested in making this novel the absolute best version of itself. My work is so much stronger for having passed through your hands, and those of the entire team at Ballantine: Debbie Aroff, Barbara Bachman, Vanessa Duque, Melissa Folds, Jordan Hill Forney, Jennifer Garza, Elena Giavaldi, Jennifer Hershey, Kim Hovey, Anusha Khan, Jennifer Rodriguez, Allison Schuster, and Kara Welsh. Thank you all for believing in this story and shepherding it into the world.

To my dear colleagues at Prism, the nonprofit news outlet that's been my professional home since 2019: through the indispensable and justice-focused journalism we've worked on together, you've taught me everything I know about movement building and enriched what I could pour into this abolition story. Thank you for your wisdom, your humor, and your camaraderie. Working alongside you all has changed my life, and this novel wouldn't exist without you.

Many thanks to my friend Emi Briggs, who has been a champion and a sounding board for this story from my first frenzied text message with a wild idea and in all the years since. You've been the most amazing company for this ride, and I appreciate you so much.

I'm grateful to my friend Amara Omeokwe, who was an early reader of this story and just about everything else I've written for the last nearly twenty years. Thank you for your expert eye, your candor, and your support—it's a gift to call you my friend.

To all my friends who've offered support and encouragement, and read early draft pages, and helped me along in ways large and small—Natasha Alford, Kristen Jones Miller, Le'Shera Hardy, Chenelle Idehen, Samantha Pierre—thank you for being the constants in my life, in this and so many other things. The friendships that form the heart of this novel are drawn from all I've learned by walking through life alongside you.

Thank you to my parents-in-law, Eloise and Michael Newsome,

for your warmth and support, always. I was able to write this story in large part thanks to your generosity of time and care, and I feel incredibly lucky to have you as part of my family and village.

To my mom and dad, Deborah and Keith Lattimore—I owe you so much, and I'm so, so grateful for your unwavering belief in me, your constant encouragement, and all that you've given and sacrificed so that I'm able to do what I love. Thank you both for your absolute certainty that this book would and should come into being even when I had doubts, for all your support along the way, and for filling my head with so many show tunes that they somehow sparked an entire book. And to my mom, my first and most trusted reader, thank you for your gentle—yet accurate!—criticism, and your perfectly timed praise.

To my beloved, favorite little folks in the world, Asa and Adrian—thank you for all the laughter you bring to my days, and the ways you expand my imagination.

Finally, thank you to my wonderful husband, Alan, whose support and unshakable faith in me bore me up during the long journey of writing this book. Your love and partnership have rewritten my notions of what's possible, and I'm grateful for you every day.

ABOUT THE AUTHOR

———

ASHTON LATTIMORE is an award-winning journalist and a former lawyer. She is the editor-in-chief at Prism, a nonprofit news outlet by and for communities of color, and her nonfiction writing has also appeared in *The Washington Post, Slate,* CNN, and *Essence.* Ashton is a graduate of Harvard College, Harvard Law School, and Columbia Journalism School. She grew up in New Jersey, and now lives in suburban Philadelphia with her husband and two sons. *All We Were Promised* is her first novel.

Twitter: @AshtonLattimore

Instagram: @AshtonLattimore

ABOUT THE TYPE

———

This book was set in Bembo, a typeface based on an old-style Roman face that was used for Cardinal Pietro Bembo's tract *De Aetna* in 1495. Bembo was cut by Francesco Griffo (1450–1518) in the early sixteenth century for Italian Renaissance printer and publisher Aldus Manutius (1449–1515). The Lanston Monotype Company of Philadelphia brought the well-proportioned letterforms of Bembo to the United States in the 1930s.